# Final Exit

# Final Exit

## The Martha's Vineyard Murders

## Raemi A. Ray

TULE
PUBLISHING

# Dedication

For Mom and Dad
You have a book dedicated to you.
Has Austin dedicated a book to you?
No? Huh, how about that?
Your turn, little brother.

# Chapter One

JUBILANT CRIES SPILLED out onto the frigid street when Tarek Collins hauled open the door to the Wraith & Bone. He ushered Kyra inside, his hand light on the small of her back. The pub was busy. Most of the tables were full. Extra televisions had been rigged on free-standing tables. A projector screen was down in front of the fieldstone wall. Apparently, all the islanders came out to support their team on the *big day*.

Kyra's gaze swept the crowd, looking for their friends. Chase Hawthorn was easy to spot. Even if he hadn't stood a head taller than nearly everyone else, one couldn't help noticing him. He was movie-star-pretty—tousled blonde waves, perpetual golden tan, and eyes the color of Lake Blausee under the sun.

"There," she said, but Tarek had already seen them.

His long fingers laced through Kyra's, and he led her through the rabble to their table. She and Tarek were the last to arrive, beaten by their neighbors, Grace and Charlie Chambers, Chase's it's-a-thing-but-not-a-thing, Dr. Gerry James, and a man she recognized as Tarek's former police colleague, Officer Mark Evans.

1

"Hi," Kyra said, her voice inaudible over the crowd, and she waved her hand.

"Kay!" Chase beamed and stumbled around the table to wrap her in a bear hug that squeezed the oxygen from her lungs and had her boots leaving the floor. "You made it!" Out of the corner of her eye, she saw Charlie grin and roll her eyes.

"Wouldn't have missed it." Kyra coughed and patted his arm.

He set her down. His lips twitched into a knowing smirk. He knew she didn't care for American football. Despite their best efforts, Chase and Tarek had failed to convert Kyra. She found the game complex and slow, unlike the Premier League matches she was used to.

Despite no love for the game, she'd told Chase the truth. She wouldn't have skipped it. When Chase learned tonight's Super Bowl fell on Tarek's birthday, he'd organized a watch party at their favorite haunt. If she had to sit through a boring broadcast, it might as well be at Gully Goulds's bar. She loved the old Edgartown pub. It reminded her of the dark drinkeries she grew up with in London.

"Tar!" a voice bellowed and the giant pub master materialized. He slid his serving tray, laden with beer glasses and pitchers, on the table before pulling Tarek into a hug. Gully pushed him back, his enormous palms encasing Tarek's shoulders. His smile widened, splitting his bushy beard. "Happy birthday!"

Tarek winced as the rest of the table extended boisterous birthday wishes. He threw Kyra a pained look and his shoulders sagged a fraction. Kyra laughed. He hated being the center of attention.

"Thank you," he said, and with amused resignation responded to the questions flying at him. "Yes. Today. Thirty-six. Mmmhmm." He shot Kyra a look. "We are the same age. For now."

Kyra stuck her tongue out at him. She might have been born nine months earlier, but Tarek was by far the more mature of the two.

"How you been, London?" Gully asked.

He wiped his hands on one of his many bar towels. One hung from each of his back pockets, and another was tucked into his belt loop.

"Well. And you?"

"No complaints. Business is good. It's been better than ever since that docuseries was announced. Thanks again for helping with all that." The ruddy skin above his shaggy beard flushed.

"Don't mention it, really. I was happy to do it. The Wraith's story is fascinating. I'm glad it's being shared and getting the attention it deserves."

Gully was a bit of a local maritime history expert. He'd been interviewed for a docuseries about a recently discovered shipwreck, one he'd been obsessed with for years. Kyra had helped him with the legal contracts.

"We should be thanking you." She waved at the pub, dressed up like a sports bar for the night. "For letting us use your bar for the match."

"*Game!*" At least four people corrected, and Charlie added an exaggerated eye roll.

Gully guffawed. His laugh, like everything about him,

was unceremonious and over-large. "Don't be an idiot, London. You're always welcome, even if you keep questionable company." He side-eyed Chase. "And since you're here, I can join you for some of it."

"You're a football fan?" Kyra couldn't picture the surly giant hooting or high-fiving.

Gully blinked, affronted. "What do you mean?" He shook his head either in disbelief or disappointment. He nodded to a chair. "Take a load off. I'll bring you a drink."

Kyra shrugged out of her leather moto jacket and hung it on the back of the chair next to Charlie.

"Hey, neighbor!" Charlie crowed and rubbed her hands together like an eager Disney villain. "This is going to be awesome. Arizona's cornerback is playing with a broken finger, and their tight end has a sinus infection."

"That's … great," Kyra hedged, unsure how to respond. An unhelpful razor commercial played on the giant projector screen. She pointed to Charlie's over-sized jersey, personalized with CHAMBERS across the shoulders. "Nice strip."

"Isn't it fab? I got it just in time." She held the shirt out by the bottom hem. "I had one made for Grace too, but she hates it."

"I don't hate it, Char." Grace heaved a weary sigh. "I only said it's a little juvenile." She turned doleful eyes on Kyra. "Thank ye gods, I talked her out of choosing sexually suggestive numbers."

"I didn't think you knew what it meant!" Charlie protested, and Kyra sputtered a laugh.

"I'm not that out of touch, Char." Grace reached across the table and gave Kyra's hand a squeeze. "Hi, dear, it's lovely to see you. When did your detective get in?"

"Not a detective anymore, Grace." Tarek leaned down to give her a hug. "I got in a few hours ago."

"Quick trip this time?" Grace didn't notice the slight dimming of Tarek's smile.

His most recent assignment with his consultancy firm, Greyscale Security, had been short by investigatory standards. He'd only been in Toronto providing profiling services to the human trafficking division for ten days, but from his terse phone calls and cryptic texts, Kyra knew whatever he'd found there had been harrowing. He compartmentalized, and became distant when his cases were upsetting, but he made a point of checking in, even if only to tell her he'd talk to her later. It was frustrating to be shut out, but the few times she had pried, she'd heard the pain in his voice, as if sharing the details made him relive the horror of what he'd witnessed.

"Tarek, we got you something," Charlie said and brandished a rumpled envelope. "Happy birthday!"

Tarek's expression immediately turned wary. He accepted it with a soft thanks.

"Go on, open it," Grace urged. She turned to Kyra and mumbled, "I hope he likes it. It was Charlie's idea."

"And mine," Chase interjected, his eyes sparkling. "It's from me, too. And Gully, technically. But it's more from me. And Charlie."

Tarek's eyes widened, alarmed, and Kyra bit back a laugh. He tore open the envelope and pulled out the folded piece of paper. The little W between his eyes eased away as he read, and when he looked up, he was grinning.

"This is great. Thank you."

Charlie let out a whoop and clapped her hands together.

"What is it?" Kyra asked, and he passed her the page. She read it. She glanced between Charlie and Chase, confused. It was a membership certificate to something called the Cottage City Club. "They've gifted you a membership to a private members' club?" Kyra pushed her hair behind her ear. She pictured the clandestine, soft lit lounges dotted about London.

Charlie roared with glee and pointed. "You should see your face." She shook her head, her wild curls bouncing with the movement. "Cottage City was the old name for Oak Bluffs. The Cottage City Club is a community organization. They run a rec center with pool tables, a bar, and old televisions. They also support a lot of local charities."

"Oh, that sounds nice." Kyra schooled her features, but felt her cheeks burn. She handed the certificate back to Tarek. "That'll be fun for you."

Charlie turned to Grace. "She thought it was a sex club." Grace pressed one hand to her heart, and the other covered her mouth. Her shoulders shook with her chuckles. Chase sputtered his beer, hiccupping, and Gerry slapped him on the back.

"I didn't," Kyra muttered, a half-hearted protest, but it wasn't that far off.

When he finally stopped coughing, Chase draped an arm across her shoulders. "What did you do in London?" he teased. She tried to shrug him off, but he only held her tighter. "Charlie and I became members when Tar was out of town. We thought it'd be fun. Gully sponsored us all."

"Oh, that's nice," she repeated, apparently unable to come up with anything that sounded more sincere. She tried to swallow back the sting that they didn't want her at their special club.

"You're not missing anything, dear. Unless, of course, you like all this." Grace gestured to the surrounding room, and to the projector screen, where the players were preparing for the coin toss.

"And chili-fries," Charlie said, her eyes raised to the heavens. "The club serves chili-fries all day, every day. And mozzarella sticks." She pressed her hands together.

"Chili-fries and mozzo-sticks?" Gully appeared behind her and crossed his arms over his broad chest. "Good game day food. I think we can make that happen. Do not tell anyone you're ordering off the menu." His lips disappeared under his beard and his brows knit together.

Charlie bopped up and down in her seat and drew an X on her chest. "Cross my heart."

Chase pulled Kyra closer and ducked his head to whisper in her ear, "Don't look so pathetic. I got you a membership, too."

"You did?" she asked, pulling back, half annoyed with herself for her intrusive thoughts and half annoyed that she sounded so hopeful.

"Yes, you jackass."

"Thank you," she muttered, embarrassed. She should have known better. Chase had his own family history that made him sensitive to her abandonment issues. He'd never let her feel excluded.

"You're welcome." He winked.

The broadcast blared over the speaker system. A man in an obnoxious green and gray plaid suit announced the coin toss. The pub erupted when the Patriots accepted the ball.

Kyra tried paying attention. She couldn't follow the gameplay and one-by-one Chase, Charlie, and even the ever-patient Gerry, tired of explaining it to her. Eventually, she ended up at the far end of the table, with Grace and Officer Mark Evans.

Mark was peppering Grace with questions about Martha's Vineyard. He asked her about the different towns, what they were like, how they changed in the summer and off season. Kyra's curiosity was piqued when he asked about the Martha's Vineyard Community Council, the island's quasi-political leadership organization, and its members, where they lived, what they were like, what was it like working with them and the executive director, Ida Ames.

"Mark, are you moving here?" Kyra asked.

"Oh." He pushed his hair off his forehead. "Collins didn't tell you?" Kyra shook her head. "I've been restationed in Oak Bluffs, supporting the island forces' community relations. I started a few weeks ago."

The year before, Officer Evans helped Tarek investigate a series of violent crimes on the island. Kyra remembered how uncomfortable he'd been with the more gruesome aspects of the case. A role as a community liaison would suit the cheerful man who reminded her of an overgrown puppy.

"That's brilliant, Mark. What a great opportunity. Congratulations."

"Thank you." Evans's cheeks turned a rosy pink. "I'm excited. And it'll be nice to spend more time here. You know," he said, his voice lowering and his tone turning serious. "It was all thanks to Collins and the letter of commendation he wrote. I wouldn't have been transferred without it."

Tarek was sitting between Chase and Gully. He caught her eye, and the side of his mouth hitched into a half smile. He turned back to the game. It didn't surprise her that Tarek helped Evans or that he never mentioned it. He probably never even considered it a kindness.

"So, you've moved here, then? Or are you commuting?"

Evans shook his head. "I moved, at least for now."

"He's been staying in one of my summer cottages," Gully said, referring to the modest compound he ran for summer rentals and off-season temporary housing.

"Gully has been a lifesaver. Finding housing on the island, especially to stay through the summer, has been challenging." Evans pressed his mouth into a thin line.

"It's one of the council's biggest priorities," Grace said with a nod. "This island needs housing accessible to the people who live and work here."

"It does, but don't worry, Evans. I'm not going to throw you out. You'd never survive the mean streets of Martha's Vineyard." Gully slapped the smaller man on his back, causing him to squeak.

"Of course not." Grace huffed, not getting Gully's joke. "The council has been pushing for closer collaboration with the island's public safety departments for years. The state finally listened. Now that you're here, we'll make sure you have a place to live."

"Thank you, ma'am," Mark said, his voice thick.

"Call me Grace, dear."

Gully leaned down between Kyra and Mark. "Did you hear what London got Tar for his birthday?"

Evans shook his head and grimaced. "Collins isn't a big fan of birthdays." He palmed the back of his neck. "The department got him a cake once. They say he shot it."

"What?" Kyra laughed, but it fell away when she took in his expression. "Seriously?"

Mark shrugged. "I think he started the rumor so folks would be too scared to sing 'Happy Birthday' to him, but they stopped getting him cake after that, too." His gaze shifted to Tarek before zipping back to Kyra. "It was a real shame. The department always got really good birthday cake, the kind with both chocolate and vanilla frosting."

Gully snickered. "That sounds like him. I doubt he'll be shooting anything this time. Tar's going to meet *Murder & MayFemme*. He and London are going to shadow them on one of their investigations." His fingers twitched in air quotes.

Tarek loved true-crime podcasts. He devoured them and his favorite, *Murder & MayFemme*, hosted by a female duo, happened to be doing a special investigation into a decades old Martha's Vineyard cold case. Kyra had made some calls and arranged to interview the hosts. She'd been excited to tell Tarek about it, but she took in Mark's dismayed expression and worried she may have mis-stepped.

"What is it? Do you think he won't like it?"

Gully let out a big belly laugh.

"On, no. I'm sorry." Mark ducked his chin, breaking eye contact. "I'm sure Collins will love it."

Kyra studied the young man. He was staring into his beer glass, his shoulders slumped, defeat in his brown eyes.

She reared back in her seat. "My god, how many times did he make you listen to them?"

"Many, many times. Over and over."

Gully's laugh deepened. His shoulders shook, and he wiped at the tears collecting in the corner of his eyes with one of his bar towels. "He's obsessed. Has been since we were kids. It started with reruns of 'Unsolved Mysteries.'" He turned to Kyra. "Have you told him yet?"

She shook her head and took a long sip of wine. Now, she was debating whether she even should.

"Don't let the kid get in your head. Tar will love it." Gully dropped a paw on her shoulder and gave it a gentle squeeze. He released her after a second and excused himself to attend to other patrons.

"How are you enjoying writing the column for *The Island Times*?" Grace asked Kyra.

"It's been going well, so far," she said, grateful for the subject change.

After the discovery of the shipwreck, Kyra had written a mildly successful article about the *Keres* and its pirate captain. Since then, she'd submitted a few articles to the local paper, mostly as a lark, but Han Park, the paper's editor-in-chief, had accepted and printed all of them. She reckoned Han's interest in her was predominantly because of her last name and local address, but when she'd quit her law firm job last December, Han had offered her a weekly guest columnist spot. The pay was abysmal. The research was tedious, and networking with the locals for fresh stories each week was time consuming and often fruitless, but writing wasn't unfulfilling.

Han had given her near free rein to write whatever she wanted, but his hints were far from subtle. He wanted her to follow in her late father's footsteps, write gritty stories exposing the dirty truths hidden under the island's glossy veneer of class and privilege, but Kyra wasn't sure it was the right path for her.

"I'm working on a story about the high school's freshman hockey teams. Their funding was cut, making it difficult for them to travel off island for games."

"No!" Grace replied, her eyes widening in horror. "That's unacceptable." She reached for her purse. She pulled out her phone and jabbed out a message with her pointer finger. "I'll let Ida know. She won't stand for that." Kyra sighed. Bringing the kids' funding woes to one of the managing community council members' attention might have just fixed their problem and killed her story.

"Yes!" Charlie screamed and jumped to her feet.

Her chair flew back. Kyra flinched. Suddenly, everyone was standing, screaming, hollering. The celebratory clamor drowned out the racket of chairs skidding across the floor and toppling over. Charlie yanked Gerry into a one-armed hug, jumping up and down, hanging on him. Grace set her phone down and clapped her hands.

"What's happened?" Kyra asked, her head swiveling around, taking in the bedlam.

"They just won." Grace leaned closer and let loose a resigned breath. "And now there'll be the after party."

# Chapter Two

*Monday, February 6*

KYRA'S EYES FLUTTERED open, and she turned, reaching for Tarek, but his side of the bed was empty and cold. She sat up, pulling the sheets to cover her chest. She blinked against sleep, letting her vision adjust, and focused on the clock sitting on her nightstand. Not yet eight. It was still early on the island, even if it was late for her, but it had been a rare late night. After the game, they'd stayed at Gully's until close, then followed the crowd around the corner to The Crow's Nest, the dingy dive bar on Main Street. It'd been well past one when she and Tarek finally got home.

She slipped into her silk dressing gown, and, ignoring the piles of clothes carelessly discarded on the floor, padded across the room to the wall of windows that made up the back side of her house. Outside, the sky was a dirty gray. The dark waters of Crackatuxet Cove swirled and spun. Sea foam gathered at the banks, soft and snowlike. Kyra squinted. It was snow.

It was snowing. Flakes so tiny they could be mistaken for dust fluttered to the ground where they stuck to the vegetation in patches. So far, the winter had been mild, or so she'd been told, with only the occasional snowfall. She wondered if they were due for a bigger storm.

Downstairs was quiet, the soft *pat* of her bare feet on the hardwood the only sound. But unlike yesterday morning, and the ten before that, the house didn't feel empty. The lights had been turned on against the shadows and Cronkite's kibble and water bowls were full.

She placed a pod in the coffeemaker and pulled down a mug. While the machine whirred, she pulled a birthday card from her purse. The brightly colored envelope was creased, and she tried to smooth the wrinkles with her palms against the granite. Inside the card was her birthday gift to Tarek. He had insisted he didn't celebrate and made her promise she wouldn't make any fuss.

She'd lied.

Last fall, Kyra learned that *Murder & MayFemme* was considering investigating a cold case on the island. She mentioned it to Han and suggested she could interview them for the paper. He'd jumped at the idea. Lucky for her, *Murder & MayFemme's* production company was a subsidiary of the newly formed Omega Global, Inc. Kyra called in a favor with its new CEO, her ex-client, Asher Owen. Asher snapped his fingers, or did whatever leaders of multinational conglomerates did, and as of last week, she and Tarek were going to meet Marjorie and Kelsey, the hosts of *Murder & MayFemme*. If Tarek wanted to. Kyra ran her fingers over the envelope, remembering Mark Evans's expression when he told her about Tarek's last office birthday. She hoped she hadn't made a mistake.

The machine sputtered to an end. She added vanilla almond milk to her mug and gave it a quick stir. Coffee in one hand, envelope in the other, she glanced at the clock over the ovens. She sucked in a deep breath. *It's now or never.*

Kyra tapped her knuckles against the glass and inched open the study's French door.

"Tar? Are you busy?"

"No, come in."

The study couldn't have been more different from the contemporary, clean lines of the rest of the house. It had been the space her father Ed Gibson had made fully his own—dark, cluttered, and worn. Cozy.

There was a large stone hearth, where a gas fire flickered. Kyra's inherited house demon was splayed out in front of it, soaking up the heat. His soft snores were just audible over the crackling flames.

At the back of the room, a set of French doors opened onto the patio and on warm days, Tarek left them ajar, letting in the sea breeze. Opposite, with a direct view of the cove, sat her father's ancient desk. Kyra's mother had bought it in Nimes. It was at least a hundred years old, and although not inherently valuable, it was unique. It was also where Ed had written his best pieces, including the one that had won him a Pulitzer. The medallion had since moved to a shelf at Tarek's insistence.

In the corner, half concealed in the bookshelves, was the gun safe Kyra had installed last fall. It'd been a compromise for the firearms Tarek was required to keep, and not one she was entirely comfortable with. Her gaze skittered over it to the man in the chair.

"Morning." Tarek's normally melodic voice was still rough from disuse. His hair was damp, and the sharp scent of chlorine pierced the air. He'd already been to the YMCA pool.

"How long have you been up?"

"A while," he said with a shrug, and stretched his arms over his head. "You made the front page." He held up a copy of *The Island Times*. Kyra recognized the photograph of Lisa and Sophia Mackey as the one she'd chosen to accompany her article. "It's good."

Kyra shrugged. It was … fine, at best.

"No, I mean it." Tarek wasn't quick or generous with compliments. Still, she knew that the piece she'd written about the sisters-in-law's new sea-to-table restaurant in Menemsha wasn't exactly riveting journalism. "We should try it one night. I think they'd give us a reservation."

Kyra mumbled something noncommittal and crossed the room. "Happy birthday."

"It was yesterday."

"I know, but I didn't get to give you your gift." Kyra held out the card.

"What did you do?" he asked, not reaching for it.

She huffed a soft laugh. "Don't look so worried. You'll like it. Probably." She grimaced.

His gaze remained trained on her as she rounded the desk to stand beside him. She perched on the edge and sipped her coffee, humming at her first hit of caffeine.

"Go on." She held the card out, and he took it between two fingers. "Open it."

"I told you not to get me anything."

Kyra shrugged, but her nonchalance was feigned. She really wanted him to like the gift. "I didn't *get* anything. I just took advantage of a connection, you could say."

Tarek's eyebrows furrowed like that didn't please him, but he didn't ask what she meant, to her relief. Tarek didn't care for Asher Owen.

He sliced through the envelope with a letter opener and slipped out the card. She'd chosen one of the cheap, humorous ones, trying to downplay her desire to make him happy, but the photo of the wrinkly elephant wearing a birthday hat with AGE IS IRRELEPHANT scrawled across the top made her feel like a complete tool.

Tarek opened it. He read the short paragraph she'd written in her tidy cursive. He looked up. His dark green eyes shined as he scanned her face.

"Seriously?" he asked, his voice barely a whisper, and he cleared his throat.

"Mmmhmm." Kyra took another sip of coffee.

He reread it. "No. Really?" He was grinning, his cheeks stretched further than she'd ever seen them.

"Yes, really." She chuckled.

Gently, he took the cup from her hand and placed it on the desk. He pulled Kyra into his lap.

"This is unbelievable," he said, his voice muffled against her shoulder. "How? When? *Murder & MayFemme* is coming to the island? And I'm really going to meet Marjorie and Kelsey?" He pulled back; his eyes were bright. "*I* am meeting *them*? Oh, gosh. I can't believe it. This is incredible."

"Gosh?" Kyra laughed at his rapid descent into fanboy-at-a-comic-convention. "Yes. We're shadowing and interviewing them. We meet them in a few hours."

Tarek stilled. "What? You mean *today*?" Tarek raked his

hand through his hair. "Where? Do you know the case? How?" His questions came too rapidly for her to answer, and Kyra laughed again, her whole body warm.

"I don't have specifics. They're sending over NDAs. We have to sign those before they'll share more."

"We should relisten to last season." Tarek reached for his phone.

Kyra bit her lip, wondering how she could decline without hurting his feelings. He'd already made her listen to their back catalog and really, one play through was enough *Murder & MayFemme* for her. For most people.

Thankfully, Tarek's phone rang with a video call. He checked the caller and pressed the screen to his chest. "It's my mom. I told her I'd talk to her today."

"Answer it," Kyra said and pressed her lips to his. She untangled herself from his grip and slid off his lap. "We have lots of time."

# Chapter Three

"WHAT TIME DO we need to leave?" Tarek asked for the third time in less than ten minutes.

He stood in the walk-in closet, scowling at a row of nearly identical button-down shirts.

"Twenty minutes." Kyra struggled for patience.

She'd never seen him like this, nervous, jittery. It was both endearing and a little alarming. He had a list of questions he wanted to ask about his favorite episodes. He'd read them to her multiple times, altering the phrasing to get it just right, worried the questions were stupid. *No.* Or if it made him sound like a super fan. *Yes.*

"What about this one?" he asked, holding a dark blue shirt against his chest.

"The one you're wearing is fine, Tar."

"You don't think it's too cop?" He tugged at the hem of his light blue chambray shirt and frowned.

"Honestly, I've no idea what that means," she lied, turning away to hide her smirk.

Tarek's wardrobe was the disgruntled detective starter kit. Ninety percent of his side of the closet was dark denim, wrinkly oxfords, and plain, cheap ties. Tarek grunted and thrust the hanger back on the rod.

Kyra took pity on him. She reached up and pulled down the sweater her Aunt Ali and Uncle Cam had gifted him for Christmas. "Here, wear this." She handed it to him. He turned it in his hands. "I assure you; no cop is wearing cashmere."

That seemed to convince him, and he cast off his shirt, pulling the sweater over his head. He smoothed the front, his elegant fingers sliding across the kitten-soft fabric. His brows slanted in a silent question.

Kyra had to give Ali credit. The woman had impeccable taste. The slim cut of the sweater fit him perfectly, highlighting his athletic swimmer's build, and the rich hunter green color brought out the gold flecks in his eyes.

"Perfect. Not cop at all." She sat on the bed and pulled on a pair of thick socks. "Why are you so nervous, anyway? This is just a chat at a coffee shop. You've spoken to more intimidating people. You've interviewed murderers and given press briefings. Hell, you've spoken to the director of the FBI."

"I know." Tarek's frown deepened. "But Kelsey and Marjorie don't have the highest opinion of law enforcement, and I don't know—" He broke off.

The podcasters often depicted the official investigators as a bunch of puffed-up idiots on power trips. Kyra knew, in part from her law degree and in part from screwing up Tarek's cases, that it was often more complicated than that. Sometimes the police's hands were tied, bound to the rules of a complex and imperfect legal system. Unlike true crime enthusiasts, they didn't have the luxury of ignoring due process and rules of evidence.

"You're technically not law enforcement anymore, you know."

He shrugged, and Kyra stood. She put her hands on his shoulders, smoothing his sweater over his biceps. Tarek was tall enough she had to tilt her head back to look into his eyes.

"Listen actively. Repeat what they say in your own words. Don't offer advice or your opinion unless they ask for it and never say *should*." She offered him the same advice she'd received as a junior associate. "But, most importantly, Tar," she said, going off script. "Just be you. They'll love you. Everyone does."

"And you?" he asked, staring down at her, his gaze intense.

Kyra's body flashed cold, then hot. She batted his chest with the back of her hand, laughing at him like his question was absurd, and stepped back, ignoring the flicker of hurt in his eyes.

She made a show of checking at her watch. "We should go, or we'll be late."

Tarek was quiet for a beat. "You said we're meeting them at Crepes 'n Crème?"

Kyra felt a pang of guilt at his subdued tone, but she pushed it away. When she finally looked at him, her smile was too bright. "Mmmhmm. That's what Marjorie said. They're staying close by. Do you know where it is?"

"I do. It's a breakfast place in OB, across the street from Claire's."

They took Tarek's beaten-up old Jeep. He preferred it to Kyra's luxury SUV in the snow, and she happily deferred to him. Most of Kyra's adult life had been spent living in large cities. She'd never really taken to driving, even in good weather, never mind the snow.

They drove into town, taking Beach Road. Under the overcast sky and soft snow flurries, State Beach was deserted. The water was dark. Ice and snow clung to patches of wet sand. On clear days, the mainland across the sound and the elbow of Chappaquiddick were visible, but today they were shrouded in mist, just dark lines above the water.

She faced forward and looked toward OB, turning her back on the shadows of Chappy. The memory of their horrific Thanksgiving dinner at the historic mansion hadn't yet faded. Sometimes, especially when she was alone, she'd have nightmares about that night. Kyra ran her hand down her thigh and reached for Tarek. She gave his warm fingers a squeeze.

Oak Bluffs was a ghost town. The giant Victorian houses on Seaview Avenue were closed for the winter, the windows and doors boarded up against the gales that battered them with waves and rocks. The festive decorations that had brightened Ocean Park over the holidays had been removed, the fountain drained. Even the flocks of Canada geese, a near constant complaint of the islanders, were absent. Only a few businesses remained open year-round, restaurants and shops that served the islanders' immediate needs. But parking was plentiful, and Tarek found a spot a few yards from the restaurant. Kyra was grateful. She wasn't properly dressed, and the wind was brutal. Each gust felt like being stabbed with a blade made of ice.

A bell tinkled as the door swung open, and Kyra pushed

aside the heavy curtain protecting the interior from the cold. Crepes 'n Crème was small and blissfully warm. The air was thick with the sweet scents of sugar, cinnamon, and vanilla. A waitress paused taking an order and waved her pad at them.

"Sit anywhere you like."

"We're meeting people." Kyra scanned the room, but realized she didn't know what the podcasters looked like. She shrugged an apology.

The waitress cocked her head, and let it drop with a sigh. She straightened, and called out, "Anyone waiting on two more?"

"We are."

The waitress pointed to a four-person table with a pair of women sitting side-by-side.

"*Murder & MayFemme?*" Kyra asked, stopping at their table.

The closer one stood, followed much more slowly by the other. The second woman was petite, at least a few inches shorter than Kyra. Her blonde hair fell to her shoulders in untamed waves that didn't flatter her round, full face. The first woman was tall, nearly as tall as Tarek, with a thick mass of black hair she'd pulled back into a tight topknot wrapped with a colorful silk scarf. She wore thick glasses that enlarged her brown eyes, giving her an owlish appearance.

"Yes," the owlish one responded, scowling. "I'm Marjorie. This"—she waved to the woman beside her—"this is Kelsey. And you are Miss Gibson?" She stuffed her hands into the kangaroo pocket of her sweatshirt.

"It's just Kyra, please. It's lovely to meet you. This is Tarek Collins."

Tarek extended his hand, his eyes bigger than Kyra had ever seen them. "Hi" he said, his voice a little breathy. He cleared his throat. "I mean, hello."

After a moment that felt too long, Kelsey reached forward and shook his hand. Marjorie's hands remained in her pocket.

"Nice to meet you," Kelsey said and shot her cohost an admonishing look. Marjorie's scowl deepened. Gripping the table, Kelsey lowered herself into her chair. She pointed to the two across from her. "Have a seat. We were waiting for you to order."

Tarek held the chair for Kyra before taking his own. Once seated, Kelsey spread her hands wide on her paper placement and her gaze traveled over Tarek. "We were told you were experts on the history of the island and criminology?"

Kyra gritted her teeth. *Fucking Asher.*

"Before we get to all that," Marjorie said, pulling a folder from her tote bag. "We need the signed NDAs." She eyed Kyra, her mouth twisted to the side. "We don't normally work with the press." Her gaze shifted to Tarek. "Or self-proclaimed experts."

Kyra stiffened, but Tarek nudged her with his knee. She pasted on a saccharine smile and pulled the pages from her pocket. "Of course. Here."

Marjorie took her time reviewing the documents. She checked, then double-checked their signatures, and Charlie's notary stamp. Finally, seeming satisfied, she slipped the pages into the folder and set it aside. Only then did she acknowledge the waitress and motioned they were ready to order.

Once three steaming mugs and one iced coffee were deposited on the table, Kelsey renewed her question. "So, you're criminology experts?"

Tarek coughed and cleared his throat again, and Kyra tried not to laugh. He was so nervous. "I work in forensics, and Kyra has a column with the local paper."

Marjorie's expression soured.

"But that's not why we're here," Kyra interjected. She raised her hand, anticipating the women were about to walk out. "This"—she motioned between the two sides of the table—"it's a birthday gift. For Tarek."

"I'm a huge fan."

"You are?" Marjorie eyed him like she thought he might be lying.

"I am. I've listened to every episode, some multiple times. I got hooked about four years ago. My favorite was the third series. Connecting the Winslow robbery to the robberies of those three other victims was some excellent investigatory work. Figuring out it was a feed delivery route." He shook his head. "Random-looking crimes are the most difficult to solve."

Marjorie's scowl thawed and Kelsey beamed.

"You think?" Kelsey asked.

"Mmmhmm. It was really impressive."

"I still can't believe the sheriff's department didn't put it together that all the victims lived next to hobby farms," Marjorie said. "I mean, come on, right?"

"It was so obvious." Kelsey's grin was smug.

"I doubt it even occurred to them to search the rural areas. The crimes occurred in wealthy suburbs. The victims weren't involved at all in agriculture. It was an incredible discovery." Tarek spun his coffee cup. "What happened to the sheriff?"

"He was replaced," Kelsey said. "That was one of our first big cases. It was recast on all the major outlets."

"The thieves didn't just take cash. They took jewelry, artwork, anything they thought they could sell. They took an old woman's engagement ring. It was all she had from her life with her dead husband. Because of us, she got it back. *Murder & MayFemme* made a difference. We helped people and legitimized the genre. True crime podcasts are just as valuable to investigations as traditional law enforcement now." Marjorie's nod was emphatic.

"That's a wonderful end to the story," Kyra said.

Tarek had made her listen to the series. She'd looked up the string of robberies on her own later. The actual story wasn't as compelling as the podcast's version. The woman in question had been in her forties and had left her very much alive husband years earlier. But Kyra had to give the podcasters credit where it was due. *Murder & MayFemme* saw a connection that no one else did.

A silent communication passed between the hosts.

"So, what sort of forensic work do you do?" Kelsey asked.

"I'm a profiler."

Kelsey's eyes widened, and she leaned forward. "Like with the FBI? Like in those crime scene shows?"

"Something like that. Although, it's a lot more statistical research than you see on television."

"You probably would have some thoughts about the case we're looking into. It's fascinating."

"Wait, Kels." Marjorie held up her hand. "Before we tell you what we're investigating and why we're here, I will remind you that everything about the case is off the record." Marjorie glared at Kyra. "This isn't part of your story."

"We understand. I haven't committed to writing an article yet, but if I do, it'll be subject to your approval."

Han wouldn't be pleased. He didn't like puff pieces, but if it got Tarek an opportunity to spend an afternoon with his version of a nineties boy band, it'd be worth the verbal thrashing.

Marjorie nodded and tilted her head, giving Kelsey permission to continue. Kelsey took a long sip of her iced coffee. She licked her lips. "Have you ever heard of the Martha's Vineyard Playhouse Tragedy?"

# Chapter Four

"**N**O," TAREK ANSWERED. "I don't think so."

Kyra stirred her coffee, watched the liquid make a tiny whirlpool. The Playhouse Tragedy sounded vaguely familiar, but she couldn't place where she'd heard it.

Kelsey's eyes brightened, and she inhaled a deep breath, one that expanded her chest. When she spoke, her voice was deeper, her words crisper, and her cadence slower. "Forty years ago, a man named Tobias Gillman moved from New York to Martha's Vineyard."

"Forty-four years ago, to be exact," Marjorie interrupted, her own tone measured.

"Sorry, Marj. You're right. Forty-four years ago, Tobias Gillman moved from New York to Martha's Vineyard." She paused.

*What's happening right now?* Kyra glanced at Tarek out of the corner of her eye, but all his attention was focused on the podcasters. He was enthralled.

Kyra set her spoon down on a napkin. The silence stretched on, grew heavy. "Oh," she said, straightening in her seat. "Should we know him?"

Marjorie's eyes narrowed behind her thick frames. "Tobias Gillman was a bit of a local celebrity."

Kyra shook her head. "Sorry. Never heard of him."

"Gillman had been a successful theater actor in New York. Very well respected."

"Really? What was he in?" Kyra asked, not that she could name a single Broadway play from forty-four years ago, or any Broadway actor, ever.

"Mostly off-Broadway productions, but he did well enough," Marjorie said through gritted teeth.

*Oh.* Apparently, this wasn't a dialogue, but a presentation. An agonizingly slow one. Kyra mumbled an apology and Tarek picked up his coffee mug, hiding his smile behind it.

"That's right," Kelsey said, her voice low and conspiratorial. "But as Tobias Gillman got older, the roles that drove his passion dried up. He found himself spending more time coaching the fresh talent. He became a mentor, a guru, for the younger generations. People came from all over to learn the craft from him. He was so sought after he opened a drama school in Tarrytown. It became famous for its yearly productions, often showcasing actors and actresses whose names later headlined the marquis on Broadway." She raised her hands and spread them wide.

"That's right, Kels. Names like Lawrence, Carey, and Nigel."

Kyra didn't know who they were talking about, and by his expression, neither did Tarek, but it was clear from the podcasters' weighted pause they were supposed to be impressed. Silently.

Marjorie and Kelsey took turns telling the history of Gillman's Tarrytown school, interrupting each other to add detail. It was a verbal tag team, and it was exactly like they spoke on the podcast, a sort of frenetic, slow-burn energy that kept the listener engaged while dragging out the tale. In person, Kyra found it annoying, and she bit back the urge to demand they get to the fucking point.

"Gillman noticed that attendance was low during the summer months, when his wealthy patrons traveled to their summer homes in the Hamptons, Cape Cod, Martha's Vineyard, Nantucket, and up north," Kelsey volleyed.

"He recognized an opportunity to create a dramatic arts program in one of those vacation spots," Marjorie returned.

"A sort of summer camp." Kelsey set Marjorie up.

"But so much more. Much, much more. He wanted to create a mainstay for the community. Something people would travel to but also want to stay for. Ultimately, he settled on Martha's Vineyard. It was larger than Nantucket, easier to get to and leave, but still far enough away to feel exclusive. It was famous and wealthy, but not limited to the super elite like the Hamptons or Hilton Head."

"The first year, the camp was run from a church base-ment." Kelsey leaned forward. She pressed her hands down on the table and focused somewhere above Kyra's left shoulder. "The camp was incredibly successful. Locals and vacationers signed up. The end of season production sold out. Tobias made more cash in one summer than an entire year in Tarrytown. At the end of that first summer, he sold the New York school and made Martha's Vineyard his permanent home."

"He purchased a swath of land in an area of Oak Bluffs, called East Chop, and built a compound. It included seasonal living quarters, rehearsal space, and a dining hall. There was also an outdoor amphitheater and a playhouse. For himself, he built a grand year-round residence. He called it the Gillman Center for the Dramatic Arts." Marjorie pulled out her phone and showed them a grainy photograph of a man in a suit standing on an open-air stage.

"The Gillman Center was an instant success. It filled up every summer. The campers came from up and down the East Coast."

"And it wasn't cheap," Marjorie said, putting her phone away. "Tobias charged a premium to attend. In exchange for a hefty tuition, the camp provided room and board for the summer months, as long as the students committed to performing or working the tasks they were assigned for the week-long end-of-summer production in August."

"There was even a scholarship program funded by the National Endowment for the Arts," Kelsey added. "Gillman was legit."

Having spent a summer on the island, Kyra knew firsthand how magical it was. It was busy and vibrant, teeming with visitors. If she'd been a drama kid, she'd have jumped at the opportunity to spend eight weeks living and performing on the island.

"It sounds like an amazing way to spend the summer," she said.

Marjorie's nostrils flared, and she pushed her glasses higher on the bridge of her nose. "It should have been, but it was anything but. The camp was cutthroat. Gillman didn't let just anyone in. Applicants had to audition, and Gillman used talent scouts. There were rumors parents bought seats for their kids."

"Really? Bribes?" Tarek asked. It was the first time he'd spoken in a long while.

Marjorie frowned at the interruption and sat back in her chair with a shrug. "Why not? It wasn't an academic institution. There were no fairness or equality rules. Gillman's was the only voice that mattered." Her voice had gone higher, less intense. With her shrug, she'd shed her podcast host persona.

"This is what our preliminary research team put together," Kelsey added. "They've been digging into the records for weeks, but there isn't much to go on. Just a few disgruntled complaints with the Better Business Bureau and the state's Office of Consumer Affairs and Business Regulation, but nothing unusual."

Marjorie jutted out her bottom lip out and glared at her cohost. She cleared her throat. Kelsey grabbed her coffee and sucked it to the dregs until it bubbled. She shook it, rattling the ice against the glass.

"Those primary sources will be the framework for the narrative we spin when we record the intro episode. It sets the scene, but the history of the summer camp isn't relevant to the actual case," Marjorie explained.

Kelsey set her glass down. "The case." Kelsey's pause was all drama, and Kyra pushed her hands under her thighs, lest she wave at them to *get on with it*. Kelsey cleared her throat and dropped her voice. "Our case is about two teenage girls, Abigail Koch and Elodie Edwards. And how they died." Another pause and again Kelsey's gaze focused somewhere behind Kyra's left shoulder.

There was nothing there. Kyra had checked. Twice. She wondered if this was a podcaster quirk, an audio medium thing that had the women telling the story like playing an aggressive ping-pong match, adding in dramatic pauses, repeating facts they felt were important. That they rarely made eye contact while spinning their story made Kyra feel like a spectator to their oh so, so, *so* long show.

"Abigail and Elodie were campers and roommates one summer, forty years ago."

"Thirty-nine," Marjorie interjected.

Kyra stiffened and Tarek's steadying hand found her thigh. He gave it a gentle squeeze, and his thumb traced a line across the top of her knee.

"Thanks, Marj. Thirty-nine years ago. *Thirty-nine* years ago, Abigail Koch returned for her third season at the Gillman Center for the Dramatic Arts. She'd been cast as the lead in the end of season production. It was Elodie's first season, but she was a genuine talent, and she was cast as Abigail's understudy."

"More coffee?" The waitress interrupted, holding a carafe.

"Please," Kyra begged. Her blood was probably seventy percent caffeine at this point, but she'd mainline jet fuel if it'd make this experience less tiresome. *Murder & May-Femme's* multi-part series structure was clearly by design rather than necessity.

The waitress filled their cups and walked away. Marjorie resumed her podcaster persona. "Before opening night, the actors and their understudies attended a final dress rehearsal, and a preopening cast dinner. It was the last time either girl was seen alive." Marjorie nodded at Kelsey, who took over.

"They missed breakfast in the morning, then lunch. Abigail missed show call, and when they called for Elodie to sub, she couldn't be found. Right before the show was due to start, someone was sent to check their room. The door was forced open. What they found was a bloodbath." Kelsey paused. Kyra bounced her leg under Tarek's palm. "Abigail had been beaten to death in her bed. Her head, her face. Gone. Bashed in with a fire poker."

"And the other girl, Elodie?" Tarek asked.

Kelsey pressed her fingertips together. She spread her hands, palms to the ceiling. "Disappeared into the night. Never to be seen or heard from again."

"The police alleged that Elodie, in a jealous rage, murdered Abigail and escaped out the open window. She drowned trying to leave the island in the middle of the night. Her body was never recovered." Marjorie's eyes glittered.

"Jealous of what?" Kyra asked, unable to stop herself.

"Elodie wasn't content being Abigail's understudy, so she killed her to take the lead." Marjorie made a sour face.

Kyra pressed her lips together. *That doesn't make sense.*

"And you disagree with those allegations?" Tarek prodded.

"You tell us, Mr. Collins. You're an expert, aren't you?" Marjorie raised her chin and arched her eyebrow in a challenge. "Do you think a fifteen-year-old girl could beat her roommate to death, climb out a second-story window, make it into town, and off the island by herself in the middle of the night?"

Tarek rolled his lips, thinking. "I think it depends on a

lot of factors, but I wouldn't say it couldn't have happened. I'd like to know why the police came to the conclusions they did. How do they know Elodie used the window and didn't walk out the front door, or that she and Abigail were alone in their room?"

"Or why Elodie would kill her and run away if she wanted to play the part?" Kyra mumbled, and Tarek's hand tightened on her leg.

"That's not in the police report," Kelsey said.

"That's why *Murder & MayFemme* is here." Marjorie peered down her nose at Tarek. "The police did a shitty job. They walked onto the crime scene and walked right out. They didn't care about the truth, but Kelsey and I do. *Murder & MayFemme* will find the answers."

*I bet.* Kyra snorted, then forced herself to cough to cover it up. She pressed her hand to her mouth and sniffed. "I'm sorry. Wrong tube." Tarek patted her thigh. Kyra refused to look at him. If she did, she'd wouldn't be able to keep herself from laughing. These women were ridiculous. She feigned another cough and schooled her expression. "What happened to the summer camp?"

"It never recovered from the tragedy." Kelsey played with her straw. "News of the murder got out, and the attendance dropped."

"The wealthy weren't keen to send their future stars to Camp Murder."

"Oh! Marj, that's an awesome sound bite. We should totally use that." Kelsey turned to Kyra. "Gillman closed it and left Martha's Vineyard."

Tarek spun his coffee mug. "Why are you looking into

this now?"

"I'm sorry?" Marjorie asked.

"I'm just wondering. Why dig up this old story now? You'd said it was a cold case, but it sounds like it's been solved."

"It was solved on paper only. Neither girl's family was from here. The summer ended. The tourists went home. Gillman left. No one investigated it further, and since Elodie was presumed dead, no charges were ever filed. They didn't want to waste precious Martha's Vineyard resources. No one cared about justice for Abigail Koch."

"And that's our tagline!" Kelsey laughed and raised her hand to high five her cohost. Marjorie ignored her and Kelsey dropped her hand to the table. Her cheeks reddened, and she cleared her throat. "We'll workshop it." She turned to Tarek and Kyra. "We're doing this case because a Broadway production company, the Pāru Group, bought the campground. They're building a huge event space there. They plan to market it as Tanglewood for theater arts. The Koch case had always been on our list, but when we learned about Pāru's plans, we wanted to investigate the story before the old campsite was reno'd." The side of her mouth dipped down, and she raised her hand in a conciliatory gesture. "They said yes, provided we give them a little publicity. It's a win-win."

It was a win-win. A production company opening a theater on the same site as an old drama camp with a gruesome past was the stuff public relations people would kill for. People loved macabre histories, and a theater with an unsolved murder, or better yet, a celebrity-solved murder?

That sort of publicity couldn't be bought.

"Pāru's plans include a complete redesign of the site. They're demolishing everything, so it made sense to come see it before it was leveled," Marjorie added.

"Actually, we're meeting the project manager in about twenty minutes. We were told you were going to shadow us?"

Marjorie's lip curled in annoyance. She clearly wanted nothing to do with them, but Kyra had called in a favor of Asher-fucking-Owen to get this afternoon for Tarek.

"Yes, that was the arrangement, and we'd love to see it with you," Kyra confirmed before Tarek could decline. She'd ensure he got everything the podcasters would give them.

"Did you drive?" Tarek asked.

"Walked." Kelsey shook her head. "We were going to call a taxi."

"My car is right outside. I can take us."

"That would be great. Thank you." Marjorie almost sounded sincere. She tapped her empty coffee mug and blinked expectantly at Kyra.

Sighing to herself, Kyra signaled for the bill and paid for their coffees.

"Are we ready? We should go." Marjorie stood and stepped away from the table to pull on her coat. She reached out and gripped Kelsey's biceps. Kelsey set her hands on the table and pushed herself up, while Marjorie steadied her. Kelsey's shoulder dipped awkwardly as she stepped back, her movement stiff and jerky.

"Thanks," she said to her cohost and pulled on her jacket.

She lumbered around the table. She walked with a pronounced limp for two or three steps before her movements smoothed out to a shifting, wobbling shamble. To Kyra's mortification, Kelsey caught her watching, and she tapped her calf against the table leg. "Prosthetic. Car accident when I was a kid. The cold weather makes me stiff. Once my muscles warm up though, I'm right as rain." She shrugged as if to say, *What can you do?* "Good thing I'm in audio content, right?" Kelsey joked, but there was a challenge behind her eyes.

Kyra forced a strained laugh, at a loss for the correct response, and held the door open for her and Marjorie. "We're the dark green Jeep, just over there."

Tarek blasted the heat and turned on the defrosters. Kyra rubbed her hands together, the tips of her fingers and toes pinching, just from the short walk to the car. They drove up New York Avenue, past the harbor, and away from OB's town center. Tarek turned right at a gas station. Except for a short, but ill-conceived road race along the bluff, past the lighthouse, Kyra hadn't explored this part of the island. She had never ventured into the spiderweb of streets that made up the bulk of East Chop.

From the snow-dusted drives and shuttered windows, Kyra gleaned that many of the houses were summer residences. The roads were haphazardly maintained, and puddles had frozen solid in places. Some roads hadn't been cleared at all from the autumn or the winter's meager snowfall and the tires crunched over dead, frozen leaves.

"Turn here," Marjorie called from the back seat, her brow creased as she studied her phone. "Map says it's about three hundred feet up on the left."

Tarek made the turn onto a narrow road, bracketed by walls of spindly trees.

He braked hard at a gap in the brush and Kyra flew forward, her seatbelt cutting into her collarbone. "Ow!"

"Sorry," Tarek mumbled.

"This must be it. I think," Marjorie said, her voice rising with uncertainty.

Beside her, Kelsey was squinting out the window, her hands cupped on either side of her eyes.

Between two crooked granite posts was an unkept dirt road. The chain that had once barred entry was on the ground, caked with mud and ice. Tree branches hung low, weighed down with icicles. Tire ruts and potholes in the mud had frozen, creating a chaotic mountain range in miniature. If Kyra lived in a Saturday morning cartoon, there'd have been a sign warning them, CURSED. KEEP OUT.

"Are you sure this is it?" Kelsey asked, her voice breathy.

Kyra glanced back. The podcasters were sitting closer together. They seemed ... *almost nervous*. The women's behavior didn't reconcile with the *Murder & MayFemme* hosts' intrepid-warriors-for-justice image.

Tarek turned onto the dirt road. The tires rumbled over the chain and bounced against the frozen mud. They progressed slowly but steadily. Suddenly, the car lurched to the right and Tarek spun the wheel against it. Kyra grabbed the dash as the left side of the Jeep dipped low, throwing her off balance, and came to a shuddering halt.

"Whoa!" a voice in the back yelped.

"Oh, shit!"

Tarek pressed the gas, and the engine revved, but the car didn't move.

"Dammit," he muttered and tried turning the steering wheel and gassing the car again. Kyra felt the tire spin beneath them, but the car didn't budge.

"Are we stuck?" she asked.

"Yeah," Tarek said, grimacing. "I can get us out. One sec." He reached down and pulled the transfer case shifter.

He pressed the accelerator. With a concerning *clank*, the engine roared, and the wheels engaged. The Jeep leaped forward, and Kyra bounced against the seat. Hard. She winced.

"Four-wheel drive," he said, as his mouth pulled down apologetically.

The Jeep moved both slower and with more power than before. Kyra's teeth clacked against each other as they bumped down the drive, but they didn't get stuck again. Still, her knuckles turned white around the grab handle.

Tarek rounded a gentle curve, and the trees fell away. The forest had been cleared to create a staging area for the construction crew. An excavator and a dump truck were parked in the clearing, and just beyond were two identical, but derelict buildings positioned in an *L* shape, around a courtyard that had long ago gone to seed. The buildings were long structures, each two stories high. Windows were spaced evenly on both floors facing the courtyard. The panes were cracked, broken, or missing altogether.

Kelsey leaned between Tarek and Kyra and pointed. "I think those buildings are the dormitories. And over there would have been the rehearsal building." She pointed to the right.

Kyra's gaze followed Kelsey's finger. But if there had been a building there, it was gone now. Only a large hole remained. It was deep and surprisingly square. The crew must have been preparing to pour a foundation for whatever structure the Pāru Group had planned for the space.

"According to the map we found, the theater would have been just on the other side of the rehearsal hall." Marjorie pointed, but beyond the giant hole, Kyra couldn't make out more than trees and shrubs.

Tarek continued past the dormitories to another clearing where more construction vehicles were parked in neat lines. Just beyond were two trailers standing in parallel. Behind the trailers stood the remains of another structure, its gabled roof collapsed in sections.

"They're expecting us?" Tarek asked Marjorie.

"Yes. Our contact at Pāru said we'd be meeting with their site manager."

"What was that building?" Kyra asked, pointing to the destroyed structure behind the trailers.

"According to Marj's map, that was probably the dining hall or a field house."

Even in its half-collapsed state, it was easy to tell the building had been large, large enough to act as a gathering space for the campers for meals and recreative activities.

"How many people did the camp accommodate?" Tarek asked.

Marjorie scrolled through the notes on her phone. "Between the residents, the day trippers, and the staff, about four hundred. Around two-thirds of that boarded."

"You said Tobias Gillman lived on campus?" Kyra said, turning around in her seat. Kelsey nodded. "Did he have any family with him?"

Marjorie slipped her phone in her pocket. "Not that I know of, but Kent might."

"Kent?" Tarek repeated.

Marjorie pointed to the trailer, where a man stood in front of the open door, his hand raised in a wave. "The Pāru rep."

# Chapter Five

THE MAN LOPED down the temporary metal staircase and pointed to an empty parking spot next to a Mercedes SUV. Tarek pulled in and the man walked up to Kyra's window. He wasn't wearing a coat over his half-zip fleece and his cheeks were pink from the cold. Tarek pressed the button, and Kyra's window descended with a soft *whir*.

"*Murder & MayFemme?*" He stared at Kyra and Tarek, his bushy eyebrows hitched together.

"That's us." Kelsey popped her head between the front seats. "I'm Kelsey." She pointed to herself, then thumbed behind her. "That's Marjorie."

The man's wide mouth stretched into a veneer-flashing grin. "Yeah, that makes more sense. Podcasters. Come on in. It's freezing out here."

Kyra watched Marjorie's expression, wondering if the man's comment had landed like the insult she assumed he'd intended, but Marjorie either didn't hear him or chose not to. She pushed open the door and stepped outside. "Come on," she muttered and assisted Kelsey. Then, leaving the car door open, she followed the man up the stairs.

"Welcome. Welcome," the man boomed as he held the door open for them.

They slid inside the trailer, and Kyra moved to the far wall, away from the drafty door. It was set up as an office. Cluttered tables were lined up one behind the other in a row along the length of the right-side wall. Cheap metal folding chairs were shoved beneath them, and more were stacked in a corner. A small kitchenette had been set up in the rear. The space smelled of printer paper, stale coffee, and aftershave, but it was warm. Three space heaters were working overtime against the near-freezing temperatures outside. A man sat at one of the makeshift desks, staring at the laptop in front of him.

The man from outside shut the door and spun around with a flourish. He wasn't tall exactly, but he was bulky, and his presence looming. He vaguely reminded Kyra of the Cowardly Lion with his bushy, red-gold hair and beard.

"Kent," the lion called to the other man, his voice too big for the cramped space. It bounced off the walls and the flat surfaces, reverberating through the trailer. "Kent! *Murder & MayFemme* are here."

Kent, the man behind the computer, dragged his gaze away from the screen. He let loose an audible sigh and snapped it shut. His less than friendly gaze scraped over them. He stood up, sliding his hands into his pockets.

"Nice to meet you," Kent said with a blank expression.

"That's Kent," the lion said. "I'm Alvin." He jutted his hand out at Kelsey. She blinked at it before giving it a firm shake. "James Alvin, actually, but everyone just calls me Alvin."

"I'm Kelsey. This is Marjorie. We're *Murder & May-Femme*. This is…" She gestured to Tarek and Kyra.

"Our tagalongs," Marjorie sniped.

"This is Tarek Collins. He's an FBI consultant, like CSI."

"Yeah, and that's Kayla. She's not FBI." Marjorie hopped up onto one of the desks and swung her legs back and forth.

"It's Kyra. Kyra Gibson. I'm with *The Island Times*." She figured that was the easiest explanation. Kyra shook Alvin's hand. "Thank you for giving us your time today."

"Press? Already?" He beamed, and the fluorescent lights reflected off his too-white teeth. "You girls work fast. I like it." He pulled Kyra a little closer, leaned into her space, and shut his eye in an exaggerated wink. "When you need a quote, pretty girl, I'm your man."

Kyra stiffened and took a step back. His smile flickered, but he recovered quickly, letting her go, and turned to Marjorie. "So, you gals are going to solve an old murder?"

"That's the story they've sold to corporate," Kent said as he walked over, his mouth turned down.

"It's what we do," Marjorie snapped at Kent. "Kelsey and I solve the unsolvable." Her gaze flicked back to Alvin, and she straightened her spine. "We were told we'd be getting a guided tour of the camp."

"I'm aware of what you've been told," Kent said. "And you will have one. As if I've nothing better to do," he muttered.

"Alright, alright," Alvin said, raising and lowering his hands. "Ignore Kent. He's just in a bad mood. We had a budget meeting earlier." Alvin settled his considerable girth into one of the folding chairs. "Why don't you young ladies tell us a little about what you're looking for and then we'll show you around the property?"

Marjorie gave him a flat look, but she and Kelsey told them a blessedly short version of the story about Abigail Koch and Elodie Edwards.

"The girls' dorm, you say?" Alvin said, rubbing his chin.

Kelsey nodded. "That's where she was killed."

"Okay, okay. That we can do." Alvin stood and walked to the back of the trailer. He stooped to rummage in a storage bin and returned with a stack of hard hats. He handed one to Marjorie. "Put that on, darling. Don't want to give OSHA a reason to show up."

"What's stopping them?" Kent barked and yanked a fleece with Pāru branding off the back of his chair. "Apparently, anyone can just walk onto this shithole jobsite."

If the podcasters were confused by Kent's hostility, they didn't show it, but as professional busybodies, they might be accustomed to less than welcome receptions. It was the difference between Kent and Alvin's behavior that struck Kyra as strange. Kent's overt irritation with their intrusion was at such odds with Alvin's aggressive friendliness. It reminded Kyra of how the podcasters told their story. It felt like a performance. She peeked at Tarek from the corner of her eye, wondering if he'd picked up on the Pāru personnel's strange behavior.

He was leaning against the wall, his hands in his pockets, with an ankle crossed over the other. He was the picture of half-bored, aloofness, but a muscle in his cheek jumped, one of his tells that he wasn't as relaxed as he pretended to be.

Once Alvin had passed out all the hard hats, he stood in the middle of the floor. His good humor fell away, and he eyed them one-by-one.

"The buildings aren't structurally sound, so you all listen to me and Kent. If we say stop, you stop. We say go; you go. Got it?" He paused, waited for any objections. He seemed to accept their silence as agreement, because his toothy smile returned, somehow bigger. "Good. You guys ready?"

"Yep," Kelsey said.

Alvin looked between the podcasters... "Do you have recording equipment?"

"Not today," Kelsey shook her head at the same time Marjorie raised her phone.

"We got what we need."

Alvin rubbed the heel of his palm along his jaw. "Okay. Kent, you ready?"

"Mmmhmm." Kent put on a Pāru-branded hardhat, adjusting it so it sat squarely on his head. He gave the room a sweep, chewing on his lip. "Alright, let's get this over—" He broke off, his gaze snagged on Kelsey. The metal of her prosthetic was visible where her pant leg had ridden up her calf. "You think you should go?"

Kelsey stiffened.

"She's fine," Marjorie snarled, and Kelsey hurried to straighten her pant leg.

Kent shared a look with Alvin, who shrugged. "Whatever. As I told corporate, if any of you get hurt, even *you*, it's not on me."

"Understood," Kelsey said weakly, her gaze trained on the floor.

With another irritated grunt, Kent pushed the door open and stepped outside. Marjorie and Alvin followed behind him. Kyra stopped at the door, waiting for Tarek, but he held back. He was saying something to Kelsey that caused her lips to curve into a shy smile.

Kyra zipped up the neck of her jacket and hurried downstairs. Kent was pacing between the parked SUVs. He yanked his sleeve back to check his watch.

"Is there a problem?" Marjorie snapped and tucked her phone into her bag.

Kent halted. He was a slight man, with dark hair, high cheekbones, and piercing eyes. He narrowed them at Marjorie.

"Not at all." He sneered. "I love spending my afternoons giving tours of my jobsite to amateur detectives. You all think you're in your own production of *The Mouse Trap*."

"We're professionals." Marjorie's eyes flashed behind her glasses. "We're nationally recognized and have been granted permission to investigate this case."

"I couldn't give less of a shit about you or your case, lady. I just don't want anything disrupting my schedule. We're already behind."

Alvin clasped a hand on Kent's shoulder. "Don't be such a grump. You worry too much. Every production has delays. One stalled afternoon while we're waiting on the materials delivery isn't going to matter."

A noise on the metal staircase drew their attention. Tarek was helping Kelsey descend, her hand on his arm.

Kent made a noise in the back of his throat and shrugged Alvin off. "Whatever. Let's just go." He strode away; his boots crunching on the frozen mud.

The dormitories weren't far, just a few minutes' walk

back down the drive, but Kyra regretted not driving immediately. First, it was *freezing* and like the stubborn ass she was, she only had her thin moto-jacket. Second, the dirt and gravel drive was beyond treacherous. The heavy machinery had torn it up, leaving giant divots and potholes in the mud. The clay had filled with water and was frozen in some places, turning the puddles into mini ice rinks. She had to take care not to turn an ankle or slip and fall on her face. She sneaked a look over her shoulder. Kelsey was more than managing. Her arm was firmly around Tarek's. She trilled a high-pitched giggle at something he said. Kyra stuffed her hands farther into her jacket pockets and closed the short distance between her and Kent.

"Per the original plans, that one was the boys' dorm." Kent pointed to the first building parallel to the drive. "This one, over here, was designated for the girls."

They continued past the boys' dorm and crossed the overgrown courtyard to the girls' building. Kent gripped the enormous combination lock hanging from the chain slung between the door handles. He cycled through the numbers; the action slowed by his thick gloves. Kyra hunched her shoulders against the cold. She clenched her teeth to keep them from chattering.

The lock popped open, and Kent gave the chain a firm yank. It clanked as the links skidded through the handles and fell to the ground.

Alvin gripped the handle and shifted his weight to pull. He hauled on the door and, with an awful hair-raising *creak*, it opened. Kyra shuddered against the nails-on-a-chalkboard screech.

Alvin tapped his hard hat. "Me first." He stepped inside and motioned for them to follow. He held his arms wide. "Ladies and gentleman, welcome to Merman Hall."

Merman Hall was dark and gloomy. Just enough light filtered in from the holes and cracks in the hallway's grimy windows for them to see. The floor was littered with debris. Branches, clusters of decaying leaves, and rubbish lay scattered around the narrow space. Water stains climbed up the bubbling walls, telltale signs of the insidious mold beneath the plaster. In the corners were mounds of straw, fabric, and other unidentifiable, half rotten things. Kyra had lived in a squalid apartment in New York City while in law school. She knew what made those sorts of nests, and the diseases the vile creatures carried. *Rats.* She pressed her hand to her mouth and tried not to gag.

"Both dorms were built with the main hallway running up and down this side. All the rooms are on the other side, with views overlooking the courtyard." Kent's flashlight played along the floor of the hallway. "The new facility will have living quarters as well, but those will be apartment style."

"Do you know where Abigail and Elodie's room was?" Kyra asked.

Marjorie checked her phone. "No, the information we have just says it was the second floor."

"Is it safe to go upstairs?" Tarek asked, motioning to the narrow staircase.

Alvin deferred to Kent with a nod.

Kent frowned, considering. "I think we can try it."

"Alright," Alvin said and slapped his hands together in a

*clap.* "We'll go one at a time. I'll go first." He set his heavy boot on the first stair.

·They watched as Alvin ascended, slowly testing his weight on each tread. The railing had long since fallen away, and the rotted wood groaned and creaked under his weight. When he reached the top, he turned and waved them forward.

Kyra stepped forward, but a hand on her elbow stopped her. Tarek tipped his head toward the podcasters and motioned for them to go first.

"Don't lean on the wall, Kels," Marjorie said. "Be careful." The last bit came out as a shaky whisper that surprised Kyra.

Kelsey climbed the stairs at a glacial pace, her movements slow and jerky. One hand remained on her thigh as she self-assisted her injured leg. Alvin reached for her and helped her up the last two steps. At the top, she turned and gave Marjorie a thumbs-up.

Kent huffed out an annoyed sigh, earning a glare from Marjorie, who went up next. Then Kent and Kyra followed last by Tarek.

It wasn't as dark upstairs. Many of the rooms' doors were open or missing, letting in the early afternoon light. They crept down the hallway, pausing at each door, so Marjorie and Kelsey could take a peek inside. Alvin and Kent stood aside as the podcasters stuck their heads in, made an idle comment, and motioned for them to proceed.

By the third room, it became clear to Kyra that Marjorie and Kelsey weren't interested in seeing or searching the dorm rooms.

When Marjorie caught Kyra watching her, she shrugged. "What? They're all the same."

It wasn't quite true. The rooms were identical but for their state of ruin. Some still contained furniture, beds, or dressers turned on their sides. Others were empty. Some had walls, and in others the plaster had collapsed or rotted away. But collectively, Kyra got a decent picture of what the double occupancy rooms would have been like.

They stopped at the doorway of one of the middle rooms, but when Marjorie and Kelsey moved to the next, Kyra stepped inside for a better view. It had been cleaned out and was empty, or as clean and empty as a room that'd been abandoned for decades with a blown-out window could be.

The carpet had rotted away in places and the subfloor below was dipped and bowed with rot. With each step she took farther into the room, the floor groaned.

"Termites, I'd wager," Alvin said with a grating cheerfulness. "The Martha's Vineyard Community Council and the local historical society wanted us to salvage as much of the old timber as we could." He kicked the wall, and the plaster fell away, leaving a hole. "Lucky for us it was so cheaply built and in such bad condition it's not worth saving. Reclaiming costs a fortune."

Kyra walked the perimeter. The occupants would have had to push their beds against opposite walls, with the small window between them. It could have held two small dressers, but it'd have been tight. There was no closet and no overhead light fixtures.

She peered out of the window and down to the courtyard below. She counted the windows on the boys' dorm, one floor stacked above the other, all with views of the same would-be green space. Kyra spun in place, taking in the four walls, the low ceilings. She exited the room and checked the one to the left.

The window in this room was in better shape. Some creature had taken advantage of the modicum of shelter. Recently, Kyra discerned from the condition of the nest in the corner, and the smell.

"Are all the buildings this bad?" Marjorie's voice carried from down the hall.

"Couldn't say. I haven't been inside many of them." *Kent.* "This is the first time I'm in here, actually."

"How long will the renovation take?" Kelsey this time.

Kyra tapped her finger against the rotting windowsill.

"Tar?" she called without raising her voice. She heard his footsteps in the room next door, in the hall. She turned around as he appeared in the doorway. His eyes gleamed when they met hers and his mouth hitched into a wry half smile. He'd already come to the same conclusion. Kyra beamed. *The police's story was wrong.*

# Chapter Six

"WHERE TO NEXT, girls?" Alvin asked. "Sorry, and gent." He shot finger guns at Tarek, who just stared at him. Alvin swallowed. "So, next?" he asked Marjorie.

She pushed her jacket sleeve up, exposing her bare wrist, and examined it like a watch should have been there. "It's getting late, and this building was the only one we needed to see."

"We can get everything else we need from the police report," Kelsey added with a firm nod. "Thanks for the tour. It was super interesting."

*The police report?* Kyra's gaze pinged between them, confused. Why were the podcasters declining to continue the tour? She was just getting started. She wanted to see the rest of the camp. Obviously, the police report was total crap, and Kyra was surprised the famous *Murder & MayFemme* hadn't figured that out yet. She opened her mouth to object, but Tarek's hand on her hip stopped her. He gave a near imperceptible shake of his head when she raised her eyebrows in a silent question.

He turned to Kelsey. "We're heading back through OB. Would you like a ride home?" She accepted with a coy smile.

"Well alright," Alvin said. "Glad you enjoyed it. We'll walk you back."

At the car, Alvin and Kent stopped to say goodbye.

"It was nice to meet you folks," Alvin said to Kyra with a nod to Tarek. He slid his hands into his jacket pockets and turned to walk away.

"Alvin?" Kyra asked, stopping the Pāru representative at the base of the trailer stairs. "If I need some more information or context for my article, can I come back for another tour?"

"Sure. We'd love to have you. Just call ahead so someone can be onsite to show you around." Alvin winked and followed Kent inside.

Tarek turned on the ignition. He placed his hand on the back of Kyra's seat to reverse out of the parking spot.

"Do you have plans tonight?" he asked *Murder & May-Femme* as he spun the car around.

"Our sound engineer is coming today. He'll set us up with a recording space," Marjorie said.

"Oh, do you do most of your recording on site?" Kyra asked as she fiddled with the heat, trying to point the fans down at her frozen feet.

"Some of it. Interviews and sound bites mostly. But we'll record most our narrative in our studio in DC," Marjorie explained, her tone amiable for the first time.

The camp shrank and disappeared in Kyra's side mirror. "Do you have any leads on people who lived on the island when Abigail was killed that you're planning to interview?" she asked, trying to sound nonchalant.

She caught Tarek watching her from his peripheral. Yes,

she was testing them. Something about their behavior annoyed her, and it wasn't just Kelsey's obvious admiration for Tarek.

Majorie made a noncommittal sound in the back of her throat. "We already have a lot of what we need. The story practically writes itself."

Kyra turned in her seat. "You don't intend to speak with the locals while you're here? Then why set up a recording space?"

Marjorie shared a look with Kelsey. "It's complicated podcast production stuff." Marjorie waved her hand, dismissing Kyra's question. "And it's unnecessary. We have enough content from the police report, and our other research. Unless you know a local who is alive and was in the room when Abigail was killed, there isn't much more they can tell us."

Kyra tilted her head to the side. "But you know the police report is shit, right?"

Marjorie gave Kyra a blank stare, and Kelsey turned to look out the window. Neither woman responded. Kyra glanced at Tarek. Should she bother trying to explain? His gaze didn't stray from the road, but he nodded his encouragement.

"There's no way someone could have climbed out that window that night with no one seeing them." Marjorie's permanent scowl deepened and Kyra continued. "Every window of both the girls' and boys' dorms face out onto that courtyard. And those rooms were tiny. A person would need to be standing against the wall to have a disrupted view. Someone would have seen her."

"It could have been late," Kelsey said. "Or early. We don't know what time the murder happened."

"No." Kyra shook her head. "You said they were last seen at a dinner and first missed at breakfast. So, the period of time when the murder could have occurred is what? Between seven p.m. and eight or nine in the morning?"

"Probably," Kelsey said, raising a hand.

"Okay." Kyra nodded. "For argument's sake, let's say it happened sometime after curfew, even if no one was looking outside, or they were sleeping when Elodie escaped, someone would have heard Elodie attack Abigail."

"Abigail could have been asleep."

"Possibly." Kyra considered it. "But I don't think it'd matter. Sounds carried in that place. In the room, I could hear your conversation down the hall. Tarek heard me through the wall. The assault would have had to have been fast and very quiet, not to alert the other campers. If she'd screamed, or protested, someone would have heard. Were there no witness accounts?" She tried to remember what the podcasters had recited over coffee.

"I ... well. We haven't..."

"We can't talk about that," Marjorie interrupted Kelsey and glared at Kyra.

But Kyra wasn't ready to let it go. "You said she was beaten to death with a fire poker?"

"Yes, according to the police report." Marjorie slumped against her seat and let out a huff. "It was found beside the body."

Kyra turned back in her seat to face forward. "Aren't you curious where it came from?" she asked, the question as much for them as for herself.

She looked over at Tarek. He was smiling, soft and to himself. Kyra felt a bloom of pride. He'd thought it, too.

"The fireplace, probably?" Marjorie harrumphed.

"The Gillman Center was a summer camp. The dorms wouldn't need to be heated."

"And the dormitory, at least the girls' one, didn't have fireplaces," Tarek added. "I didn't see a chimney on the roofline of the boys' dorm, either." Someone had brought the weapon into the dorm. "Did the report say anything about questioning the other campers?"

"No." Marjorie sighed, the sound ragged and annoyed. "Nothing. The report said the other boarders were in such hysterics they couldn't be questioned, and then the show was canceled, and the dormitory was closed off for the investigation. Many people left for home that night."

"And the boys, too? Were they shut out of their sleeping quarters?"

"I don't know," she snapped. "I assumed they all left."

"You guys really are crime experts, aren't you?" Kelsey said and leaned between them. "Have you thought about doing a podcast, Tarek? You'd need to work on your delivery, but you should think about it. You have a great voice."

"Kels." Marjorie's voice was stern.

"Yeah, I know. It's a saturated market. Hmmm, but you know, you could probably do video." She giggled and sat back.

"Something to consider if my current role doesn't work out."

Kyra stared out her window. She didn't think one needed to be an expert in criminology to see the flaws in the police's story. What was even more confusing to her was the podcasters' attitudes. At the coffee shop, they'd been so animated, talking about the story, playing off each other, but once they arrived on site, it was like they'd completely lost interest. Was it part of their strategy? Throw off Alvin and Kent? Or had they already come to all the same conclusions Kyra had and weren't willing to share their findings?

"Kyra's right. The locals probably have their own theories about what happened that night, especially if some of them were attendees. If I were going to open up a cold case, I'd start with people who remember the night of the crime." Tarek turned onto a side road.

"And that's not you guys?" Kelsey asked.

"No," Kyra said, unable to hide her annoyance. "I'm not from here and even if I was, I wasn't born yet."

Tarek smirked. "Kyra and I are fairly new residents."

"Oh, that makes sense. I thought you had an accent."

"I lived in London for a long time. I only moved here last summer."

"And you, Tarek? Where are you from?" Kelsey asked.

"Central Mass, originally." He slowed the car and pulled to the side. "Is this one yours?" He pointed across the street to a two-story house.

It resembled one of Oak Bluffs' famous Gingerbread Cottages, the colorful, nineteenth century tiny homes built by a community of Methodists, but it was larger, more suitable for year-round living. It was painted a pretty lavender, with plum and indigo accents. The house was charming.

"Yep, that's us. Thanks so much for the lift."

Tarek turned around to face them. "If you're interested in pursuing the story," he said, the slightest hint of challenge in his tone. "One of the best places to interact with the locals is the Cottage City Club."

Marjorie eyed him warily. "The what?"

"It's an unaffiliated members' club. It's popular with the residents here, especially some of the older crowd."

"Oh, but you have to be a member to get in?" Kelsey said and pulled a perfect frown. "That's too bad. We're not members."

"Kyra and I are. We're meeting friends there tonight. If you wanted, we could sign you in as our guests."

There was no mistaking the challenge. He was calling them out. They couldn't decline his offer for access to the islanders without giving it away that they weren't legitimately interested in the Koch murder.

Marjorie pushed open the door. "When our sound engineer gets in, if it's not too late, maybe we'll stop by. Kels?"

"Yeah, that could be fun. We should go. I mean, if Benny wants to." She giggled behind her hand, a tinkling sound that set Kyra's teeth on edge. "Thanks so much for the invitation, Tarek."

"You're very welcome, Kelsey."

Tarek waited until the women entered the house and the purple door closed against the cold, before he put the car in gear and pulled onto the road.

"We have plans tonight? When did that happen? And you invited them out ... with us?" Kyra asked.

"Chase texted while we were at the campground. He and Gully are going tonight." He grinned. "Why? Don't you like

Kelsey?" Kyra glared at him, and he laughed, a warm, rumbling chuckle. "I wasn't making it up, though. There's a chance someone at the CC Club remembers the theater camp and Abigail Koch."

"Do you think they'll actually talk to anyone?"

"I don't know. They don't seem that interested in the case, do they?" His brow furrowed. "When I walked with Kelsey, she told me about winters in DC versus where she grew up in Chicago. She talked about her siblings, her degree—an MFA in drama—and how she aspires to do more than audio work. She didn't mention or ask about the case at all."

"No, she wouldn't. She was flirting with you." Kyra made a face.

"I know." He grinned and Kyra hit his arm with the back of her hand.

Her knuckles slid off his coat. "You're an asshole."

He shrugged, unapologetic. "I can't help it." He laughed at her incredulous expression. "The curiosity. I want to know what happened to Abigail Koch, and I want to know why the true crime podcasters don't." His mouth twisted to the side. "It may not be a mystery. It's possible that Marjorie and Kelsey aren't who I thought they were."

Kyra's heart sank. Her birthday present hadn't gone the way she'd thought it would. She'd wanted him to enjoy it, perhaps embarrass himself a little by meeting his idols.

"I'm sorry I ruined it for you," she said, her voice coming out small.

"You didn't ruin anything, Kyra."

"If it makes any difference, I want to find out what happened to Abigail and Elodie, too."

He glanced at her, and his mouth spread into one of his rare, full smiles. "Tell me, how's your darts game?"

# Chapter Seven

"Yes!" Kyra shrieked, jumping in place when her dart hit the board, closing out the seventeen on a triple.

Tarek's laugh was half astonished, half dejected.

She batted her eyelashes at him. "You asked if I played."

"You said you're, and I quote, 'not terrible.'"

Kyra shrugged. She wasn't terrible. She was quite good. Afternoons in English pubs had a few upsides. "Does that look terrible to you?" She waved to the scoreboard.

"You won by sixty points."

She'd hit the bull's-eye. First.

Mirth danced in Kyra's eyes, and she grinned. "You owe me another drink. G and T, please."

Shaking his head, he retreated to the bar on the other side of the Cottage City Club, and Kyra retrieved her darts.

The club was just two large rooms, the original building and an obvious extension. The front room was busy with patrons sitting at mismatched, second-hand dining tables or lounging on saggy couches or armchairs. Along the back wall of the original structure, just to the left of the doors, was a long bar and a small enclave that had been outfitted as a kitchen.

The extension held pool tables, bar-acceptable arcade

games for people who liked to play at shooting deer or teeing off, and two dartboards. It was haphazard feeling, but the effect wasn't shabby. It was unpretentious and homey. She saw right away why the islanders liked it.

"You didn't tell Tarek I could play," Kyra said, taking a seat at the round table Chase and Gully had claimed.

"And miss seeing his face when you kicked his ass? Never." Chase pushed his hair off his forehead.

"You've created a monster, London. He'll be in here every night practicing until he can beat you."

Kyra laughed and spun a dart between her fingers. "Do you want to play?"

Gully put a hand to his ear and leaned away. "What's that, Tar?" He dropped his hand and his mouth pulled to the side, shifting his bushy beard. "Sorry, no can do. Sounds like he needs help." Gully finished his pint in a single swallow and pushed back from his seat.

"One of these old guys is going to proposition you to marry them or join their weird dart league," Chase said, biting back his grin.

"Why not both?"

Chase laughed. "How was the sleuthing adventure today?"

Kyra's elation dissipated. "It was ... interesting?" She hedged, not quite sure how to explain the afternoon. "It wasn't what we expected." She looked over, searching for Tarek. He was at the bar, talking to people she didn't recognize.

"That good?"

"Perhaps there's something to be said for never meeting

your heroes." Kyra finished the watered-down dregs of her drink.

She'd wanted the experience to be a positive memory. Instead, she felt like Toto pulling the curtain back on the not-so-great-or-powerful Oz. She hoped Tarek wasn't too disappointed *Murder & MayFemme* turned out to be duds.

"You can see for yourself. Tarek invited them to join us."

Chase leaned back in his chair. He picked up his beer bottle and raised it, moving in a semicircle, motioning to the other patrons. "That will be interesting."

"What will be interesting?" Tarek asked, and he set down their glasses.

He handed Kyra her victory drink with a mock scowl. Gully passed Chase a fresh bottle and sat.

"The podcasters may be coming. And you know how the members feel about outsiders."

"Don't be an asshole, Hawthorn." Gully gave him a bland look. "The islanders will talk to Marjorie and Kelsey. They're practically celebrities after that serial killer case out west."

Kyra gaped at him. "*You* listen to *Murder & May-Femme?*"

The sliver of skin above Gully's beard turned bright red. "Tarek got me hooked a few years ago." Tarek patted his friend's shoulder and raised an eyebrow at her. A silent *See, everyone likes it.*

"And do you?" she asked Chase.

"Nope," he said, his lips popping on the *P*. "I don't really do podcasts."

He'd never admit it, but Chase was an avid reader. Kyra

had seen the piles of books around his house. He ate through Penguin Classics at the same rate he consumed tubes of Pringles.

"So, did they tell you why they're here?"

"Mmmhmm." Tarek hummed and shared a look with Kyra.

"We signed an NDA, so we really can't say." When Chase opened his mouth to protest, Kyra cut him off with her hand. "Just don't tell them we told you." She motioned for Tarek to continue.

"You know that abandoned summer camp over in East Chop?" he asked, and Chase nodded. "Apparently it was a theater camp. About forty years ago, a girl was killed, and another went missing."

Gully sucked on his bottom lip and stroked his beard. "I've heard that story. It's a dark blip on OB's safety record."

"Do you know what happened?" Kyra asked, but Gully shook his head.

"No. Just the basics. A girl was killed. The camp was closed. I think I read it was sold to a developer a few years ago."

"The Pāru Group," Kyra said. "It's an entertainment company. They're going to be building a new performance facility on the site."

Chase stilled. "Pāru?" But before Kyra could confirm, his gaze shifted over her head to the front of the club. His expression smoothed out. "I think your podcasters are here."

Kyra turned around. Marjorie and Kelsey, their noses pink from the cold, stood in the doorway with an older, scruffy-looking man. Unlike them, he didn't seem bothered by the weather. He wore no heavy coat, just a hoodie with the hot pink *Murder & MayFemme* logo—the silhouette of a woman in a deerstalker hat holding a magnifying glass.

Kyra raised her hand in greeting, and Marjorie zeroed in on her. She tapped Kelsey's elbow and pointed.

"Hi," Marjorie said, her voice cheerful when she arrived at their table. Her gaze zeroed in on Chase, pinged to Kyra, and back to Chase again. Then, to Kyra's utter shock, she actually smiled. "Hi," she said again, her voice breathy. Tarek chuckled.

"Marjorie, Kelsey, this is Gully Gould and Chase Hawthorn."

"Nice to meet you," Marjorie said, never taking her eyes off Chase and she slipped onto the chair beside him.

"Hi, Kyra. Tarek." Kelsey raised her hand in a halfhearted wave and took the seat on Chase's other side. "This is our audio engineer, Benny."

"He just arrived in the white creeper van outside with our sound equipment."

Benny shook his head a little, as if clearing his mind. He raised his hand, mumbled an indiscernible greeting, and pulled an empty chair up to the table, forcing the group to shift.

"I'm so sorry," Kelsey trilled from behind her hand as she bumped Chase.

Kyra smirked around her straw. Chase glared at her, and she blinked her innocence. Better him than Tarek.

"I was just telling them about your podcast," Tarek said, throwing Chase a bone. "Gully has lived here for a while. He runs a pub in town and knows a lot of locals."

"Mmmhmm." Marjorie hummed; her eyes trained on Chase. "Yes, Kels and I host a crime podcast, *Murder & MayFemme*." She fluttered her lashes at him. "It's a play on words."

"Mayhem," Kelsey clarified. "The podcast community loves puns."

"Interesting." Chase reached for another beer.

"It is," Marjorie said with a solemn nod, missing Chase's sarcasm. She leaned in close. Her voice dropped to a stage whisper. "We're investigating a cold case from years ago. A girl was beaten to death while she slept in her bed at theater camp."

Kyra blinked. Apparently, the NDA was just for show. "Tar thought some of the club's patrons may remember it," Kyra said.

"Probably." Gully nodded.

He gestured to a group of weather worn men sitting at the bar. By Kyra's estimation, they'd have been old-timers forty years ago.

"Those gentlemen over there grew up here. They'd be your best bet tonight. They're friendly enough, but you'll pay for their stories." He tapped his pint glass.

"Thanks for the tip." Kelsey turned back to Chase. "Have you heard of the Playhouse Tragedy?"

"It's a harrowing story," Marjorie added.

Chase's gaze shifted between them, uncertain. "Uh … yeah, I've heard the story. Do you have any leads?"

"A few." Pink spots bloomed on Kelsey's cheeks, making her freckles more pronounced.

"But nothing we can share." Marjorie jumped in. "For

obvious reasons." The podcasters laughed.

Kyra was used to men and women alike falling all over Chase, and honestly, most days Kyra couldn't blame them. He was striking. But Kelsey and Marjorie were acting like hormonal teenagers. It was a little hard to watch.

She glanced out of the corner of her eye at the audio engineer, curious if he found his coworkers' flirting uncomfortable. He wasn't paying attention. At some point, he'd shifted his seat away and was watching the game being played on the pool table next to Chase.

He caught Kyra watching him and stood. "Excuse me. I need a refill," he said, and walked toward the bar.

Marjorie stared daggers at his back.

"Oh, don't mind Benny." Kelsey laughed. "He's just a grump."

"Not a fan of the Vineyard?" Kyra asked, her gaze following him as he ordered and paid for his drink.

Kelsey laughed again, but this time it sounded forced and high pitched. "No, not really. But it's not just the Vineyard. He doesn't like any site visits. He prefers to work out of the sound studio in DC."

"It's our poor luck that we were assigned a homebody jerk for our audio guy." Marjorie made a face. "We'd request someone new, but unfortunately, he's excellent."

"He really is." Kelsey sighed. "He's the best sound guy we've ever had. You should hear our early stuff. It sounds so amateur." She leaned closer to Chase. "He brought our production up to the next level. He's the best, even if he is crabby."

"We normally let him stay home, if we can, but he asked

to come on this trip." Marjorie pursed her lips and shrugged. "You'd think he'd be in a better mood."

Kelsey put her hand on Chase's arm. "So, how do you spend your time on Martha's Vineyard?"

Marjorie turned back to the table. "Yeah, Chase, what is there to do here in the winter?"

Kelsey and Marjorie took turns asking Chase questions about Mander Lane Farm, his life on the island, and in DC. He answered each question with half-truths protecting his privacy but giving them what they wanted, a glimpse into a high society life of wealth and privilege.

Drinks and food kept arriving at their table, and by the podcasters' second order of buffalo wings and waffle fries, it became obvious to Kyra that they had no interest in talking to anyone except Chase. He tried to steer the conversation back to Abigail Koch a few times, but the podcasters clumsily changed the subject.

Kyra yawned behind her hand and checked the time. It wasn't late, just after nine, but the day had felt long, and she was ready for it to end.

"Ready to go home?" Tarek asked, leaning in close to her ear.

"I am."

He pushed his chair back. "We're going to head out," he said to Chase, and turned to Marjorie and Kelsey. "Thank you for this afternoon. It was really very special meeting you both and seeing your process. I can't wait until the season airs."

"Thank you for all your help," Kelsey said. "Are you leaving, too?" she asked Chase.

Kyra said goodbye to Gully and gave Chase a quick hug, earning a possessive glower from Marjorie that she pointedly ignored. "Get home safe."

# Chapter Eight

KYRA STARED AT her blank computer screen. Her coffee had gone cold. Beside it, her half-eaten, blackened toast sat abandoned on the kitchen island. She'd been trying to get something down, an outline, notes—anything that she could use as a basis for the story she'd pitched to Han about *Murder & MayFemme*. For the life of her, she had no clue where to start.

Last night, she'd tried to give the podcasters the benefit of the doubt. She conceded it was possible she and Tarek just weren't privy to their research activities behind the curtain. But now she wasn't so sure. After listening to recent episodes and reading interviews with the hosts, Kyra believed *Murder & MayFemme* dedicated significant time and resources to becoming experts in the cases they covered. They spent months researching and preparing their narrative, collecting witness accounts, data points, reviewing evidence, and submitting Freedom of Information Act requests. When they finally arrived on the scene, Marjorie and Kelsey presented themselves as investigators who were in it. They were the ones in the dirt, hunting through old evidence, reading files, and interviewing witnesses. They did the type of investigatory work her father had been famous for. Those women would have toured the entire campground and never would have wasted an opportunity to question the locals. It made Marjorie and Kelsey's unenthusiastic behavior all the more confusing.

She'd come to two possible conclusions. *Murder & May-Femme* was an overproduced farce, and Marjorie and Kelsey were just the voices supported by a behind-the-scenes team of actual true-crime investigators. Or Marjorie and Kelsey had no actual interest in solving the Abigail Koch case.

It was the latter she found bizarre. The story—the lack of media attention, the slipshod police work, and that no one questioned what happened to Elodie—was ideal for a true-crime special. In a matter of minutes both she and Tarek had become invested. Kyra wanted to know what happened to the bunkmates. If Marjorie and Kelsey weren't interested, though, why come to the island at all?

Kyra closed the blank document and turned her attention to the articles she'd retrieved from *The Island Times*'s digital archive.

Before Abigail died, the Gillman Center for the Dramatic Arts had been a mainstay in the local paper, especially regarding its performances and its attendees' post summer camp successes. There were at least a half dozen articles about an ex-camper and his Broadway debut. The paper had printed a character piece, an interview, and multiple reviews of the play, singing the young man's praises.

Martha's Vineyard was a sleepy place. News didn't run hot like in the cities. When something big happened, it was front page news. For days. The violent death of a young woman would have qualified as something big. It should have received tons of local news coverage, but there was only a single article published about Abigail Koch's death, and it had been buried in the weekend section the day after her body was discovered.

The article was vague. It briefly mentioned the police's interest in questioning the missing roommate, but the majority of the article was about the cancellation of the much-anticipated end-of-summer production of Shakespeare's *Much Ado About Nothing*.

Tobias Gillman had been interviewed, and he was quoted expressing his heartfelt condolences to Abigail's family. The paper commended him for his ongoing support of the arts and the Oak Bluffs community. It was a puff piece. And it was total crap.

She called her editor.

"Gibson."

"Han, do you have a minute?"

"I have three."

"Do you remember the old theater camp in East Chop? A young woman was killed there about forty years ago."

"No," he scoffed. "How old do you think I am? I was cutting math class at Valley Middle School forty years ago. I'd never heard the story before Ida Ames told me about the podcast coming to the island. Why?"

"I'm sending you the article the paper published on Abigail's murder. It's just very … uninformative." She heard Han rustling through the phone, probably shifting whatever pile of papers were covering his keyboard to the side. He was quiet for a minute while he read.

"Huh. You're right. Strange. Hold on…" More rustling. "Back then, the paper was run by Marchant. He was old school, a stickler for *journalistic integrity*." Kyra didn't miss Han's sarcastic tone. The article didn't sound like something the old editor would have approved.

"And how do you feel about journalistic integrity?"

"It's why god gifted us the word *allegedly*, Gibson."

"Does he still live on the island?" she asked, ignoring Han's questionable ethical perspective.

"In a manner of speaking. He's interred at Oak Grove Cemetery."

Kyra blew out a breath. A dead end. Literally. Her phone buzzed with an incoming call from an unknown five-o-eight number.

She debated sending it to voicemail. "I've another call, Han. I'll ring you back?"

"For sure. Talk soon." He hung up.

"This is Kyra."

"Kay?" Chase's voice was hoarse, raspy, like it'd been overused. He coughed.

"Chase? Is everything alright?"

"Yeah, everything's fine. But do you think you can come pick me up?"

She stood, already reaching for her purse. "Where are you?"

Chase let out a long, weary sigh. "The OB police station."

Kyra froze. "What?" she demanded. "No. Don't say anything. If anyone asks, you're represented by counsel. I'll be there in fifteen."

A year ago, Chase's sister had attempted to frame him for the murders of Kyra's father and Chase's then boyfriend, Brendan. He'd spent months hounded by police and the press. He still suffered from panic attacks.

"Kyra? Going out?" Tarek emerged from his office as she hurried to lace up her boots.

She yanked on the laces, cursing. "Chase is at the police station. I have to get him."

Tarek didn't hesitate. "I'll come with you." He rounded the console table, grabbing her keys from the bowl and handed her his phone. "I'll drive. Text Evans."

Tarek pulled into the small parking lot in front of the Oak Bluffs Police Station. He'd barely stopped the car when Kyra burst out.

"Kyra, stop!"

She ignored him. She threw the doors open with more force than necessary and barreled into the lobby.

"I'm Kyra Gibson here for my client, Chase Hawthorn." She couldn't help the sharpness in her tone. The woman behind the counter blinked at her, and Kyra's temper spiked. "I said…"

"Hey, Mel," Tarek said, as he entered the lobby and nodded to the woman behind the plexiglass. Kyra gritted her teeth, but she waited for him as he closed the door and came to stand beside her. "What's Chase Hawthorn here for?"

"Routine questions, as far as I know." Mel shrugged and Kyra glared at her.

"Routine questions for what?" Kyra asked, annunciating each word.

Mel returned her attention to the crossword puzzle on

her desk. "You can take a seat."

Kyra sucked in a breath, ready to unleash a verbal lashing of epic proportions, but Tarek gripped her arm. He gently tugged her to the hard plastic chairs lined up in the center of the room.

"Snapping at the front desk officer won't earn you any favors. She has no authority, and they tell her nothing."

Kyra threw herself into a chair and crossed her arms over her chest. Her knee bounced up and down. The rubber sole of her boot squeaked against the tile floor, earning her an annoyed frown from front desk officer Mel. Kyra met her gaze and the side of her mouth twitched up, daring Mel to say something.

They didn't have to wait long before Chase was escorted through the doors behind the reception desk. An officer spoke a few words to him, and Mel buzzed him through security, releasing him into the lobby. Kyra scrambled to her feet and studied him. He wasn't in last night's clothes. He was in sneakers and sweatpants. His hair was a mess, rumpled and standing on end. Under his farm coat, he only had on a ratty T-shirt. He looked dead on his feet, but at least he hadn't been there all night.

Chase opened his mouth, but Kyra hushed him. "Outside." She herded him through the doors and to the car.

"What happened?" she asked, when OB was far behind them. Theirs was the only vehicle on the twisty road to Chilmark. Any other time, Kyra would have marveled at the beauty of the fields blanketed with light snow. As it was, she barely noticed. She leaned between the front seats. "Are you okay? What were you doing there?"

Chase pushed his hair back and rested his head against the headrest. "What time is it?" he asked. His hands fell to his lap.

"Two-thirty. Where's your car?" Tarek asked.

"Home. I was home when they knocked on my door. That was at ten, I think? I had the early shift and had gone back to bed. They woke me up and brought me down to the station."

Chase was often up at ungodly hours doing rounds, caring for the farm's menagerie of animals.

"And? What did they want with you?"

Chase shook his head. "They wouldn't say. Two cops brought me in. They read me my Miranda rights then…" He paused. "Then they asked me where I was last night. Who I was with."

"What did you tell them?" Kyra asked.

"The truth. I was at the Cottage City Club with you guys, and then the *Murder & MayFemme* people showed up. You and Tar left first, Gully shortly after. The podcasters finished their drinks, and I walked them out ten or fifteen minutes later." His mouth pressed into a straight-lipped frown. "Don't give me that look. I went home. Alone. The police asked if anyone could corroborate my story." Chase shrugged.

"Can someone?" Tarek asked with a grim expression.

"You guys, and when I got home, I turned off the security system. That must be logged somewhere, right?"

It was something, at least.

"Did they say why they questioned you?" Kyra asked.

"No," Tarek answered for Chase. "That's not procedure.

They don't have to tell you."

"Did they ask you anything else?"

"They asked me questions about *Murder & MayFemme*. What they were doing here. If I'd met them before. If I was a fan of the show." Chase's shoulder lifted and fell. "It was weird."

"Did they say anything else?" Tarek asked.

"No. Just the *Don't leave the island in case we have more questions for you*," he said, mimicking a deep, authoritative voice. "Then they let me call you."

Kyra sat back and crossed her arms over her chest. This was police abuse of power and harassment. They could have asked Chase those questions from his front porch or by phone. There was no reason for them to drag him across island, perp-walk him through the station, and leave him in an interrogation room for hours. It was pure intimidation.

Tarek pulled onto the gravel drive and under the brambly Mander Lane Farm arbor. He circled around the back of the property and up the hill to the Hawthorns' house, a postmodern Franken-Victorian monstrosity complete with metal turret. Chase unbuckled his seatbelt.

He paused his hand on the door handle. "Did something happen at the club?" he asked Tarek, a tightness around his eyes. "Or to the podcasters?"

"I haven't heard anything. Have you?" he asked Kyra.

"No." She shook her head. She pulled out her phone and dialed Marjorie's number. The call went straight to voicemail. "Marjorie isn't answering."

Tarek turned back to Chase. "If the police come back or call, tell them you've retained an attorney and give them

Kyra's number. Get some rest."

"Okay." Chase's nod was slow, and he blinked a few times. "Thank you for coming to get me." He opened the door and set one foot on the ground. He stopped and turned to Kyra. "Oh, Kay, I remembered something last night. Abigail, the murdered girl, her last name was Koch, right?" Kyra nodded. "I don't know if it means anything but Greta from yoga? Her last name is Koch."

"Do you think they knew each other?"

"Dunno, but thought you should know." Chase got out. He disappeared, leaving the car door open, and Kyra took his place in the passenger seat.

"Who's Greta?" Tarek asked.

"I think he's talking about the pair of older ladies, Dot and Greta. They go to yoga at Daphne's studio in Vineyard Haven. I've met them a few times. They've been regulars on the island for decades."

Tarek gave her a noncommittal frown.

His phone rang, and he answered it over the car's Bluetooth. "Collins."

"Collins, it's me."

"Evans, I'm in the car. I've got Kyra with me. We just dropped Chase Hawthorn off at Mander Lane. What the hell happened last night?"

There was a long pause. "It'll be better if you come and see for yourself. I'll text you the address."

# Chapter Nine

THE ADDRESS WAS familiar, as was the purple ginger-bread house, except now it was awash in pulsing red and blue lights. Tarek parked behind one of the many emergency response vehicles lining the street. Kyra counted six police cruisers, an ambulance, and a fire truck. Traffic cops stood at either end of the road, directing people away.

"What's going on?" Kyra couldn't help asking, knowing Tarek knew no more than she did.

"Crime scene protocol," he muttered, and Kyra's heart skipped. *Crime scene?* "Stay close to me and don't touch anything."

The command prickled, but she didn't argue. She was both surprised and thrilled he hadn't dropped her off at home or told her to wait in the car. Not that she'd have listened. She didn't have to. She had press credentials.

Since their first *case* together last spring, they had a tenuous sort of partnership. Tarek was reluctant to include her. Probably because she had a habit of getting herself kidnapped or shot at. He would say she could be reckless. Kyra preferred the term *enterprising*.

"Collins." A man in a police uniform approached and shook Tarek's hand. "Good to see you. Evans is inside. Socks are by the door." He jerked his chin toward a box sitting on the front porch.

Tarek mumbled a thanks and motioned for Kyra to follow him. He handed her a pair of polyethylene shoe covers. Kyra fumbled, pulling the sticky fabric over her snow boots. Once secured, she followed him inside.

The house's layout was traditional. Just beyond the entry was a narrow hallway. To the left was the staircase to the second floor. Everything was in shades of purple, ranging from rich aubergine to pale lavender. Kyra peeked inside the first room to her right. It was a formal sitting room just large enough for two purple loveseats on either side of an electric hearth with a magenta mantle. A television was mounted above it. On the ultraviolet lacquered coffee table was a vase filled with fabric irises.

A uniformed police officer spoke in soft tones to Tarek and pointed to the back of the house.

"Thanks. Kyra, this way."

She fell into step beside him, but paused in the doorway of each room. There was an office, the bookshelves filled with books covered in purple-colored wrapping papers, and a dining room with a table for six underneath a chandelier covered in amethyst crystals. The purple-on-purple-on-purple went from kitschy to disconcerting quickly. Kyra felt like she was in a Technicolor *Twilight Zone* episode.

The kitchen was at the back of the house, and like everything else, was miniature but functional. And purple. The grape retro-style fridge matched the stove. The cabinets were lilac with a deep indigo trim. A tiny dinette sat under the violet curtained window.

Kyra turned and looked down the hall, then back at the kitchen. She felt unsettled, but couldn't quite pinpoint what was bothering her. There were too many stimuli—the monochrome color palette that made everything not purple hurt her eyes, the emptiness of the house despite all the emergency response people, the faint antiseptic and rancid meat smell that permeated the place, like someone had tried to bleach something rotten.

Her gaze swept the kitchen. Again. The floors, the counters, the stovetop all were clean, buffed to a shine. There was nothing on the counters except for a few pristine appliances. There were no dishes in the sink, none drying in the rack. No dish towels hanging on the oven handle or the hook next to the window above the sink. The kitchen was immaculate, but not just in a recently-been-cleaned way. It was the type of clean reminiscent of empty hotel rooms or staged model houses. There was no sign of anyone living here. There was no sign of life.

"Evans," Tarek said when the younger man appeared beside her.

He bobbed his head at her. "Miss Gibson." He shook Tarek's hand. "Thanks for coming." He ran his hand down his face. His eyes were rimmed red, and he was pale except for the pink splotches at the tops of his cheeks and along his neck. "Investigations just left," he said and dropped onto the dinette's bench seat. "They sure do it different here." He let out a long breath. "It was pretty disorganized."

"Mark, what's going on?" Kyra asked and waved toward the front of the house. "And what does all of this have to do with Chase?"

Evans's eyebrows slanted, and he shook his head. "I'm sorry about that. I only found out they'd brought Mr. Hawthorn in for questioning when Ms. Ames called me. She wasn't too pleased, either. I'll call to apologize to him."

"But what did they want with him?" Kyra pressed.

"We got a call through dispatch this morning at nine thirty-seven. The property manager, Manuel called 911. It was followed by a direct call into the station from the homeowner." Evans pulled a small notebook from his pocket and checked it. "Edina Horvath called us at nine forty-three. She owns this house and three others on this road. All rental properties. Around eight a.m. this morning, Edina received a message from her smart home company that one of the fire alarms was malfunctioning. She called the renters, but they didn't answer, and she asked Manuel to stop in. He told the first responders that he could hear the alarm going off from outside. He knocked, but when no one answered the door, he entered and checked the house. That's when he found it." Evans placed his hands on his knees and stared down at the floor.

"Found what?" Kyra asked.

"Come see for yourself."

They followed Evans back to the front of the house and to the staircase. Evans's boots clomped up the treads. Kyra placed her hand on the plum-painted balustrade and followed Tarek. Her stomach sank with each step up. Foreboding weighed heavy in the quiet. The rotten smell grew stronger as she ascended. She could taste it, bitter and decayed.

"What about the fire alarm?" Tarek asked.

"Manuel disabled it before the first responders arrived."

"And he said *Murder & MayFemme* weren't here?" Kyra asked.

"He said the place was empty. He wasn't sure they even checked in."

Kyra's brow furrowed. She'd seen Marjorie and Kelsey enter the house when she and Tarek had dropped them off yesterday.

Upstairs was a wide landing that opened up to three modest bedrooms, two with full-size beds, and a third larger one with bunk beds. The beds were made; the bedspreads pulled taut over the mattresses. Upstairs, too, was all purple. Purple walls, purple furniture, purple bedding.

"He searched the house and found that." Evans pointed to the only closed door on the landing, its doorknob wrapped in plastic. "Then, he called 911. You'll want to see it for yourselves."

Tarek gripped the doorknob, turned it, and with a gentle pull, the door *creaked* open.

At first, Kyra's brain only processed more purple. Walls. Tile. Vanity. Then she noticed the stains, dark splotches, and splatters everywhere. Her gaze fell on the porcelain sink and her breath caught. It was covered in a thick, rusty red substance, now dried and cracked. *Blood.* The room was covered in blood. So. Much. Blood. Then the smell hit her. It was stifling, filling the small bathroom with a meaty, metallic scent that was tangy and fetid.

Kyra stepped back and pressed her hand to her mouth, holding in her gag. Tarek moved forward, stepped inside the small bathroom. He turned in a circle, his gaze sweeping the space. He pulled his phone from his pocket, and took photos of the walls, the ceiling, the tub, everywhere there was blood.

"What happened in here?" Kyra asked, her voice shaking.

Tarek peered closer to the splatters covering the wall opposite the sink. He squatted down and studied the blood on the floor. It looked like someone had been hacked to bits.

Kyra squeezed her eyes shut, forced herself to remain calm. She opened them. *The blood.* It was in great sprays on the wall, dried pools on the floor, and vanity. All left to dry where it fell. The purple towels hung straight on the towel bar. More were neatly folded on a shelf in the bath. Sample-size shampoo, body wash, body lotion, and a bar of beach plum soap sat on top of the vanity, still wrapped with a purple ribbon, now dark with blood.

Kyra inched forward and paused on the threshold. *No footprints. No handprints, no struggle. Did the victim not fight back?*

"Tar?"

But Tarek raised his hand, quieting her. "Evans, did they take samples?"

"Yes, sir. It'll be sent to the lab on the mainland."

"Okay. I've seen enough. Let's go back downstairs."

They stopped in the entryway, and Tarek leaned against the front door. "Why was Hawthorn brought to the station for questioning? Does someone think he had something to do with that?" He pointed to the ceiling.

Evans ran his hand across his forehead. "One of the responding officers was at the Cottage City Club last night. He saw Chase leave with the podcasters. He took it upon himself to speak to him. According to the officer, Chase was the last known person who'd seen them."

"Wait, no one has spoken to Kelsey or Marjorie today?" Kyra asked, and Evans shook his head.

"We haven't been able to reach them. Have you spoken to them?"

Kyra pulled out her phone and dialed Marjorie's number. She got her voicemail again, and this time she left a message stressing the urgency that she return the call as soon as possible.

"You think something's happened to them and Chase was involved?" Tarek asked, his brow creasing.

"No, sir. It's too early to speculate what happened. The officer acted without authority and will be reprimanded. His misconduct was the reason I was called in to consult. Ida insisted." Evans spread his hands wide in a helpless gesture. "If Chase wants to file a complaint, he'd be within his rights to."

"We'll see," Kyra said, knowing Chase would sooner chew off his own arm. "Does this mean that you've been assigned to lead this case?"

"No," he said with palpable relief. "I'll supervise and manage the communications and activity between the investigations team, the community, and the press. Ida doesn't want the police harassing other prominent islanders."

Evans's phone rang. The twang of early years Taylor Swift blasted through the empty house. He unlocked the screen and his expression flattened into a resigned grimace. "I'm so sorry. I have to take this. Collins, if you think of anything that could be helpful, please let me know. I'll be in touch?" It wasn't just a question, but a gentle plea. Evans was in over his head.

"We'll talk later," Tarek agreed.

Outside, they peeled off their shoe covers and dropped them in the waste bin beside the door. Except for Kyra's Range Rover and Evans's black and white police-issued SUV, the street was empty and eerily quiet.

"Do people live here year-round?" she asked. The houses were dark, the driveways icy.

"It doesn't look like it, but generally, yes. There are around five thousand year-round residents in OB, give-or-take."

Tarek pulled away from the curb. His fingers tapped out a staccato rhythm on the steering wheel. He turned onto Lake Avenue toward the beach.

"Do you think something happened to the podcasters?"

Tarek glanced at her from the corner of his eye. He frowned. "I don't know. You saw the house. It was almost like they were never there. Except for the bathroom, and that was just weird."

The bathroom was weird. The gruesome scene had felt artificial somehow.

"Weird because there was no sign of a struggle? No footprints. Handprints. Just blood?"

"I figured you'd notice that. I'm no expert, and there is a science to that sort of forensics, but it's almost like someone stood in the doorway and hurled blood across the room. There was almost none near the door, just little drops. But the splatters on the walls, the bathtub, and across the sink were upward." He mimed an underhanded throw. "It's almost like it was intentional, for maximum effect. And there was that smell. Blood doesn't smell like that."

"What do you think that means?"

"I don't know, but I'm curious to see the lab results."

When they arrived home, Tarek headed straight to his office, probably to call his supervisor at Greyscale. Kyra wandered into the kitchen, worrying her lip. She poured herself a glass of water and sipped it as she leaned against the counter.

"They could have had some sort of emergency, or maybe they were called away late last night?" she whispered, wishing her mini-yeti was with her. She preferred to pretend she was talking to Cronk and not to herself when working through her thoughts, but the cat would be with Tarek. He was never far from his favorite human.

Her nails tapped against her glass, sending little ripples through the water. The Steamship Authority ran ferries at night. Kyra thought the last one left around eleven. It would've been tight, but it was possible they could have made the last boat.

She sat and pulled out her phone.

"Steamship Authority."

"Hi, this is Kyra Gibson with *The Island Times*. I was wondering if you'd answer a few questions?" She heard the man's sharp intake of breath and hurried to clarify. "I'm not asking about this winter's service record."

"Oh, okay," he said, drawing it out.

"I am trying to find out if a white van was on one of the late ferries last night to Woods Hole."

"License plate number?"

"I don't have one. But there would have been three passengers, two women in their twenties and a man, older."

"Hold on." There was a fumbling noise, like he was jostling the phone. "Yo, you were on shift last night, right? You see a white van?" He came back. "What make and model?"

Kyra didn't know, but Marjorie had described it as a creeper van. "I'm not sure, but it was a cargo van."

"She doesn't know. Says a cargo. Three passengers." More rustling. Then silence. Minutes passed and Kyra was just about to hang up when the receiver crackled, and the man came back online. "Lady? No one remembers a white van. I checked the reservations list and there weren't that many cars on the last two boats. Only four of them were in the full-size category. No vans. Sorry."

"It's okay," she said, unable to mask her disappointment. She'd known it'd been a long shot. "Thank you. I appreciate the effort."

Kyra crossed the living room and knocked on the door to the office.

"Come in."

Tarek was standing behind the desk. Cronkite was lounging on the floor in front of the fire. His open green eye tracked her as she crossed the room.

"I just got off the phone with the Steamship Authority. I asked if they had any late ferry reservations for a white cargo van." She perched on the arm of her father's old leather clubman chair. "No vans, white or otherwise, had reservations on the late boats last night."

Tarek pressed his lips together. "If they didn't have a reservation and stood in standby, their information wouldn't have been collected. But a white cargo van might be memorable, if only for the novelty kidnapper factor."

That had been Kyra's thinking. Tarek came around to the front of the desk and leaned against it, crossing his arms over his chest.

*A cargo van is memorable enough. There can't be that many unrecognizable ones on the island. If one's been driving around, someone would have seen it.*

"What are you thinking?"

"I could call Jimmy. If anyone has seen the van on island or going off island he'd know, or he'll find out."

Tarek's eyebrow rose a fraction. "Jimmy Blau? From the Shack?"

"Mmmhmm."

Jimmy Blau worked at a tiny fish fry in Menemsha, but thanks to a shortwave radio and his slippery personality, he heard everything that happened on the island. He and Grace Chambers were opposite sides of the same coin. What Grace knew about the elite society who played on Martha's Vineyard, Jimmy knew about the people who lived here year-round, the people who worked the water, the land, and for the summer people. If there was a van, no one recognized driving around the island, Jimmy would have heard about it.

"Do you call him often?"

Kyra shrugged. "On occasion. Why?" she teased. "Jealous?"

"Of your ability to put everyone at immediate ease, so they innately trust you with their deepest, darkest secrets? Desperately. It'd make my job much easier."

"That's not true."

Tarek uncrossed his arms. He leaned forward, his hands

resting on the edge of the desk. "How long did it take before Chase confided in you about a hidden murder weapon?"

Kyra didn't respond. About twenty minutes, but the situation had been unique.

Tarek counted down on his fingers. "And Lisa Mackey? Gully? Hell, me?"

"You don't have any dark secrets."

"Not that you know of. Yet." His green eyes sparkled. "But in twelve years in law enforcement, I never once considered bringing a civilian into an investigation. And yet, not ten minutes after meeting you..." His voice trailed off.

Kyra shook her head and back stepped toward the door. "I'll text Jimmy," she said and closed the office door behind her.

The implication that she manipulated people to get her way, or for information, made her a little uncomfortable. Sure, people trusted her, but that was her job, or it had been when she was at the law firm. Even now as a pseudo-journalist, she didn't ask questions intending to mine information, or not only to mine information. She asked, because she was interested.

Jimmy responded immediately. *"Haven't heard anything. Will alert my little birds. Be in touch."*

"The fuck does that even mean?" Kyra blinked at the screen and tossed the phone onto the couch cushion beside her.

She rarely understood Jimmy's obscure pop culture references. She scraped her hands down her face and massaged her temples. At least with Jimmy asking questions, she and Tarek would learn if anyone had seen the podcasters since the CC Club. On the downside, so would everyone else. Jimmy might have been excellent at collecting secrets, but he was terrible at keeping them.

She settled back into the cushions and reached for the television remote. She paused the show she was half-watching when she heard Tarek's soft footsteps approaching, followed by the louder, but more succinct *pfft, pfft, pfft, pfft* ones of his tiny, demonic shadow.

He held up his mobile phone. "Evans. There's a hit on the blood samples."

"Already?" Kyra asked. It'd only been a few hours since the blood-bathroom had been discovered.

"Biologic samples from crime scenes are flown over to Mass General, but occasionally, the pathology lab at MVH will take a look if the sample is big enough and someone there has time. Someone on the island did a preliminary review. The blood found at the scene today? It's not human."

Kyra's mouth fell open. "Pardon?"

"It's animal blood."

Kyra immediately thought of animal sacrifice and her eyes widened. "*What?*"

"It's being sent to a veterinary pathologist for more tests, but the doctor at MVH says it's probably cow's blood. He thinks it's probably food grade. It'd been frozen and thawed out and cow's blood is pretty easy to purchase at specialty butcher shops, apparently."

"Frozen and thawed?" She made a pinched face. "Ew."

"I knew it smelled weird." Tarek's expression twisted into mild disgust that mirrored her own.

"Marjorie and Kelsey bought a container of frozen cow's

blood, brought it to the Vineyard, thawed it out, and splashed it all over the bathroom of their short-term rental property?" Kyra scrunched her nose. "That's insane."

"That's what it looks like." Tarek said with a helpless shrug.

She sat back. Tarek joined her, scrolling through his phone. "Did Mark say anything else?"

"Only that he'll request the ferry manifests for the last few days."

That instruction would have come from Tarek.

"And the OB Police? Do they have any thoughts?"

"No. As far as their chief is concerned, this is a civil matter between the podcasters and the landlord for the cleaning fees. No one has reported anyone missing. There's no evidence of anything happening to them." He looked up. "They're allowed to leave without telling anyone."

"But Mark is still searching for them?"

"Technically, no, but Ida and the council are concerned about the bad publicity and rumors getting out that the podcasters intentionally vandalized island property, or worse, they were disappointed or run off by unfriendly islanders. Their podcast was pitched as a tourism and marketing opportunity for the island and the new Pāru project. That they left so abruptly has upset some people, in particular, the council members who voted to rush permitting approvals. They've tasked Evans with finding out why they left. I want to know why they vandalized a bathroom."

"And Mark wants your help?"

"Actually, he asked *us* to help him."

"Really?" She grinned. She'd gladly help Mark find *Mur-*

*der & MayFemme.* "And Abigail and Elodie? Do they want to know what happened to them?"

"I suspect it's less of a priority. For them. But I want to know."

Kyra propped her feet on the coffee table and resumed her show. "And thanks to Chase, I know just where to start."

# Chapter Ten

*Wednesday, February 8*

KYRA RUBBED AT her dry, sleep deprived eyes and held her phone close to her face. She squinted at her contacts list, scrolling for Chase's number. The beginning of a headache pulsated at her temples. She hadn't slept well. She couldn't stop thinking about the blood splattered bathroom, missing *Murder & MayFemme*, or Abigail Koch.

It was one of her more annoying psychological quirks. She'd lay awake at night for hours, obsessing over her to-do list, problems that needed solving, or mistakes she'd made. She was sure a therapist would have thoughts, but she couldn't deny her overanalytical brain had made her an excellent, if often tired, attorney. It wasn't much of a liability when she was sleuthing—as Chase called it—either.

"Kay." Chase answered before the first ring completed.

"Hey," she said, concern softening her voice. "How are you?" She hadn't spoken to him since dropping him off at home. She hoped it was because he'd been sleeping, not enduring a panic attack alone.

It took him a moment, and then he huffed a dry, humorless laugh. "Oh, because of yesterday? I'm fine."

"Chase."

"No really. It wasn't the first time I've been in an interrogation room, you know." She could picture his lazy shrug. "It's no big thing."

Before his parents returned permanently to DC, amid a political scandal, when they still forced their son to live in the public eye as the heir apparent to a political dynasty he wanted nothing to do with, Chase had been a bit of a troublemaker, albeit an irresistible one.

It was only since meeting Kyra that he'd been a suspect in a murder investigation, shot at by an ecoterrorist, and hunted by a deranged chef. She supposed that for civilians, she and Chase spent an unusual amount of time in interrogation rooms.

He let out a sigh. "I promise. No panic attacks. I didn't even need to do the breathing thing. I'm okay. More annoyed than anything. And tired."

Annoyed was good. At least Kyra thought it was better than the alternative. "Alright."

"What's up?"

"Are you going to yoga today?"

"I could. Why?" He inhaled. "Oh, Greta. Yes. I'll sign us up. It's in an hour. See you there."

Kyra poured herself a glass of water and gulped down half. She'd been to Daphne's morning classes enough times to know they were a special level of sweat-drenched hell. It didn't matter how much she hydrated; she always left the studio feeling like a microwaved raisin.

She refilled the glass and returned to the living room where she'd been working.

Cronk had commandeered her place on the couch and

was nestled into her still warm blanket. She slid in beside him. He half-opened one sour apple eye and turned on his back, inviting a belly rub.

"No way. I have scars from the last time you tricked me." She reached out and rubbed his velvety ears instead and was rewarded with the soft rumbling of a contented purr. "Have time for your spare human now, do you?"

Cronkite allowed Kyra to cuddle with him until a noise at the front door announced Tarek's return and the alpine gremlin zipped to meet him.

"Hey, bud," Tarek greeted the cat.

She heard his soft murmurs and the little fiend's friendly chirps. Cronk never chirped for her.

"Hey to you, too." Tarek appeared in the living room, holding a coffee tray and a paper bag. He leaned down to give her a quick kiss. She wrinkled her nose against the sharp scent of chlorine. "I brought breakfast." He opened the paper bag, and heavenly buttery scents wafted on the steam.

"They're warm?" She eyed the bag of tempting pastry, questioning her life decisions.

"Nina had a batch in the oven when I got there. I waited." He pointed to his face and mimicked her pained expression. "What's that about?"

"I can't have one. I'm going to yoga with Chase." She wouldn't risk throwing up and humiliating herself in front of a room of octogenarian contortionists or Chase. "We're going to talk to Greta Koch."

"You sure?" he asked. Kyra's nod was forlorn. "Well, they'll be here when you get back, but I'm going to eat." He pulled an enormous breakfast burrito out of the bag and flopped on the couch beside her. He unwrapped it and took a massive bite. "It's good," he murmured, and Kyra chuckled. Swimming made him ravenous.

She excused herself to change into her workout clothes. When she came back downstairs, Tarek was in his office, hunched over a stack of papers. His phone lay beside it.

"I'm going to go."

He closed the file he'd been reading and ran his hand through his still-damp hair. "You don't sound too excited."

Kyra made a face. "Daphne's class probably violates the eighth amendment and the Geneva Convention. I'm subjecting myself to a lot of pain, and I'm not sure Greta will even agree to speak with me. She's not the friendliest and doesn't trust off islanders."

"Did you want me to come?"

"To yoga?" She couldn't picture him bending over a yoga mat or submitting himself to shavasana. Admittedly, she barely survived those five to ten minutes.

"I've attended a few classes."

"Really?"

He hesitated a half-second before expounding. "Rachel was an instructor while she was in grad school."

*Oh.* The ex-wife. Kyra wasn't thrilled to learn that in addition to competing with the memory of smart, successful, gorgeous Rachel, the woman was also a yoga instructor. *Bloody brilliant.*

Tarek rarely talked about his marriage or his ex-wife. When Kyra had asked, he'd shrugged and said he almost never thought of her, but the lack of information left Kyra feeling insecure. She couldn't help comparing herself to a woman she'd built up in her mind.

All she knew was that Rachel walked out of their marriage when Tarek was recovering in the hospital from a stab wound. Kyra didn't have the details, but had pieced together that he'd been attacked in what should have been a routine raid. He'd almost died. Rachel couldn't handle the constant worrying over whether he'd make it home each night, and she'd left. Kyra sympathized.

"Kyra?"

She took in the stack of files to one side of his laptop, the phone he'd placed on the desk, either in anticipation of a call or because one had just ended. He was busy.

"No," she said, shaking her head. "I can do it myself."

"I don't doubt it," he said, and reopened the file.

# Chapter Eleven

"I SWEAR, CHASE..." Kyra grumbled.

"Yes, I know. If you die, you'll claw yourself back from hell and drag me down with you." That wasn't what she was going to say, but *yes*. "It's a power class. You've done it before." Chase stretched out on his mat, his long body folding in half like he had no organs.

Or bones.

Kyra, beside him on her own mat, could barely get her fingers past her shins. He reached over and pressed a flat hand to the space between her shoulder blades and pushed, gaining her a few inches and a pleasant but painful stretching sensation down the backs of her thighs.

"You'll live."

"I doubt it," she snapped, earning a laugh.

·They'd arrived early enough they'd had their pick of spots in the studio, and they'd chosen to set up their mats near the back of the room where Greta and Dot preferred to be. There were three other masochists in the class lined up in front. At least she wouldn't have to endure them witnessing her flailing about and falling on her ass.

"Tarek almost came with."

"Seriously?" Chase turned, his blond hair falling into his

eyes. "I'd pay good money to see that."

"Oh, Chase!" a woman's voice called. "You're here!" Dot set her mat next to his, and her companion set hers next to Dot's. "We missed you last week, didn't we, Greta?"

Greta didn't answer. She just shook her head and continued setting up her space, grabbing yoga blocks, a band, one of the thick woolen blankets. Kyra didn't know what those were for. The room would soon be hotter than the Sun's corona.

"I pulled the later shift. How was it?"

"Daphne had us do the most amazing sequence last week. What did she call it?"

"Vinyasa."

Dot waved a dismissive hand at Greta and blew a raspberry. "It's all Vinyasa."

"Hiya, Greta. Sunshiny as usual today, aren't you?" Chase peered around Dot, his playboy smile firmly in place. "I like the new mat and water bottle combo. Are those hummingbirds?"

Greta paused her organizing. Her rosy cheeks deepened in color. "They're my favorite. I saw these at Target when I went off island last week. Couldn't resist."

"Good choice," he said, and made an overt show of looking over at Kyra and back. "You ladies remember my friend, Kyra?" Dot studied her. Greta ignored them. "She moved here last summer from London. She's been to class a few times."

"Oh, yes," Dot exclaimed, her eyes widening with recognition. "You wrote the article about the pirate ship they dug up last fall."

"I did."

"And now you're with *The Island Times*?"

"I freelance, yes."

"Mmmhmm." Greta's features sharpened; suspicion written all over her face. "And you're reporting on yoga?"

"No, Greta. She's here to work out, align her chi, and because she's my friend. Same as you and Dot," Chase said. "Kay just happens to be a writer."

Kyra opened her mouth to object. She wasn't a writer.

Chase shook his head, the slightest movement. "Just like her dad, actually. He won a Pulitzer. She will too, one day."

"No," Kyra interjected. "I'm not—" She broke off. Not what? Good enough? Talented enough? Like her father? The list of her shortcomings was a long one.

"Who is your father? Does he live on the island?" Greta asked, her attention focused on Kyra.

"He did. He died last year. Ed Gibson."

"Oh, no." Dot covered her heart. "I remember that."

"Me too. That was an awful tragedy. And then to find out later it wasn't an accident." Greta's voice was soft, but heavy with emotion. When she met Kyra's eyes, Kyra saw raw empathy there. "I'm sorry for your loss."

"Oh, thank you." Kyra swallowed, realizing why Chase led them down this path.

His chin dipped, encouraging her. Tarek's comments from yesterday invaded her thoughts, and she waited for the sting of guilt to keep her from using their shared loss to manipulate Greta into telling her story. She felt it, the smallest hint of heat below her rib. She dismissed it and it dissipated in an instant, as if it'd never been there.

"It's easier now that I know what happened to him." She paused. "You've lost someone too."

"I'm old. I've lost many people." She laughed, but it was dry and forced. "But a long time ago, my younger sister Abigail was killed. Murdered."

Kyra's heart thumped. *Sister.*

"We never found out what really happened." Greta's eyes were on her hands as she folded and refolded them in her lap. Dot reached over and rubbed her friend's shoulder.

"That's kind of Kyra's thing. She solves murders. She solved her dad's case. She caught my sister and saved my life. That nut bag bird watcher and the Verinder House killer? She caught them, too. Maybe she can help you."

That really wasn't how it happened. "Chase…" Kyra warned, but before she could clarify, Daphne walked in, clapping her hands together.

"Alright, let's get started. Please lay back on your mats."

Chase gave her a thumbs up and reclined. Kyra groaned and tried to mentally prepare herself for the next ninety minutes of pain.

Kyra gulped down half her water bottle. Her body felt exhausted and loose in that way before the aches set in. She was pre-sore. After class had ended, she'd half stumbled, half crawled out of the studio to the lobby. Greta and Dot were still inside, talking to Daphne. She tried to glare at Chase, but didn't have the strength to lift her head.

"I hate you," she said to her boots sitting below the bench, trying to muster the energy to tie them on her feet.

"Love you, too," Chase murmured from his seat beside her, his head resting back against the wall, his eyes closed. "I think she made it harder for us on purpose."

"Again. She did it again." Kyra coughed. "I'm going to die."

"It was a wonderful class, don't you think, Chase?" Dot asked.

Using every ounce of strength left in her body, Kyra raised her head. Dot was humming while she packed her mat into her bag.

"The wonderfullest. Can't wait for next week."

At least Kyra now understood how the two women left Daphne's classes so fresh faced and rosy. They spent most of it prone on their backs doing deep breathing. "Meditating," Dot had called it.

"Do you think you can really help find who killed Greta's sister?" Dot asked.

Kyra attempted to straighten her back, each of her muscles protesting. Chase opened his eyes. Greta was staring at them, her arms wrapped around her yoga bag, clutching it to her chest.

"We can try," Kyra said to Greta. "We'd need to know more about what happened that night. More about Abigail, the drama camp, and her life that summer."

"You know the story." Greta pursed her lips and a slew of emotions rippled across her face: wariness, fear, hope.

"Some of it."

"And it'd be you two?" Greta gestured between Kyra and Chase.

"And my partner, Tarek Collins."

"He works with the FBI, sort of," Chase added.

Greta's frown deepened, the lines on her forehead becoming more pronounced as her mouth dragged down. Her chin shifted as she thought. She let out a long breath and her shoulders straightened. "Okay. Come by the house tomorrow. I'll tell you what I know. But this isn't for the paper." Before Kyra could agree, Greta stomped out into the cold.

Dot shouted a goodbye as she scurried after her.

The spark of guilt Kyra had smothered in the studio flared. She shared a look with Chase. His hand found hers and he gave it a squeeze.

"If you figure out what really happened, it'll be worth it." Kyra hoped he was right.

At home, showered and dressed, Kyra heated her croissant and set about the calming English ritual of making tea. Her pre-sore muscles had settled into fully sore, and she rolled her shoulders, seeking relief. The left one twinged and crunched, an old injury that flared up with overuse. She dry-swallowed three ibuprofen. When the kettle flipped off, Kyra poured her tea and settled at the island with her breakfast and her laptop.

Her mailbox was full of new messages. The most recent one was from Mark Evans. She opened it.

DR. COLLINS / MISS GIBSON:

ATTACHED PLEASE FIND THE LIST OF ALL VEHICLE RESERVATIONS TO AND FROM WOODS HOLE SUNDAY THROUGH TUESDAY.

THANK YOU,
MARK

The list had been sent to him from someone with a Martha's Vineyard Community Council email address and it was labeled CONFIDENTIAL.

"That's interesting," she murmured to herself.

The council was powerful on the island. Made up of representatives from all areas of the Vineyard, it was an unofficial but effective and respected island-wide advocacy group and one of its highest priorities was maintaining the island's economy. With the council's support, Mark could forego proper legal processes without consequence. Kyra wasn't comforted by the thought.

She opened the spreadsheet and scrolled. The list was long. It'd take someone hours to go through each reservation, check each license plate against the registration information.

"Kyra?" A hand pressed gently against her shoulder.

She gasped, jerking in her seat.

"You didn't hear me? I called you."

"No. I didn't." She reached for her tea.

Tarek refilled and turned on the kettle. "How was yoga?"

Kyra filled him in. When she told him that Greta had agreed to meet with them, he chuckled.

"What?"

"You seem surprised you convinced Greta to speak with you."

"I suppose I am, but I can't take any credit. It was Chase that persuaded her." Tarek cocked an eyebrow at her, but she shook her head and asked, "Did you see the email from Mark?"

"I did. I forwarded it to Greyscale. Hopefully, they'll have some information for us in a day or two." He took the seat beside her and shifted her laptop so he could see the screen. He ran a few word searches for vehicle makes and models of popular cargo vans.

"No registered cargo vans came over on Monday." Tarek cocked his head to the side, thinking. "It's a strange lie to tell. If Benny wasn't driving over, why mention it at all?" He changed the search criteria to narrow the reservations down to those in the commercial classes. Still no cargo van with DC plates. "It's possible they didn't declare the correct class. The Steamship Authority's website isn't the most intuitive."

Tarek shifted the computer, so it faced her. His phone buzzed. "It's Evans. He sent me the evidence files they collected from the purple house. Let me get my computer."

Tarek returned with his laptop and booted it up.

"Can Mark share that with us?" she asked.

"Mmmhmm. Once the blood was identified as animal blood, the OBPD closed the case file. They're holding the evidence in storage in case Edina, the landlady, sues, but there's no criminal investigation."

Tarek logged into his work account and downloaded the massive file. It contained dozens upon dozens of photographs—pictures of the living room, the study, the dining room, from different angles, closeups of the décor, all exactly as Kyra remembered it. The next set of images were of the kitchen, its empty pantry, organized drawers, cabinets with stacks of purple dinnerware, and matching glasses. There were even images of the empty fridge, the empty freezer, and icebox.

"They didn't even make ice?"

"What's that?" Tarek asked.

She pushed a loose strand of hair behind her ear and pointed to the empty ice trays stacked in the freezer. "I don't know. To me, that seems like one of the first things people do in new places, make sure there's water and ice. But they did none of that. No milk for coffee, no tea. Not even a dirty glass. It's just weird. They said they arrived on Sunday, and they didn't bother with any supplies?"

"They may have eaten out Sunday."

She shrugged. "They didn't seem like big sports fans to me."

"The Super Bowl isn't just a game. It's one of America's most-watched events. It's about the party, the food, the commercials. Also, remember, we saw them Monday morning. If they'd just arrived Sunday, they may not have had a chance to purchase supplies."

Tarek had a point. There was only a small grocery store in Oak Bluffs, and it kept short hours, even in the summer season.

"What else?"

Tarek clicked through images of empty bedrooms, empty closets, and empty dressers.

The next were images of items laid out on a stainless-steel table, a plastic number beside each one.

"What's this?" Kyra leaned closer.

"Contents of the trash and recycling bins."

Cans, newspapers, water bottles. At least it was evidence they had been there. "And all that was from Marjorie and Kelsey?"

"Maybe." Tarek drew closer to the screen and zoomed in on the pile of soda and beer cans. "Or from a previous renter and the caretaker hadn't taken the trash to the recycling center yet."

Tarek clicked through more images, moving through them quickly. More garbage, paper towels, cleaning rags, empty bottles of laundry detergent and takeaway containers.

"Wait, what's this?" He clicked back to the pint-size food containers. Three of them—the clear plastic kind that takeaway soup came in. He enlarged the photograph. The insides were caked in a dark brown residue, but the labels were readable. BUCKLEBURY MEATS AND SUNDRIES, NEW HAVEN.

"Did those contain the blood?" Kyra's voice came out in a whisper.

"One way to find out." Tarek picked up his phone.

"Evans, it's Collins. Yes. Thanks for the images. There was something. Can you ask the pathologist who identified the animal blood to test the samples in the three takeout containers? I'm sending you the images. Evidence items three twenty-four through three twenty-six. Tomorrow would be great if he can do it." Tarek gave Kyra a nod. His brow creased. "Wait. Evans, I've got Kyra with me. Let me put you on speaker." Tarek set the phone down between them. "We're here."

"Hi, Miss Gibson."

"Hi, Mark."

"Go ahead. What were you saying?"

"Oh, yes. Ida Ames called me. The community council is worried about bad publicity. The podcasters had been active on social media and posting about their secret project. They never came out and said what they were doing or where they were, but they posted pictures of Woods Hole, the Steam-ship Authority, and one of them in front of the Flying Horses. People will know they are … *were* here. And they'll know they left the island without finishing their podcast, leaving behind that bathroom."

A light bulb that felt more like a dunce cap flicked on in Kyra's mind. She hadn't even thought to check their social media. She pulled out her phone.

Leading up to their visit, Marjorie and Kelsey had posted photos of their road trip from DC to Martha's Vineyard—selfies in front of a WELCOME TO MYSTIC CONNECTICUT sign, lunch in Woods Hole, photos on the ferry, even a few of the exterior of the purple house. The last one, on Sunday night, was a picture of side-by-side pints of beer at a place Kyra didn't recognize.

She turned her phone to Tarek, but he only nodded without looking. *Of course. He would have checked that first.* Kyra ran through the photos again, silently chastising herself for her error.

"What was that?" Evans's voice was muffled, like he'd covered his phone's microphone. When he came back on the line, his tone was apologetic and a little harried. "Collins? I have to go. I have a meeting about crossing guards in Vineyard Haven. I'll drop the containers off at the hospital on the way."

"We'll talk later." Tarek hung up.

"Do you know where this place is?" Kyra asked Tarek, pointing to the image with the two beers.

"I'm pretty sure it's a brewpub in OB. It's one of the few places open year-round."

"Do you think someone there would remember serving Marjorie and Kelsey on Super Bowl Sunday?"

"I couldn't say." He didn't sound optimistic. "It would've been busy." His eyes searched hers. "Do you want to ask them?"

Kyra stood. "Let's go."

# Chapter Twelve

TAREK FOUND A parking spot in Ocean Park near the restaurant. Kyra pulled her worn leather jacket tighter around her shoulders, but the wind still sliced into her, peppering her with icy shards of seawater and sand.

"Tar," she gritted out through clenched teeth as another blast hit her, making her stumble.

He opened his mouth but then clamped it shut like he reconsidered saying something, not that he needed to. Kyra knew she was being ridiculous. She needed a proper winter coat. She was being stubborn, or stupid, but she couldn't bring herself to purchase another. The image of her aunt lying in the sand on Thanksgiving night, wearing Kyra's horrible bright blue parka, still haunted her. Ali, the person who'd been her entire family—her mother, her sister, her rock—since she was a girl, had almost died because of Kyra and that stupid jacket.

Tarek grabbed her freezing hand in his warmer one, swiped his thumb across her knuckles. "It's just there." He pulled her down Healy Way, stopping under a wooden awning. "Inside." He held the door open.

She pushed back a heavy drape to reveal a rustic but cheerful restaurant within.

It was built like a barn. A mezzanine ran around the perimeter, drawing attention to the antique racing shell suspended from the ceiling. The air was warm and heavy with the heady scents of yeast and malt. Wood smoke from the hearth chased away the winter chill. A shiny bar with brass accents was directly across from the entrance. Behind it, and behind a wall of cross-hatched windows, were the silver beer tanks. A chalkboard listed what was brewing, along with the name of the brewmaster.

Tarek peeled off his coat and took Kyra's. He hung them on one of the entryway hooks. "Let's get you warm." He steered her across the room to the bar. Their boots crunched on discarded peanut shells.

Despite the early hour, the pub was busy. Another chalkboard boasted the day's happy hour menu, dollar oysters and half-priced pours, explaining the bar's weekday popularity.

Tarek pushed her into a seat. "Two East Chops, please."

The bartender, a woman with long blonde hair pulled into a ponytail, wearing a Wicked Island Ale sweatshirt, gave them a friendly nod.

Tarek took Kyra's hands in his and rubbed warmth back into them, massaged her chapped reddened knuckles. They'd only been outside a few minutes, but she felt like she'd been assaulted by Boreas himself.

"It's freezing out there," Kyra chattered, unable to stop shivering.

"Just going to get colder. And now they're predicting snow." The bartender set their glasses down on cardboard coasters. "There's a storm watch. It's gonna be a big one."

She spoke in the twangy accent unique to southern New England, her vowels elongated and nasally. She pushed back her long sleeves, revealing dozens of woven bracelets, some made with purple wampum beads. "Can I get you anything else? Menus?"

"Actually, I was hoping you could help us," Tarek said, releasing Kyra. The bartender wiped her hands on a bar towel and nodded for him to continue. "Were you working Sunday night?"

"Yup. I work every night." The woman straightened her sweatshirt. "This place is mine. Well, mine and Raf's." She pointed to the name of the head brewmaster on the chalkboard. "My husband. I'm Ellen."

"Nice to meet you, I'm…"

"You're Gully's cop friend and you're the Gibson girl." Ellen's smile was more of a smug smirk.

"That's right. I'm Tarek. Tarek Collins. I grew up with Gully. This is my partner, Kyra."

"We were hoping to ask you a few questions, if you don't mind?"

Ellen assessed Kyra and pursed her lips before nodding slowly. "Jimmy said you were good people. He doesn't vouch for just anyone."

*Jimmy Blau?*

Kyra was surprised, and perhaps a little flattered. "Oh, that was nice of him." Tarek raised an incredulous eyebrow at her, like she'd sprouted a second head. *What?* she mouthed, but he turned back to Ellen.

"So, you were here on Sunday?"

"Yes, I was here from noon to close. Why?"

"Do you remember serving these two women?" he asked, holding up his phone.

Ellen squinted at the screen for barely a second before her forehead smoothed out. "The podcasters. Murder and something? They came in for an early dinner before the football crowd. Nice girls."

"They told you they were here researching a podcast?" Kyra asked.

Ellen tipped her head to the side, and her ponytail shifted, sliding against her shoulder. She ran her tongue over her top lip and her mouth hitched to the side. "You going to order something?"

"Sure." Kyra scanned the menu. "We'll share the fish and chips."

"Good choice." Ellen keyed in their order and poured them each another pint. She set them beside their still mostly full glasses. She leaned back against the counter opposite them. "They told me they were looking into that murder at the old East Chop summer camp, asked me what I knew about it."

"They told you they were here to find out what happened to Abigail Koch?" Kyra asked, annoyed.

The feigned secrecy, and the NDAs were clearly part of whatever game the podcasters were playing.

"Mmmhmm. I told them my dad used to tell my brother and I that story when we misbehaved. He'd tell us there was a madman who lived on the island who stole away bad children at night. Not that it had any effect on my brother." Ellen shook her head with a resigned sigh. "As teenagers, we'd break in and drink in the old camp buildings. It's a miracle no one was hurt, but other than being a scary story told around campfires..." Her voice trailed off.

"Did they mention how long they intended to stay?" Kyra asked.

"No, but I got the impression they weren't on the island long. They asked what there was to do here in the off season and when I mentioned visiting Edgartown and Vineyard Haven, they said they wouldn't have time."

The island was small. One could easily experience all three little towns in half a day, especially in the off season when many of the shops and businesses were closed.

"Hmm." Kyra hummed. "You didn't see what kind of car they were driving, did you?"

Ellen gave Kyra a look not unsimilar to the one Tarek had just given her, a little surprised, a little disappointed. "You mean from inside the bar?" She pointed to the thick paned wavy glass windows to her left that looked out onto a distorted street, made worse by the streetlamp's glow.

Kyra sat back in her seat. "Ah, no. Right. Thank you."

Another couple took seats at the corner and Ellen excused herself to wait on them.

Kyra let out a long breath. She tapped her fingernails against her pint glass.

"What are you thinking?" Tarek asked.

She pressed the pad of her finger to her lip. "I'm beginning to doubt *Murder & MayFemme* were here to investigate Abigail's death."

"Me, too."

"But if not for Abigail, why would they come here? What were they doing?"

"And why did they want everyone to believe they were investigating a decades-old murder?"

That was the question, wasn't it? Why go to all this trouble, make public declarations, all to just disappear?

"Fish and chips?" asked a young man in a stained Wicked Island Ale t-shirt holding an enormous plate of fried food.

"That's us," Tarek said and made room on the narrow bar. He dipped a fry in tartar sauce. "What time are you and Chase meeting Greta tomorrow?"

"Midday sometime. Will you be able to come with?"

"I wouldn't miss it."

# Chapter Thirteen

*Thursday, February 9*

"ARE YOU READY?" Kyra called down from upstairs. She looked out the windows, past her backyard, to the cove below. The snow that had started when they'd left Wicked Island Ale had kept falling overnight. At least a foot, probably more, had accumulated, and it continued to fall, but big, sloppy flakes had replaced the stream of tiny ones. Tarek said it meant it was getting warmer. Kyra couldn't tell the difference. At some point, cold was just cold. She pulled on one of Tarek's wool sweaters and a thick pair of socks.

"Tar?" she called again.

Still no answer.

She muttered an expletive and traipsed downstairs. She came to a stop in the living room. "What's going on?"

Tarek was lying on the couch, the white nightmare curled up on his chest. "I didn't want to wake him." Tarek stroked the cat's forehead and Cronk stretched out his paw, extending his claws so they shimmered in the firelight before retracting them. A reminder that even ensconced in floof, he was still a fearsome predator. She glared at the sociofluff.

"We have to go." She picked up the paperback splayed

on the floor. *Jane Eyre.* She held it up. "Brontë?"

"Chase recommended it. He said I'd identify with Mr. Rochester."

Kyra grinned. "I don't think that was a compliment." She dropped the book on the coffee table. "He just texted. He's already on his way." Tarek extracted himself from beneath the sleeping terror and moved Cronk to the sofa. He wrapped the throw blanket around the cat, creating a little nest, and walked to the coat closet. He held his thick winter coat out to her.

"No." She shook her head and pushed it back. "I can't." She should suffer for being an idiot.

"Take it. It's freezing out." He pressed the coat to her chest.

"But what about you?" she asked, relenting and accepting it.

"I'm a New Englander. I'm used to it." He pulled his faded canvas field jacket, the one he'd worn last spring, and wasn't nearly warm enough, off the hanger. He wrapped his arms around her and pressed a quick kiss to her temple. "I'll be fine."

Tarek skillfully reversed the car out of the drive, but stopped when the wheels hit the snow-covered road.

He looked right, then left. "Shit. I'd forgotten the plows don't always clear the side streets."

Kyra took in the expanse of unmarred white in both directions. There weren't many houses on her street and most of her neighbors were seasonal. Of course, her street wasn't prioritized.

"Can you get through it?" she asked.

"Yeah," he said and put the Jeep in four-wheel drive. "We'll stick to the main roads." Tarek drove slowly, but the snow didn't impose a significant obstacle, and the Jeep moved smoothly through the drifts. He stopped at the intersection with Herring Creek Road. It had been plowed and treated. The thick wet flakes melted on impact with the pavement.

Unfortunately, the improvement was temporary. The gentle snowfall became an onslaught once they were moving at thirty miles an hour. The wet snow clung and caked to the windshield and the wipers, rendering them useless. With each pass, the wipers slid clumps of snow across the glass, distorting their visibility.

"Is it always like this?" Kyra asked, angling for a better view through her foggy passenger window. Theirs was the only car on the road. The parking lots were empty, and even the houses seemed darker than usual. The islanders were hunkered down, waiting out the storm.

"This isn't even that bad," Tarek said, slowing the car to turn onto Cooke Street. "Where I grew up, we'd get twice as much snow as Boston. Three times as much as here. And it's always colder."

"I'd die." She couldn't imagine that kind of winter. She was already in a permanent state of half-frozen.

"You get used to it. Oh, I forgot to tell you. I spoke with someone at Bucklebury this morning."

"The butcher shop?"

"It's more of a specialty gourmet goods store." Kyra waited for him to continue. "It's run by a couple, Alan and Michel. Alan was working Sunday and Monday."

"He remembers Marjorie and Kelsey?"

"No. He remembers selling blood to a man Monday. Alan said that he stocks it for one regular customer, an artisanal sausage maker. The man who asked for it wasn't his regular."

Kyra thought. "Do you think it was Benny?"

"It'd be one hell of a coincidence, otherwise. Unfortunately, Alan wasn't able to confirm it was Benny from a photo. He couldn't provide a description either."

Kyra had spent a few hours with Benny, had even shared a few polite words with him, and she barely remembered him. He'd been a normal, somewhat dull, nondescript guy. She couldn't blame the store owner for not noticing.

"What about receipts?"

"I asked, and he checked his purchase history. He sold three pints of blood at 2:46 p.m. on Monday. The customer paid with cash."

*Of course he did.* Kyra made a frustrated noise in the back of her throat. "Did he see Benny's van?"

"No. He doesn't remember seeing one."

Kyra pressed her lips together. People often weren't paying attention to their surroundings unless they made a point to. It was one of the many reasons lawyers hated eye witness testimony. It wasn't reliable.

"He sent a photo." Tarek handed her his phone.

Kyra opened the photo app. She scrolled past too many to count pictures of Cronkite before she came to the one Tarek must have been talking about. The image was a fisheye view of the interior of a storefront. It was taken from behind the counter, showing the checkered floor, shelves lining the walls, and beyond, the large picture windows with a view of a parking lot.

"Bucklebury isn't part of a strip mall or retail cluster. That's their private parking area." Kyra bit her lip and stared at the photo. "Look at the building across the street."

Kyra zoomed in, but the image was too blurry. She used her own phone and found the street on her maps app. She blinked. "A dispensary? They have a lot of security, right? Like cameras."

"Mmmhmm. I already called them. They were surprisingly helpful and shared the footage with me. No cargo vans parked at Bucklebury on Monday, but there were a few Subarus in the morning, a pickup truck right after lunch and a black sedan."

Tarek made a left into the Dodger's Hole community and pulled to the side of the road. He took the phone back from Kyra and pulled up a grainy video. "Look."

The camera lens was focused on the entrance to the dispensary, but at the top edge was a partial view of the butcher shop's parking lot. An older model, black four-door sedan pulled into the lot and Kyra paused the video. She checked the time stamp: 2:38 p.m.

"That's just about the same time the blood was purchased. You think whoever was driving this car bought it?"

"I think it's a fair assumption."

She zoomed in on the car's license plate. She couldn't make it out. "You were able to get a license plate from this?"

Tarek's mouth flattened, and he quirked an eyebrow at her. "You know *CSI* isn't real, right?"

Kyra made a face at him. "I know." Still, how disappointing. She zoomed in further. The back of the car was blurry, but she made out a swipe of pink on the black bumper. And a white license plate with blue or back lettering. She couldn't make out the state. Kyra huffed and handed his phone back. "So, what does this mean? If that is Benny's car, and he bought the blood, you think they lied about what car Benny drove over?"

"Actually, I'm questioning if Benny drove over at all."

# Chapter Fourteen

TAREK PULLED BACK onto the road. It curved deeper and deeper into the interior of the island, but at least these roads were cleared. Kyra squinted through the windshield and out her window.

"I haven't been over here before."

"Behind us is the interior side of Sengekontacket Pond. State Beach is across it."

Kyra tried to picture it in her mind. The island was small, but she still hadn't explored all of it. There were miles and miles of walking trails that crisscrossed through forests and parks that she hadn't yet seen.

He pointed forward and to the left. "We live over that way. There's a golf course in between us. We can technically get home using back roads, but they're private. I didn't know if they'd be plowed." He pointed further left. "Gully lives about a mile that way."

The road curved and Tarek reduced his speed.

"That's Chase's car." Kyra pointed to the Bronco stopped on the side of the road. It was in front of a snow-covered driveway.

A mailbox decorated like a lobster trap was attached to a stake and stood at the top of the drive. To the left was a saltbox style house with cedar shingles. It'd been built on an angle not quite facing the road. Flower boxes covered in snow hung from each window.

Tarek parked behind the Bronco and Kyra opened her door just as Chase exited his car.

"You made it!"

Kyra hopped down. The snow was deeper inland and kissed the tops of her boots. She swore it felt colder here, too. Tarek apologized to Chase for being late, blamed the poor road conditions.

"I know. Chilmark is a fucking disaster." Chase shook his head. "You guys ready to do this?"

"Yep," she said, feeling ill prepared. Kyra followed Chase and Tarek across the snowy driveway, stepping in their footprints.

Chase rang the doorbell and stood back. A wooden wreath painted like a lifebuoy hung on the front door. Kyra squeezed herself between Chase and Tarek, seeking warmth. Even with Tarek's coat, she was cold. It was too big. Drafts of frigid air flowed in at her wrists, the neckline, and the hem, leaving her chilled. She fisted her hands in her pockets and silently chastised herself for her issues that kept her balking at ordering a proper coat.

The door cracked open, and Greta's wrinkled face appeared. Her pale blue eyes narrowed to slits. Kyra steeled herself, anticipating Greta shouting at them to get off her property, but the crack widened, and Greta stepped to the side. She blinked at them. Again.

"Well?" she snapped. "Don't just stand there. You're letting out the heat." Greta turned on her heel and disappeared down the hall.

"I think we're allowed in." Chase gave them a thumbs-up and entered the house. He wiped his boots on the mat and stooped to remove them. "Hi Greta!" he crowed. "How are you feeling after yoga yesterday? Daphne did not hold back, did she?"

Kyra and Tarek followed Chase's example, removing their boots and hanging their coats on the wall hooks above the mud trays.

"I'm back here." They followed Greta's raspy voice down the hall and into a warm kitchen with a cozy breakfast nook. Greta sat on one of the cushioned benches, a cup of tea clasped between her hands. She stared out the window. The silence dragged on until she motioned for them to sit.

"This is your FBI friend?" she asked Tarek.

"Tarek Collins, ma'am. I consult for them, yes."

"And they're interested in my story?"

"I ... *we* are interested," Tarek said. "If you're willing to share it."

"Is it for the papers?" She shot a disdainful look at Kyra.

"Only if you want it to be," Kyra said, trying to emulate Tarek's gentle tone.

"Come on, Greta. We wanna help." Chase took the seat next to her and bumped his shoulder against hers.

Greta heaved a shaky sigh. It was both annoyed and resigned. Kyra felt a twinge of guilt. They were here because their curiosity had been piqued. Greta had been grieving, seeking the truth for nearly forty years.

"Alright. What do you want to know?"

"How about you just tell us what you remember about

your sister, that summer, and the night she died?" Kyra said.

Greta pressed her thin lips together, considering. "Alright." She nodded. "I'll tell you what I know. It isn't much. Abigail was my sister, but we were never close. I was eight years older than her. When she started at that summer camp, she was a young girl. She always said she wanted to be a star. When it opened, I bet she was the first one to sign up." Greta's smile was sad. "The first year, she won a small part in the end of summer play, and she was hooked. She attended every year and in the off season, she signed up for drama and dance at school." Greta took a sip of her tea. "My family wasn't wealthy. They really couldn't afford it, but my father couldn't say no to Abby.

"For the first few years, she attended as a day-camper. Our house wasn't far away. She walked over every morning, and back after class or practice ended each afternoon. She took evening jobs babysitting, mending sails or fishing nets, cleaning, anything to help my parents pay the fees." Greta picked up her teacup. Her hand shook, sloshing liquid over the rim, and she set it down. "But that last summer, I'd gotten married in May. Robert and I stayed with my parents while he finished building our house. This house. Abby decided she wanted to board at camp. She said it was so Robert and I had privacy, but I think she hated being around us. Abby wasn't a romantic. She was much too practical. She told me I was throwing my life away, marrying Robert." Greta spun a gold band on her ring finger and her expression darkened.

Kyra wondered if Abigail might have been right.

"I think she was nervous to live away from her family for

the first time. She was only fifteen. But it only took her a few days to settle in and then she loved it. Sundays were free days, and she'd come home for lunch or dinner. She was so full of stories." Greta paused and turned her face to the window. Her eyes became glassy, unfocused.

"What kind of stories?" Kyra asked.

"Oh." Greta chuckled. "Just regular fifteen-year-old-girl stories. What happened with the play. Her acting and voice coaching, what so-and-so said to so-and-so. The part she was assigned, the leading part, she said. Boys."

"Did she ever mention her roommate, Elodie Edwards?" Tarek asked.

"Elodie? Sure. She and Abby were thick as thieves. Wore those silly broken heart necklaces. The one where each girl has half? They traded in their arcade tickets for them."

"You met Elodie?"

"A few times. Sometimes she came with Abby on Sundays."

"What was she like?" Kyra asked.

"Oh, shy, quiet. I was surprised they made her Abby's understudy. It was a big role and Elodie didn't seem the type to want the spotlight. But Abby drew her out. They were inseparable. At least for the first half of the summer." Greta grunted. "So much for best friends forever."

"Did something happen between them?" Tarek asked. "An argument?"

Greta shook her head and let out a long breath. "Abby never said, and Elodie stopped coming on Sundays. I hardly noticed, to be honest." Greta's voice grew hard. "Abby was just a silly teenager, and I was busy picking out furnishings and curtains, starting my life with my new husband." She stared into her cup, straightened it on the saucer.

"The police alleged Elodie killed your sister and escaped out their dorm room window. She was never found after that night, and they thought she could have drowned trying to reach the mainland. Do you think Elodie could have hurt Abigail?" Kyra tried to soften her tone.

Tarek's toe touched hers, warning her not to go too far, but Greta seemed to have been expecting the question.

"I don't know," she said, her tone weary, weighted. "That was the story we were given, and then the Edwards family had the case closed and the police refused to answer any more of our questions. Abby was just some poor girl who got herself killed. They didn't care about her, or us."

"What do you mean?" Chase asked.

Greta gave them a look like they were stupid. "Because Elodie was an Edwards and Abby was a Koch."

Chase's eyebrows hitched up, and he shared a look with Kyra.

"And that's important, because..." Kyra prompted.

Greta scowled. "The Edwardses were a rich family from Connecticut. The Koches? We were just a family who came for seasonal work each year. My father worked the lobster boats in the summer. In the winter, he did maintenance work up at Cougar Mountain in Franconia. No one cared what happened to Norbert Koch's girl. They just needed to protect the island's reputation for their rich summer folks."

"But if Elodie's family was so important, why did no one try to find her?" Kyra ran her hands down her thighs.

"After they found my sister dead, and realized Elodie had

disappeared, they searched for her or said they did. After, there were the whispers that Elodie had run off with a boy. That wouldn't do for the family, so they washed their hands of her."

"She had a boyfriend? Do you know who it was? Did Abigail ever mention him?" Tarek asked.

Greta shook her head. "I don't know." She swallowed. "We heard it was a local boy, but no one ever reported their son missing. It didn't matter who it was to the Edwardses. Elodie being dead was less of a scandal for their high society circles."

Kyra frowned. "Her family said that? They said she was better off dead?"

Greta shrugged. "That's what the police and the community council said when the case was closed."

"Anything else you can think of?" Tarek asked.

Greta's mouth twisted, but after a pause, she nodded. "There was another rumor going around at the time—that Elodie hadn't run off, but that something had happened to her. That was early on though, and the police paid him no mind."

"Him?" Kyra repeated.

"Charles Harris. He made claims that his wife Loretta had information about the case. I don't know whatever came of that."

*Harris?* Kyra caught Chase's eye, and he gave her a nearly imperceptible nod.

Harris was Charlie Chambers's maiden name. Greta was talking about Charlie's parents. Charlie's very unsupportive, very estranged parents.

Greta cleared her throat, recapturing Kyra's attention. "The police would have kept looking for her, but the Edwards family wanted it to go away, so…" Greta shrugged.

Kyra turned to Tarek. "Is that normal?"

He shook his head, but Greta spoke. "The police were told to stop, to let it go. And then my parents had to leave the island. Go back to work up north. Robert and I stayed, but he worked in the shipyard. He was threatened that if I made trouble, kept after the police or the community council, he'd lose his job. What choice did I have but to let it go? The police said the case was solved. I was told to bury Abby and move on. So, I did, as best I could. Until I received that phone call a few weeks ago."

Kyra felt Tarek tense beside her.

"What phone call?"

Greta blinked as if the call still confused her. "A person left a message saying they wanted to ask me questions about Abby's death, that they'd make it worth my time, and to call them back."

"Do you remember who they said they were? Or if they were calling on behalf of someone or a company? Was it *Murder & MayFemme*?" Kyra sat forward in her seat.

"I don't think the woman left a name, but Murder-and-whatsit, doesn't sound familiar." Greta sounded uncertain.

"What about the Pāru Group?" Tarek asked.

Greta pressed her lips together before shaking her head, a slow, deliberate movement. "Maybe?" Her mouth slanted down.

"Do you still have the voicemail?" Tarek asked.

"No. I deleted the message after listening to it. I wasn't

going to talk to them."

"And yet you agreed to speak with us?" Kyra gestured to herself, Tarek, and Chase, her curiosity overtaking her good sense to keep her mouth shut.

Greta blinked at her, and an emotion Kyra couldn't place flashed and disappeared across her face. When she spoke, her voice was high pitched, and wavered. "But you help people like me." She pointed a shaky finger at Chase. "You helped him. Charlie Chambers. Lisa Mackey. The Ramos girl. You and him." She jerked her chin at Tarek.

Kyra didn't know what to say, but Chase saved her from having to come up with anything. "They do help people, Greta. They'll help you, too."

Kyra wasn't confident there was anything she and Tarek could do, but she'd do her best. She placed her hand on top of Greta's wrinkled one. "If we're able to help, we will."

Chase stood and leaned over the table to get a better view of the backyard. Kyra followed his line of sight. The snow had finally stopped.

"Who's coming to do your driveway?" he asked.

"Oh, my neighbor. He has a plow contract with the town. When he has time, he'll do it."

"Are the shovels in the shed?" Chase asked, straightening. Greta's brow furrowed, but she nodded. "Tar?"

"Yeah, let's go."

The men left, leaving Kyra sitting at the table with Greta. "It's not like I'm going anywhere," the old woman muttered, but she was smiling.

It was the first genuine smile Kyra had seen her make. Kyra imagined it'd been a long time since someone had taken care of Greta Koch. "Would you like another cup of tea?" she asked.

"Oh. Okay. Bags are in that cannister."

She took Greta's cup and set an old-fashioned kettle on the electric stove. When the water boiled, she poured it over the tea bag and let it steep before bringing it back to the table.

"Does Dot live close by?" she asked.

"Just round the corner." Greta pointed over Kyra's shoulder. "She and her husband bought their house three years after me and Robert moved in. They moved here full-time when they retired. Dot's son lives in Atlanta, so they spend some time down there when it gets too cold."

"And your husband, Robert?" Kyra asked gently.

The last vestiges of Greta's smile faded away. "He left."

Greta lapsed into silence and stared out the window. Kyra didn't pry. She sat with her, while her untouched tea went cold.

# Chapter Fifteen

"JESUS SHIT," KYRA griped and rubbed warmth into her arms. The house was freezing. The snow might have stopped, but the temperatures had plummeted. She'd been wrong before. There was cold, and then there was *New England cold*. The wall of windows overlooking the cove, the showpiece of the house, did little to retain the heat. She blew on her red, stinging fingertips and pulled the old afghan from the back of the couch. Wrapping it around her shoulders, Kyra turned on the gas fireplace. She stood in front of it and held out her hands, letting the flames ease away the bite.

She and Tarek had driven straight home after leaving Greta Koch's house. Chase and Tarek were half frozen when they finally finished clearing the old woman's driveway. That Tarek had shoveled Greta's drive in a canvas jacket ate at Kyra.

Chase had gone home to Mander Lane to warm up and dry off. She assumed Tarek would have bee-lined for a hot shower and dry clothes, but as soon as he turned off the Jeep's ignition, his boss had called. He'd been locked away in his office with the resident rakshasa since.

She eyed the office doors and rolled her shoulders against a phantom weight. Long calls from Greyscale set her on edge. They often meant one of two things—his testimony was needed at a trial or deposition, or he'd been assigned a new case. Either way, it meant he would be leaving. The thought troubled her more than last time. He'd been home less than a week, and she hadn't planned on being invested in a forty-year-old murder. She didn't want him to leave before solving it. At least, that was the reason she was telling herself.

Kyra checked her laptop. There were no updates about the podcasters' whereabouts. She tried calling Marjorie again. It clicked straight to voicemail. Her phone was still off.

Kyra knew plenty of journalists. She'd spent the first decade of her life surrounded by them. Technically, she could call herself one, she supposed. In her experience, they were attached to their devices. They needed constant and immediate access to information and unrestricted lines of communication. The podcasters weren't official news people, but they were close enough. That Marjorie's phone was still off made Kyra uneasy.

She dropped the blanket on the ottoman, shot a glance at Tarek's closed door, and grabbed her phone. On wool-clad toes, she slunk upstairs, pausing at the bedroom entrance. She strained her ears listening, but downstairs was quiet. She slipped inside, shut the door, and leaning with her back against it, she dialed.

It only rang twice. She was one of only a select few who had Asher Owen's private number. In all the years they'd worked together, she'd never once used it.

"Kyra?" Asher said her name, his posh public-school accent sliding over the R. "Is everything alright?"

"It's fine."

"Ah." She heard the smile in his voice.

"I had a quick question for you. It won't take long. I know you're busy."

"I appreciate your consideration."

"The podcasters *Murder & MayFemme*. We met with them on Monday."

"I'm aware. Did your policeman enjoy his birthday gift?"

Kyra ignored his question, half-intended to bait her. "Have you heard from them since?"

Asher was quiet for a long moment. "No, but I'm not in the habit of conversing with the audio talent."

"I know. But can you ask if anyone's heard from them since Tuesday?"

He dropped the teasing lilt. "What's this about, Kyra? Should I be concerned?"

"No, not yet. I have an off feeling. It's probably nothing, but can you ask around?"

"An off feeling?" She could picture him tipping his chin at her. "I'll see what I can do."

"Thank you, Asher." She moved the phone away from her ear to hang up when his voice carried through the speaker.

"But Kyra, love." Kyra sucked in a breath. "Now, you owe me." Asher hung up.

Kyra stared at her phone. She questioned whether she'd been rash in reaching out to the Omega Global CEO again. But, she tried to convince herself, when Asher confirmed the podcasters were safe, taking an unauthorized holiday, or following up on a different, better story, the anxious, unsettled feeling that had been steadily increasing over the past seventy-some odd hours would dissipate. Possibly, she'd even laugh at herself and her ridiculous paranoia, and laugh again when Asher called in his favor. She let out a sigh. Unlikely.

"Kyra?" Tarek called. "Where are you?"

"Upstairs. One minute."

Tarek was already on the couch, his feet kicked up on the coffee table. Cronk was on the ottoman. He'd commandeered the blanket she'd abandoned and was kneading it into his desired shape.

"What is it?"

"I had an interesting call with Evans. He pulled the Abigail Koch case file. It took a while for him to find it, since it wasn't in the Archive."

"Archive? What's that?"

"Closed cases are put into long-term storage. It's nicknamed the Archive, but Abigail's case wasn't there. It was with the active cases. Contrary to everything we've been told, the case wasn't solved or officially closed. The investigatory team at the time just set it aside."

Kyra's mouth hitched to the side, and she waited for him to explain. Outside of what she saw on *CSI*, she knew nothing of American police procedures.

"It means that the case is open." Kyra shook her head, still not following. "I mentioned it to Briscoe, my supervisor. He's arranging it as we speak. Greyscale will be engaged to consult on the Abigail Koch case at the request of Officer Mark Evans and Ida Ames."

"You weren't talking to him about a new case?"

"I was," Tarek said, his enthusiasm wanning. "He's given

us permission to work on this until I leave." Kyra's heart dropped at his tone.

"When do you go?"

"Monday. Tuesday, the latest."

"Where?"

"I can't say." He shook his head.

That was new. Normally she at least got a state. She nodded and did her best to ignore the sense of disappointment sinking in her stomach, hollowing her out. She gave herself a mental shake.

"You said us?" She took the seat beside him.

"Well, officially, it's the Greyscale consultant, so me." He smirked and pointed to his chest. "You know the forensic psychologist and investigatory expert but seeing as you're right here…" Kyra swatted at his finger, but he caught her hand.

He turned serious. "I'd hoped I'd have more time at home. I'm sorry."

"Nothing to be sorry about." She shook her head and pulled her hand back. "What does that mean for Abigail's case? That Greyscale is involved?"

Some emotion flickered behind Tarek's eyes before he blinked it away. "We have access to all of Greyscale's databases and other no-cost resources."

She bit her lower lip, thinking. "No-cost resources?" Tarek's chin dipped. Her mouth stretched into a grin. "Meaning you have full access to the unredacted files, the evidence, the investigation notes? Everything?"

Tarek opened his laptop. She hadn't noticed it sitting on the coffee table. "Yup. Evans had everything sent right over.

Want to see?"

Kyra practically climbed into his lap as Tarek opened the files. But her eagerness died and turned to horror when he pulled up the crime scene photographs.

"Gods," she whispered, a hoarse, strangled sound and pressed her fingers to her lips.

"Kyra." He reached for the screen, but her hand on his arm stopped him.

"Don't." Barely any sound left her lips.

The dorm room was the same as the rooms she and Tarek toured, except it was lived in. Two twin beds sat on either side of the window. Clothes were on the floor. Framed pictures, a hairbrush, and an empty glass sat on the shared bedside table. Abigail's, at least she assumed it was Abigail's, bed was on the left.

The photos weren't the highest quality, but there was no mistaking the pulpy lump on Abigail's bed was a body. She was on her back. One bare foot hung off the end of the bed. The other, still in a pink sneaker, was bent at the knee. The coverlet was askew, pulled down, revealing the sheet beneath. Her dress, that once might have been a pale blue, was dark with blood and tissue. Where her head, her face, should have been was just a mess of gore and chunks of hair, lying on her pillow.

Kyra gasped.

Tarek pulled the laptop away and hurried to close the images. "Fucking hell. I'm so sorry. I didn't open it first. I didn't…" His eyes met hers, full of regret.

"No," she said and reached for the computer. "We need to see it. I'm … I'll be okay." He let her take it.

She felt his gaze on her as she reopened the files and flipped through the images.

Each one was worse than the last. Close-ups of the damage done to Abigail. Her chest, concave where the assault had crushed her ribs, her hand hung limp, splattered with blood, her face, unrecognizable as anything once human. The right side of her skull had been crushed; the orbital bone collapsed.

Kyra's mouth went dry, then it filled with saliva as she fought off nausea. Tarek appeared unaffected, but for the tense set of his jaw, and Kyra suspected that was more about his concern for her.

She continued, moving onto the next set of images.

These were better, clinical. Photographs of the contents of their room, a catalog of the scene. Abigail's open dresser drawer, broken glass on the floor in front of the bedside table.

Then it got so much worse.

The last image was of a metal rod. It was about three feet long, with a hook on one end and an intricate swirling metal handle on the other. It was covered in blood. Bits of skin and hair clung to the hook. It lay discarded on the floor, next to the bed, like it was nothing.

Tarek closed the images folder and hovered his cursor on another set of files. "The case notes are here." He pulled his hand away, but he watched her, the corners of his eyes creased with tension.

"Have you read them?"

He shook his head. "I haven't. Maybe we shouldn't…"

"I want to." She opened the documents folder.

The police reports were sparse, containing the most basic information. It was surprising, especially when compared to the sheer number of gruesome photographs. The photographer had either been an overzealous try-hard or a sadist. Perhaps both.

There was almost no crime scene analysis, just bland descriptions of the photos. The medical examiner's report was the last document.

"They did forensic autopsies on the island?" Kyra asked.

"No." Tarek shook his head. He pointed to the man's name printed at the top and scrolled down to the bottom of the report, where he'd signed it with a flourish. EMMET BLACKWOOD. "There was no forensic inquest. This report is from a coroner and the owner of Blackwood and Burke. It's the only funeral home on the island."

The name was familiar. Her father's body had been cremated there the year before, while she'd been in London. There'd been no service, and he had no burial requirements. His ashes were sent to wherever unwanted ashes go.

Kyra looked up the funeral home. The website was tasteful, the business name at the top, along with the address and contact information and a map.

"Oh my god." She sputtered. "It's next to a kiln house?" Kyra couldn't hold in her giggle. "Seriously? Fire your clay works pot and your loved one while you wait?"

"Kyra." Tarek's returning smile was crisp with worry.

He squinted at her, but she hadn't gone mad. Kyra knew it wasn't funny. It was morbid and crass, but she couldn't stop laughing. It was like her brain needed to counteract the horror of what it'd been forced to process with lots of dopamine.

"Are you done?" he asked.

When her giggles subsided, she wiped a tear from her eye. "Grace and Ida could not have approved that for zoning purposes."

That at least earned a slight twitch at the side of his mouth, and he turned back to the screen. "They have separate street addresses." He pointed to the map.

"They're literally next to each other."

Tarek sighed. "You spend way too much time with Chase," he mumbled. "You're both a little sick, you know that?" he teased, but concern still pinched the corners of his eyes.

Kyra leaned closer to the screen and read the coroner's report more closely. She felt Tarek's chest at her back as he read over her shoulder. Like everything else in Abigail's file, it was short on detail. Much of the information crucial to an investigation was missing. None of Abigail's ghastly injuries were described. It only said that she was fifteen, female, and her death was attributed to severe head trauma.

*No shit.*

Kyra had read a similar report after her father's autopsy. It had gone on for pages, cataloging everything in minute detail, from the descriptions of his clothes to the fibers found in his lacerations, to the peri and postmortem injuries his body sustained. At the time, she found the circumstances of his death described in scientific terms callous and cold, but at least the analysis had been thorough and thoughtful. This, whatever it was, was an insult to the poor girl's memory.

"It says she was struck *many times*." Kyra said, pointing

to the screen. "Many? Is that conclusive of anything?" Tarek averted his gaze, looked out to the cove. She put her hand on his forearm. "Tell me."

"No. *Many* doesn't begin to cover it. The condition of her body?" His eyes slid closed for a second. When they opened, they blazed. He was angry. For Abigail. "Whoever killed her continued the assault long after she died."

Kyra kept reading, scrolling down to the end of the document. There was a note, added at the end, a letter written by a hand that had been scanned into the report.

"What's this?" she asked, and Tarek pulled the screen closer.

DEAR SIRS,

I WISH TO INFORM YOU THAT PER THE FAMILY'S RE-QUEST, BLACKWOOD AND BURKE WILL HOLD THE FUNERAL SERVICES FOR THE DECEASED THIS COM-ING WEDNESDAY. I HAVE RECEIVED NO RESPONSE REGARDING THE INFORMATION I SHARED WITH YOU WHEN THE BODY WAS FIRST RELEASED. YOUR PROMPT ATTENTION TO THIS MATTER IS DULY AP-PRECIATED.

KIND REGARDS,
MARSHALL M. BURKE.

"Marshall M. Burke, as in Blackwood and Burke?" Kyra tapped his name on the screen with a nail.

"Mmmhmm. The mortician. He was, anyway."

"You know him?"

"Of him." Tarek pulled the computer closer and clicked

through the remaining unopened files, but there was no response to Marshall Burke that made it into the police record. Tarek sat back and ran his hand through his hair.

"Tar? Do you think Elodie did this?"

Tarek shook his head, but it wasn't a no, it was an *I don't know.*

The image of the fire poker covered in bits of Abigail's brain came to the front of Kyra's mind. It didn't add up. The violence Abigail endured, Elodie going missing, the community council's involvement, the public's disinterest. This was more than negligence. Someone had gone to great lengths to keep what really happened that night a secret.

"We've stumbled upon something much bigger than Abigail Koch and Elodie Edwards, haven't we?" she asked.

Tarek swallowed, a pronounced movement causing the column of his throat to undulate. His dark green eyes met hers. "It looks that way, doesn't it?"

# Chapter Sixteen

KYRA HEARD THE shower shut off and sat back on the couch with a huff. Cronkite peeked at her through a slitted eye, from his warm nest of blankets.

"You lead a grueling existence, you little beast."

He yawned and fell back to sleep.

After finishing their review of Abigail's case file, Tarek excused himself to finally shower and change into warm, dry clothes. While he was upstairs, Kyra went through the files again. Nothing more struck her. Their next course of action would be to hear the story from people who remembered that summer. Unfortunately, Kyra only had one solid lead. Charles and Loretta Harris.

She wasn't keen on cold-calling them. Everyone on the island knew she and Charlie were close friends and neighbors. Everyone also knew about their shared experience aboard the adrift *Neamhnaid*. No, she decided, shaking her head. First, she needed Charlie to be okay with Kyra and Tarek talking to the Harrises. However, Kyra wasn't confident Charlie would be okay with it. There was bad blood between Charlie and her family. She rarely saw them, despite living barely ten miles away.

"I can try bribing her," Kyra said to the sleeping cat.

Charlie would do nearly anything for apple fritters. "She's like you and T-R-E-A-T-S." Cronkite's head popped up. He stared at her with unblinking eyes, before yawning and lying back down. *Human treats, it is.* Kyra hoped it'd be enough. She reached for her phone.

"Hello?"

"Hi, Grace, it's Kyra. How are you?"

"Oh lovely, dear. It's so nice to hear from you. How are you and the detective? Are you managing with all this snow?"

"Yes. Well, Tarek is. He's been fastidious about the snow blowing. Blowing snow? I don't know what the right phrase is."

Grace laughed. "Snow blowing, I think. What can I do for you?" Grace asked, at the same time Kyra offered, "Do you and Charlie need help clearing your driveway?"

"Oh, no, but thank you. Wes Silva plows our drive for us." Grace's tone turned apprehensive, and Kyra's heart thumped at the mention of her former assailant and intimidator.

Wes hadn't hurt her, not physically, but he had scared the shit out of her. Last fall, he'd somewhat redeemed himself when he tried to save her from being shoved off a roof. While they'd never be friends, Kyra was glad he wasn't being ostracized by the island community.

"I hope he can make a go of it," she said truthfully.

"Me, too."

"Grace, I'm calling because I need a favor."

"Whatever you need, dear."

"From Charlie." Grace remained quiet, and Kyra sighed. "It's about the murder at the theater camp. It turns out

Charlie's parents had some information that no one listened to at the time. I'd like to ask them about it."

"I see."

"Do you think she'd be okay with me meeting them?"

"Honestly? No, but she wouldn't let you face those awful people alone. I won't either." Grace paused. "I'll talk to her."

"Tell her I'll get her apple fritters."

"Hmmm." Grace hummed, resigned. "You'll need quite a few, dear."

Kyra hung up and blew out a breath. She hated putting Charlie in an uncomfortable position, but she didn't see a better option.

Her phone buzzed with an incoming call. She blinked at the name on the screen in surprise.

"Asher?" She hadn't expected to hear from him so soon.

"Kyra, love."

"What did you find out?"

Asher chuckled. "What no, *How are you Asher? How's the company I could have helped you run, Asher? I've missed your delectable wit terribly, Asher.*" Kyra bit her cheek, silencing her retort. "No? It's a good thing I have confidence in spades, Kyra, or you'd wound me."

"Doubtful."

He huffed a laugh. "Alright. I'm putting you on speaker. My assistant has information for you."

"Hi, Miss Gibson," a voice Kyra didn't recognize came over the line. "Per your and Asher's request, I made some calls. No one has heard from any of the *Murder & May-Femme* crew. They've been called, emailed, and messaged. No response. I also reached out to their emergency contacts.

148

Marjorie and Kelsey's families have not heard from them since Saturday. We have no emergency contact info for Benny Perez." The assistant paused.

"What are you saying?" Asher asked, all humor gone from his tone.

"There's more. I had their Omega Global issued phones checked. They've been turned off since early hours on Tuesday morning. We didn't issue a phone to the sound engineer."

Kyra's stomach soured. This hadn't been the news she'd been hoping for. "Has anyone tried reaching them at their homes?"

"Yes. I had the local police do a wellness check. They're not home. Human Resources would like to file missing persons, but I told them I'd speak with Asher first."

"Kyra, what do you advise?" Asher asked.

Kyra heard Tarek on the stairs behind her, and she sucked in a breath. "Let me speak with Tarek. I'll call you right back."

"Bated breath."

Kyra hung up. She felt the heavy weight of Tarek's gaze. His hands slid into the pockets of his jeans as he waited for her to explain.

"That was Asher." She set her phone down on the coffee table.

"I heard. You still speak with him?"

Kyra tensed. "Occasionally." She didn't like the gnawing feeling building in her chest. It felt a lot like guilt, and it made her defensive. Tarek had never warmed to Asher. Her old client had a way of irritating people. He could be an arrogant bastard. He *was* an arrogant bastard, but she'd worked with him for years. She trusted him.

Kyra sighed. "Omega acquired *Murder & MayFemme's* production company in the merger last fall. I asked Asher to arrange for us to meet them." She pulled on one of the old afghan's tassels. "It didn't quite turn into the birthday experience I'd intended." Kyra raised her gaze to meet his eyes, mentally prepared for his reprimand, but Tarek wasn't angry or annoyed. He looked a little baffled, like he was surprised she'd gone to the effort.

"After Marjorie and Kelsey disappeared—" She broke off. "It's just so strange. The house, the blood. The van that never made it to the island. I had a bad feeling, and I couldn't let it go. I called him and asked him if he could get in touch with them."

"Was he able to?"

"No. No one from Omega can find them. They've been no contact since Saturday. Omega wants to file missing persons' reports."

"They should. Immediately." Tarek ran his hand through his damp hair. "Tell Asher to give the authorities the license plate numbers for the vehicles they were driving. If he has them, he should also provide their trip itinerary, drivers' licenses or passport numbers, access to the podcast's social media, anything that will help identify them or their location. If he can share that information with us and Evans, the OBPD can open a case here. It would also be helpful if we had a list of who knew about their trip." His eyes found hers. "Don't tell him this, but, Kyra, the first seventy-two hours after a missing person's claim is filed is crucial. After that, the likelihood of the victims' retrieval decreases."

"Decreases?" she repeated.

"Exponentially."

"I'll call him back now." Kyra unlocked her phone.

Asher and his assistant were quiet as she relayed what Tarek told her. He promised to call the local authorities and the company's contact at the FBI and to keep them apprised of information he received.

"I expect the same courtesy." Kyra hedged, and he interrupted her. "I'm serious, Kyra. I have enough shit to deal with right now and missing podcasters is not how I want to spend my time or my public relations budget. The moment you hear anything about those people, you alert me."

"I promise."

"Give my regards to your policeman." Asher hung up.

"He'll take care of it," Kyra said to Tarek.

Tarek gave her a nod and took a seat next to Cronk. "Hey there, buddy," he murmured. The snowy fiend stretched, and his emerald eyes slid open. He made a soft chirping noise and crawled into Tarek's lap, where he nestled down, his purr intensifying to a low-pitched rumble.

She stared daggers at the little menace and his favored disciple. Tarek smirked. Her phone buzzed with an incoming call. Han. She declined it. Whatever he wanted could wait. The phone began buzzing again.

"You'd better answer."

"Ugh." She slid her thumb over the screen. "Han?"

"Kyra, I have something. Well, I may have something."

"What is it?"

"About *Murder & MayFemme*."

A spike of adrenaline shot through her system. "Hold on, Tarek's here. I'll put you on speaker." She changed the audio output and angled the phone between them. "Okay, we're here. What is it?"

"I'll get right to it. I found *Murder & MayFemme* on social media, and I recognized one of them, Marjorie. She was a rookie in the Lifestyle section when I was on the features desk in Jersey eight years ago. I didn't realize it was the same person."

"Are you sure?"

"Positive. She left after only a few months. The rumor was she was caught citing fake sources. The fact-checkers reported her. Last I heard, she'd left the news business. Faking sources isn't something a reporter recovers from."

Kyra kept her gaze trained on her phone, the seconds ticking up.

Han cleared his throat. "There's another thing. I found the names of Elodie Edwards's parents. George and Cora Edwards of Bridgeport, Connecticut. Deceased. I'm emailing you their obituaries. They were survived by a son, Peter."

"How'd you find them?" Edwards wasn't an uncommon name. Her own rudimentary searches had turned up thousands of results.

"Experience, Gibson. Good luck."

# Chapter Seventeen

"HOW MANY FRITTERS did you buy?" Tarek asked, taking the enormous paper bag from Kyra so she could wrangle herself into the car.

"All of them." They'd made it to the small OB bakery just before it closed for the day. Their apple fritters were famous, and it was a miracle there'd been any left. "I also ordered six more for tomorrow. The woman said they freeze well."

"And that?" he asked, pointing to the two boxes in her hands.

"Apple and cherry pies? For the Harrises."

"Kyra, I work with law enforcement. I don't bring hostess gifts to interrogations."

She balanced the pastry boxes on her knees. Her Aunt Ali believed pie was a universal unifier. Apparently, Kyra was going to test that theory.

"They'll appreciate the sentiment," she said with a conviction she didn't feel.

She knew next to nothing about Charlie's family. It was very possible they wouldn't appreciate her peace offering, but she felt like she needed to bring something, especially because she didn't feel prepared to meet with the Harrises.

She'd barely ended her call with Han, when she'd received a text from Grace notifying them, she'd arranged for a visit with Charlie's parents at their home. Kyra hadn't had time to draft up questions or research Charles and Loretta. It was a rookie move to walk into an interview without all available information. Making it worse, the Harrises hadn't actually agreed to the visit. Grace just hadn't given them the opportunity to decline. This was an ambush, and those rarely went well. Kyra hoped her bakery miracle extended to the pies.

The Harrises' house was in Tisbury, on a pretty, residential street a few blocks away from the village center. From the appearance of the homes, modest but well maintained, Kyra suspected the neighborhood was mostly islanders. Tarek pulled behind the Chamberses' Subaru. Kyra peered out the window, taking in the house where Charlie grew up. It wasn't flashy or opulent, but it was obviously cared for. The snow had been cleared from the drive and the walkway. Someone had wrapped burlap around the bushes and trees, protecting them from the cold. The furniture on the wraparound porch had been covered and tied down for the winter.

"Ready?" Tarek asked and Kyra nodded, not at all ready.

They walked up the path and to the front door. Tarek pressed the doorbell button, and it chimed through the house. They waited. The cold seeped inside Tarek's too-big jacket. Kyra shivered, jostling the pie boxes.

"I can take the pies," Tarek offered, but Kyra shook her head.

With gentle fingers, he brushed her hair away from her cheek.

The door opened. A man, taller than she'd expected,

scowled down at her. His dark eyes shifted to Tarek and narrowed to slits.

"Mr. Harris? My name is Kyra Gibson. This is Tarek Collins. We're friends of your daughter." That was the wrong thing to say. Charles Harris's expression twisted. "And we're investigating a cold case. Your name came up in our initial inquiries and we thought you may be able to help us."

Tarek began reaching for his wallet, presumably to show Mr. Harris his credentials, when a petite woman appeared from behind him. She looked like Charlie, warm brown eyes, full mouth, but where Charlie kept her curls wild and natural, Mrs. Harris's hair had been tamed into shiny, black layers that brushed the curve of her jaw.

"Let them in, Charles." She assessed them with none of Charlie's cheerfulness.

"We brought pie." Kyra held out the boxes.

"Hmmm." Loretta accepted them with something akin to politeness. "Well, come on. We're in the family room." Charles stepped to the side to let them pass.

The house was simple, homey. Faded and yellowed family photos in outdated chrome frames hung on the walls. One was of a wedding. The bride and groom stood on the church steps; hands clasped together. Another was of two children, both wearing tennis outfits. Kyra recognized a young, smiling Charlie standing next to an older boy, presumably her brother.

They followed Loretta to a large den at the back of the house. A pellet stove sat at the end, heating the room. There were more family photographs on the walls, but these were more recent, and less posed. Charlie wasn't in any of them.

Charlie and Grace sat next to each other on the far side of the reclining sectional. When Tarek and Kyra entered the room, they stood to greet them.

"Hi," Kyra said softly as she gave them each a hug. "Thank you. And I'm so sorry." Charlie shrugged and squeezed her back.

"Charles, bring in some plates and a pie cutter, please," Loretta called to her husband and set the pies on the coffee table. She sat down in the center of the long side of the sectional, directly in front of the television. "Have a seat."

Kyra took one of the two wooden, stiff-backed chairs. They could have been borrowed from a dining set. Tarek took the other.

They sat in silence. Loretta clearly wasn't ready to start the visit without her husband, and neither Grace nor Charlie seemed inclined to fill the quiet. Tarek shifted in his seat, and turned toward Loretta, but Charlie shook her head, a quick movement that sent her curls rippling.

Charles returned with a tray. He placed it on the coffee table and handed his wife a pie knife before taking a seat beside her. Loretta scooted forward and, with the precision of a surgeon, began cutting the pies.

Kyra glanced at Charlie, who rolled her eyes, for once with no humor.

"Alright, Charlene," Charles said, placing his hands on his knees. "Why don't you tell us why you and your…" His nostrils flared. He accepted a plate with slices from both pies. "Friends are here."

"Dad, these are our neighbors, Kyra and Tarek. They're looking into what happened to Abigail Koch and Elodie

Edwards. They thought you could help."

"No." Charles shook his head.

"Dad."

"No, Charlene, I'm not selling that poor girl's story to some tabloid."

Kyra stiffened. *The Island Times* wasn't the same caliber as her father's nationally distributed papers, but it was far from a tabloid.

"Sir," Tarek said, his voice low. "I assure you, my partner and I are not here to exploit anyone's story. I am a forensic psychologist and law enforcement consultant with Greyscale Security." He pulled out his wallet and passed Charles his card. "Kyra and I have been engaged to assist on this case by the OBPD and the community council."

Charles read the card. His scowl deepened. He shot Grace a nasty look before his gaze returned to Tarek. "Ida knows about you? She wants you asking questions?"

"Yes, sir."

"And her?" he jerked his chin at Kyra.

"I freelance with *The Island Times*, but I don't report on active investigations."

"Charles," Grace said, her tone unusually formal. "Kyra and Dr. Collins were the ones who found the man who killed the Mackey brothers. They uncovered Senator Hawthorn's involvement in the wind farm scandal and, don't forget, Kyra saved your daughter's life."

Kyra tensed. She didn't like how Grace made her sound like some sort of hero. She didn't see herself as one. Apparently, neither did Charles. He stared Grace down, his expression steely, but Grace met his gaze straight on, her chin raised.

"From what I hear, she was also the cause of the Silvas' financial problems. The Silvas are good island folks and now look at what's happened to that family."

Kyra opened her mouth, ready to defend herself. She might have come to a tenuous truce with Wes Silva, but that didn't change the fact that he had threatened her and ran her off the road, or that his mother had tried to kill her. Charles held up his hand, silencing her.

He handed Tarek back his card. "What do you want to know?"

"Do you remember the night Abigail Koch was killed?" Tarek asked.

"Of course I do." He waited while Loretta handed plates to Grace and Charlie. Tarek declined for both he and Kyra, earning them a tight-lipped nod.

"Were you there?"

"No."

Kyra wasn't a litigator, but she'd sat through enough depositions to identify a hostile witness. They could derail the conversation, make getting the tiniest bit of information as painful as possible. But this wasn't a deposition, she reminded herself. There were no rules of evidence or procedures to follow.

She threw caution and decorum to the wind. "I'll get right to it, Mr. Harris. We've been talking to islanders and from contemporaneous accounts, we heard that when the police concluded Elodie had murdered Abigail, you disagreed. We'd like to know why. What do you think happened?"

Charles Harris's nostrils flared again, and he set his plate down on the coffee table. He sucked in a deep breath. Kyra forced herself not to whither under his imposing gaze. Mr. Harris was an intimidating man.

"Charles, it's alright." Loretta folded her hands in her lap. "I was the one who told him to speak to the police." She blinked down at her hands. "In the end though, no one cared to hear what we had to say. The council demanded we keep quiet. They threatened our contracts."

"Your contracts?" Tarek repeated.

"Charles was the vice principal at the high school, and I was a school nurse. I worked at the Tisbury School. Without the council's support, our contracts wouldn't have been renewed. We'd have had to leave Martha's Vineyard."

"My family has made this rock our home for generations," Charles said. "Leaving was never an option, not three hundred years ago, not forty." His gaze flicked to Charlie and back to Tarek.

"Can you share with us what you tried to tell the police that summer?"

Loretta rolled her lips and looked at her husband. He shrugged, but his hand gripped his knee.

"During the summer months, some of the school nurses took seasonal work with summer camps. It was a nice arrangement where we could sign up for dayshifts and we'd be dispatched all over the island. Tobias Gillman's program was one of the camps we'd work at. We were assigned our preferences based on seniority. No one wanted Gillman's camp because of all the paperwork. I wasn't as new as some of the other girls, but I still found myself at Gillman's at least once a week."

"Paperwork?" Kyra asked. "What do you mean?"

"Oh, the theater camp may have had fewer bug bites and sunburns than the other island programs, but they had more serious injuries requiring visits to the ER. The set design kids were always getting hurt." She shook her head. "I treated smashed thumbs, gashes deep enough for stitches, concussions. There were even a few broken bones, toes mostly. ER visits require lots of forms. Paperwork and notation weren't included in our daily wages. We weren't paid for that administrative work.

"Most of the injuries were minor." Her tone was laced with an emotion that had Kyra inching to the edge of her seat. "But there was something off about that place. Too many unsupervised teenagers, I suppose."

"What do you mean, Mrs. Harris?" Tarek asked.

"Each summer, there was at least one camper, sometimes two, who were sent home early." Her gaze traveled to the wall behind Kyra and Kyra turned around to see the small Latin cross hanging next to the window. "They complained of the stress of performing, or some unidentifiable illness. We'd call their parents, and they'd come retrieve their children." Her eyes met Kyra's, and she sucked in her cheeks. "Their daughters."

"Daughters only? What happened to them?" Kyra asked.

Loretta pressed her lips together. For a second, she looked like she was going to say something more, but she just shook her head. "I couldn't say."

"Mrs. Harris, please go on," Tarek said. "That summer?"

"Right. That last summer, one of the newer nurses, Rita,

had more shifts at the camp than the rest of us. In one of our weekly update meetings, she told us about a fifteen-year-old girl who'd come to the infirmary complaining of nausea. The girl claimed she was nervous about her role, and stressed from the rehearsal schedule, but Rita thought the young woman exhibited strange behavior. She expressed concern for her, and as a group, we agreed to keep an eye out for her. The girl's name was Elodie Edwards.

"Elodie's name didn't come up again. I assumed she'd gotten over her nerves. But about a week before Abigail was killed, she came to see me. I was the on-call nurse that day." Loretta stared down at the floor and wiped her cheek. Charles rubbed his wife's shoulder.

Loretta swallowed and cleared her throat. "Her friend, a girl about her age, brought her in. Elodie was in crisis. She was shaking and crying. She wouldn't let me touch her, much less perform any examination."

"Crisis?" Charlie asked from the corner. "What does that mean?"

Loretta didn't spare a glance for her daughter. "Elodie refused to say. She insisted she was just tired. Said there was nothing wrong. I gave her some Tylenol and let her rest until she was calm enough to return to her room." Loretta twisted her hands in her lap. "There wasn't anything more I could do to help her."

Kyra bit her lip to keep from saying something she'd regret. *Tylenol?* Loretta Harris had just admitted to witnessing the aftermath of some kind of trauma, and based on her earlier insinuation, Kyra suspected it'd been sexual. And yet, she'd done nothing.

"Mrs. Harris, nurses are mandated reporters under state law." Tarek's voice was steady and polite.

It was only by the slight flex in his cheek, Kyra knew he wasn't unaffected. He was furious. He was just better at concealing his emotions than she was.

"Don't you think I know that?" she snapped.

"My wife told me, Mr. Collins. But we had no facts, no proof, nothing but a hunch. And the Edwards girl wouldn't tell Loretta the truth. Even so, I made the call to the Oak Bluffs Police Department myself. I told them we had reason to believe the girl had been or was being harmed or abused. They promised to take care of it. When I called back a few days later, they told me that this was an Oak Bluffs matter, and it no longer concerned us.

"Less than a week later, the Koch girl was dead and Elodie Edwards was missing."

"I called the police when we heard the news." Loretta's voice shook. "I urged them to investigate the summer camp. I told them about the other female campers who were sent home. I told them that Elodie presented with behaviors consistent with sexual abuse or assault. Later that day, we received a call from the community council saying that there were problems with our school contracts."

"You're saying the community council obstructed the investigation?" Tarek asked.

"The camp was a real boon to the town back then," Charles said. "It brought in a lot of tourism money from the mainland. I'm sure Tobias Gillman had a few members in his pocket. It wouldn't be the first time the local authorities stepped in to protect the money makers."

"I can't believe you." Charlie gripped the edge of the couch and shook her head at her parents. "You just let it go? A girl was dead, and another was missing and you just said, 'Oh well, not our problem?'" She threw her hands up in mock resignation.

"There was nothing more your mother or I could have done, Charlene. Elodie insisted she was fine. We went above and beyond what was required of us as we always have. And what did we get for it? Our livelihoods were threatened." Charles glared at his daughter.

"As long as you and mom are good, right?" Charlie shook her head at her parents and stood. "Kay, do you have what you need?"

Kyra's gaze shifted between her friends and the Harrises, their steely expressions, the disgust and disappointment tinged with sadness etched on Charlie's face.

"Yes. I think so."

Kyra and Tarek followed Charlie outside, Grace trailing behind them. Charlie stopped beside their car and whirled around. "I'm sorry for that. For them." She flung her hand at the house. "If they'd done something, maybe those girls would be alive."

"No, I'm the one who's sorry. I hate that I asked you. Thank you." Kyra offered her friend a wan smile. "You really didn't have to come."

"No, I didn't." Charlie barked a dejected laugh. "Grace did. They wouldn't have spoken to me, you, or even you, Tarek, but they're terrified of Grace."

"Grace?" Kyra repeated, turning to her friend.

Grace was frowning, looking down, patting the pockets

of her Canada Goose parka. "What's that, dear?" she asked, pausing her search.

"Grace ran the investment bank my brother worked at out of business school. She trained him up. It's how we met, actually. He gave Grace my name when she was searching for a new apartment. Something happened, and he lost a lot of money. He could have been in a lot of trouble. Grace covered for him. When she met my parents for the first time, they were their usual, awful selves."

"They insulted her. Called Char a terrible name. They made my beautiful, successful wife doubt herself, doubt us." Grace glared at the house. "So, I may have threatened them. A little. I said if they ever spoke to my Char like that in front of me again, I'd destroy their precious Levi's career." Grace clasped Charlie's hand. "Since then, I just happen to be around when they are. Char deserves better than those people."

Charlie reached up and gave Grace a kiss on her cheek. "Thank you."

"Thank you, both." Kyra grabbed the bag of fritters and handed it to Charlie. "There are six more coming tomorrow, and we owe you dinner. Anywhere you like."

Charlie took the bag, opening it to inhale the apple cinnamon scents. She feigned her eyes rolling back in her head. "Yuuuummm." She bounced up and down. "It almost makes it worth it. Almost. And I want Gully's."

"Name the day and I'll tell him we're coming." Tarek back-stepped to his car. "Thank you, both." He paused, his hand on the handle. "Hey, Grace?"

"Hmmm?"

"Do you have information that could ruin his career?"

"Whose?"

"Levi Harris's?"

"Oh." Grace's blue eyes gleamed. "Nothing I remember. Ready, Char?"

# Chapter Eighteen

"CAR, STOP."

"Hmm?"

"Stop the car. Pull in there." Kyra pointed to the black and silver Blackwood and Burke sign. The parking lot was visible from the street. It was empty except for two cars, a dark sedan, and a darker hearse. "I want to ask if anyone there remembers Abigail."

The door to the funeral home wasn't locked. When they entered, a buzzer sounded somewhere deep inside. They waited in the vestibule on a wide welcome mat, the door at their backs. An ineffective light fixture fought against the funeral parlor's somber decor. The place felt heavy and suffocating. It pressed in on all sides, and Kyra shifted her weight. She'd never been great in enclosed spaces and her discomfort with them had only intensified since her and Chase's spelunking misadventure last summer.

"Do you think anyone's here?" she whispered. "It's late."

Tarek leaned close and spoke in her ear. "The car outside."

*Right. The reason we stopped.* Tarek straightened as a man stepped out from the gloom.

"Can I help you?" His feet glided over the thick carpet.

FINAL EXIT

Kyra put his age in the mid-to-late-forties, and her heart sank. The man was probably too young.

"Hi, we're looking for Marshall Burke."

The man's head tipped to the side. "My father?"

"Umm, yes?"

The man shook his head. "I'm afraid he passed. Eight years ago. Is there something I can help you with?"

Kyra sighed. "I'm not sure." She summarized why they were there, who they were, and that they were investigating what happened to Abigail Koch. As she spoke, the man's expression grew troubled, a crease forming and deepening between his brows. "In the case file, we found a letter from Marshall Burke, your dad, to the OB police reminding them to respond to something he'd discovered and shared with them. We were hoping to ask him about it." Kyra raised and dropped her hand.

"Did he ever mention Abigail Koch? Or did he keep records?" Tarek asked.

The man sucked in a breath, his cheeks hollowing out. He studied them for a moment and Kyra bit back a pang of disappointment, certain he would refuse to help them, cite some undertaker-dead guy confidentiality.

"You'd better come on back." He waved them forward.

Tarek motioned for her to go first. They followed the man down the long hallway, past large empty rooms where the scents of decaying flowers lingered. About halfway, the man stopped at a closed door and pushed it open, revealing a tidy, elegant business office.

He gestured for them to sit and took the chair behind the desk. "I'm Alexander, *Xander* Burke. I took over after my father died." Xander folded his hands on the blotter in front of him. "I was a child when the Koch girl was killed, but it affected my father long after he buried her. In this business, you're exposed to a lot of death. You grow a thick skin. My father treated all his clients and their loved ones with respect, kindness, and without judgment. Abigail Koch was the only time he'd been..." He trailed off and pursed his lips, tight. "Disturbed."

"Did he tell you why?" Tarek asked, and Kyra gripped her chair's armrests tighter.

"Occasionally, it'd come up. We don't provide services for the families of many murder victims, and Abigail's death was brutal. He'd been upset when the police refused to listen to him. It caused a rift between my father and the officials in OB. When they dismissed him, they hurt his pride, I think."

"Did he ever say what he tried to tell them?" Kyra asked.

Xander pushed back from the desk and walked over to one of the tall metal filing cabinets. He unlocked it with a key he pulled from his pocket. After a few minutes of flipping through the contents, he withdrew a manilla folder with Abigail's name printed on a label at the top.

"Here." He handed it to Kyra.

Inside, there were only three sheets of paper. The invoice to the Koch family for the service and cost of the casket, a copy of the letter that they'd found included in the police file, and another piece of lined notepaper with a jagged edge.

She turned it over. It was a handwritten note.

—PETECHIAE IN CONJUNCTIVA AND NECK

—CYANOSIS OF LIPS AND EARLOBE

—BRUISING AROUND THROAT

—POSTMORTEM CONTUSIONS

Kyra read it out loud.

"Can I see that?" Tarek took the paper. His eyes moved back and forth as he read. He did it again. His brow was furrowed when he looked up. "Burke thought Abigail Koch was strangled? Then someone beat her corpse?" He glanced at Kyra. "Petechia, burst blood vessels and cyanosis, blue skin are signs of asphyxiation. It'd explain why no one heard the assault. Strangulation would be fast and quiet. The assailant could have mutilated her body when the dorms emptied or even while people slept."

Kyra shuddered at the thought.

Tarek turned back to Xander. "Was your father qualified to make those determinations?"

"I think so. We can easily differentiate between perimortem and postmortem wounds. We see a lot from boating accident victims."

"But we saw the coroner's report in the file. It was signed by someone from here and it said she died from blunt force trauma, not strangulation." Kyra pointed to the paper still in Tarek's hand.

"That would have been Emmett Blackwood. His father and my grandfather started the business. When Dad took over, Emmett became more of a silent partner. He was involved in local politics, and, for a while, he was appointed as coroner, which allowed him to funnel more business to Blackwood and Burke. As the coroner, he only certified cause of death. He would have written whatever the police told him to." Xander held out his hand for the file.

"He lied?" Kyra said.

"I doubt it was intentional." Xander shrugged. "He'd have no reason to question the police, and he didn't see the deceased. He signed off on all the death certificates from his council office."

"Emmett Blackwood was on the community council?" Tarek asked.

"Yes, sir. An Oak Bluffs representative." Kyra returned the file. "I'm sorry. I don't have anything more helpful."

"No," Tarek said. "This has been very helpful, actually." He stood and held out his hand to shake Xander's. "Thank you for your time. We can show ourselves out."

Tarek strode down the hall. Kyra had to hustle to keep up with his long strides.

"Tar, what's going on?" she asked, but he ignored her.

His phone was in his hand, and he was typing. It wasn't until she buckled her seatbelt that he finally put the phone away. He started the car, and the headlights illuminated the hedgerows in front of him.

Tarek thrust the Jeep into reverse and his hand came to the back of her seat as he steered the car. "I want Greyscale to send the case file to Dr. Khaleng." Dr. Khaleng was a medical examiner in Boston that Tarek had worked closely with when he was with the Massachusetts State Police.

"Doesn't Greyscale have their own medical experts?"

"Of course, but this isn't a priority for them. Bhakti will look at it for me." His grip on the steering wheel tightened. "If the police lied about how that girl died, I want to know why."

# Chapter Nineteen

*Friday, February 10*

KYRA'S LEGS FELT wobbly as she pushed open the YMCA's glass doors. The crisp chill of the early morning bit into her sweat-slicked skin, and the wind shredded through her damp running clothes. She'd just finished a long, grueling run on the treadmill. She shivered and tried hustling to her car, but it was more of a slow shamble.

"Hey, Kay!"

"Shit," she hissed, her sneakers slipping on the icy pavement. She righted herself, just before falling on her ass.

"Whoa!" Jimmy Blau jogged over; an enormous hockey bag slung across his back. He stopped beside her, too close to be comfortable. "That was a close one. You good?"

"I'm fine. Thank you." She took a step back, careful not to lose her footing again.

"I thought it was you." His smile was oily. "I was at practice." He pointed to the ice rink behind him. "I've been meaning to text you. I haven't had any luck finding your kidnapper van." His unburdened shoulder rose and fell. "No one's seen one on or going off island. I'm real, sorry."

Kyra exhaled and gave him a rueful shake of her head.

"It's okay, Jimmy. It was a long shot, anyway. Thank you for asking around."

"For you?" His languid perusal from her face down her body left a film on Kyra's skin. "Anything."

She suppressed a shudder. "Right. Well, I'll see you later," she said, but his hand on her biceps halted her. He stepped into her space, close enough she could smell stale sweat and mildew. His hot breath slid over her cheek. Her heart thumped against her sternum.

"I'll let you know if I hear anything. I promise." He released her and hitched his bag higher on his shoulder. "How long is the cop in town this time?"

Kyra started at the question. "He's back for a while," she lied. That Jimmy was keeping tabs on her and Tarek made her uneasy.

"We should get together. Get drinks at the CC Club? I heard you were a new member. Or I could show you my bikes. Just restored a Shadow. I think you'd like it."

With her teeth clenched tight, Kyra forced her expression to stay neutral. She didn't want to insult him, or worse, encourage him. "We'll see, but I have to go."

"Cool. I'll see ya around, Kay."

She hurried to her car, feeling his eyes on her back. She rolled her shoulders against the dirty feeling that had settled over her. Chase had told her often enough that Jimmy was socially inept, but he was mostly harmless. Still, he gave her the creeps. She kept to the main roads going home, even if it took a few minutes longer.

She almost relished the stinging blasts of wind battering her body as she jogged back from dropping off the extra fritters at the Chambers's house. It was like a natural cleanse washing away the memory of Jimmy's touch. She shivered and entered her lock code with half-frozen hands. It took her two tries before it disengaged, and she stumbled inside.

"Where've you been?" Tarek asked, emerging from the kitchen, holding a steaming cup of coffee.

"The gym." She pointed to her disheveled appearance. "I saw you at the pool. I waved." She opened the closet door and unzipped her windbreaker.

"I didn't see you. I'm sorry. How was it?"

"Awful." She didn't like running on a treadmill. It made her feel like a Sisyphusian hamster, but it was better than the alternative, freezing to death on a beach run.

Tarek didn't smile and on closer inspection, he appeared troubled. The lines at the corners of his mouth and eyes were deeper, his posture more rigid. She stilled; her left arm still half-inside her fleece.

"Tar? Is everything alright?"

"Evans called. He needs us at the station as soon as possible. There's been an update with *Murder & MayFemme*."

"Okay, I'll be fast."

Less than an hour later, Kyra was in the front seat of the Range Rover with her seat warmer on high. She'd showered and dressed as quickly as humanly possible, but she couldn't bring herself to go out into the arctic with wet hair. Tarek had had the good sense not to object, but now he was driving a little too fast. As a chronic speeder, fast for him was terrifying. Kyra gripped the grab handle with one hand and her seat with the other.

"Slow down!" she yelped when he took a turn and the

car slid on ice, or sand, or icy sand. Kyra squeezed her eyes closed. "Please."

The car slowed to Mach 4. "Sorry."

Tarek stopped at the front door of the OB station. "I'll park. Wait for me inside."

"It's you. Fantastic," desk agent Mel muttered when Kyra entered the station's lobby. She heaved a martyr's sigh. "Officer Evans mentioned you and Dr. Collins may be stopping by." She made a show of looking around the empty room. "Doesn't look like Dr. Collins has arrived. You can wait over there."

"Tarek is parking the car."

Mel's mouth twisted to the side, and she grimaced. "You came together?"

Icy air blasted through the room, and Tarek yanked the door closed behind him. When he turned around, his cheeks and nose were red. He rubbed his bare hands together, blowing on them.

"Dr. Collins," Mel cooed.

Irritation prickled the back of Kyra's neck and shoulders. She was used to women appreciating the men she dated. She wasn't used to caring much about it.

"Evans asked that I buzz you right through." She waved. "Go on back."

"Thanks, Mel." Tarek ushered Kyra through the doors. Kyra clenched her fist, lest she show Mel her favorite finger.

Tarek led her down bland, indistinguishable hallways and stopped at one of the many nondescript, nearly identical doors and knocked. She was thankful he knew where Evans's office was. She'd never have found it.

"Come in!" Evans called from inside.

The small office was toasty warm thanks to a space heater blasting beside his desk. Leaning towers of files were stacked high on every available surface in outward defiance of the laws of gravity.

"Collins." He shook Tarek's hand. "Miss Gibson," he said with uncharacteristic formality. "Thank you for coming." He motioned for them to sit.

"What did you find?" Tarek asked, cutting the small talk short.

Mark rubbed his forehead with the back of his hand and pulled a notebook from a pile. He flipped through it until he came to the page he wanted. "Omega Global sent over the podcasters' license plates. The cargo van was registered to Neverfull Media in DC. It's a subsidiary of Omega. Marjorie L. Fallon's is a 2003 Toyota Corolla. Black. Kelsey's car is still in her parking spot in DC."

Kyra stilled. The car on the dispensary's security tape could have been an old black Corolla.

"Were you able to determine whether Marjorie's car or the van got on the ferry?" Tarek asked.

"No. We can't confirm it. The Steamship Authority doesn't have a registration that matches either vehicle. But we were able to track Marjorie's car driving up from DC on the I95. She crossed the GW Bridge Monday morning, and then we lose her for a few hours through Connecticut. We pick her up again at New London when she gets back on 95, around two p.m. We lose her again around three, when she exits in Providence, probably en route to Woods Hole."

"No," Kyra said, shaking her head. "Tarek and I were

with Marjorie. She and Kelsey were on the island Monday afternoon."

"Benny may have been driving Marjorie's car," Tarek said. "We can put a similar car at Bucklebury's Monday afternoon, and we know a man bought the cow's blood."

"But what about the van? Where is that if Benny was in Marjorie's car?" Kyra asked.

Tarek blinked. "Evans, did you pull toll information for the van on Saturday or Sunday?"

"I did. The van hit tolls from DC to Connecticut on Saturday. It made its way to Massachusetts on Sunday morning. The van took a straight shot up 95 from DC to New York, but after leaving the city, it got on and off the highway multiple times."

Kyra pulled her phone from her purse. "Marjorie and Kelsey took pictures of their trip. They stopped in places along the coast." She pulled up *Murder & MayFemme's* social media account and passed the phone to Mark. "Can we verify if these photos match the van's trip?"

Evans cycled through the images, glancing between the phone and his notebook. "It could be," he said, handing the phone back. "I'll run it past my team."

"If Marjorie and Kelsey drove up in the white van, why lie about Benny driving it?" she asked out loud.

"It's part of the game. The blood, the missing van, their whole strange, convoluted story. They played us from the beginning. They wanted us to discover them missing and to search for them." Tarek shook his head, annoyed. "Evans," he said. "Have Falmouth PD do a sweep of the Palmer and Thomas Landers lots for cars matching Marjorie's or the cargo van's license plates and descriptions."

Evans bit his lip and wrote it down on a Post-it. He stuck it to the bottom of his monitor, where it joined at least thirty others. Tarek shifted forward, ready to stand.

"I don't think they'll find the cargo van in the ferry lots, sir."

"What?" Tarek froze halfway out of his seat.

Evans opened his phone and handed it to Tarek. The image was pixelated and distorted, taken while the photographer was moving, but there was no mistaking it. It was a photo of a white, windowless van parked on a street.

"One of the mapping companies happened to be in the area. They caught this. We could only get a partial on the license plate from the image, but the last two digits are a match for the Neverfull vehicle. I had local PD check it out, but the license plates have since been removed."

"When was this taken?" Kyra asked.

"Yesterday."

"Where?" Tarek asked.

"Bridgeport."

Kyra blinked. "Connecticut?"

Evans nodded.

Her gaze met Tarek's. "That cannot be a coincidence."

"No."

"What?" Evans asked, his eyebrows raised.

"Bridgeport is where Elodie Edwards is from."

"Tar," Kyra started, but he interrupted her.

"Evans, get us on the next ferry. And order Bridgeport PD to close access off. No one touches that van."

# Chapter Twenty

TAREK SET A coffee and a stale, soft pretzel in front of Kyra. He heaved a weary sigh and slid into the seat opposite her. They were sitting in the café of the *Nantucket*, sailing into Woods Hole. After leaving Mark's office, Tarek had tried to convince her to stay home, but she'd argued with him, refusing to be sidelined, pointing out it was her contacts with the podcasters and Omega Global that had Tarek involved at all. Eventually, he'd relented, but apparently, he was going to pout about it for a bit longer. She tore off a hunk of bread. It was chewy and crumbly at the same time, and over salted, but she was starving. She opened the pop-tab on her coffee cup.

"Careful," Tarek warned, wincing, and licked his bottom lip. "It's really hot."

She took a tentative sip and bit back a grimace. *And terrible.* Tarek's eyes glinted with the faintest light of smug amusement, and he turned his attention to his phone.

He'd been on it nonstop, making travel and hotel arrangements, talking with contacts at the Bridgeport police headquarters and with his superiors in DC who sent instructions, ones that could not be ignored, to Bridgeport PD to keep away from that white van.

"What's the plan when we get there?" Kyra asked and swiped her tongue over the raw roof of her mouth.

"We'll go straight to the van. If we have time, I think we should speak to Elodie's brother, Peter."

"You have an address?"

"Yup. He still lives in the house he grew up in. The address is the same as the last one on record for both parents, except for a short stint in hospice for his mother."

"When did she die?"

"Cora Edwards died about eighteen years ago. Her husband, George, two years before."

Kyra felt a pang of sadness for Peter. She knew what it felt like to lose your whole family. She at least still had Ali.

It took about three hours to get to Bridgeport, well under the GPS's estimated time, thanks to Tarek's lead foot. Speeding down long, uninteresting highways, weaving between cars and tractor trailers, left Kyra feeling both nauseous and jittery. She mumbled a relieved thanks to any listening deity when they finally entered the city center, forcing Tarek to slow down.

Kyra had lived all over the world as a young girl. She had vivid memories of her times in France, Peru, and Singapore, and less vivid ones of Egypt, Germany, and Nicaragua. As an adult, she'd traveled as frequently as she could to any place with a direct flight out of Heathrow that had a beach. But other than New York for law school, and the four years she lived in Providence for undergrad, she had seen little of the United States.

Last spring, she visited Boston for a few days, and from the interior of an SUV, she'd seen the appeal. It was American-old, and it simmered with a latent sedition borne of a long history of rebellion. It felt similar to England and yet entirely different.

She had expected that all cities in New England would be much the same. She was wrong.

Thanks to her architect aunt, Kyra could tell that Bridgeport had an industrial-era history. This was masonry with purpose, monstrous and utilitarian. By the sheer size of the old buildings, Kyra guessed the city had been a successful center of business. Once. Now, it looked like it was in a desperate fight for its life, holding on with mortar and nails.

"We need to check in at the station, then we'll go see the vehicle."

Following the GPS, they wove deeper and deeper into downtown Bridgeport. Tarek stopped in front of a brown building that resembled an old radiator. A rectangle with vertical windows situated like stripes between the stonework sat atop a base embellished with arches.

"Not all police headquarters are as picturesque as the little buildings on the island."

"No, but that's just ugly," she said, her nose scrunching up, and Tarek laughed.

She followed him inside, standing to the side when he spoke to the desk agent, and showed his credentials.

"What about her?" The uniformed man pointed at Kyra.

"She's my partner."

The policeman ran a skeptical eye over her. "She got clearance?"

"If you have a question, you can bring it up with Grey-scale."

The policeman blew out a breath. "Nah, go on back. Interrogation room twelve." He pressed a button, unlocking the security door with a *buzz*.

It took them a few minutes, wandering up and down identical hallways, past holding cells, and locker rooms, before they found the right room. Inside was a metal table and four chairs, all bolted to the ground. Kyra eyed the one-way mirror that took up most of the back wall. It reminded her of a police station from the movies, sparse and clinical. She perched on the edge of one of the metal chairs. The cold steel bit into her thighs.

The door opened and a man in a rumpled suit entered. "Agent Collins and Miss Gibson?" the man read from his phone.

"I'm a consultant with Greyscale Security. Not an agent."

"Oh, right. I'm Sergeant McCathy. I've been assigned to not do anything with an abandoned van on North Ave. Don't often get assigned a case and told to not do anything."

"What would you have done?" Kyra asked before she could think better of it.

McCathy stared at her. He cracked a grin and touched his finger to his forehead. "Touché, Miss Gibson. We'd have done nothing. It would have been towed." He turned back to Tarek. "What's the deal with it?"

"It may be part of an investigation into a missing-persons case."

That got the sergeant's attention, and his expression turned more serious. "Who's missing?"

"I can't say yet, but if this is the right van, it's supposed to be in Massachusetts. We'd like to see it."

"Yeah. Okay. I'll go, too. I'm curious what the fuss is about. You can follow me."

The sergeant led them through the winding streets of Bridgeport and Kyra took in the city that she found less and less appealing. Finally, he pulled over, and Tarek pulled behind him, blocking in a rusty Honda Prelude that by the state of its deflated tires hadn't moved in a long, long time.

Tarek pulled two pairs of nitrile gloves and a flashlight from the kit he kept in both cars. He gave her a pair and slipped the other onto his hands.

Tarek and the sergeant first circled the van. Tarek took pictures. McCathy peered inside the driver's side window, his hands cupping his eyes. He stepped aside when Kyra approached to let her see.

Inside, the van was blanketed in shadows, made worse by the late afternoon light. Paper cups sat in the cup holders, and takeout bags lay crumpled on the floor. She tried to get an angle to see behind the seats, but she wasn't tall enough, and it was too dark.

Kyra tried the handle. Locked.

"Here, miss." McCathy shined his flashlight inside the car. "No alarm." He swept the beam across the dashboard, the front seats, and behind. "Huh, is that? Electronics? What is this?"

Kyra's heart thumped. This was it, *Murder & May-Femme's* missing van.

"It's a sound studio. It belongs to Neverfull Media, a podcasting production company. It was loaned out to podcasters recording a special on Martha's Vineyard," Kyra explained as she moved to the back of the van, stooping to see underneath. "But we're not sure it ever made it to the island."

"Stolen?"

"I don't think so." Underneath was nothing more than a dirty city street. Kyra straightened. "The podcast hosts and their sound engineer seem to have gone missing. We're trying to find them."

There were no other windows, so Kyra returned to the front of the vehicle.

"Tar, hand me your torch?" She asked and hauled herself onto the hood.

"Hey!" Sergeant McCathy protested, but Tarek handed her his flashlight. Kyra crawled across the hood and kneeled in front of the windshield. She shined the light all over the interior. The beam danced over the sound and mixing boards, and other electronics Kyra couldn't identify. She brought the light down to the floor of the load area. It flew over a dark lump and Kyra paused, moved it back. It could have been a blanket. She squinted. *No.* It was *a pile of laundry?* Purple laundry. Covered in dark stains.

"What the fuck?" she mumbled.

She angled the light farther away, toward the back doors. The light fell on a tangled mass of black, and Kyra gasped. *Hair.*

# Chapter Twenty-One

"SHIT, TAR!" KYRA scrambled down and to the driver's side. She yanked uselessly on the handle. "There's a person in there!"

"What?" McCathy asked at the same time Tarek barked, "Where?"

"In the loading area, in the back. Wrapped up. Hurry!"

"Sounds like probable cause to me," McCathy said and then there was a loud *crack* that had Kyra ducking as he broke through the window with the butt of his flashlight.

Tarek ran to the back. "Unlock it!"

McCarthy reached inside, released the locks, and yanked the door open. Kyra scrambled to the back, where Tarek had pulled open the barn doors.

Kyra halted. Both hands flew to her mouth, holding in her scream. "Oh, my god."

She stared at the unruly mess of curly black hair matted with blood and gore protruding from the shroud of purple towels and matching sheets. She reached for the edge, stiff and crusty, but Tarek's hand on her wrist stopped her. He shared a grim look with McCathy.

"Already on it." The sergeant motioned to the phone he was holding.

Kyra heard him speaking to dispatch, calling in the … whatever this was.

Tarek pulled back the towel and Kyra held her breath. The woman's face and skull had been bashed in. She was almost unrecognizable. Almost. Her blood had soaked into her *Murder & MayFemme* sweatshirt, turning the hot pink of their logo a gruesome brown. Marjorie's thick-framed glasses lay on the van floor. They'd been broken; the lenses shattered.

"Victim is a black female, deceased. Possible COD is head trauma."

"McCarthy, we have a possible murder weapon," Tarek said and pointed to a bloodied tire iron packed next to the body. He replaced the towel and stepped back, surveying the interior of the van. He pointed to the walls and the ceiling. "This could have been where she was killed. Look at the blood splatter. We're going to need a full crime scene unit here."

McCathy gave him a curt nod. Tarek stepped back, shut the barn doors. He turned to Kyra.

"You okay?" he asked, pulling his gloves off.

"Yes." As surprising as it was, it was the truth. Marjorie's wasn't the first body she'd seen, not even the first murder, or the most horrible.

Months ago, Tarek told her seeing death never got any easier. It wasn't exactly easier, but unlike the last time she'd found a body, she didn't think she'd spiral into a panic attack or hyperventilate. The shock, the disgust, and the horror were somehow manageable. She only felt an overwhelming sense of sadness and regret for the woman in the van.

"She took towels and bedding from the purple house?" Kyra murmured.

"Looks that way." Tarek gripped her elbow. "Go sit in the car, Kyra. Stay warm."

She turned on the ignition and let the car idle. Tarek and McCathy stood near the van talking, and after a few minutes, Tarek joined her.

He held his hands to the heating vent. "The police are on their way. I've let Greyscale know what we've found."

"And Asher? Marjorie's family?"

"Those responsibilities will be handled by local law enforcement. They'll contact her next of kin, find someone who can officially identify her." His eyes bore into hers. "I'm so sorry you had to see that."

Kyra reached out for his hand. It was ice cold in hers. "There's nothing to be sorry about, but, Tar, I have to tell Asher. I promised."

Tarek huffed, but nodded.

She dialed Asher's private line, and in as few words as possible, informed him of discovering Marjorie's body.

"I'll notify HR and legal." Asher's voice was serious and brittle over the car's speaker. "Any word about the other woman? And the sound engineer?"

"Bridgeport Police will put out an APB for them. The FBI is being called, too, since we're crossing state lines. I imagine I'll get a call for a debriefing soon," Tarek responded.

"Good man. Keep me informed. Thank you, both." Asher hung up.

An ambulance arrived, followed by more vans tagged with Bridgeport Police banners. Soon, the area around the van was swarming with people in white hazmat suits. A perimeter was set up around the vehicle and the road was closed to traffic. It was like something out of the BBC crime shows Kyra and her aunt used to binge.

The sun completely disappeared, and spotlights were brought in. The bustle attracted the attention of locals and the news media, but the police kept them corralled at the ends of the street, out of sight of the van and the crime scene activities.

Eventually, she was asked to give a statement to the Bridgeport detective assigned to the case. After, she was given a cup of lukewarm coffee and told to wait.

She waited. And waited. The minutes stretched into hours and Kyra was keenly aware of the day, and the opportunity to speak to Peter Edwards, slipping away. She debated catching a cab to Peter Edwards's house, but knew Tarek would lose the plot if she disappeared. Instead, she sat in her car. When she felt restless, she walked up and down the street, trying to stay out of the police's way. Eventually, Tarek joined her, but he was quiet, distracted with messaging Greyscale and the FBI.

A rap on the car window startled Kyra, and Tarek rolled it down. "Sergeant?"

"Just got word. You two can go. We have your contact information if we need it, but as this whole mess will probably be handed over to you and the feds, anyway." He shrugged. "I'll let you know if we discover anything else of note in the van."

Tarek thanked him.

"No thanks necessary. This could have been a lot worse if you hadn't come down."

Tarek put the car in gear. "Goodnight, Sergeant."

McCathy patted the top of the car and stepped back. He motioned to a uniform. The officer pulled a cone out of the way, allowing Tarek and Kyra to exit the street.

# Chapter Twenty-Two

"I THINK THIS is it." Kyra paused at the edge of the property and double-checked the house number. It matched. "Not exactly what I pictured when Greta said Elodie was from a wealthy family."

"No, definitely not."

The darkness couldn't hide the American foursquare's shabbiness. Where once a gate had been, there was just a gap in the rusty, chain-link fence. The roofline bowed and sagged. The porch stairs were rotting away, and the treads slanted in different directions. Kyra wasn't confident the steps could hold a person's weight.

"They might have fallen on bad times?" Tarek said with a slight frown.

Kyra didn't think so. The house looked like it'd begun falling down the day it went up.

She pointed to a second-story window, where a sliver of light was visible under the drawn shade. "Someone's home."

She picked her way across the yard, and, ignoring Tarek's protests, scurried up the precarious stairs to the porch. At the top, she pointed down. "Watch it. The middle one is missing."

"Really, Kyra?" Tarek side-eyed her and pushed past her

to knock on the door.

They waited.

Tarek knocked again.

He banged on the door with his fist. "Mr. Edwards? Police. Open up!" Kyra raised a questioning eyebrow, and Tarek shrugged. "Law enforcement consultant is a lot to yell."

Noise came from the other side of the door, a shuffling sound, like things being moved. A dingy porch light flickered on, and the door finally cracked open on squeaky hinges.

A man peered at them from behind wire-frame glasses. He scowled. "What?"

"Peter Edwards?" When the man dipped his chin in a stilted nod, Tarek continued, "My name is Tarek Collins, and this is my partner, Kyra Gibson. We wanted to ask you a few questions."

"Badge."

Tarek pulled out his wallet. Peter studied Tarek's credentials under the meager light. "This doesn't say you're police. Says you're a law enforcement consultant. What's that? Who are you? What are you doing here?" His voice rose with each question.

"I'm a special investigator contracted with the FBI. We are looking into the death of Abigail Koch and the disappearance of Elodie Edwards."

All color drained from Peter's already pallid face. "No." He tried to push the door closed, but Tarek's boot held it open.

"We won't take up much of your time, Mr. Edwards.

And I'm sure you'd rather talk to us, not the FBI agents, who will come to question you." Tarek returned his wallet to his pocket. "Mr. Edwards?"

Something a lot like fear flickered across his features, but he shook it off and pulled his shoulders back. "Fine," Edwards barked. He stepped out onto the porch and yanked the door shut behind him. He crossed his arms over his chest and glared at them. "I don't know anything."

"Can you tell us about your sister, Mr. Edwards?" Kyra asked, hoping she sounded kind.

He frowned at her, then stared down at his work boots. Minutes ticked by.

"Mr. Edwards, should I let the FBI know you were unwilling to cooperate with us and that they should follow up with you?" Tarek pulled his phone from his pocket and scrolled through his contacts.

"No." Edwards shook his head. "I'll answer. Elodie was a normal girl. She went to school, preferred art to math, had a few friends, but I don't think she was one of the popular kids. She was quiet, shy."

"And yet she wanted to be an actress?" Kyra asked.

"No, a dancer. Ballet. She didn't like speaking in front of people."

"Then why go to a drama camp?"

He gave a helpless shrug. "We were as surprised as anyone when she said she wanted to go, but she was accepted for a spot there, and she had her heart set on it."

"Did she like it? Camp, I mean," Kyra asked.

"I think so, at least at first."

"At first?" Kyra prodded.

"She was excited when she left here, and for tryouts in the first few weeks. She'd wanted one of the backup group roles, one without a solo, you know?"

"The ensemble?" Kyra supplied.

"Maybe? Yeah. But she received an understudy role, instead. She was nervous about it."

"You spoke to her often before she disappeared?" Tarek asked.

"No, not me. She called home Sunday mornings until she stopped. The last time my mom spoke to her was in early July."

Meaning, the last time Elodie had contact with her family was about six or seven weeks before Abigail was killed.

"Do you know why she stopped calling?" Tarek asked.

"I don't think so. Mom said the last time she called, Elodie was quiet. When Mom asked, she said she was just tired. Then she stopped calling and she wouldn't return my mom's calls. Mom was worried, but Dad and I told her Elodie was just busy having fun and not to bother her." Peter shook his head, the motion sad, regretful.

"Did the police tell you what happened the night Abigail, Elodie's roommate, was killed?" Kyra asked.

Peter's expression sharpened, then slackened with sorrow. "They called us. Said Elodie killed a girl then she got herself drowned trying to escape. We didn't believe it. Elodie wouldn't hurt a fly, but them rich people on their fancy island didn't want to hear from the likes of us."

Kyra pressed her lips together, thinking. Peter's story didn't align with what they'd been told about a wealthy family abandoning their daughter. She shared a look with

Tarek.

"We believe that Elodie may have been a victim of assault before she disappeared. Do you remember her saying anything? Mentioning someone bothering her?" Kyra asked.

Peter reared backward and his heel hit the door. "No," he said, shaking his head. "Elodie never said anything like that to Mom. She only had nice things to say about her friends and the camp counselors. She was even signing up for extra rehearsals with the camp director. If we'd heard someone was harassing her, or she'd been hurt, Dad would have gone up there and brought her home."

"Your father would have gone to the island?" Kyra asked.

Peter's eyebrows flew up, and he shook his head. "Of course. When we heard she'd disappeared, Dad wanted to go search for her, but the police threatened him. They said if he stepped foot in their town, they'd arrest him for interfering with their investigation. They said she was lost and to move on. We didn't even have a body to bury. There's just an empty casket in the ground next to my parents. My mother was never the same."

"Peter, were your parents wealthy?"

"No." He laughed without humor.

"Influential?"

Peter looked at them like they were simple. "I don't know where you got your information, lady, but my mom was a seamstress and Dad worked at the marina, same as me. They had enough to put food on the table and oil in the tank, but that's about it. The only reason they could pay off this house is because of the insurance money." He gave the wall a soft kick.

"Insurance money?" Tarek repeated.

"Yeah, from the camp. A few weeks after Elodie was pronounced dead, we got a letter. Said all the attendees at the fancy summer camp had life insurance policies. When the police determined Elodie drowned, we received a payout. With the letter came a check for seventy thousand dollars." His voice softened. "It also said that because she was dead, and in respect of the family, they weren't charging her with any crime, but if the case was reopened and Elodie was charged with killing that girl, it'd void the insurance coverage. We'd have to pay the money back."

Kyra stared at Peter Edwards, not sure she believed what she'd heard. If he was telling the truth, the Edwards family hadn't abandoned Elodie. They'd been paid to go away.

Peter stuffed his hands in his pockets. "It wasn't our proudest moment, but Elodie was dead. Fighting some rich folks wasn't going to change that." He scowled, but it was tinged with anxiety. "I don't want you saying you spoke to me. I can't afford to pay that money back."

"You needn't worry," Kyra said, shaking her head. "You won't be required to."

"How would you know?" he demanded.

Tarek gestured to Kyra. "My partner is a lawyer."

Peter glared at Kyra. "If you're a lawyer, you can't lie to me."

Kyra had no idea what Peter was talking about. Most of the lawyers she knew were excellent and prolific liars.

"She wouldn't dream of it, Mr. Edwards. Do you remember who sent your family that letter?"

Peter shook his head. "Nah. Not the person, but it had a

fancy official logo on it. Some sort of council?"

Kyra blinked. "The Martha's Vineyard Community Council?"

Peter shrugged. "Maybe?"

Tarek pulled out his wallet and withdrew a business card. "That answers all our immediate questions. Thank you, Mr. Edwards. It's been helpful." He held out the card but didn't release it when Peter's fingers touched it. Tarek cocked his head to the side. "In forty years, no one has contacted you about what happened to your sister?"

Peter sucked in a breath and let it out. "No. No one."

Tarek released the card. "If you think of anything more, or if anyone else reaches out to you with questions about Elodie, please let me know."

Peter turned the card in his hand, once, twice. He slid it into his pocket.

Kyra turned to follow Tarek down the stairs.

She stopped, turned back. "Peter?" He paused; the door half closed. "How did your family pay for Elodie's summer camp?"

"We didn't. She had a scholarship." Peter Edwards closed the door.

# Chapter Twenty-Three

THE SUV'S HEATED seats soothed away the tension and tightness Kyra held in her shoulders. She stared out the window, barely noticing as they drove through neighborhoods and back through the city. The conversation with Peter Edwards replayed over and over in her mind. The Edwards family wasn't the prominent, wealthy one they were led to believe. They'd been a normal, hardworking family. One that had been lied to and manipulated.

She hadn't paid the closest attention in her criminal procedure class, but it was true that posthumous charges weren't often brought. However, she didn't need her law degree to know that the insurance explanation was complete and utter crap wrapped in a loose sheet of legitimacy. Summer camps did not insure their campers for the benefit of their parents.

No, someone had paid the Edwardses off to keep them from looking into their daughter's disappearance, and that someone probably knew, or was protecting the person who knew, what had happened to Abigail Koch and Elodie. Kyra would bet one of Cronkite's nine lives the someone who knew had been on the community council.

"Out with it."

Kyra's head snapped around. "What?"

Tarek pointed to his head. "I can practically see your brain working." He nodded to her hand on her thigh. "And you tap your fingers when you're thinking. So? What is it?"

Kyra made a fist. "I was thinking that someone knows what happened to Abigail and Elodie and went to great lengths to cover it up. I'm also wondering if they're still covering it up." Marjorie's battered face flashed behind her eyes, then Marjorie's face morphed into Abigail Koch's. Both women had been brutalized. Kyra closed her eyes. Tarek's hand found hers and squeezed. "What do you think?"

"I think you're not wrong, but I'm not sure how *Murder & MayFemme* fit in. What connection could there be between the podcasters and the Koches or Edwardses?"

"I know." She sighed. "I can't make sense of it either. Have you heard news about Kelsey? Benny?" Tarek shook his head. "What about Marjorie's car?"

"Not much. Evans texted earlier. Falmouth PD checked every black car in the lots. None had a plate matching Marjorie's. They're running the VINs on all the Corollas, but I don't think they'll find anything. Greyscale is obtaining Kelsey and Benny's bank and credit card information and tracking their cellphones for tower pings. Hopefully, we can locate them."

Kyra wasn't optimistic. If Marjorie's phone had been turned off, she suspected Kelsey's and Benny's were off, too. She rubbed her forehead. The long day was taking its toll.

"Where are we going?" she asked.

"The hotel. It'll take three hours to get to Woods Hole."

"It's in Bridgeport?" Kyra tried not to sound disappointed. She wanted to get out of this depressing place as soon as possible.

"No. Just north. Is that okay? We can try to push through if you want. We might make the last boat."

"No." Kyra shifted back in her seat. "Hotel sounds nice."

The hotel Tarek booked was one of those chain places. The kind that hosted conferences and corporate meetings. It was bland but clean, and it had everything Kyra needed, namely a bed.

Tarek got their keys, and they rode the elevator up to their room. They hadn't spoken much on the drive. After a while, Tarek had put on one of his podcasts, but after a few minutes, switched to a radio station. Kyra hoped that meeting *Murder & MayFemme* and Marjorie's violent death hadn't ruined true crime for him.

Kyra dropped their overnight bag on the desk, unzipped it, and rummaged inside for her toiletries.

"Are you hungry?" Tarek asked. "I'll order room service. Unless you wanted to go to the restaurant?"

Kyra hadn't eaten since the pretzel on the ferry, and she'd consumed enough coffee to kill a horse, but she wasn't hungry. The caffeine was suppressing her appetite, or it could have been seeing the aftermath of a deadly bludgeoning.

She hadn't liked Marjorie. The podcaster had been rude and unpleasant, but Kyra still felt the loss. She wondered if there hadn't been more she could have done. If she'd asked the right questions or called Asher sooner, maybe Marjorie would still be alive.

Kyra clutched her cosmetics case and sleep shirt to her chest. She raised her eyes to Tarek's. "No, thank you. I'm just going to grab a shower and go to bed."

She retreated into the bathroom, stripped off her clothes, and turned on the water. She let it heat to scalding. Tarek's voice was just audible over the stream, but his words were indiscernible. He was probably on another debriefing call.

When she emerged, he was gone. After today, he'd need to decompress. He'd either work out his frustrations at the gym or drown them at the bar. Alone, she slid under the covers, switched off the light and curled up, hugging the pillow to her chest.

"Kyra?" A hand gently shook her shoulder. "Hey, wake up. It's a dream."

Her eyes flew open with a gasp. She could still picture Marjorie's face in vivid detail. Her bashed in cheek and orbital bone. Her expelled eye hanging by threads of tissue. The clumps of hair. The stolen bedsheets the killer had used to wrap her up, stiff with blood and brain matter.

A tear leaked out of the corner of her eye.

"Hey." Tarek wiped it away with his thumb. "You had a nightmare. Do you want to talk about it?"

She shook her head. It'd been awful, but she wasn't frightened, just full of regret and grief. She wrapped her arms around him, pressing her body to his, seeking comfort.

He trailed soft kisses along her neck, her jaw. Her hands found his waist. Her fingers trailed the hard plains of his stomach, needing more, needing to block out the slideshow of horrors playing on repeat in her mind.

He moved over her, pressed her into the mattress. Kyra looked into his eyes, bright but tinged with sadness. She arched against him, wanting him closer. He hitched her thigh around his waist and his mouth found hers.

After, tucked against his chest, his heart a steady rhythm beneath her cheek, Kyra fell into a deep and dreamless sleep.

# Chapter Twenty-Four

*Saturday, February 11*

SUNLIGHT STREAMED IN through the hotel window, highlighting the red undertones in Tarek's dark hair. He held his cellphone at arm's length.

"Mom?"

Kyra stepped back into the bathroom, tightening the towel around her chest. The last thing she needed was to flash Liya Collins on video chat.

"You're tired." Liya's vowels stretched, softened by her accent. Her voice, like Tarek's, was almost musical.

"It's been a long few days. What's up?"

Liya hummed, the universal mom sound of concerned disapproval. "I received a letter from a court appointed liaison."

"What?" Tarek's tone was sharp. "What do they want?"

"It's about your father. He's asking to see you."

"No."

Kyra leaned against the counter, hovering near the door. She felt a little guilty for eavesdropping, but she had nowhere she could go, and she was curious. She knew next to nothing about Tarek's father, only that he abandoned his wife and son when Tarek was a boy. Tarek never spoke about him.

"But, Tarek…"

"I said no. Does he have your address? Your phone number?"

"No, I don't think so. He's not…"

"The restraining order is still in place. He's not allowed to contact you."

"He didn't. The letter is for you."

"Then why did you open it?"

"Because it was sent here." She made an exasperated noise. "He's still your father, Tarek."

Tarek responded, but not in English. Kyra pushed herself off the counter. She inched closer to the door and peeked out. He was sitting on the unmade bed, his elbow resting on his knee, holding the phone. The other hand ran through his hair as he stumbled over his words.

Liya responded, her tone sharp. She heaved a sigh. "Where are you?"

"On a case."

"You've left Kyra again? She's alone in that big house?"

"No, she's with me," he said and looked up. A smile ghosted over his lips when he saw her lurking in the doorway. "She's right here." He flipped the phone around so Kyra could see the screen. Liya resembled her son, wide-set eyes, hers brown, high cheekbones.

"Kyra!"

"Hi, Liya." Kyra waved at the camera, maintaining a death grip on her towel.

Tarek turned the phone back around. "We have to get going. Ignore the letter. Throw it away."

Kyra rummaged through her bag. She waited until he'd

hung up. "I didn't know you spoke Swahili."

"I don't. Well, I do, I guess. Barely. My Arabic is even worse."

"What was that about your dad?"

Tarek stiffened. "Nothing."

"It didn't sound like nothing."

"Just drop it."

She winced and turned away. Suddenly, she found the interior of her overnight bag fascinating.

He clasped her elbow and gently pulled her back to face him. "I'm sorry. I didn't mean it like that. I don't like talking about him. It's not a nice story," he said, his voice soft, but rough and edged with pain. "It's not you. I just..." he trailed off.

"It's okay," she said. "But you can tell me if you wanted to."

"I know. Thank you." His expression was so contrite. She resolved not to let it bother her, for now. She knew better than most about disappointing fathers.

Her phone buzzed, and he released her so she could retrieve it from the bedside table.

Jimmy Blau. "*The 5-0 are all over the radio. Something big is going on in East Chop. Thought you'd want to know. Call me for deets.*"

She swiped it away, not at all inclined to call Jimmy back. Her phone buzzed again, this time with an incoming call. "It's Grace."

"Go head. I'll check us out."

Kyra answered the call as he slipped from the room. "Grace?"

"Oh, thank goodness. Are you on the ferry?" Her voice was breathy, high pitched.

"No, not yet. We're about to leave. Is everything okay?"

"No, I don't think so. The Pāru construction crew found something. Ida asked me to call you. We need you and Tarek here as soon as possible."

It must have been serious. Grace called Tarek by name.

"What did they find?"

"I don't know. Ida's at the OB station now, but it didn't sound good, Kyra."

"Okay, Grace. We'll get there as soon as we can."

She hung up, threw on her clothes, and hurried downstairs.

Tarek pulled the car up just as she exited the revolving doors.

"Grace said…" she began, but Tarek interrupted her.

"Evans called. We have to hurry."

Kyra froze. One hand on the door, the other on her purse strap. "What did they find?"

Tarek's gaze met hers, his mouth set in a grim line. "Kelsey."

# Chapter Twenty-Five

"THANK YOU, MEL," Officer Evans's smile was more of a grimace. The desk agent set the fresh pot of coffee on the sideboard with a nod.

As soon as they'd arrived at OBPD, Tarek and Kyra had been directed to a windowless conference room.

"Coffee, Miss Gibson?"

"Please. Thank you, Mark." She accepted the thick ceramic mug, snaking her chilled fingers through the handle.

"Sir?"

Tarek shook his head and kept scrolling through his phone, mumbling under his breath. Every few minutes, he'd shift in his seat or huff with impatience.

They'd rushed back from Connecticut. Tarek's blatant disregard for the posted speed limit had Kyra biting her nails and her tongue. She was positive they'd broken many laws of state and physics. Upon arriving at Woods Hole, they'd talked themselves onto an unscheduled freight boat and arrived on island in record time.

Kyra thought they'd be sent to see Kelsey immediately, instead they were stuck waiting for the OBPD to authorize their visit. After their mad dash to get on island, the waiting around was particularly unbearable.

At first, the lack of urgency by the OBPD appalled Kyra. It was only after the first hour of fidgeting in her hard plastic chair that she realized what Tarek had known since receiving Evans's phone call. Kelsey was dead.

"What's the holdup?" Tarek asked for the third time, dropping his phone on the table.

Evans deflated. He opened his mouth to no doubt repeat the same ambiguous nonsense about protocol and jurisdictional bureaucracy, but Tarek's phone rang.

He smirked when he read the screen and answered the call. "This is Collins."

Kyra waited while Tarek hummed agreements interspersed with *yes, sirs* and *no, sirs*. From his deference, she assumed he was speaking to his superior at Greyscale. She turned to Officer Evans to confirm, but he was watching Tarek with pure adoration, a puppy to the guy with the kibble. It was exactly how Cronkite looked at Tarek.

Tarek hung up and stood. "We can go over now."

"Sir?" Evans scrambled to his feet.

"This is officially FBI jurisdiction, and Greyscale will be taking lead."

Evans's face fell, and he began to lower back into his seat. Kyra nudged Tarek with her toe. She gave him a pointed look, then glanced at Mark and back. Tarek arched an eyebrow at her. She rolled her hand, motioning for him to get on with it.

*Don't be an asshole*, she mouthed, and Tarek let out a long-suffering breath before turning to Evans.

"But, Evans, having the community liaison's support would be really helpful. It's a delicate situation with the crime scene being at the new Pāru site. It'd be great if we could work together."

Evans broke out into a grin rivaling a child's on Christmas morning. "Yes, sir! Like old times, right? Do you want to ride with me?" *Too far, Mark.* Kyra bit the inside of her cheek.

"Umm, no. We can take our own car."

Tarek followed Evans's SUV and turned onto the camp's drive. The recent snowfall had turned it into a mess of mud and slush. The tires slid, making Kyra's heart thump. She white-knuckled the grab bar.

The construction site was crawling with police and emergency personnel. People were huddled in groups, their hard hats in their hands, or still on their heads. The field in front of the rehearsal building had been turned into a makeshift parking lot full of mostly pickup trucks.

"The construction crew found her?" Kyra asked as Tarek pulled into an empty slot.

"That's the story."

Just as they exited their cars, a man in a police uniform raised his hand and approached. He shook Evans's and Tarek's hands. He bowed his head to Kyra and turned his back to her. His obvious dismissal rankled, and it took her a significant effort not to react with a snide comment. She didn't want to get kicked out.

The officer gave Tarek and Evans a short briefing. OBPD had arrived at the camp after a 911 call. They'd been on site since, trying to keep the crime scene from being contaminated while the local and state police forces fought with the FBI over jurisdiction.

"The FBI pulled rank when the victim in Connecticut was positively identified by her mother." He motioned for them to follow. "The vic is over here."

They followed him across the service road to the dormitories. The courtyard in front of the buildings was trampled, cluttered with police and emergency response vehicles. The ambulance stood dark and idle; an eerie intimation that dashing to the hospital wouldn't be necessary.

"She's in one of the dorm rooms?" Kyra asked.

The policeman halted and swung around.

He glowered at her. "How do you know these buildings were dormitories?"

"We toured the campgrounds Monday afternoon with *Murder & MayFemme*. Which dorm was it?"

The officer pressed his lips together, like he was reluctant to answer.

"Which one, Officer Coscioni?" Evans asked with a professional assuredness Kyra didn't know the cheery man possessed. "Miss Gibson's consultation has been specifically requested by the community council."

Officer Coscioni pointed. "The one on the left."

"The girls' dorm," Kyra muttered, earning another look of disdain from Coscioni.

At the door, they donned hard hats and followed him inside. There weren't many people in the building. A few uniforms had taken positions guarding the doors. Emergency responders were off to the side, speaking to two men in expensive clothes and Pāru branded hardhats.

Alvin spotted them first. He raised his hand to them and tapped Kent on the shoulder.

"Over here," he said, his expression grim.

They followed Alvin and Kent into one of the first-floor rooms about halfway down the hall. Kent held out his hand to Tarek, then to Kyra. His handshake was firm.

"I'm glad to see you," he said seriously, and Kyra blinked back her surprise.

"Evans, these gentlemen are with Pāru. Alvin, Kent, this is Officer Evans with the Massachusetts State Police. He's a community liaison on the island and represents the council's interests," Tarek explained.

Kent slipped his hands into his pockets. "When they told us the FBI's consultants were going to be assigned to the case, I won't lie, I was hoping it'd be you two." He swallowed and let out a long breath. "Those poor women. The office is freaking the fuck out. This isn't what they meant when they told us to drum up publicity." He shook his head.

Kyra couldn't get her head around Kent's change in behavior. He was acting professional, polite, nothing like the rude jerk she'd met earlier in the week. Alvin too was different. He was less than, like he'd slid the dimmer switch down on his personality.

Tarek cleared his throat. "Can you tell us what happened?" Kent gave Alvin a nod.

"My crew arrived just before seven. We were supposed to demo the old theater, but someone noticed that the door chain on the girls' building had been cut. We assumed it was kids, partying, drinking, or whatever. I sent a few guys in to make sure they were all out, hadn't left anything, and to lock it back up."

"Left anything?" Kyra asked.

"Yeah, if they'd started a fire or were smoking. These buildings are old, all rotting timber and mold. It wouldn't take much for them to go up like that." He snapped his fingers. "I don't know what possessed my guys to check the old utility room. But that's where they found her. They called me right away. I ran over to check. I trust the crew, but…" He shook his head and pressed his lips together. "Even in the poor light, I recognized her. That's when I called 911. Then I called Kent."

"We thought it best to leave her and the room as undisturbed as possible. We asked some guys to stay close by to help the emergency response teams, but no one from our crew has gone inside that room again," Kent said.

"Okay. That's good." Tarek nodded. "We'd like to see the body. Can you show us where it is?"

"Us?" Alvin asked, and Tarek nodded as he pulled a flashlight from his pocket. "Yeah, alright. It's this way."

Alvin led them down the hall. The utility room doorway was open, the door, no longer attached to the frame, was propped against the wall.

"What else is in there?" Kyra inhaled the dank scents of moisture, mildew, and decay.

"Nothing," Kent said with a shrug. "The electrical box, hot water heaters, probably the laundry, would have been in there, but all of that was stripped out ages ago. There's access to a crawlspace, but even that's empty."

Kent shined his light on the warped tread below their feet. "Watch where you step."

"Wait here," Tarek instructed them and motioned for Kyra to follow him down.

The distance was short, only four steps. Kyra's foot hit the hard packed dirt floor. She felt the cold emanating from below through her boots' thick rubber soles.

The utility room was large, twelve by fifteen feet. There were no windows. The only light came from the three work lights that had been set up around a tarp-covered lump on the ground. Tarek was already squatting down. He motioned to a first responder dressed in a white hazmat suit.

"Kyra." His tone held a warning, but she ignored him.

She stepped right up to the edge of the white plastic and stood, her body rigid with dread. The man in the hazmat suit slowly rolled back the tarp.

Kyra stared at Kelsey's body. Her blond hair fanned out around her head like some macabre, wavey halo. Her eyes were half open, just enough to see a sliver of milky blue irises below the gaping hole in her forehead. Bits of bone, blood, and brain clung to her hair, her cheeks, her eyelashes. Her coat and jeans were dirty with more than just blood and gray matter.

Someone handed Tarek black gloves. He lifted the woman's head. "Gunshot wound to the back of her skull. Singed skin and hair at the entrance wound. Close range, probably a contact shot. Did you find casings?" he asked the closest hazmat suit.

"No, sir."

Tarek stood, moved down to Kelsey's single shoe, and lifted it. He pointed at the heel. Scuff marks. "She was dragged." He pointed to the mud caked to her knees, her chin, chest, and thighs. "Looks like she was kneeling when she was shot and fell forward." He picked up her hands, studied her fingers. The tips were jagged and bloody. "Rats."

Kyra's stomach roiled, and she swallowed against the bile rising in her throat.

Tarek replaced Kelsey's hand and eased back on his heels. "Has she been moved since she was found? Did anyone touch her?" he asked the room.

"Alvarez found her first. He's outside," Alvin said from the doorway.

"Do you have a time of death?" he asked the hazmat suit closest to him.

"I'm just a paramedic. That's not in my wheelhouse, but from muscle rigidity and decomp, I'd guesstimate she's been dead at least three days."

"There's no evidence of a struggle." Tarek gestured to her hands. He frowned as he scanned Kelsey's body again. Kyra could almost see his mind cataloging what he was seeing, making deductions.

Tarek pulled out his flashlight and swept it along the floor, the walls. "No blood spatter, no casings." He looked over at Kent and Alvin. "Were people on the work site the last few days?"

"During the day, but we close up when it gets dark," Alvin said.

It got dark early, right around four. That would give someone plenty of time to dump a body before the construction crew returned in the morning.

"Mud on her knees." Tarek was muttering half to himself. He stopped. "I don't think she was killed here. I'd guess she was executed somewhere else, then dumped."

*Executed? Close contact?* Kyra sucked in a ragged breath.

Death wafted over her tongue, and she bit down hard on her lip to keep from gagging.

Compared to the violence Marjorie endured, this was tame. But to be forced to kneel in the dirt while someone placed a gun to the back of your skull? Kyra couldn't imagine how terrifying this woman's last moments were.

Tarek turned to Alvin. "And the chain across the door was only cut last night?"

Alvin bit his cheek. "We noticed it this morning, but I couldn't say that it hadn't been cut the day before or earlier. We haven't been working on this side of the property. It could have gone unnoticed."

"I locked up after you left Monday. But no one's been authorized to be here since," Kent confirmed.

"Is there any other way to get into the building?" Kyra asked.

Kent shrugged. "You've seen it. None of the windows are intact. If someone wanted to break in, they could have."

That was what Kyra thought. "So why cut the chain?"

"The body." Tarek nodded. "It'd be too difficult to manage a body through a window. Going through the door would be the easiest. And the killer wanted her found."

"But why? Why not dump her in the ocean?" Kyra asked.

Tarek didn't answer. He moved to the far end of the room and splayed his light on the square panel near the floor. "This is the access to the crawl space?"

Kent nodded and Tarek squatted. He motioned for Evans to move the wood panel and inched forward. His light disappeared into the gloom.

"Tar?" Kyra's voice was loud in the near silent room.

Tarek scooted back, stood, and stowed his flashlight. "It's empty, but Evans have forensics do a full sweep just in case."

Evans nodded.

Tarek turned his attention to another man in a hazmat suit. This one holding a camera with an enormous flash. He motioned for the camera and flipped through the images.

"Evans, did the bureau say when the forensics and crime scene teams will arrive on island?"

"They're coming from the field office in Boston," Evans replied.

"And no one's found anything else? Anywhere in the building? Outside?"

Alvin rubbed his chin. "No, I don't think so. What are you looking for?"

It was Kyra who answered. "Kelsey's prosthetic leg."

# Chapter Twenty-Six

"ALVAREZ?" ALVIN CALLED to the group of work-booted men. "Get a word? Over here?"

A slight man, Alvarez, stubbed out a cigarette. He stuffed his hands into the deep pockets of his work pants and walked over, his shoulders hunched by his ears.

"Mr. Alvin?"

Alvarez wasn't much taller than Kyra and his cheeks were still full and round, his jawline soft. Despite his innocent, boyish appearance, his dark brown eyes remained wary.

"Alvarez, this is Officer Evans with the OBPD. Mr. Collins and his partner Ms. Gibson work with the FBI."

Alvarez took two steps back, and he paled.

Tarek raised his hands. "Mr. Alvarez, we work with violent crimes. We're only interested in finding the person responsible for the body in that building. Isn't that right, Evans?"

"Yes, sir." Evans gave an emphatic nod.

"We heard you were the one who found her. Can you tell us what happened?" Tarek asked.

Alvarez didn't appear reassured, and he looked to Alvin, asking a silent question.

"It'll be alright. Just tell these folks what you know."

Alvarez swallowed. It was loud enough for Kyra to hear. "When Mr. Alvin noticed the chain to the dormitory had been cut, he asked me, Hal, and Goodwill to check it out."

"Goodwill?" Kyra repeated.

He turned wide eyes on her and nodded. "Yes, ma'am." Kyra tried her best to keep her expression neutral, but sometimes she couldn't help it. She hated being called ma'am. "'Cause he's from Cambridge and likes Sudoku."

She bit down on a smile. "Fair enough. Please, continue."

Alvarez angled himself toward Kyra as if he found her the least intimidating. "Hal checked upstairs, and Goodwill and I checked the first floor. I noticed the door to the utility room had been moved. I'd been inside the dorm a few times. Before the door was closed. I'd noticed because it'd rotted off the hinges but was still wedged into the door jamb, just sitting on the floor. I thought it was cool." He pulled his phone from his pocket. His thumb passed over the screen. He handed it to Kyra. "See?"

Alvarez had taken pictures of the derelict building. The one he'd pulled up was in black and white, a study of light. A beam of dusty sunlight shined through the broken window, creating a fractured pattern on the door standing but crooked in the door jamb. Closed, but not functional.

She didn't think. She swiped to the next image. It was of a room with a collapsed ceiling. Sunlight filtered through, illuminating a floor covered in debris.

She handed his phone back to him. "You took these?"

He nodded. "They're beautiful."

The tops of Alvarez's cheeks turned pink. "Gracias." He

repocketed the phone.

"So, you noticed the door had been moved," Tarek prodded.

"Yes, sir. It was leaning against the wall. It couldn't have fallen that way. Someone moved it. Goodwill and I went inside. I was first. It was real dark in there and all we had were our phones. At first, we didn't see anything. Just dirt, you know? But then I saw what I thought was a garbage pile. We got closer, and it was a woman. I turned her over, but she was cold. Dead."

"You turned her over?" Tarek asked, but there was an urgency to his voice that caused Alvarez to flinch. "No, you did nothing wrong, but it is important. Tell me exactly what happened."

"Uh ... she was lying face down. I saw her hair. At first, I didn't think she was real, but she was heavy when I rolled her over."

"And you're certain she was face down?"

Alvarez nodded.

"And her arms? Legs?"

"I think she had one arm under her. It flopped when we rolled her over. Hal said she was unconscious. Then we saw her face." Alvarez's shoulders tensed and he blinked rapidly. "I checked her neck for a heartbeat. Her skin was cold."

Tarek was pensive. He held out his hand. "Thank you, Mr. Alvarez. You've been very helpful." He pulled a business card from his pocket and handed it to him. "If you think of anything else, this is my direct line."

Alvarez pocketed the card, and with a nod, returned to the group of crew members.

"Let's discuss this inside?" Kent said.

He unlocked the trailer door. Kyra sagged a little when he shut it behind them. The trailer was warm. Alvin took a seat behind a desk, and Kent perched on top.

"Did that mean something to you? What Alvarez said about Kelsey being face down?" Kyra asked Tarek, as she tried to rub warmth back into her arms.

"It gives me some insight into the killer's mind set. If she'd been laid out with intention, that would indicate emotional attachment. That he dumped her, and she was found how she fell? That's detachment. This wasn't about Kelsey, but there is a message there. Whatever the killer is trying to tell us, it's not about the victim. It wasn't personal."

She wasn't sure she agreed with his last statement. Execution sounded very personal to her.

"What happens now?" Kent asked.

"Evans," Tarek said, turning to the officer. "Make sure when the forensics team gets here, they get samples of the dirt on the victim's knees. See if we can get a location for the crime scene. We'll also need a time of death. I'll call Dr. Khaleng in Boston to get that expedited."

Evans jotted the instructions down in his little notebook. "What else?"

"We'll need official statements from everyone who has been on the site for the last few days. Make sure they get Alvarez, Hal, and the other guy, Goodwill's, prints. We want to eliminate them as potential persons of interest right away. Alvin, if either the OBPD or FBI give them trouble, let me know."

Alvin nodded. "Thank you."

"I also want the door taken into evidence. There may be DNA on it."

Evans nodded and pulled out a pad and pen.

"We need to make sure this stays out of the press." Tarek eyed each of them. Kent made a face but dipped his chin in a curt nod. "I don't want to spook the killer, send them into hiding, or worse."

"I'll make sure everyone here and in Connecticut knows that this is to be kept quiet. Is there anything else?" The pen stopped moving.

Tarek shook his head, but Kyra spoke up. "Ask Alverez for copies of the photos he's taken of the construction site. There may be more that we missed."

"On it," Evans said, his pen moving across the pad. "I'm going to check in with the office, put in these requests, and get some more uniforms to take statements." He pocketed the notebook and with a nod left the trailer.

When the door closed, Kyra turned back to Alvin and Kent. "What did you mean when you said publicity earlier? About drumming it up?"

Kent and Alvin exchanged a look, and Alvin cleared his throat as Kent shifted on the top of the desk.

"About that." Alvin ran his hand down his face. "When we were told about the podcast, it was supposed to be part of a publicity stunt arranged by Pāru. At the time, it sounded like a good idea." His voice trailed off.

"Stunt? What stunt?" Tarek crossed his arms over his chest.

Kent raised his hands. "This wasn't our idea. Alvin and I do what we're told."

Tarek stared at him, waited for him to continue. Alvin's shoulders hitched in a sheepish shrug.

Kent blew out a long breath. "The higher ups wanted to create buzz. Something that'd go viral, super meta." He swung his hands in a wide circle. "You know how it is."

Kyra did not know how it was and from Tarek's thunderous expression, he didn't know either.

"What's more meta than murder podcasters being murdered on an old murder scene where we're building a stage for a murder play?"

"It would have been unreal." Alvin grinned. Then his smile wavered, and as if realizing who he was speaking to, it melted away.

"Yeah, the whole thing was staged." Kent pressed his lips together and stared at the floor.

"Well, not quite." Alvin's toothy grin was back. "You guys weren't part of the plan, and, Kent, remember the podcasters were supposed to *die* in the old theater. I don't know why they did the killing in their house. That was off script."

Kyra gaped at them.

"You're saying Pāru killed them?" Tarek asked, his brow furrowed.

"What no!" Kent blustered. "The first play is *Dial M for Murder*. Marketing thought staging a fake killing of the murder podcasters would be a fun way to announce the production. We were supposed to live stream discovering the blood all over the theater on Thursday on social media, make a show of it. The podcasters were supposed to turn up a day later and announce the production. We all had parts to play."

"Right." Alvin nodded. "It was performance art. Kent and I were supposed to act unwelcoming to the podcasters, like we didn't want them digging into the history of the place. The podcasters were supposed to record bites for their social media during the tour, leak them before they fake-died. But when you guys showed up, I guess they decided against it."

"But why? Why would they agree to that?" Kyra asked, frowning. "It makes them look like frauds, like their podcast is faked."

Alvin raised his hand and rubbed his thumb against the pads of his pointer and middle finger.

"How much?" Tarek demanded.

"Hundred and fifty grand." Kent pursed his lips. "Each. Pāru has been working toward this project for nearly a decade. They're pulling out all the stops, and they needed a media blitz."

"They got one," Alvin said, his expression tight.

"And Benny Perez? What did he get?" Tarek asked.

Alvin's brows pulled together.

Kent shook his head. "Who?"

"Never mind. Who else knew about the stunt?" Tarek ground out through gritted teeth.

Kent shrugged. "Marjorie and Kelsey, obviously. The Pāru execs. It was hush-hush. We had to sign NDAs. I'm pretty sure no one ran it by legal."

"Definitely not. The lawyers always shut down the good ideas." Alvin scoffed and leaned back in his seat, causing it to creak.

Kent hopped down from the desk. "Corporate was adamant that to keep the performances convincing, they controlled who knew what. We only had a general idea of the plan. Be unfriendly to the podcasters, be believable when we discovered the murders, and wait for the reveal. When the podcasters went off script, staging the attack at their house, we assumed it came down from HQ. It wasn't until Marjorie was found…" Kent broke eye contact and blinked at the floor.

"I'm going to need the names of everyone who was involved," Tarek said.

Kent's head snapped up, and he sucked in a breath.

Tarek's responding smile wasn't friendly. "Or I'll get a warrant and make it all public record."

"Ah fuck." Alvin sighed.

# Chapter Twenty-Seven

TAREK LET THE door to the trailer shut with an unapologetic *bang* and stalked down to the car. Kyra chased after him. She shot off an angry text to Asher. If he'd known about the podcasters' plans, and lied to her, she'd never forgive him. She stuffed her phone back in her bag and slumped against the seat. Her gaze drifted to Tarek. There was a tense set to his shoulders, but it was more than just anger with Pāru.

"Tar, what is it?" Kyra asked when they rounded Ocean Park. A minute stretched, then two. "I can't help if I don't know."

When he spoke, his voice was low. "I'm wondering how Benny fits. The media blitz, the camp killings, the hosts' deaths. It doesn't sound like he was a part of whatever Pāru was planning." Tarek gripped the steering wheel until the tops of his knuckles paled.

"Do you think the killer has him?" Kyra asked. A knot formed in her stomach as something dawned on her. "Do you think something's happened to him?"

"I don't know. It's possible he isn't involved at all and is on the mainland doing whatever he does when he's not in DC. Or he's another victim, or..." His voice trailed off. The look he shot her was weighted. Kyra heard what he left unsaid. Benny could be the one responsible for what had happened to Marjorie and Kelsey.

"You think he could have killed them? But why? And why now? Why go all the way to Connecticut and then come back here?" she asked.

"I don't know." Tarek raised a shoulder with a shake of his head.

"I don't think so, Tar. Benny worked with Marjorie and Kelsey for years. He had plenty of opportunities to hurt them without drawing so much attention." Another thought entered her mind. "Could this be revenge by someone from the podcasters' series? Someone they wronged?"

"Unlikely. That was the first thing I had Greyscale check when we found Marjorie. Assuming their investigations aren't complete bullshit," he said bitterly. "None of the accused, or the victims, were in New England over the past week."

"And their families?"

"Greyscale is looking into it, but I don't think so."

Tarek's hands tightened on the steering wheel. He swallowed. "I just can't stop thinking about the difference between the two murders. Marjorie's death was messy, emotional. Her face took the brunt of the assault. That tells me the killer knew her and there was a reaction to something. The ME's report will confirm, but I'd bet that it wasn't until her face was fully bashed in that the killer struck her body." He glanced at Kyra and back to the road. "There was so much rage there. But with Kelsey? An execution is a different kind of kill. Holding a gun against a person, making them walk, kneel, then pulling the trigger. That takes control. Restraint.

"And even how the bodies were treated? Again, so different. Wrapping Marjorie up so carefully in the van surrounded by her work? It's almost like she was entombed. That's another sign of emotion. It could have been regret."

"Are you saying the killer didn't plan to kill Marjorie?"

"Maybe. It's consistent with a crime of passion, a violent person pushed too far. That can't be said for Kelsey, though. An execution, a relocation, and dumping the body in the building where the crime she was investigating occurred? That was intended to send a message. For whom or what the message is, we don't know." Tarek sucked in a deep breath. "I haven't worked out what the killer is thinking yet, but the escalation is concerning."

Kyra listened, half horrified, half transfixed. She'd worked with Tarek on cases before and she'd watched him process, but he'd never walked her through a profile. She'd known he was brilliant, but it was different seeing it.

"Concerning? More concerning than finding them dead?" Kyra asked, and Tarek nodded, his expression grim.

"It's the change from wild, emotional, spontaneous to premeditated and calculated. The switch has flipped. The killer is in it now. They have a plan, and they're committed to seeing it through. If that plan includes more people…"

"We'll find more bodies," she whispered, filling in what Tarek left unsaid. "Shit."

Kyra sat back against her seat and stared out at the road ahead.

# Chapter Twenty-Eight

"WHAT DID YOU find?" Chase answered Kyra's call after the first ring.

She tucked her feet under her on the couch and gave him a short version. When she told him about Marjorie's brutal beating and Kelsey's execution, she heard his sharp intake of breath.

"What the fuck?"

"I know. It's horrible."

He was quiet for a few minutes. "What now?"

"I could use your help if you're not busy."

"Whatever you need."

"We spoke with Peter Edwards in Bridgeport. He mentioned that his family received a payout from the community council a few months after Abigail was killed. It came with a warning not to question the circumstances around Elodie's disappearance. I'd like to ask Ida Ames about it."

Kyra could have spoken to Ida on her own, but the head of the community council could be hard to pin down. However, the staid councilwoman had a soft spot for Chase. She seemed defenseless against his charms, and Kyra suspected Ida wouldn't say no to a request coming from him.

"Tarek doesn't want to go?" Chase asked.

"He might, but finding the person responsible for killing Marjorie and Kelsey is his priority now."

When they'd arrived back at the house, Tarek had dropped their bag by the front door, shot her an apologetic look, and disappeared into his office. From the scraps of conversation she heard, Greyscale had its lawyers working on motions and they were escalating the search for Benny.

"Okay," Chase said. "I'll call Ida and come to you."

Forty-five minutes later, Chase let himself into the house.

"I'll let Tar know we're leaving." Kyra tapped a soft knock on the glass door and poked her head inside. Tarek looked up and ran his hand through his hair. It was standing on end in places. He'd been messing with it. He was stressed. His brow creased as he took in her moto-jacket, the purse on her shoulder.

"Where are you going?"

"Chase and I are going to talk to Ida Ames about the council and its involvement with the payment made to the Edwards family."

Chase appeared over Kyra's shoulder, his eyes glittering. "I'm the Mulder to her Scully, the Ninety-Nine to her Eight-Six."

Tarek's lips twitched.

"What does that mean?" Kyra asked, looking between them and Tarek huffed a laugh.

Chase shook his head, disappointed. "Seriously? Did you grow up under a rock? Or did Ali only let you watch *Masterpiece Theatre?*"

Her Aunt Ali had hoarded the TV remote, but she was

more inclined to watch *Love Island* reruns than period dramas.

"He's referencing television shows about secret agents. Old shows." A soft bleep from Tarek's laptop announced an incoming communication. He glanced at the screen and sighed. His computer made another noise. This one somehow sounding more insistent. His hand inched toward his mouse.

He made a fist. "Do you need me to come with you?"

"No, we can manage."

Tarek's shoulders dropped, relieved. "Okay. You'll be careful?"

"No, Tar, I'm going to sneak onto a yacht where a murderer is living and hide in a closet."

Chase snorted.

"Kyra, that's not funny." Tarek didn't look amused at all, and she grinned.

"I thought it was pretty funny."

"It was funny," Chase agreed. "Don't be such a worrywart. We'll be back before you know it. And I'll be hungry."

The Martha's Vineyard Community Council was headquartered in a converted house in Edgartown. The only clue that it was a business was the nearly full parking lot with assigned spaces.

Kyra pointed to a familiar Subaru. "Did you know Grace would be here?"

"Probably? When I called, the woman who answered the phone said Ida was in a council meeting."

"Good afternoon. I'm afraid today's meeting is closed to the public." The receptionist, a white-haired woman in thick glasses, smiled at them. She sat behind a wide desk facing the front door. She pulled her glasses off her nose and let them drop. They dangled from the chain around her neck and rested on her chest.

"We're not here for the meeting. I'm Kyra Gibson and this is Chase Hawthorn. We're here to see Ida Ames."

"I called about an hour ago."

"Chase Hawthorn?" The receptionist peered up at him. She replaced her glasses and broke out into a wide grin. "I remember you, but the last time I saw you, you were knee high. You've grown." She wagged a wrinkled finger at him.

"Time works that way," Chase said with a cheeky smile and the old woman chuckled.

"It does. It does. Go on, take a seat. I'll let Ida know you're here. The meeting should be just about done."

Kyra and Chase moved into the small waiting room. An electric space heater sat in the fireplace, radiating warmth into the room. Photos of Martha's Vineyard over the years decorated the walls. Kyra studied a picture of the Old Whaling Church. Below the black-and-white photograph was a plaque with a brief history of the building. She moved down to the next frame. It was of the same church but taken more recently. A man in a tuxedo was bent over his new bride, his arms supporting her in a low dip.

"Bye, Marilyn!" A woman's voice crowed, followed by a more subdued male one. People, many in business attire, filed out of the community council offices with polite parting words. Kyra heard the creak of floorboards above as council members returned to their offices upstairs.

"Bye now. See you next week," the receptionist called, as

the last of the members departed. She appeared in the doorway, her glasses down again. "Ida's gone up to her office. She'll see you now. It's at the end of the hall."

The historic images of Martha's Vineyard continued upstairs where the council members' offices were. The communities they represented were identified by the nameplates beside each door.

Chase tapped on the open door to an empty office where the sign for Katama sat above one for Chappaquiddick. "Grace's?"

Kyra pointed to the pink Kelly bag sitting on the neater of the two desks. "She's still here."

"Marilyn said Ida's office was at the end."

"Come in!" a husky voice called when Chase tapped a knuckle against the director's door.

Ida Ames and Grace Chambers were sitting at a small conference table. Grace stood when they entered and clasped her hands together. Her rings glinted under the overhead lights.

"Kyra, Chase! So lovely to see you." She gave them both rib-crushing hugs. "Sit. Sit. Do you want anything? Coffee? Tea?"

"A coffee would be lovely."

"That sounds good. I take it the same as Kay."

"Right away." Grace bustled out as Kyra and Chase took seats at the table.

"So, what brings you here today?" Ida asked. "I don't think you've ever sought me out, Mr. Hawthorn. This must be important." Her smile slipped. "Is this about Mander Lane?"

Chase shook his head. "No, the farm's great."

"Actually, we're here about the Gillman Center for the Arts."

Ida's expression turned somber. "We just called an emergency meeting about the poor girl who was found there. This is terrible for the island and our family-friendly image. It's a strange sort of blessing that we've been told not to discuss it publicly. At least we can come up with a public relations strategy before the news runs away with claims that the island is unsafe for visitors."

"Yes," Kyra said, choosing her words. "It's really awful what happened to Kelsey and Marjorie. Tarek is working closely with Mark Evans and the authorities to find the person responsible."

"Mmmhmm, Officer Evans has been keeping us informed. We're lucky to have him."

"Kay wanted to ask you about the other murder at the camp. The old one."

Ida sat back in her chair. The movement made her long chandelier earrings sway.

"What did I miss?" Grace asked and set a tray down on the table. She passed out steaming mugs.

"Miss Gibson was about to ask some questions about the Koch girl."

"Oh, dear." Grace took the remaining empty seat.

"I'm not sure if Mark told you," Kyra said. "But Marjorie's body was found in the same city where Elodie Edwards grew up. Her older brother still lives there."

"Is that so?" Ida asked.

"You may know that the story on the island was that Elodie Edwards murdered Abigail, escaped out their dormitory window, and drowned trying to leave Martha's Vineyard." Ida nodded. "It was also part of the story that her wealthy parents were ashamed of Elodie and the allegations against her and they persuaded the OBPD that further investigation was unnecessary."

"That is the story," Ida said, enunciating each syllable.

"Tarek and I saw the house where Elodie grew up. She attended Gillman's camp on a scholarship. The Edwardses weren't wealthy." Kyra stirred her coffee. "Peter, the brother, told us that after they received news of Elodie's disappearance and her implication in the murder of Abigail, the family received a letter from the council with a check for seventy-thousand dollars. The letter claimed it was a life insurance payout and that the amount would be repayable if it was determined Elodie died while committing a crime."

Ida frowned, creating a perfect W between her eyes, but it was Grace who spoke, "That's ridiculous. No summer camp takes out insurance policies on their campers."

"We're thinking it was a payoff," Chase said.

"And you think the council was involved?" Ida's voice rose. "Do you have this alleged letter?"

"No." Kyra shook her head.

"Then there's no proof." Ida crossed her arms over her chest.

"I don't think Peter was lying. I can't think of any reason he would."

"What do you need from us, dear?" Grace asked and Ida glared at her. Grace placed a hand on Ida's forearm. "Loretta Harris suspected that the Edwards girl was being abused, Ida.

She tried to notify the police, but no one at the time listened to her or Charles."

After a long moment, Ida let out a long breath through her nose. "Alright, for argument's sake, let's say this letter does exist. What does that mean?"

"Do you know who was on the council back then? Perhaps one of the members was somehow connected to Elodie or Abigail."

Ida stood and crossed the room to a filing cabinet. She rifled through the files. "We're supposed to get these records digitized, but it just hasn't happened yet." She pulled one out, flipped through the pages. "Ah, here we are," she said and handed Kyra the file.

Kyra scanned the list, then she passed it to Chase, but he shook his head.

"We weren't on the island yet. Shit, my parents hadn't even met. Do you know any of these people?" he asked Ida.

Ida took the list back and she and Grace leaned over it.

"I'm sorry, dear. This was well before I came to the island. I could ask Char. She may remember some of these people."

"I recognize some of them, but I wouldn't know if any of these people knew Abigail or Elodie. Oh." Ida tapped a name with her crimson lacquered finger. "This man."

"Who?" Kyra asked, leaning forward.

"Arthur Skada. He represented East Chop."

"What's so special about him?" Chase asked.

"He owned the land where the summer camp was. Where the new entertainment venue will be. Technically, his estate still owns it."

"I thought it was owned by Tobias Gillman," Kyra said, trying to remember the story Marjorie and Kelsey told her.

"No. It was a fifty-year lease-to-own." Ida stood and grabbed her computer from her desk. "When Pāru submitted their plans to redevelop the land, the council was asked to weigh in on some variances. That's when I learned about the strange set up." She placed the computer on the table so they could see the screen.

The Skada Charitable Trust was listed as the owner of the property with registered occupancy by the Pāru Group.

"Pāru took possession and occupied the summer camp property six years ago?" Kyra asked.

"Appears so. Of course, they didn't do anything with it for a while."

"Is this kind of arrangement unusual?" Chase asked.

"Lease-to-own on the island is rare, but not unheard of. It was the long term that struck me as curious."

"It is long," Grace said, her mouth scrunched to the side. "But it creates a fixed and stable income and with the nonprofit status of the camp, it could have positive tax implications."

"How did Pāru assume the lease?" Kyra asked.

"I couldn't say." Ida shook her head and squinted at the screen. "Tobias Gillman held the occupancy certificate prior to Pāru. He or his estate must have sold it?"

"Do you think this is important, dear?"

"I'm not sure. I don't know how the property ownership would fit into what happened to Abigail and Elodie." Kyra tapped her fingers against the table. She pointed to the computer screen. "Something like this would have had to be registered with the Registry of Deeds, right?"

Ida nodded. "Oh yes. Those are kept at the town hall on School Street, but they also have an electronic record if you want to pay for it."

Kyra motioned to the laptop. "Would you mind?"

"By all means." Ida pushed it to Kyra. Chase fished his wallet from his back pocket.

Kyra quickly found the registry of deeds and looked up the address.

"Fifteen dollars?" Chase scoffed and handed her his credit card.

"Don't get me started," Ida huffed. "The town even charges the council to access its records. Absurd."

The documents landed in her mailbox and Kyra downloaded the files. She scanned the contents.

"Huh." Kyra sat back.

"Dear?"

"The contract is a lease-to-own with no vesting until the balance is fully paid."

"In English, Kyra. American preferably." Chase nudged her.

"Gillman was paying down his debt, but he never gained equity. He was truly renting the property until he paid off the entire balance. If he missed a payment, the property automatically reverted to the Trust."

"You're saying that the rent was still being paid even after Tobias left the island?" Chase asked. "When he could have walked away?"

Kyra nodded. "Yes. All the payments are recorded. Twice a year, every year for the past forty-three years, a payment of fifteen thousand dollars was made. The last six years' payments were made by Pāru."

"And before that?" Chase pulled the computer closer to him.

"It's the same account number, so I'd assume Tobias Gillman?"

Chase tapped the screen with his finger. "After fifty years, Gillman would have owned the property outright for just one point five million?"

"How much is that property worth now?" Kyra asked Ida.

Ida tipped her head to the side. "I'd say easily ten times that, potentially much more."

"And not counting what they paid to buy the lease, Pāru has bought a ten-plus million-dollar property for less than four hundred grand paid out over thirteen years." Chase made a smacking noise and sat back in his chair. He stared up at the ceiling. "Well, that fucking figures."

"Chase?"

He turned his blue-green eyes on Kyra. They were full of apology. "Pāru means pearl in Japanese." Kyra gave him a quizzical look and shook her head. "It's one of Margot's companies."

Kyra gaped at him. "Your mother owns the new theater project?"

"I'm sorry. I should have told you."

Kyra waved his apology off. "But how did she get the land from Tobias Gillman?"

"I don't know. I could ask." Chase's mouth slanted down.

Kyra doubted Margot would tell her son anything, and if she knew it'd be helping Kyra and Tarek, she'd outright refuse. "Not yet," she said, and turned to Grace and Ida. "We should go. Thank you for everything." Kyra stood and shook Ida's hand.

"If you need anything more, dear, don't hesitate to ask," Grace said and gave Kyra a squeeze.

In the hall, Kyra checked her phone. She had two text messages.

Asher: "*I did not know. You have my word. But now that I do, be assured whoever had knowledge of this scheme will be sacked forthwith.*"

"Formal, isn't he?" Chase asked, peering over her shoulder.

"When he's furious, he can be." Kyra swiped to the next message.

Tarek: "*Heading off island. Call you later.*" She read it twice more, each time her stomach sinking further.

"He left?" Chase studied her face and put his arm around her shoulders.

"Looks that way." Kyra bit her lip, pinching the soft tissue between her teeth. Her gaze fell on the framed photograph across the hall. "Oh, one second." She turned back to Ida's office.

"Ida?" She poked her head inside, interrupting her and Grace.

"Yes?"

"Sorry, one more thing. Do you know if the council has any old photos of the Gillman summer camp when it was in business?"

"I'm sure we do. I'll have someone check the archive. We'll send you whatever we find."

"As soon as possible. Thank you."

Kyra took the stairs, her movements slow. She wanted to analyze what she'd learned from the council about the camp property, but her brain was stalled on the fact Tarek had left and she was alone. Again.

Chase was waiting for her by the reception desk.

"You kids have a nice evening," Marilyn said.

"Marilyn, before we go, I have a question for you." Chase leaned his hip against her desk. Marilyn's eyebrows rose over her frames. "How long have you been working at the council?"

Marilyn's nose wrinkled. "Oh, ages. Since I was a teenager. The council members come and go, but I'm always here." She motioned to her desk. "It's like my second home."

"Do you remember a councilman named Arthur Skada?"

"How could I forget him?" She leaned forward and whispered, "He was a bit of a J-E-R-K."

"Do you know anything about him owning a tract of land in East Chop?" Chase was all nonchalance, like he questioned old women about land ownership all the time.

Marilyn made duck lips and nodded. "Oh yeah. Art Skada fancied himself a land developer. He bought himself a big chunk of property out there. It used to be a farm. He thought he'd subdivide it up and build houses for summer people." Marilyn shook her head. "But the town wouldn't give him a zoning variance. That's when he joined the council. He tried to change the laws every year until he died." She shook her head. "He was never successful. It was a lucky break when he leased it to the summer camp. Then the camp went out of business. Everyone thought Tobias was a fool to keep paying the rent on that land. I guess now he's laughing all the way to the bank."

"What do you mean?" Kyra asked.

"About eight years ago, the zoning rules changed. I bet Tobias sold the lease for a fortune to that entertainment company that's in there now." She shook her head. "Some people have a golden thumb, you know?"

Kyra caught Chase's eye.

"Yeah," Chase said. "Some people are just lucky like that. Thanks, Marilyn."

"Oh anytime. Don't be strangers."

# Chapter Twenty-Nine

"DO YOU HAVE food?" Chase asked from the passenger seat. He fiddled with the radio.

"I think so." Kyra tried to recall the contents of her fridge.

When Tarek was home, he did the grocery shopping, but she wasn't sure if he'd been. When he wasn't on the island, she subsisted on fruit and dodgy toast.

Kyra used the code to unlock the house and Chase unarmed the alarm.

"Mew!" a soft little voice called, and the white terror emerged.

He twined himself between her legs, then Chase's. Chase eyed the cat with suspicion until he finally gave in and gave Cronk's ears a good scratch.

"He already misses Tar, huh?"

"Yes," she sighed. "He sees him bring out his bags and gets anxious. He'll be clingy for a few days, then remember he loathes me."

Chase laughed and headed to the kitchen. "Food."

"Help yourself to whatever we have." Kyra followed him and collapsed onto a barstool. She rested her forehead on her folded arms and sucked in a deep breath.

Chase moved through her kitchen like he owned the place. He assessed the contents of her fridge and pantry and began pulling out ingredients, piling them on the counter. He fed the cat, opened a bottle of wine, and set a stockpot of water on the stove. For someone who'd lived his entire life with staff, he was surprisingly self-sufficient.

"How do you know how to cook?" she asked.

His blond head appeared from behind the fridge door, and he flashed her his smarmy playboy smile. "I knew a chef. She taught me things." His smile turned wicked.

"Why do you make *knew* sound like you mean in the biblical sense?"

"What she taught me wasn't in any bible." He winked and Kyra couldn't help it. She laughed, and his grin widened. He'd been trying to coax her into a better mood. He poured her a glass of wine and ran a knife through whatever was on his cutting board.

Her phone buzzed, and she fished it from her purse. "It's Tarek."

Chase wiped his hands on a towel.

"Hello?"

"Hi." It came out long and breathy. He was tired. Given how exhausted she was, she could only imagine how he felt traipsing back to the mainland.

"You're on speaker. Chase is with me."

"Hey, Chase. How was your meeting with Ida?"

She and Chase took turns telling Tarek about the meeting.

"Margot owns the theater company?" Tarek said.

"Part of it, yeah." Chase pulled a face. His knife began

moving again, perhaps with a bit more force.

"Interesting."

"Is it really, though?" Kyra shrugged, even though Tarek couldn't see her. Margot being invested in a multimillion-dollar entertainment venue wasn't that surprising. She and her husband Phil had their hands in everything. It was what rich people called a *diversified portfolio.*

"Maybe. Maybe not, but that's not why I called. I received Dr. Khaleng's preliminary report. Marjorie died of blunt force trauma to the skull, causing massive brain hemorrhaging." Kyra didn't need a medical degree to have come to that conclusion. The woman's face had been bashed in.

"Kelsey was executed. Gunshot wound to the back of the skull with a nine-millimeter. Contact shot. Ballistics will review her report to confirm.

"Time of death for Marjorie is sometime Wednesday morning. Kelsey's was about the same. There was blood spattered on Kelsey's clothes, underneath her jacket. It'll be tested, but I bet it's Marjorie's."

"You think Kelsey murdered Marjorie?" Chase asked.

"No. Khaleng found ligature marks on Kelsey's wrists. My guess is that Kelsey witnessed Marjorie's death. Then she was killed."

Kyra tapped her nails against the granite. "What about the dirt on her pants and coat?"

"It's being sent to the lab. Based on the condition of the body and de-comp, plus the lack of physical evidence on the scene, Khaleng thinks Kelsey was only in the utility room for two or three days.

"If the blood on her clothes is a match for Marjorie, we can safely assume she was killed somewhere between the island and Bridgeport."

"If they were killed on Wednesday, where has Kelsey been the past three days?" Chase asked.

"I don't know. But it's not all bad news. Forensics found a receipt from a gas station in Manchester in the van."

Kyra blinked at Chase. *Manchester?*

"That's in New Hampshire," Chase supplied. "Is that where you are now?"

"I'm heading there."

"Why you?" Kyra asked. As a forensic psychologist, Tarek wasn't often deployed as a field investigator.

"I'm the closest available Greyscale operative, and I have the case background. It's routine stuff. Shouldn't take long."

"*Oh-kay*," she said, drawing out the word. "When will you be back?" Tarek was quiet for a while. "Tar?"

"I'm not sure. After I'm done in Manchester, probably tomorrow or Monday, I'll head north and then I have to report in for my next assignment." Kyra's heart sank. He could be gone for weeks, and he couldn't even tell her where he'd be.

"What's north?" Chase asked.

"Benny Perez is from a town up there. A place called Errol."

Chase's knife stopped moving. He'd gone white as a sheet.

He cleared his throat. "Say the name of the town again."

"Errol. You've heard of it?"

Chase nodded, the motion slow. He swallowed. "Yeah,

I've heard of it. That's where Penny and Adele Wolkowyski were born."

Kyra's mouth fell open.

When Tarek's voice came over the speaker, it was staticky. "Your mother and sister are from Errol, New Hampshire?"

"Margot doesn't want people to know. They left when Adele was seven. Penny changed her name. They never went back. Adele mentioned it. Once."

"Could it be a coincidence?" Kyra asked, knowing the answer.

"Nothing involving my mother is a coincidence." Chase wiped his hands on his jeans and reached for his phone. "I'll find out."

"Wait, Chase." Kyra raised her hand.

"No, don't call her," Tarek said. "I don't want her having time to craft some bullshit story. I'll call Greyscale, have someone from the bureau, or DOJ go talk to her. She won't be able to say no to them." His voice crackled. "Shit. Service is getting spotty. I'll call you tomorrow. Chase, don't talk to Margot or your father." Tarek hung up without waiting for a goodbye.

Chase pushed his hair away from his face and tipped his head back, staring up at the ceiling. He sucked in a long, ragged-sounding breath and let it out slowly, as if counting. Breathing exercises for when he was anxious.

"Chase?" Even if they were horrible, Chase could have some loyalty to his family. "You don't have to listen to him. If you want to call your parents, do it. He won't blame you."

"No." He lowered his head. "It's fine. I'm fine." He

looked down at the counter, cluttered with the ingredients he'd been prepping. The pot of water boiled on the stove. He grabbed a box of pasta. "We're making dinner."

Kyra sipped her wine while Chase banged around her kitchen. She'd offered to help, but he'd waved her off and told her to go into the living room. A cabinet door slammed shut louder than necessary, and she flinched but stayed on the couch, giving him the space he needed.

She opened her laptop to search for Errol, New Hampshire. Margot hadn't come from privilege despite the image she'd cultivated. Chase's half-sister, Adele was a shameful reminder to Margot of the life they'd lived before becoming part of the Hawthorn dynasty. It was one of the reasons Adele had killed Kyra's father and Chase's boyfriend. She'd wanted to destroy the Hawthorn name, and she'd targeted their legacy, Chase.

Chase entered the living room carrying their dinner, two plates piled high with pasta. He set them down on the table, retreated to the kitchen, and returned with a salad and the wine. He sat beside her, his leg against hers, took a long drink, and refilled both their glasses.

"*Cacio e pepe.*" He picked up his fork and pointed. "And that's a salad."

"You made this?" she asked, taking in the artfully plated pasta garnished with a sprinkle of fresh herbs. As long as she'd known Chase, he'd always demanded she bring snacks. "It looks and smells amazing." He shrugged off her compliment, but Kyra could tell he was pleased. She leveled him with a mock glare and brandished her fork at him. "You've been holding out on me."

"Don't tell anyone." Chase took an enormous bite, filling his cheeks like an overgrown chipmunk, and jerked his chin toward the laptop on the table. "Whatcha looking at?" he asked around a mouthful of food.

"Errol," Kyra said, pulling the computer closer.

"What's it like?"

"You really want to know?"

Chase chewed and his expression turned thoughtful before he nodded. "Yeah. Show me."

Kyra angled the screen so they could both view it. Chase scrolled through photographs, none of which painted a very nice picture.

Errol was a small logging outpost far to the north, just thirty miles from the Canadian border. It was in the middle of the wilderness, surrounded by state parks and wildlife refuges. The photographs were of dilapidated houses set deep in the woods, or clusters of trailer homes just off the highway.

"You've never looked it up before? Or been there?" she asked.

"Nah," he said, reaching for the salad. "Margot wanted to forget that place. So did Adele." He scrolled further down the search results. His expression softened, turned almost regretful.

"Hey, you okay?"

He shook his head. "Yeah. Fine. Just tired."

Kyra cleaned up their plates. When she returned to the living room, Chase had turned on the fire and pulled one of the throw blankets over his legs. His lanky frame took up most of the long side of the sectional.

"Do you want to watch a movie or something?"

Kyra recognized the request for what it was. He didn't want to be alone. He didn't want to suffer through the memories of the trauma his sister and parents inflicted on him, and honestly, she wanted his company, too.

She settled back into the soft cushions and passed him the remote. "Yeah."

# Chapter Thirty

*Sunday, February 12*

TAREK'S PHONE RANG through to voicemail. Again. Kyra rubbed her temple and left a message. It wasn't like him to not answer, and even less like him to not call when he said he would. She'd expected his call in the morning, but the morning had come and gone, and then the early afternoon and still no word. She was waffling between worry and irritation, worry for Tarek and irritation with her obvious overreaction. It wasn't like she'd never gone half a day without speaking to him before.

Her phone buzzed.

She answered without checking the screen. "Tar?"

"No, it's me." Chase. "Still haven't heard from him?"

"No, not yet," she huffed, settling on irritation.

"Hmm." Chase hummed.

Tarek often withdrew when he was on a case, but not since last spring had he missed calling her when he said he would.

"It's at least a three-hour drive, Kay, and it's been snowing up there. He's probably stuck on the highway. Cell reception in the White Mountains is shitty. I bet he has no signal."

And now she was back to worried. She pictured Tarek's crappy Jeep stuck in a ditch in the middle of nowhere.

As if realizing that he'd made it worse, Chase said, his tone softer. "He's fine. Give him at least a day or two before you freak out."

Chase was being sensible. They chatted for a few minutes more, and she promised to call when she heard from Tarek.

He ended the call, and she stared at the darkened phone screen. She couldn't remain idle. Sitting at home, waiting for Tarek to call, would drive her mad. She yanked her hair back into a ponytail, laced on her running shoes, and grabbed her car keys.

She'd developed a habit or *a masochist's coping mechanism* according to her aunt, of running whenever she was overwhelmed, stressed, or just stuck. Something about the slap of her feet on pavement, the air in her lungs, settled and quieted her busy mind in ways that shavasana or meditating never could.

It was a sunny day, but too cold and windy to run outside. She drove to the YMCA and set up at her least-despised treadmill overlooking the pool, but watching the members do laps only made her feel Tarek's absence more acutely, and she switched to a machine that looked outside.

An hour, and seven miles later, there was still no call or text from Tarek. She trudged back to her car. The cold air chilled the sweat on her body, and she shivered in her fleece that wasn't warm enough for a fall day, much less the dead of winter.

"For fuck's sake." Her forehead hit the steering wheel. "Enough." Her run-swollen hands gripped the steering wheel, and she steered the car into downtown Edgartown in search of a coat.

Kyra parked at the bottom of Main Street, in front of the Yacht Club, and next to the slip where the *Island Pearl* had docked. It'd been just over a year since her father's body was pulled from the water, eventually bringing her to Martha's Vineyard. Back then, she never could have predicted that she'd fall in love with the island and make it her permanent home.

She turned her back on the harbor and walked up Water Street. Few stores were open, and even less had winter wear, but determined, she scoured the available inventory. She wandered up and down the streets, checking any open shop, and moving farther away from the little town center.

Down North Water Street, traffic increased. A small crowd was gathered outside of the Heritage Center Museum. Kyra crept closer, curious what had drawn out the islanders on a freezing Sunday afternoon.

The double doors had been propped open and inside, the crowd was well-dressed, sipping on champagne and sampling canapes. Realizing she was gate-crashing some sort of event, she tried to backtrack, but a large party jostled her through the front doors, their voices too loud with alcohol. Unable to get around them, Kyra stumbled inside, deeper into the museum, very aware of her sweaty ponytail, her leggings, and pilly fleece. She scanned the crowd, and to her relief and delight, spotted Charlie. Kyra's neighbor was leaning against the mezzanine balcony railing, holding a half empty champagne flute, her expression beyond bored.

Keeping to the perimeter, trying to draw as little attention to herself as possible, Kyra made her way over to her friend.

"Charlie?" she whispered when she was close enough to be heard but not smelled. She liked Charlie, after all.

"Kay?" Charlie's eyebrows flew up, and she grinned. "What are you doing here?" She cocked her head to the side. "Did you *run* here?"

"No, I just happened upon it. What's going on?"

"A dedication of some art piece that we're all supposed to fall head over heels for. It's a fish made of scrap metal Hank Elliot collected from the dump." She rolled her eyes and lowered her voice. "Doesn't even look like a fish. It's just a big triangle." Kyra bit her cheek to keep from laughing. "Let's get you a drink." Charlie waved at one of the waiters and plucked a champagne glass off his tray. The man in an ill-fitting polyester waistcoat pursed his lips at Kyra, taking in her workout clothes and messy hair. "She's the artist," Charlie hissed.

"Oh, I'm so sorry, Miss Elliot. The piece is stunning. If you need anything else." He bowed his head and backed away.

"Charlie!"

"What? Hank isn't even here. He lives in Naples. Florida." She clinked her glass against Kyra's and turned around, resting her elbows on the balcony ledge. Kyra did the same.

"What were you doing in town?"

"Trying to buy a coat. I didn't find much."

"No." Charlie shook her head and her mouth twisted to the side. "You won't find anything in Edgartown. Maybe OB or Vineyard Haven, but you're better off ordering something online or going off island."

"I know." Kyra sighed, and her gaze fell to the level below. An enormous raised-relief map of Martha's Vineyard sat in the center of the room, lit from beneath. People stood around it in small groups.

Her attention was drawn to a man with shaggy auburn hair. She almost didn't recognize him in his business casual pressed khakis and plaid button-up shirt.

"Is that Mark Evans?" She pointed.

Mark was standing next to a woman who was speaking, her mouth moving rapidly. His posture was erect and stiff. He checked his watch.

"Who?" Charlie leaned farther forward. "Oh, Officer Evans. Yeah. He comes to all these things now. The council insists. Although I can't think of any reason, a bunch of middle-aged, bad-art enthusiasts would need to liaise with the police."

"Can I get down there?"

"Sure. The stairs are through there." Charlie motioned with her champagne glass.

Kyra thanked her and made her way downstairs to Mark. When he saw her approach, his face lit up. Not as bright as it did for Tarek, but close enough.

"Excuse me, Mrs. Reed," he interrupted the woman's lambasting. "I must speak to Miss Gibson. It's urgent." He stepped around her. "Miss Gibson, what are you doing here?" he asked. He ushered Kyra to a corner away from the crowd. "I should thank you. I don't think I could have discussed the Barnes Road traffic patterns any longer."

"It's a long story, but I'm glad I caught you. Have you

heard from Tarek or Greyscale today?"

Evans's brow creased, and he shook his head. "No, but it is Sunday. I don't expect to hear from Greyscale until tomorrow, unless it's important."

"He didn't check in from Manchester?"

He peered at her from under his floppy hair. "No, but that probably means it was a dead end. We're waiting for a judge to rule on a motion filed by Greyscale. That won't come through before tomorrow, so I expect we'll hear from him then." He gave her shoulder a sympathetic pat. "You know how Collins can get wrapped up in his cases. I can't tell you how many times he forgot to check in with HQ. It drove the captain nuts. It's also what makes him very good at his job." His cheeks flushed with embarrassment.

"I know." Kyra heaved a sigh, both frustrated and worried. She swallowed and gave herself a mental reproof. "I'm sure he'll check in tonight."

"He will," Mark said, then straightened his posture. "Oh, I can cheer you up. I was going to call you when I left. I received the link to Alvarez's photography portfolio. Let me share it with you." He dragged his pointer finger over his phone's cracked screen and Kyra's phone buzzed.

"Thanks. I'll take a look when I get home. I'd better get going before someone realizes I wasn't invited. Will you let me know if you hear from him?"

Mark promised and Kyra slipped out. She felt a little better having a task to keep her mind busy. Her fingers itched to see the images, but she forced herself to drive home and shower first.

Dressed in one of Tarek's ratty Boston University sweatshirts, she padded downstairs. The house demon blinked his absinthe eyes at her and rubbed against her calves. She scooped him up and buried her face in his soft fur. For once, he didn't struggle.

She booted up her laptop and clicked on the link Mark sent. Alvarez's website was bare bones and was organized by his different photography series. One looked like all the images had been taken at the campground. They were in black and white and played with the juxtaposition of light and shadow. The images were beautiful. And eerie. She clicked through each one, studying the subjects. She recognized the images of the girls' dorm. Alvarez had photographed the collapsed playhouse, and the other camp structures, all slowly being reclaimed by the woods.

She clicked to the next one. It was of a house hidden in the forest. The two-story replica gothic revival was ornate compared to the other buildings' utilitarian designs. There was a wide covered front porch that appeared to disappear around the sides. The windows were arched or shuttered. The trim, once dark, was chipped and broken in places. An overgrown hedgerow lined the walkway to the porch stairs. She zoomed in. Kyra's heart thumped against her chest. She squinted at the darkened shape partially concealed by the angle of the pitched roof.

"Is that a chimney?" she asked aloud.

She scrolled to the next photograph, an image of the porch. Another, the entryway. The next one was of a window, but this image had been taken from inside, looking out through the glass to the yard beyond. In the reflection, Kyra could just make out a mantel and the darkened space below.

*A fireplace.*

She hurried through the last three photographs. She re-reviewed them. They were closeups of subjects in the house. The last one was of a staircase, ascending into blinding light, like Alvarez had stood in complete darkness, when he took the image from below.

Kyra tapped her finger against the screen. "Do you think it's a cellar?" Cronk blinked at her.

She called the community council and left a message, reminding Ida that she needed the photo archive.

Then she tried Tarek again. The call rang to his voicemail. "Tar, call me back. Tobias Gillman had a fireplace in his house. That could explain where the murder weapon came from."

She looked at the front door. Her instinct was to get in her car and drive straight to the campgrounds to see the building. She flipped through the photographs again. Unlike the dorms, the house had been cleaned out. There was no furniture, no draperies, nothing to suggest she'd find anything there but rotting rooms. She dialed Mark Evans instead and left a message suggesting he send a team to search it.

Kyra studied the design of Gillman's house, the ornate detailing and woodwork. She texted her aunt.

"*Ali, do you know if cellars are common in gothic revival houses?*" If anyone would know, it'd be Ali.

Little blue dots indicated her aunt was responding.

Ali: "*?*"

Kyra: "*These are pictures of a house on Martha's Vineyard, built about forty years ago. It seems out of place.*" She forwarded the images. "*WDYT?*"

She waited. Minutes ticked by. Her phone buzzed with a response.

Ali: "*Weird choices. I don't know about the cellar specifics, but I can find out. Send me the address? Love you.*"

Kyra sent her aunt the address and set her phone aside. She gazed out her back windows to the cove below. An icy film had formed around the edges, creating a dark contrast against the snowy banks.

She threw herself on the couch and picked up the remote. She surfed the channels without seeing. This was the part of Tarek's job she couldn't stand. He had a begrudging patience for the legal and scientific processes and procedures that took hours, days, or more. She was used to doing the work, not waiting around for others. It made her twitchy. She could feel the answers were out there, in front of her, just out of reach. It was infuriating.

# Chapter Thirty-One

*Tuesday, February 14*

"HI, MY NAME is Kyra Gibson." Kyra squeezed her eyes shut. Her grip on her phone tightened and her fingers ached. She forced her voice to remain calm. "Yes, that's right. I'm looking for my partner, Tarek Collins."

"Shouldn't you know where your partner is? It's standard protocol." The man on the line was much too snide for Kyra's fracturing patience. "No, I'm not with Greyscale. Tarek is. He and I are ... we're ... er..." She held in a frustrated scream.

This was the third person at Tarek's consultancy firm that she'd spoken to. No one knew what the hell she was talking about, and they couldn't seem to fathom why someone would be looking for one of their employees.

"Louis? Wasn't that your name? Look, Louis, it doesn't matter what my relationship with Dr. Collins is. I'm just asking that you put me in touch with his supervisor. Please."

"Uh-huh. Please hold."

Elevator music began playing. It stopped. The call ended. They'd hung up on her. Kyra let her scream out through her teeth. She threw the phone down and flopped back on the couch. Tarek still hadn't called, not Sunday or Monday, and not this morning, nor had he checked in with Evans. Kyra was officially worried.

She'd found phone numbers for two motels within twenty miles of Errol, New Hampshire. Neither had been helpful. They'd refused to confirm if he was staying there or transfer the call to his room, but both took messages. Messages she was positive were not written down and would never be delivered.

"There's nothing else for it, Cronkers," she muttered to the cotton ball curled up beside her. He'd been her constant shadow, like he knew she was worried about his favorite person. She hauled him into her lap and pressed her cheek against his furry little head. "I'm going up there."

It was a terrible, stupid idea. It couldn't even be called a plan. She didn't actually know where *there* even was, or what she'd do once she got there, and yet, it was better than sitting at home, doing nothing.

Her phone buzzed.

"Hello?"

"Has he called?" Chase.

"No. No one's heard from him, and his stupid company won't help me. Chase, I'm going to Errol."

"Fuck." He sucked in a long breath. "No, not yet."

"But, Chase, I can't…"

Chase interrupted her. "Pack a bag, bring something lawyerly, and meet me at the private airfield in an hour."

Kyra sat up straight. "Where are we going?"

There was a long pause. "To see my sister."

Kyra ran upstairs, taking two at a time. She burst into her closet and began tossing things onto the tufted bench. A gray garment bag with a subtle YSL embossing was first, followed by a pair of jeans, sweater, underthings, socks, her toiletries bag, and finally, the unworn, red-soled black patent leather pumps Asher Owen had sent at Christmas. If she had to go as Chase Hawthorn's high-powered lawyer, she'd commit to the role.

Kyra yanked her father's old leather overnight bag down from the top shelf. She hadn't used it since that disastrous night on Chappaquiddick. She unzipped it, pressed the sides wide open, and froze. At the bottom was the card Tarek had given to her that Thanksgiving night, the one with his security clearance number written on the back. She picked it up, ran her finger over it, felt the depressions made by the pen. She stuffed it into the outside pocket.

The private airfield was a separate building at the Martha's Vineyard Airport. It took Kyra three circles to find it, and then it was only because she spotted Chase's Bronco parked out front.

Chase was inside talking to a man in a pilot's uniform. He shook Chase's hand and retreated through the sliding doors.

"Chase?"

He turned around. "We just got the flight plan."

Kyra's head swiveled back and forth, taking in the tidy office where the likes of her were probably unwelcome. She scrambled for something to say. "Flight plan?" she said, weakly.

"Yeah. We'll fly into the airfield at Tipton. It's the closest we can get to Jessup. Where my sister is."

"But how?" Chase shrugged, but the strain at the corner

of his mouth gave him away. "Chase." Her voice came out stern, an almost Ali-voice—the one her aunt used when she was serious—and Chase smirked.

"I made the request last night. Billy flew in this morning from Reagan." He waved to the windows lining the back of the building, and beyond to the runway. "It's always been available. I just don't like to use it." This time, his shrug wasn't forced. "I don't leave the island much, anyway. But it's the fastest way to Maryland."

Kyra was at a total loss for words. This was too much. And what if Tarek was fine? He'd be furious that they'd gone to see Adele without him.

As if reading her mind, Chase nodded to her handbag. "Call him again."

She put the phone on speaker. Straight to voicemail. Kyra waited through the automatic recording, intending to leave yet another message.

"*The user's voicemail box is full.*"

"Right. Let's go." Chase grabbed Kyra's bag from the floor. She scrambled to keep up with him as they ran for the plane.

Kyra's relief that the Hawthorns' plane was not one of the little propellered death traps that flew between the island and Boston, but a proper private jet, the kind she'd only seen on reality shows, was short-lived. Guilt set in when she took in the luxurious leather seats, the conference table with video set-up, a fully stocked bar, and the woman who stood at the back wearing a flight attendant's uniform.

*This is not me.*

"Masha." Chase dropped their bags and crossed the

plane. The woman broke out into a wide, maternal smile. "It's good to see you." He stooped to hug her, and Kyra swore the woman's eyes misted over.

"Billy didn't say it was you who called." She swiped a hand at him and ran a finger under her eye.

"Billy's an asshole."

Masha laughed, a strange hiccupping sound. She peered up at him and pressed a hand to his cheek. It was the same look Kyra had seen Beth, the Hawthorns' house manager, give him. It was full of love, and ... distance. Masha, Kyra realized, was one of the many Hawthorn staff members who'd helped raise him. His parents' employees had been the people who tucked him in at night, told him stories, made sure he attended school.

Kyra's mother died when she was twelve, and her father left her on her aunt's doorstep, but at least for a little while she'd had parents who wanted her. She wasn't sure Chase ever had that.

"Masha, meet my friend. This is Kyra Gibson. Kyra, Masha."

Kyra awkwardly jostled her garment bag so Masha could take her free hand in both of hers. "It's so nice to finally meet you."

"It's lovely to meet you as well. Thank you for taking us to…" Kyra looked to Chase. "Where are we going, again?"

"Maryland."

"Right, Maryland."

Masha let her go and smoothed her skirt. "Go on, take your seats. I'll talk to Billy and get our taxi time." She stopped in front of the cockpit door and turned around, pointing at Kyra. "And I want to know everything about this Gryphon."

"I'll tell you anything you want to know."

Masha's eyes sparkled with delight, and she disappeared inside the cockpit.

"Traitor," Chase grumbled and threw himself into the larger-than-commercial seat.

"You haven't told her Gerry's real name?" Kyra asked, taking the seat across from him and buckling in. *Gryphon* had been Gerry's dating app username when he and Chase first met.

"Of course not. She and Beth would have called Home-land Security to run a background check." Chase threw out his hand.

Kyra peered at him from under her lashes, and blinked, the image of innocence.

His mouth popped open, then stretched into a surprised smile. "You had Tarek run a background check." She raised a single shoulder. "You're as bad as they are."

"Mr. Hawthorn," a voice blared over the intercom. "We're preparing for taxi and takeoff. Please stow all loose objects. We'll be airborne in ten minutes."

"Billy, I'm right fucking here!" Chase hollered just as Masha came out of the cockpit.

"Would you like anything before we take off?" she asked, her hands folded in front of her. "A beverage? Snack?"

"Ugh, no." He pinched the bridge of his nose. "If we want anything, we'll get it ourselves." Masha gave him a cool-eyed stare, but the wrinkles at her eyes and mouth deepened as she fought a grin. He dropped his hand. "We're

fine. Go read whatever porny book you have in your bag."
Masha sucked in a short breath and her face went red. Chase
snickered. "You thought I didn't know? Everyone knows."

"You're horrible," Masha said, without bite. She found
her seat and pulled out an eReader.

"Chase." Kyra wasn't sure what her next words would be,
but she felt compelled to say something, a thank you, an
offer to help pay for something she knew she'd never be able
to afford in ten lifetimes, insist they take a normal-person
flight. She shifted in her seat.

He raised his hand. "The flight is about two hours. We
can spend that time making you feel better about all this, or
we can decide what we're going to ask Adele. She's in a high
security ward. We won't have much time."

"Fine," Kyra said and pulled a legal pad and pen from
her bag. "What are we asking Adele?"

# Chapter Thirty-Two

THE PRISON, OR *correctional facility*, as the gate guard reminded them, wasn't what Kyra had pictured when Chase said high security. The exterior was a nondescript brick building, much like any other. It almost could have been a post office or a paper supply company.

"Are you sure this is it?" she whispered, as if the fences topped with barbed wire weren't a dead giveaway.

"According to Beth." He held the door open for her.

They'd spent the flight discussing their strategy. Kyra was going as Chase's *fancy-as-fuck lawyer* and Chase would play his part as the *irreverent-but-irresistible Hawthorn heir*. Kyra wasn't convinced Adele would agree to speak to them about her memories of Errol, but Chase had a plan.

They took turns in the jet's spacious bathroom to change. When Kyra emerged in her tailored business suit, sky-high heels, her dark hair pulled back away from her face, Chase whistled.

"Is this what all London lawyers look like?" Kyra blushed. "You look like you crush hearts and jugulars beneath those spiky shoes."

Kyra waved him off and smoothed her jacket. "You look nice, too."

It was a massive understatement. Chase looked like an off-duty movie star, with his open collar and bespoke navy suit. That he hadn't had a saucy retort at the ready told Kyra he was more nervous than he was letting on.

They moved slowly through security. Kyra pulled her ID and phone from her pocket and handed it to the guard. She stepped through the metal detector, then the body scanner. She waited for Chase on the other end, as he fed his belt through the loops.

"Shouldn't you have a briefcase? Or that yellow pad or something?" he asked, eyeing her empty hands.

"People who need answers are prepared to write them down. A good lawyer doesn't reveal what she doesn't know if she doesn't have to," she said under her breath. Knowledge, or the perception of it, could be far more intimidating than blustering. It was one of the many lessons she'd learned from her old boss in England.

"Damn." Chase said it so softly she almost didn't hear.

"This is a legal visit," Kyra said to the attendant when she signed them in. "Please turn off the cameras and microphone feeds." Kyra didn't know if the prison had surveillance in the meeting rooms or if her request was valid, but she'd seen it on American crime shows.

"The inmate didn't notify us of a visit with her attorney."

"She's not Adele's attorney. She's mine. My sister did try to frame me for murder." Chase raised an eyebrow and stared down his nose at the guard.

The guard ran her pen down a clipboard and tapped it. "We'll put you in Priv Four. It's open. Follow me."

They followed her down a dingy hall. Dirt and dust were caked at the seams where the floors met the walls. The air was stale and smelled of unwashed bodies and disinfectant. The electrical hum from the fluorescent fixtures reverberated off the tiled walls. It was vile.

"This one." The guard shuffled to a stop. She pressed a button on the communication device strapped to her shoulder. "Priv Four!" A moment later, with a *click* and a *buzz*, the door unlocked, and she pulled it open.

"We're escorting the inmate now. I'll be outside. When you're ready to exit, give the door a knock or wave through the window here." She pointed. "You have forty minutes."

The door slammed shut behind her and Kyra jumped. A table and three chairs were in the center of the room, bolted to the floor. A metal ring was attached to the tabletop, closer to one side and directly in front of a single chair. The other two chairs were set further back from the table than comfortable. A grimy, barred window near the ceiling let in diffused natural light. Kyra shuddered. This was so much worse than she could have imagined.

"Adele's only request was to be as close as possible to Margot."

"She chose this place?" Kyra eyed the metal table smudged with more than just fingerprints.

"I think she thought it'd bother my mother."

"Does it?"

"Probably? But everything bothers her." Chase unbuttoned his suit jacket and took a seat. Kyra sat beside him. The chairs, at least, weren't as disgusting as the table.

The door buzzed, and a guard followed Adele Lee inside.

He looped and locked the chain attached to her wrists and ankles through the ring on the table. Adele only smiled, sweetly.

With a nod, the guard left.

Adele's face went blank, then hostile. She glared at Kyra and Chase. She ran her tongue across her teeth. "Never thought I'd see you here."

"Hi, Adele." Chase's voice was soft, and Kyra swore she heard a slight tremor. "How are you?"

"Just peachy, can't you tell?" Adele rattled her chains and Chase flinched.

"We're here about a place called Errol, New Hampshire," Kyra broke in, folding her hands in her lap.

Adele's gaze snapped to hers. "I've no idea what you're talking about."

"Adele," Chase whispered. "We need your help."

"Help?! You need *my help*?" she shrieked, and Chase jerked back. "You have some fucking nerve. Why the fuck would I help you? I don't owe you anything! Look at me!" Adele yanked on her chains again. "I'm here because of you!" Her breaths came in pants.

"No." He shook his head. "You're here because you killed two people and tried to kill two more. I wouldn't be here if it wasn't important."

"Typical." She sneered. "You selfish shit. You expect everyone to fall over themselves just because you're his son. Despite all the shit you did, you'll always be her favorite. Her perfect golden boy." Adele's mouth twisted, became the evil twin of a smile, and Kyra wanted to shield Chase from the malice behind it. "What happened? Was she mean to you?

You want revenge? Get some dirt on dear old Mom? No. Get out."

Chase shook his head. His hair shifted over his brow. "Is that what you think?" When he looked back at his sister, his gaze was full of sadness and pity. "You're wrong. I'm no one's favorite. I'm nothing but a nuisance to Phil, and Margot only prefers my last name to yours. She bailed me out to protect that name and the doors it opens for her. She doesn't give a single fuck about me. Never has. We're the same. Or we could have been. Phil would have made you a Hawthorn, had you wanted it."

"You lie."

Chase pulled an envelope from his suit jacket and set it on the table. He slid it closer to Adele. "I found it after they moved back to DC. Adoption papers from twenty-five years ago. Signed by Dad. The adoptee is listed as Adele Evangeline Hawthorn."

Adele didn't reach for the envelope. She just stared at it, blinking over and over.

"Adele, please," he whispered.

Minutes passed, and when she finally looked up, Adele focused on Kyra. She pressed her thin lips, Margot's lips, together. "What do you want to know?"

"Do you remember living in Errol? When did you move away from there?"

"Some." She nodded. "We left when I was six or seven." She'd left over thirty years ago.

"What was it like?"

Adele frowned. "Like? It wasn't like much of anything. Just a little town in the mountains. There were woods everywhere. Thick pine forests."

"Your mom," Kyra started, and Adele stiffened. "Did Margot grow up there?"

"Yeah. She was homecoming queen." Adele's lip curled. "It was her greatest achievement until she married Phil. Pregnant girls can't be prom queen."

"Did you or Margot know anyone with the last name Perez?"

"Perez? No, I don't think so, but I was just a kid."

"How about a Benny? He'd have been a little boy about your age when you left."

Adele's brow wrinkled. "Benny?"

Kyra nodded.

"There was a boy named Benny … our mothers both worked at the hunting lodge. That was the only place that'd employ people like them. Sometimes Benny and I would play together." Adele shrugged.

"People like them?" Chase asked.

"Teen moms."

"Do you remember where he lived?"

"No. I didn't see him outside of the lodge."

Kyra bit back her disappointment.

"Do you remember when Mom became involved in the Pāru Group's summer program on the island?"

Adele barked a humorless laugh. "She's still doing that? She couldn't get anyone to fund that stupid idea. Even Brian eventually withdrew."

"Margot asked your husband for money?" Kyra asked.

Adele raised an unkept eyebrow, the motion strangely similar to her brother's. "*Ex*-husband. He served me with papers before I was even sentenced. Till death or incarceration, apparently."

"You were sleeping with another man."

Adele shrugged. "We do what we do. But yes, Margot asked Brian for money. He gave it to her at first. Thirty thousand dollars a year for a few years."

Kyra's heart sped up. Thirty thousand was the annual rent on the summer camp property.

"But when she came back begging for another payment, he found out what he was really funding and refused. Can you imagine that sycophant saying no to Margot Hawthorn? I thought her head was going to explode." She glared at Chase. "We should have paid that bitch. Everything became so much worse after that. But no, even Brian wasn't stupid enough to pay for Margot to live her unrealized dreams of being a star."

"Mom wanted to be an actress?"

"She wanted to be rich *and* famous. She didn't care how."

"They broke ground on the Pāru complex in Oak Bluffs a few weeks ago," Kyra said.

"That's wonderful." Adele's flat tone implied it was anything but. "That land would be worth a fortune if they parceled it off and sold it for redevelopment, but that wouldn't stroke Margot's ego."

"Do you know how Margot and Pāru came into possession of the land?" Kyra asked.

Adele pressed her lips together. "Mom had some tip from someone she used to know. She first came to Brian six years ago. Whatever happened, it happened then."

Kyra's mind raced. She wasn't sure how it fit that Margot had been the one to bring the land to the Pāru Group and that she paid at least the first few years' rent on it, but it felt like an important piece of the puzzle.

"What do you remember about Benny?"

The question caught Adele off guard. "Not much. We were the only kids at the lodge, so we played together. I don't know what happened to him. Margot didn't keep in touch with anyone from there, not even Benny's mom, who was supposed to be her friend."

Kyra wasn't sure if Adele's Benny was Benny Perez, but she at least had a starting place. She needed to speak to someone at the Errol hunting lodge. She caught Chase's eye and glanced at the door. His chin dipped in a nearly imperceptible nod.

Kyra stood. "I don't think we have any more questions." She banged on the door to notify the guard.

The door buzzed and Chase pulled it open.

"Wait." Adele snatched up the envelope and yanked out the paper. She scanned it and her jaw went slack. "It was your first birthday." Her mouth pulled down and when she spoke again, her voice was full of emotion. "I remember. Margot threw a huge party for all of Phil's political friends. She told me to wait until she came to get me. She never came. I waited in my bedroom forever. Finally, Phil came. He said he had a present for me." She stared down at the paper. "I screamed at him. Told him I hated him, and I never wanted to see him again. He was different after that, didn't try to include me, pretended I didn't exist. I thought all of you were ashamed of me. Ashamed of the hick trash

271

Margot dragged to DC with her."

Chase straightened to his full height. "You were just a kid. Dad should have kept trying. But for what it's worth, I wasn't ashamed to call you my sister."

Adele's lower lip quivered, and tears brimmed in her eyes. "Was?" Her voice was a whisper.

"Yeah, Adele," he said without looking at her. He rebuttoned his jacket. "Was. You are nothing to me now." And Chase strode out.

# Chapter Thirty-Three

CHASE WAS QUIET while Kyra signed them out on the log and led them through the lengthy exit security process. Outside, the alarm blared as the gates slid closed behind them. Kyra took a last look at the chain-link fence, the coils of barbed wire. She placed her hand on Chase's forearm, keeping him from getting into their hired SUV.

"Chase, do you want to talk about it?"

"No. Tonight, I just want to go to the hotel bar and get very, very drunk." His blue-green eyes were rimmed red, and his hands trembled as they buttoned up his overcoat.

Kyra took his hand, laced her fingers with his, and gave it a squeeze. "Stupid drunk."

Chase drove them away from Jessup to a hotel he'd booked off the highway, in an office park. It clearly catered to the mid-level-management corporate drone and offered all the business travel essentials: questionable steakhouse, bar, twenty-four-seven coffee shop, gym, and office center. All of it dressed in shades of beige and depression.

Kyra dropped her bag on the closer of the two queen beds and beelined for the shower. She needed to scrub off the film of despair that the women's prison had left on her skin. She had little sympathy for Adele. The woman was pure evil, but she'd never forget her expression when Chase finally shut the door on their relationship. The devastation on Adele's face had been heartbreaking.

Chase was already seated at the bar when Kyra joined him. He'd changed back into casual clothes. His hair was damp, and his eyes still a little bloodshot. He was smiling his playboy smirk, arrogant and smarmy. He said something to the handsome man tending bar, making him laugh and his cheeks flush. Kyra slid into the seat beside him.

"She'll have a cab, and we'll take some menus, Tildon."

"Coming right up."

"How long have you been here?"

"Not too long. Tildon's from Fort Meade." His grin was sloppy and slow from alcohol. "I don't know what the fuck that means."

They went back and forth on what to order, and with Tildon's recommendation, settled on splitting a few appetizers.

"I'm sorry today's visit with Adele was a waste of time," Chase said, his chin dipped low.

"It wasn't a waste, Chase. I don't know how it all fits yet, but we now have a place to start in Errol. I'll call the hunting lodge tomorrow. Maybe they'll have some information about Benny Perez or Tarek." She pressed her cheek to his shoulder. "And we learned Margot had at least some connection with Tobias Gillman." She pulled away. "I'm glad we came." Even if they hadn't needed information from Adele, Kyra would have come. Chase needed the closure. He needed Adele to know that everything she'd done to him had been for nothing. He was fine, happy.

Their food came. Kyra picked at it and pretended to scroll through her phone while Chase flirted with Tildon. It buzzed with a text from Ali. Chase squinted at the screen.

"What's that about gothic revival?" He read over her shoulder.

"It's a type of architecture. Tobias Gillman's camp house was built in the style. It's known for angled roofs and dormers, ornate details and it's not contemporary at all."

Ali: "*I checked. Gothic revivals sometimes had basements and cellars in New England. But based on the topography and water tables in the area, a crawl space or cold weather slab foundation would be preferable. Anything deeper would collect water. I pulled the permitting records for the Gillman Center for the Arts. All buildings were approved for crawlspace foundations, no basements. Hope that helps. Love you.*"

"What does that mean?"

Kyra pulled up Alvarez's photographs and showed them to Chase. "See? Tobias's house had a basement." Chase shook his head, still not following. "It's not in the permit record. He did it illegally."

"So?"

That was the question, wasn't it? Why would he have an illegal basement? She tapped the side of her wineglass. "I don't know, but it's suspicious, don't you think?"

"Kay, lots of people have illegal stuff in their homes. Maybe he needed extra storage. Or maybe he was a kinky old bastard and wanted a sex dungeon."

"Chase, be serious."

"Fine, maybe he was one of those old guys with a massive model train collection or a pot farm. There are dozens of reasons you wouldn't want to pull a permit to build out a basement, the biggest one being you don't want to pay the extra permitting fees and taxes."

"I guess, but it's strange that his house is so different from all the other buildings on the property."

"Is it? Wasn't his house the only building used in the winter? He probably just wanted a nice place to live. Who wants to live like a camper year-round?"

Chase had a point. Still, she sent a text to Ida Ames asking about the status of the photographs of the Gillman Center.

Ida texted back immediately. "*Our intern is scanning them in and will send them as soon as he's done. Hope it helps.*"

"Refill?" Tildon asked, holding the wine bottle aloft.

"No, thank you." Kyra pulled out her credit card and handed it to him. "Can you put this and anything else he orders on my card?"

"Will do."

"Kay? Is everything okay?"

"Yeah, I'm fine, but I'm going to go up." She stood. "Stay. Have fun." She gave him a hug, and Chase's arms wrapped around her waist. "You're one of my favorite people, you know that, right?"

"I do." Chase pulled back. The side of his mouth hitched in the smallest smile. "You, too."

# Chapter Thirty-Four

J UST AS KYRA pressed her keycard to her room's lock panel, her phone lit up with a notification. She'd been sent access to a large file from the community counsel. She scrambled to her laptop and connected to the hotel's Wi-Fi.

The download still took forever.

Finally, the file loaded, and she opened it. There were dozens of images. From the thumbnails, Kyra determined they were from various print publications, articles, playbills, posters, and the like. The intern had scanned and cropped them. The quality was atrocious, but she could still make out the subjects.

Most were of Gillman posing with the cast of the end of the year productions. She cycled through until she found those from Abigail and Elodie's year. There were a few of Gillman with the campers eating at the mess hall. One where he was directing a rehearsal on the lawn, the campers dressed in their costumes. Three more were of the cast in the theater, his arm around the same petite, dark-haired girl. Kyra enlarged the image, squinted at the girl's face. Even decades later, she bore a resemblance to her brother. *Elodie Edwards.* In one photo she looked straight at the camera, in the other two, the floor. Kyra zoomed out. The cast were in their costumes, period pieces with lots of frills and collars. A blonde girl was dressed identically to Elodie. In one image, she stood beside Elodie. In the other, she was farther away, among the rest of the cast. Kyra chewed her lip and tapped her nail against the screen.

"Wasn't Elodie Abigail's understudy?" she murmured to the empty room.

She opened the next image. Campers sat around a long dining table. A crystal chandelier cast strange shadows over their smiling faces. Gillman sat at the head, holding a wineglass. To his right was Elodie, staring down at her plate. A few seats down and across the table was the blonde girl, whom Kyra was convinced was Abigail. She wasn't smiling.

The last image was of the same group of teenagers. Kyra recognized the room from Alvarez's photographs. It was Gillman's house. They posed in front of the fireplace. Elodie was in the center, staring at something off camera, her shoulders slumped and her expression blank. Gillman's arm was around her, his hand wrapped tight around her shoulder, holding her against him. It was strangely possessive, something more than a casual pose for a photo. At the edge, farthest away from Elodie, was Abigail in a light blue dress and bright pink sneakers, staring, no, *glaring* right down the camera lens. Behind her, almost obstructed by the flare of her skirt, was an iron stand. Kyra zoomed in and her breathing stuttered. The stand contained a set of fireplace tools—tongs, shovel, broom, and a poker, all with handles of swirling cast iron. Just like the one used to beat Abigail.

"Oh, shit."

KYRA SHOOK HER head and rubbed her tired eyes. Even closed, she could still see blue-tinged light. The laptop's glare had permanently burned into her retinas.

She heard a muted banging noise, and her eyes snapped open. She paused the music she'd been listening to and slid her headphones down around her neck. It came again. A knock, more insistent this time. Pushing herself up, she ran her hands down her face. Her legs and back were stiff from the uncomfortable chair, where she'd been sitting for the past however many hours. She looked at the clock and blinked. She did it again, not quite believing her eyes. It was past midnight.

After seeing the fire poker, and Abigail's dress and shoes, she'd emailed Mark Evans the images. She was confident those photographs were taken the night Abigail died. Maybe Evans could identify and locate the other attendees. Perhaps one of them remembered what happened at that dinner. She couldn't stop thinking about Elodie's lost expression, or Gillman's arm around her, the proprietorial curve of his fingers.

"Kay?" Chase's voice was muffled from the other side of the door. "Are you awake?"

"Coming." She stumbled across the room and opened it. He stood in the hallway, in pajama bottoms and bare feet, his hair disheveled. He clutched a pillow against his chest.

"What are you doing here?" she asked, her voice scratchy.

His toes curled into the carpet. "Tildon snores."

"Seriously?" Kyra waved him inside. "You couldn't wake

him?"

"I tried. It was easier just to come here." He beelined straight for the bed on the far side of the room, pulled back the comforter and fell onto it with a groan. "'Night."

"Wait. Don't go to sleep. I found something."

Chase yawned but sat up against the headboard. She showed him the photos, the picture of Elodie, Abigail, and the fire poker.

"You're sure it's Elodie? And why is Gillman holding her like he owns her? Creepy." He grimaced at the image on Kyra's computer.

Kyra worried her lip. "I'm pretty sure it's her. She looks a lot like her brother." She pointed. "And I'm positive that's the same fire poker."

"I guess now you know where it came from." He closed the computer and handed it back to her.

"Yeah, but how did it end up in the girls' dorm?" she asked half to herself.

She dropped her computer on her bed and walked to the bathroom to brush her teeth and wash her face. When she came back out, Chase was already fast asleep. His breathing was deep and regular. Kyra slipped into the other bed and opened her laptop.

# Chapter Thirty-Five

*Wednesday, February 15*

"KAY?" CHASE'S VOICE was gravely with sleep. "What are you doing? What time is it?"

"Not yet seven." She was sitting in bed, sipping on cold pod coffee, her laptop on her knees. "Researching."

He rubbed his eyes. "Did you sleep at all?"

She shook her head. *No.*

With a groan, he sat up. The sheets pooled around his waist. He ran his hands down his face. Even hungover with pillow wrinkles imprinted on his cheek, Chase was beautiful. She cursed the vitality of youth. "You're insane, you know that? What did you find?"

"I've been checking registrations and permits with the OB records office. Did you know that after that summer, with one exception, Tobias Gillman never applied for anymore licenses or scheduled any inspections?" He blinked at her slowly and rolled his wrist. "No occupation permits, no employment permits, or help-wanted adverts, not even marketing collateral for the next year. Nothing."

"I thought the camp closed permanently after that summer?"

Kyra nodded. "It did, but *Murder & MayFemme* said he

was forced to close down because no one enrolled, but I can't find any evidence that he even tried to reopen. And to make it weirder, he continued to pay the rents. And every year thereafter, Arthur Skada submitted a request for a zoning variance to develop the land. Every year it was denied."

Chase rubbed his hands over his face and pushed his hair back. "I'm just hungover enough that I'm going to need you to explain this to me slowly and like I'm stupid. What now?"

"I don't think Tobias ever entertained the idea of reopening the camp, but if that's the case, why keep the lease?" She clicked on the screen, her eyes narrowing. "It just doesn't make sense," she mumbled to herself.

"You said there was an exception? What was it?"

Kyra's eyes gleamed. "Every year he filed the tax return for the Gillman Center for the Arts, a not for profit, listing the camp as its sole asset."

"Kyra! Talk dumber."

"As long as that property was in a charitable trust for the benefit of a nonprofit organization, it was tax exempt."

Chase rolled his lips and leaned his head toward her. "And that is important because?"

"Year after year, Skada's variance petition was denied. The property was a continuous financial drain, but as long as Tobias paid the rents, the property remained in the charitable trust and Skada avoided paying property taxes on it. I think he was biding his time until the rules changed. He planned on terminating the lease and developing the property."

"Okay..."

"But thirty thousand dollars a year on a useless property

isn't a small amount of money. Tobias had to have gotten something for it."

"He saw an investment opportunity? That property is worth a shitload more than he paid for it."

Kyra bit her lip and swung her feet to the floor. "But why sign the lease over to Pāru?" She bit down on her lip, shaking her head. She walked to the bathroom. "No, there's something more." She squeezed toothpaste onto her toothbrush and ran it under the water. She stared at her reflection in the mirror without seeing. There was a piece she was missing.

"Didn't you say that Elodie's family was bought off by someone from the community council?" Chase's voice followed her into the bathroom.

"Mmmhmm."

"And Charlie's mom thought Elodie was being sexually abused?"

"Mmmhmm."

"Those photos don't make Tobias Gillman look good. He's practically pawing her."

Kyra's toothbrush froze in her mouth, and she stepped back into the room so she could see Chase.

His brow was furrowed. "Maybe that's what he got out of it. Skada knew about Tobias molesting his campers, but he kept his mouth shut as long as the payments kept coming?"

Kyra cringed. The thought was horrifying. "You think Tobias Gillman abused Elodie?" Kyra's sleep-deprived brain tried to process the possibility. "What's the statute of limitations for rape of a minor here?"

Chase gaped at her. "Why the fuck would I know that?"

Her phone buzzed on the bedside table. "Can you get it?" she asked and retreated to the sink to spit. She squeezed her eyes tight. "Please be Tarek," she whispered.

"It's Evans." Chase appeared in the doorway, the phone in his hand. Kyra motioned for him to continue, and his thumb slid over the screen to answer the call. "Hey, Evans, it's Chase. I'm with Kyra."

"Oh, hello." Mark sounded out of breath. "Do you have a minute?"

"Yeah, what do you need? Have you heard from Tarek?" he asked.

"No, he missed our check-in again this morning."

Kyra's stomach dropped. *Again?*

"But don't worry," Evans said, his tone rushed. "He's been in contact with Greyscale. He's fine, just busy."

"You spoke with them?" she asked.

"Yes, this morning."

"Mark, what did they say exactly?"

"That the investigation is proceeding in accordance with standard protocol, and they're monitoring the situation closely."

"About Tarek, Mark. What did they say about him? When did they speak to him?"

"Oh, they didn't say. They just said that they have the utmost confidence in their field operatives, and they promised to keep us updated as events unfurl. Obviously, Collins knows…"

The roaring in Kyra's ears drowned out Mark's voice. Her hand gripped the counter, and she sagged against it.

That was lawyer-speak for *we have no idea what the fuck is happening, and we need time to spin our bullshit.* She'd given similar statements hundreds of times. Always when something terrible had or was about to happen.

"Kay?" Chase's voice was a whisper, his expression concerned.

"They haven't spoken to him."

"Fucking hell." Chase ran his hand through his hair. "Evans, are you sure Tar was going to Errol?"

"Yes. He had a lead on Benny Perez. Actually, that's why I'm calling." He sounded hesitant. "It took a while to get the information because the records were sealed, but Benny Perez is an alias."

"What?"

"Yes, ma'am. Mr. Perez changed his name after he was released from prison five years ago." Kyra's blood went cold. "His record was sealed by order of Judge Harper in Massachusetts. His birth name is Benedick Gillman."

"Shit. As in Tobias Gillman?" Chase demanded.

"Yes, sir. We've found his birth certificate. Mr. Gillman's father is listed as Tobias Gillman, and his mother, Elizabeth Gillman both of Errol, New Hampshire."

Chase swore again, and he asked Mark another question, but Kyra was no longer listening. *Benny is Tobias's son?* Chase's hand wrapped around her forearm, and he gave her a gentle shake.

"What did he go to prison for?" Kyra asked, her voice hoarse.

"Mr. Gillman has an extensive criminal record, but he was ultimately incarcerated for armed robbery. He pled down. He held up a convenience store and assaulted the store clerk. The clerk was shot. Twice. But his wounds weren't fatal. It wasn't Mr. Gillman's first violent crime."

Kyra's hand covered her mouth. *No.*

"What happens now?" Chase asked.

"Greyscale has escalated Mr. Gillman to an official person of interest. I imagine they're going to try to locate him. They've filed for a warrant, but the judge is reluctant to issue one that uses information from a sealed record. They have to find something more to implicate Benny. They said they'd keep me informed." Mark didn't sound as certain as before. "I'll call you when I learn more."

"Okay, Evans. Thanks."

Chase ended the call. He gripped Kyra's elbows and stooped to peer into her eyes. "We're leaving. Get dressed and meet me in the lobby."

She blinked at him. "What about Tildon?"

"We have late check out. He's welcome to use it."

# Chapter Thirty-Six

KYRA CALLED TAREK again. The call clicked right over to his full voicemail box. His phone was still off. She hated herself for not following her instincts. When he didn't call Sunday, she'd known in her gut something was wrong.

She pulled Tarek's business card from the pocket of her overnight bag. She ran her fingers across the number written on the back. *925837*.

Last fall, at Verinder House, he'd told her to give this number to the police chief, and he'd pay attention to her.

She dialed the Greyscale number.

"Greyscale Security. How may I direct your call?"

"Security number 925837. I'd like to speak to the supervisor immediately."

"Right away, ma'am. Please hold."

"Briscoe." A man's voice.

It'd been that easy. "Bloody hell," Kyra murmured.

"Excuse me?"

"Sorry, yes. Mr. Briscoe, my name is Kyra. I'm calling about Tarek Collins." She heard his sharp inhale. "He gave me his code and said if there was ever an emergency, to use it. There's an emergency. I think he's missing."

He cleared his throat. "Kyra Gibson? The girlfriend? The

one from Martha's Vineyard?"

"Yes," she said, surprised Tarek's boss knew about her. "I haven't heard from him in days. It's not like him. He said he's gone to northern New Hampshire. His phone is off." She was babbling. There was some rustling and the sound of keys clicking. "Please, I just need to know if you've spoken to him."

"I cannot discuss the whereabouts of Greyscale field personnel."

"I'm not asking for a discussion. I'm asking if you've heard from him. It's a yes or no question." Each word came out stilted, through her teeth.

Biscoe cleared his throat. "No, I haven't. Collins missed his debriefing call."

Kyra squeezed her eyes shut. Tarek might not report in regularly, but he wouldn't miss an official debriefing. "When was the last time you spoke to him?"

"Is this the best number to reach you?" he asked, ignoring her. Kyra confirmed it. "Good. When I have more information, I'll be in touch. If you hear from him, notify me right away. Dial the security code he gave you. Ask for Director Dylan Briscoe."

"Wait, what are you doing to find him?"

Briscoe didn't answer right away, and Kyra wondered if he would. "A team is preparing to deploy, but we're waiting on a judge." She must have made a noise because when Director Dylan Briscoe spoke, his voice was softer, kinder. "Kyra, Tarek is a professional and before his role with us, he was a decorated homicide detective. He's the best at what he does. That's why I hired him. Sit tight and let us do our jobs." Briscoe ended the call.

Kyra was numb as she gathered her things and slung her bag onto her shoulder. She wasn't sure if she was more comforted or concerned that Greyscale was mobilizing an entire team to go after Tarek.

The elevator doors opened. Chase was there, pacing. When he spotted her, he stopped.

"What happened?" he asked. His eyes were too big as they searched hers. She recounted the conversation with Director Briscoe and with each word, Chase's expression became more troubled. He pulled her to a couch in the lobby, away from reception.

"Kay, Jimmy Blau called. He had drinks with some friends last night at the CC Club. One of the guys works the winches for the Steamship Authority."

"Okay."

"This guy asked Jimmy and the others whether they thought he should go to the police. He heard the police on the mainland were searching for an old Corolla in the Steamship lots. He swears he saw one drive over from Woods Hole on Thursday morning and the same car was on a ferry out a few hours later. He thinks it's the one they're looking for."

"How could he be sure? It's a common car."

"It is, but the guy recognized the bumper sticker, a pink silhouette of a female Sherlock Holmes."

"Send him a screenshot of the *Murder & MayFemme* website. The bumper sticker is their logo. He didn't say what the driver looked like, did he?"

Chase shook his head and typed out the message.

His phone buzzed, and he held it so she could see. The response was from an unknown number.

*"Yeah, that's it."*

"We think Benny was driving that car," Kyra said. "But why come back and leave again?" Kyra felt the color drain from her face. Violent offender Benny returned to the island and left on Thursday. "Oh god. Kelsey. Tarek was right. Tell them to call Mark Evans right now." Kyra grabbed her bags and rushed for the door.

"Wait. Kyra! Stop!" Chase grabbed her arm, forcing her to stop and face him.

"Tarek's in trouble, Chase. I know it." Her voice broke over the words. "He's chasing after a murderer. Benny must have killed Marjorie and Kelsey." She looked around the lobby, her head swiveling back and forth wildly. "I need a car. I'm going up there."

Chase's grip tightened. "We have a plane."

"I can't ask you to do that," she said, shaking her head.

"You didn't."

# Chapter Thirty-Seven

KYRA FIDGETED IN the passenger seat while Chase drove them to the private airfield.

"I need to tell you something," he said from behind his Wayfarers. His tone made Kyra's hackles rise. She could tell she wasn't going to like it. He swallowed. "I know Judge Harper."

"Okay."

"He's one of my dad's golf buddies. They went to Yale together." Kyra shook her head, not following. "I don't think it's a coincidence that Tobias's son Benny lived in Errol at the same time as my mom and sister, or that Benny's mother probably worked with mine. It also can't be a coincidence that the judge who sealed Benny's record is a close friend of my parents."

"Or that he changed his name and got a job in DC at about the same time as your mom took over Tobias's lease?" Chase nodded and his jaw flexed. "The podcast company is a subsidiary of Asher's company. Before he took over, it was run by the Elmers."

"Yeah, Mom's awful friends, the Elmers."

"You think Elizabeth and Tobias Gillman gave your mom the lease in exchange for helping their son?"

"Don't you?" He glanced at her and back at the road.

Kyra tapped her fingers against her thigh. It made sense. "But what does that have to do with the podcasters? Why kill them?" she asked.

Chase shook his head. "Dunno? Benny sounds like he's violent. He could have just snapped?"

Kyra frowned. *No.* "That only makes sense if both killings were similar. Marjorie's death was so brutal. Hers could have been a passion killing, but Kelsey's murder was meant to send a message. Benny went back to the island specifically to drop her body in the dorm. It must be related to Pāru somehow."

"There's one more thing." Kyra waited, her nails digging into her palms. "Abigail and Elodie had the leads in the play, right?" Kyra nodded. "They would both have had the part of Beatrice. Benedick is the name of Beatrice's love interest in *Much Ado About Nothing.*"

Kyra gaped at him.

"Kay, I don't think Benny's mom's name is Elizabeth."

The car suddenly veered to the right, throwing Kyra against the seatbelt. "Whoa!" she screeched. Chase accelerated, weaving across the three-lane highway. He swerved onto the exit ramp. "The hell? What are you doing? Where are we going?"

"We're going to New Hampshire. In February. Your little moto-jacket won't cut it up there." He sped into the parking lot of a shopping center and parked in front of an enormous Walmart. "You're getting a coat. Hat, gloves. All that shit. We'll need it."

Kyra found a suitable coat with a hood, gloves, a hat, and

292

thick socks. Chase picked out a pair of snow boots and a hat.

All the while, she mulled over Chase's bombshell and the significance of Benny's name. Tobias could have been a fan of the play, or he impregnated an underage girl, stole her away under cover of night, and she bore him a son. Abigail was Elodie's roommate. Had she known what was going on? Kyra thought of the photograph of Abigail staring down the camera the night she died. She didn't look like a girl excited about her big opening night. She looked pissed. Did Abigail try to protect Elodie and end up dead?

Kyra passed her card to the checkout boy while Chase bagged their items.

"You're thinking what I'm thinking, right?" he asked when the bags were in the trunk.

"I am," she sighed. "And I think Tobias killed Abigail Koch to keep it a secret."

The airfield was only a few minutes away. Kyra dropped the car keys off with the rental agent while Chase hauled their bags into the tiny office.

"Mr. Hawthorn, are you ready to return to Martha's Vineyard? I'm trying to get us a landing time, but a nor'easter is coming in, causing some delays." Billy studied his tablet.

"New plan, Billy. We're going to Errol, New Hampshire, or as close as we can get to it."

"Uh, where?" Billy frowned.

"It's north? I don't fucking know, but that's where we want to go. Right now."

Billy sucked in his bottom lip and studied them. He crossed his arms over his chest. "There's a snowstorm driving up the coast and you want to fly through it?"

"Is that a problem?"

Billy glared at Chase. "Of course it's not a problem, but it is stupid. What's in Errol, New Hampshire?"

"A friend," Chase said at the same time Kyra said, "It's important."

Billy narrowed his eyes at Chase. "How much trouble are you getting into?"

"Less than Mexico." Chase shrugged. "I'm pretty sure, anyway."

Billy smacked his lips. "Okay, I'll get us a flight plan. Get on board. You get to tell Masha she won't be home tonight."

Kyra followed Chase onto the plane where he explained to an increasingly upset Masha that they were flying out and heading north.

"Just stay here, then," he bit out, exasperated.

"You know that it's against FAA regulations, Chase."

"I wouldn't ask if it wasn't important, Masha." He spread his hands wide. "It's life or…" His voice trailed off and he caught Kyra's eye. "It's really important we get up there as quickly as possible. You and Billy can fly right home. I'll figure out how to get us back without you."

"Are you in trouble?"

"No, but our friend might be."

Masha stared at him and finally her chin dipped in a nod. "Alright."

"We good?" Billy asked, stepping into the cabin and pulling his hat on. Masha grimaced, but nodded. "There's an airport in Errol. We have a runway. Let's go."

# Chapter Thirty-Eight

"Hey." A HAND gripped Kyra's shoulder and gave her a gentle nudge. "We're about to land." She peeled her eyes open. Her lids felt like sandpaper.

"Water." Chase pressed a bottle into her hand, and she took a long sip.

She hadn't meant to fall asleep, but the lull of the engines, combined with her exhaustion, had overwhelmed her and she'd drifted off.

"Look." Chase pointed to the window.

The landscape was painted bright white. It glittered under the low sun's rays. Forests of evergreens blanketed the rolling peaks, bald in some places where the snow clung to dark granite. In the crags and valleys were mountain lakes. She inched closer, her nose almost touching the glass. Sporadically, as if dropped randomly from above, were clusters of buildings hugging the lone road snaking through the mountains. Towns.

"The parks out here are less regulated than the ones in the west," Chase said. "Hikers and campers don't need permits. There are big swaths of land that aren't supported by communications except for satellite. People get lost and die out here all the time."

"Why?" she murmured, her eyes still on the ground thousands of feet below.

"They go off the trail, rock or mudslides, avalanches. There aren't too many large predators like bears, but there have been wolf sightings in recent years."

"No." She shook her head and turned to face him. "Not why they died. Why is it so desolate out here?"

"It's not too different from the Vineyard," he said with a shrug. "Except instead of whaling and fishing, the main industry here was hunting and lumber until they decimated the forests. With industrialization, demand died down, but the people stayed. The forests are recovering and many are protected. The economy now depends on tourism. Mountain people coming up to enjoy nature. Errol sits on the edge of a refuge. Most of the businesses there are retail and hospitality, servicing hikers, kayakers, hunters…."

"How do you know all this?" Chase never failed to surprise her.

He tapped her laptop. "Someone didn't sleep the entire flight."

"You looked this all up?"

An embarrassed flush brightened his cheeks. "We're going to need a way to get around. There aren't any car rental places. But we can hire a guide at the hunting lodge. Unless we can convince someone at the airport to give us a ride, we'll need to walk. It's about a mile up the highway."

"A mile isn't bad."

"It's seventeen degrees." Kyra's brows hitched together as she tried to do the Celsius to Fahrenheit conversion in her head. "It's like negative ten in your temperatures."

Her eyes widened. *What?* She was suddenly very grateful for Chase's insistence they stop for cold weather gear.

"Mr. Hawthorn, prepare for landing," a voice crackled over the speaker.

"Billy, I'm right fucking here!" Chase yelled at the closed cockpit door and Masha's chuckle could be heard from the back.

The plane dipped and swayed as it descended. The runway was practically invisible under the snow that shrouded the land, but Billy navigated it perfectly and when the plane's landing gear touched down, snow flew up, a blizzard in reverse.

They taxied to a stop near a dark, one-story brick building. Masha and Billy prepared for deplaning and lowered the stairs.

Chase held his hand out to Billy, who took it in a firm shake. "Thanks. I owe you both. You and Masha get back to DC."

"No, we can stay," Masha interjected.

Billy's brows lowered. "If we leave now, I can fly west, go around the storm. It'll take us a little longer, but we have the fuel."

"Do it," Chase said, cutting off Masha's protest. He gave the flight attendant a hug.

"Okay," she said. "I'll send your clothes from DC. Be safe."

When the doors closed, Kyra asked, "Why the urgency?"

"I don't want them stuck here during a blizzard."

"Blizzard?" Her voice cracked over the word.

"Mmmhmm. It's moving north. They're predicting a few

feet of snow." Chase tried the door to the building with a loose sign that read AIRPORT. It was locked. He banged on it, but no one responded. Kyra peered through the window, cupping her hands around her eyes. Inside was empty and dark.

"I don't think anyone's here."

"Fuck." Chase sighed. "I guess that means we're walking."

Kyra zipped up her coat and strapped her bag across her chest. She donned her new gloves and pulled on the thick wool hat. Chase changed into his boots, careful not to let his socks touch the snow.

Trepidation settled deep in Kyra's stomach as they began the walk to the highway.

# Chapter Thirty-Nine

KYRA'S BREATHING TURNED heavy as they hiked, carrying their things through the deep drifts. In places, the snow reached past the tops of her boots, soaking her shins and calves. Her fingers and toes pinched, and the sweat collecting on her back made her shiver.

She sighed when they finally reached the highway. It'd been plowed, the brown snowbanks on either side piled high. Her relief was short-lived. Walking through a few inches of salty slush should have been easier than the drifts, but it was windy. She and Chase bent forward against the gusts. Tears streamed down her cheeks. She wanted to complain, but it didn't feel fair. Chase was probably as miserable as she was, and they were here because of her.

Chase mumbled something.

"What was that?" She had to shout to be heard.

"I'm just listing all the food I'm ordering when we get there. French fries, cheeseburger, chicken wings. Do you think they have lobster mac? I could definitely go for some lobster mac."

Kyra's stomach lurched. Ever since she was doused with scalding lobster bisque, on Thanksgiving she couldn't stand the smell or even the mention of the sea bug.

"It can't be that much farther, right?"

"Are you sure we're going the right way?" she asked.

"I think so?" Chase did a three-sixty and checked his phone. They'd been walking for at least half an hour. The hunting lodge should have been nearby, assuming it was still there.

She squinted. Her gaze followed the double yellow line down the deserted highway, up the mountains in the distance, to the horizon. Clouds darkened the sky, and the air had turned crisper. The scent of the coming snow was sharp in her nose.

"I think it must be up that way?" Chase pointed and Kyra hitched her bag higher on her shoulder. She motioned for him to continue.

She walked behind him, letting Chase take the brunt of the wind. They followed the highway around a bend and the onslaught relented. Kyra wiped her eyes. She got her first good look at their surroundings. On their side of the highway were trees. On the other was a great empty expanse covered in snow. It could have been a field, or a frozen over lake.

"Chase, look!" She pointed to the thin plumes of dark gray smoke curling above the treetops.

"Thank fucking christ. Let's go."

Route 26 gradually inclined until it flattened out and Errol, New Hampshire came into view. It was little more than a strip of modest buildings along the narrow two-lane highway. On the right, past a fishing and hunting supply and a snowmobile service center, set back from the road, was a large cabin-like structure and behind that groups of smaller outbuildings.

They made their way down the driveway. It hadn't been cleared since the last snowfall. The deep, messy tire tracks traversing back and forth were the only evidence that the lodge was open. Kyra slipped. Chase grabbed her, keeping her on her feet.

As they approached, the building's details came into focus. It wasn't a real log cabin at all. It was covered in a log cabin façade. In places, the paint and plaster had worn away, revealing the cracked sheathing underneath.

"Are you sure this is it?" she asked, hoping it wasn't.

Chase pointed to the sign carved into a piece of wood hanging above the entrance. ERROL HUNTING LODGE. His expression was almost apologetic.

He opened the door, and as she stepped inside, Kyra was blasted with blessed heat. Inside was better than outside— worn but clean. The foyer's chipped stone floor was wet in places where people had stomped snow off their boots. Beyond was a great room with wood floors covered in thick rugs. At the far end was an enormous hearth piled high with logs where a fire raged against the cold.

The great room was a reception-slash-bar-slash-lounge. Mismatched couches and loveseats were distributed around the room with no obvious rhyme or reason. Above the bar hung a massive flat screen television. A few patrons sat there, nursing drinks and playing Keno.

"Can I help you?" A man's voice drew their attention.

He was older, well into his sixties, with ruddy skin partially concealed by a patchy beard. He eyed them, his expression not quite friendly.

"Yes, sir," Kyra said. "We'd like to book two rooms, please."

"Do you have a reservation?"

"No." Chase made a show of looking around the almost empty room. "Do we need one?"

The man grunted and waved his hand, beckoning them. "This way."

They followed him to a desk set up in the corner. He pulled down a binder, flipped through the pages, and picked up the ballpoint pen tied to the desk with a piece of string. "How many nights?"

"Keep it open," Chase said.

A muscle in the man's cheek twitched, and he looked up. Chase pulled his hat off and shook out his hair. The man looked at Kyra, and she raised her chin under his inspection.

"It's one hundred twenty a night. Each." Kyra set her credit card down. "What's the name?"

"Hawthorn and Gibson."

The man stilled. His pen froze, the tip pressed into the register. "You're that Hawthorn? The ones from Washington?"

Chase cocked his head. He nodded.

"You know him?" Kyra asked, and the man's shrewd gaze snapped to her.

"Who are you?"

"She's my friend."

The man cleared his throat and pulled two keys off a pegboard. "Your rooms are here in the main lodge, third floor." He held them out. Chase reached for them, but the man didn't let go. "You look just like her." Chase's head jerked back. "What are you doing here?"

Kyra pulled out her phone. She found a photo of her and Tarek taken around Christmas, his arm around her waist. She was smiling at the camera, but he was smiling down at her. "We're looking for this man." She turned it so he could see. "Have you seen him?"

The man shook his head. "No, but I don't work here. I'm just filling in. You should ask Vance. He and Teresa run this place. They'll be back soon." The man released the keys and turned away.

"Hey, you knew my mom?" Chase asked, calling after him.

The man paused, and his gaze crawled over Chase. "Nah, not really," he said with a shake of his head, and walked away.

They found their rooms, one next door to the other. The furniture was rustic, the carpet patchy, and the bathroom dank and water stained, but it was warm and reasonably clean. It would suffice. Kyra pulled off her wet boots and draped her socks across the radiator to dry.

She quickly changed into dry clothes and knocked on Chase's door.

"One minute." He pulled it open as he slid on a thick sweater.

"Let's feed you and find this Vance and Teresa, or someone who's seen Tarek or knows Benny."

"Let's do it."

They stopped at the hotel's bar and asked the woman for dining recommendations.

"There are a few places in town, but with the storm, everything will close up early." The woman wiped her hands on a bar towel and pulled a menu off the stack near the register. "We're serving lunch. Dinner service starts at five."

"Thank you." Kyra passed Chase the menu, and he nodded. "We'll eat here."

They ordered drinks and food, and Kyra observed the people around them. Three men, at least as old as the man who'd checked them in, nursed their beers, their eyes trained on the sports channel playing on the television. They all were dressed in some sort of mountain man uniform of cargo pants, with patches at the knees, hooded sweatshirts, and thick-soled boots.

"They're snowmobilers," the woman told them as she set their drinks down. She began drying off glasses from the stack beside the sink. "The lodge is about halfway through one of the reserve's more popular trails. They stop in to warm up."

Chase donned his playboy mask and smiled. "My name's Chase. Chase Hawthorn. What's yours?"

The bartender stopped drying and assessed him. "Lainey."

"It's a pleasure to meet you, Lainey. How long have you lived in Errol?"

Lainey huffed a wry laugh and waved the towel between her and Chase. "Does this work wherever you all are from?" she asked Kyra.

Kyra smothered a laugh. "Almost every time, actually."

"Hey!" Chase protested.

"I'm Kyra Gibson. We're in town looking for someone and read that we could hire a guide here."

"A hiker?"

"No." Kyra brought up the photograph on her phone and handed it to Lainey. "His name is Tarek Collins. He'd driven up here a few days ago. He would have been asking questions about the Gillman or Perez family."

Lainey handed Kyra her phone and took a step back. She shrugged. "I haven't seen him."

"And hiring a guide?"

"Wouldn't know anything about that. Ask the owners." Before Kyra could ask her another question, Lainey disappeared into the kitchen.

"What was that?" Chase asked, keeping his voice low. "She couldn't give you your phone back fast enough."

"She was lying about something, seeing Tarek or knowing about Benny's family."

Lainey didn't reappear. Instead, a kid in his mid-teens brought out their food.

"Excuse me," she said to the busboy. "Do you know when Vance and Teresa are returning?"

"I saw Vance a few minutes ago. He was in his office. I can get him?"

Kyra handed him ten dollars. "Yes, please. Thank you."

A few minutes later, a burly man strolled into the great room and let himself behind the bar. His gaze skimmed over the snowmobilers with little interest, but halted on her and Chase. He came to stand in front of them, his thick arms crossed over his flannel-clad chest.

"You asked for me?"

"Mr. Vance?" Kyra asked.

"Just Vance."

"Uh, yes. Thank you. We're looking for someone. His name is Tarek Collins. He would have come into town a few days ago. He may have come by here?" Kyra held her phone out. Vance blinked at the photo of her and Tarek. His mouth pulled down at the corner.

"Vance, honey?" a woman's voice carried through the room. She walked in, studying the contents of a binder. "Do we have..." Her voice trailed off when she saw Vance behind the bar.

"Mom, we have some new guests." He glared at Chase and Kyra.

Chase stood, and his mouth slid up into his most charming smile. He held out his hand. "Hi, I'm..." But Teresa's eyes had gone round, and she clasped the binder to her chest.

"Penny's boy." It came out on her breath. Her eyes lit up.

"You know him?" Vance demanded.

"I'd recognize him anywhere, even if you weren't always on TMZ." She waved a finger at Chase in mock seriousness. "You look just like her. Taller. Blonder." Her laugh was tinged with sadness. "Vance, get these nice people whatever they want." She took the seat next to them and peered at Kyra. "And is this your wife?"

"Oh no," Kyra sputtered, and Chase laughed at her obvious horror.

He gripped her shoulder. "No, Kyra's my bestie. We're actually here looking for someone. Have you seen him?"

Kyra handed Teresa her phone with the image of Tarek. Teresa studied the image. Then she shook her head. She handed Kyra her phone back. "I don't think so. Vance, do you recognize that man?"

"No," he said abruptly and turned away.

Chase shared a look with Kyra, but she shook her head, a silent request not to push. Even if Vance wasn't being truthful, they needed the owners' help. Chase's expression shifted and smoothed out. "Teresa, how do you know Margot? Er ... Penny?"

Vance set a tall beer down in front of his mother and leaned against the back counter, watchful.

"Years ago, your mom worked here. That was when my dad ran the lodge."

Kyra sucked her water down through her straw to hide her reaction. She hadn't dared to hope that the Errol Hunting Lodge was the same business where Margot worked and Adele played with Benny. She set her glass down and feigned calm. "Margot worked here when her daughter, Adele was little?"

"Mmmhmm. She often brought Adele. Childcare wasn't a thing back then. Most mothers stayed home to take care of their little ones." Teresa heaved a sigh. "Penny was this town's shining star until she wound up pregnant. Suddenly, there wasn't a nice thing that could be said about her. Narrowmindedness is all that was. My dad gave fair employment opportunities to people in all walks of life. And Penny was a hard worker."

"What about another young woman that worked here? She had a son. He was called Benny."

"What do you want with Benny?" Vance asked, his voice low and gravely.

"Hush, Vance," Teresa scolded, and nodded at Kyra.

Her mouth turned down, and she rubbed the silver cross pendant at her neck. "Mmmhmm, she died. Years ago. Right after Benny came home."

"From prison?" Chase said.

Vance stepped closer to them. "What do you know about it?"

"Enough." Chase smirked and sat back in his chair. He raised a hand and began ticking off facts on his fingers. "We know he's been calling himself Perez for a while, but before that, his name was Gillman. We know that Margot, *Penny*, helped him with his legal troubles, and she may have helped him get a job in DC. We know Penny assumed Tobias's responsibility on a land lease on Martha's Vineyard, and we know Penny and Benny's mom, Elodie were close friends." Chase smacked his lips. "That would mean Benny and I are almost like cousins." He was laying it on a little thick, but Teresa didn't seem to mind. Her expression turned contemplative.

Vance frowned. "Benny's mother's name was Elizabeth."

Kyra found the photograph of Elodie at Tobias Gillman's dinner party. She pointed to her phone screen. "Is that her?"

"Let me see." Kyra handed Teresa the phone. Her eyebrows slanted. "Yes, that's her and Toby. She's so young in this picture."

"Do you remember when she moved here?" Kyra asked, taking her phone back.

Teresa's mouth twisted as she thought. "Vance hadn't been born yet."

"Thirty-eight years ago," Vance said.

"That's right." Teresa nodded. "It was the year Benny was born. Vance is two years and a day younger than Benny. I forgot about that. When the boys were children, we had parties here at the lodge for them both."

"Like Mom said though, his mom's dead, and Benny doesn't come into the lodge. He rarely comes back to Errol at all." Vance's shrug was stilted. "I don't know what you're talking about with your mom and a lease. Old Tobias bought that farmstead near Lake Umbagog ages ago and after he died, Elizabeth paid it off."

"Farmstead? Lake Umbagog?" Kyra repeated.

"It's the Gillman's house in the woods. Benny lets it for hunters and vacationers," Teresa explained.

"Where is it?" Kyra pulled up the map on her phone.

"Up the highway. It's at the beginning of the state park. There are signs. You really can't miss it."

Kyra tilted the phone so Chase could see. "We need to go."

"Now hold on," Vance interjected at the same time Teresa asked, "What's this about? What do you want with Elizabeth and Benny?"

Kyra bit her lip, debating how much to tell them, but Chase spoke. "Tobias Gillman probably raped and kidnapped the girl you knew as Elizabeth. Her real name was Elodie Edwards. She's been missing for thirty-nine years, presumed to be dead."

The color drained from Teresa's face. She blinked, a slow measured movement, before looking down at her hands clasped tightly in her lap.

"You aren't surprised?" Kyra said, peering at Teresa.

"I suppose I'm not," she said sadly. "We all knew that there was something off with that family. Elizabeth was such a quiet, shy girl. She didn't have many friends. Tobias was so much older than her and protective. Controlling. He would monitor who she spent time with, where she would go. She was often alone with Benny at their house in the woods." She shook her head. "Someone probably should have said something, tried to help, but Elizabeth never said a word against Tobias. And after he died, she stayed on at that old farmstead, took a new job. She apprenticed at Larry's, of all places."

"Larry's?"

"He makes hunting trophies."

Kyra turned to Chase, confused. He made a face. "Taxidermist."

*Yuck.* Kyra suppressed a shudder.

"How did she die?" Chase asked.

Teresa's mouth pulled down on the side, but it was Vance who answered. "She fell outside. No one was home, and she was found a few days later when Larry sent someone to check on her after she didn't show up for work. She died of exposure."

Kyra swallowed, and she reached for Chase's hand. "When was that?"

"Five years ago," Teresa answered. "So sad."

A puzzle piece slid into place and Kyra squeezed Chase's fingers. Benny was released from prison five years ago. His name changed. His record sealed. Five years ago, right when he would have learned about the transfer of the lease to Margot Hawthorn and losing a property worth millions of dollars. Her grip tightened.

"Chase, he wants the property back," she whispered. Chase let out a long breath through pursed lips. "Has Benny been back to town recently?" she asked Teresa.

"No," Vance snapped.

"I read online that we can hire a guide through your hotel," Chase said, catching on. "I'd like to make those arrangements."

"You want a guide? Now?" Vance pressed his lips together. "We're due for a blizzard."

"Yes. Right away."

"Vance can..."

"No. I'm not going out there. I don't have a death wish, but I'll loan you my truck." His lips stretched, a smug, twisted turn of his mouth. "But it'll cost you."

Kyra had no doubt it would.

# Chapter Forty

"ARE YOU SURE you know how to drive this thing?" Kyra asked.

The truck Vance had lent them was an old, rusted-out death trap. The heat didn't work, and the taillights were smashed. It stank of motor oil, sweat, and old coffee. It'd cost them five hundred dollars. Cash. But the closest car rental was more than an hour away, and no one would agree to deliver them a car during a blizzard. But now that she was inside the sorry excuse for a vehicle, Kyra thought they might have been safer walking.

"The concepts are the same. Move steering wheel, tires turn." The gears ground together as he tried to find second on the finnicky transmission.

"But can you drive stick?"

"Of course," he said, offended.

She couldn't help teasing him further. "Just remember, soft release on the clutch to change gears."

He muttered something about soft releasing her right off a cliff and pulled down the lodge's drive. The truck bounced over the snowy ruts and Kyra clutched the grab bar above the window to keep from being thrown from her seat.

"Teresa said it was six miles up, with a turnoff on the

right."

It'd begun snowing. Snowflakes the size of pinheads fell with surprising speed. In the short time it'd taken for them to get the truck warmed up, the snow had accumulated, and a thin layer covered the landscape.

The truck rumbled onto the highway; the backend sliding out on the slick pavement.

"Shit." Chase's knuckles paled as he gripped the steering wheel, manhandling it back under control. "The visibility is already terrible. Watch for the turnoff."

They crept up the highway, going well below the speed limit. The snow billowed toward them, creating near whiteout conditions, and from what Teresa had told them, the storm was going to get much, much worse. This wasn't safe. A sane person would turn back and wait for the weather to clear, but she couldn't make herself recommend it. Every cell in her body told her they needed to go to that farmstead. She leaned forward, gripping the dust-sticky dashboard, mentally urging the truck forward. She squinted against the strange white glare of the snow.

"I can barely see the road," Chase said through clenched teeth. "What does the GPS say?"

Kyra held her phone up. "Three miles." Chase shifted, and the car clanked into a higher gear. The rumbling settled into a keening whine.

Kyra kept one eye on the increasingly snow-covered road, and another on her phone. Their progress was deceiving. The wind lashed the truck, and the horizontal streaks of snow made her feel like she was hurtling at light-refracting speeds, but the speedometer, if it could it be trusted, read eighteen miles per hour.

"Slow down. We should be near the road." Kyra squinted against the glare. "There!" She pointed to a break in the trees, just wide enough for a car or truck. Chase pulled over and Kyra hopped out.

"Wait!"

Kyra ignored him and stepped closer to the break, looking for a sign or plaque, anything that named the road to Lake Umbagog. She used her boot to move the snow aside. Underneath was pavement.

"It's a road!" she called back. She walked further, cursing as the snow slipped underneath her collar and dribbled down her neck.

Just as she approached the tree line, she noticed the snow-covered bump about four feet high and just as wide to the right of the road. She wiped snow off the top, clearing it away from a giant slab of granite. She wiped the front, feeling the indentations of carvings even through her thick gloves. In three firm swipes, she cleared it.

LAKE UMBAGOG.

Kyra rushed back to the truck where an irritated Chase glared at her. "The actual fuck, Kyra! You don't go running into a fucking blizzard!"

"This is it," she said, jumping onto the seat and rubbing her hands together. The car wasn't much warmer than outside. "That way."

Chase huffed but forced the truck into gear and it lurched forward into the forest. The trees offered them some protection from the wind and snow, and their visibility improved. Even uncleared, the road was visible thanks to the higher drifts on the sides. The road curved and snaked deeper into the woods. Kyra glanced behind them. The view was identical forward and back, dark, colorless trees, stark against the white ground, and stormy sky. Her chest tightened, the feeling of being enclosed prickled her skin. Her mouth went dry. She squeezed her eyes shut and counted down from ten. Again.

*Six, five, four…*

"How much farther?" Chase asked.

"I don't know. Teresa said that it's the first driveway."

Chase slowed down to a crawl and leaned forward. Their breath steamed up the windows and his hand fiddled with the controls on the console.

"Find the defroster?"

Kyra found the switch. The icon was mostly rubbed off. She turned it, and there was a soft whir of a fan, and then … nothing.

"Seriously? How did this piece of shit pass inspection?"

Though she was loath to do it, Kyra opened her window, letting in the frigid air. The steam and condensation that had built up on the glass dissipated. Chase cursed again and rolled his window down a crack, because it could go no further.

The temperature in the car dropped to unbearable. The wind ripped into Kyra's cheeks like shards of glass. She stuffed her hands under her thighs and pulled the hood of her jacket tight around her face.

"Do you see…"

"Chase! There. Is that a fence?"

Snow clung to the tops and posts of a dilapidated split-rail fence. It was missing rails, and in some places, the entire section.

Chase pulled to a stop at a break. "Think it's through there?"

Kyra nodded. She wasn't sure what she was looking for, Tarek's car? Tarek? Benny?

"Go," she urged, and he turned onto the driveway.

Unlike the country road, the drive had been cleared and there were tire marks in the fresh snow. Chase crept forward. At the reduced speed, the visibility improved.

The driveway was long and winding. Kyra worried they'd made a mistake, but just as she was about to suggest they turn around, it widened, and the farmstead came into view. A house sat in the clearing. The driveway snaked around back.

"What now?" Chase asked. The truck came to a shuddering halt.

The big house was dark. Footprints crossed the front yard, to and from a lean-to, filled with firewood. Kyra looked up at the roofline, but she couldn't see or smell smoke.

"Knock?" She didn't know what other options they had. It wasn't like they could hide the truck. Their tracks in the snow would reveal their presence.

"Knock? He's probably a killer, Kyra. He *is* a killer."

"I know, but he doesn't know we know that. If we were just going to stand in his driveway, why bother coming?"

Chase's gaze swept the property. "Kyra," he warned.

"Please, I need to know if Tarek's been here."

Chase looked like he was going to argue with her. Instead, his shoulders sagged, then straightened. "Okay. Fine." Chase pulled his hat lower over his forehead.

The front yard was littered with snow-covered machinery, rusted and falling apart. She could just make out the metal lines of an old-fashioned plow. Icicles hung from the steel frame. The house was set back from the driveway and was in a serious state of neglect. It once might have been painted a pretty shade of blue, but now it was mostly a faded and grimy gray. The white trim around the windows and door was cracked and peeled. The door itself didn't match at all. It was stained and warped with layers of chipped paint. It might have been a salvaged replacement.

They made their way to the front door, and Kyra rang the bell. It chimed through the house. They waited. Nothing. She tried again, ringing it twice.

"No one's home," she whispered and opened what was left of the shredded screen door. She tried the doorknob. It was locked.

Kyra moved to the window. She cupped her gloved hands around her eyes and peered inside. There were four folding chairs around an upside-down milk crate set up like a makeshift table. Table lamps also sat on the floor, their chords snaking across the naked wood floors.

She angled her body so she could peek into the hallway. It was dark.

"It's empty." Her breath condensed on the glass.

"Here, let me try." Kyra stepped aside and Chase pushed at the top of the window casing. It gave the tiniest bit. With a grunt, he pushed harder, and the window inched open enough to get his fingers through and push it up. He turned to her with a gleam in his eyes. "Wait here."

"What? No!"

But Chase had already hoisted himself over the window-sill and disappeared inside.

"Chase!"

Nothing.

Kyra shifted her weight from foot-to-foot. Her breaths came out in visible puffs. The front door opened, squeaking on its hinges. Chase flashed a triumphant grin that was quickly replaced by disgust. "Ugh, you'd really have to love shooting things to want to stay in this dump. Come on."

When he closed the door behind her, she whirled on him. "You didn't even want to knock on the fucking door!"

He shrugged. "A penny, a pound. We're here. Let's find out what we're risking life and limb to find out."

Kyra seethed. *I'm gonna kill him.*

The house didn't have a traditional foyer. Rather, two rooms sat on opposite sides of the entryway. Chase had climbed through the window and into the room to the right. Across the hall was another room, a sort of parlor, that was being used for storage. Among the junk, Kyra spotted a rusty bicycle frame, golf equipment, and an old kayak that had seen better days.

She tugged on Chase's sleeve. They moved farther down the hall, peeking their heads through each doorway. Like the two front rooms, the rest of the house was made up of small, nearly identical spaces, their use designated by the rooms' contents. They found a dining room, a living room, a tiny bathroom under the stairs. At the end of the hall, there was a landing with a doorway leading to the kitchen, upstairs, and another door, this one closed.

Chase motioned to try upstairs. Kyra's boots were quiet on the ancient carpet that covered the treads. In the back of her mind, she remembered joking with Tarek about sneaking onto a killer's boat. *The irony.* If he knew what they were doing, he'd be furious. At the top, there were three bedrooms and another bathroom.

Two bedrooms were on the smaller side and were being used for storage. Only the largest bedroom was being used as such, with a double bed between two bedside tables and a dresser pushed against the wall. Unlike the furniture in the rest of the house, the pieces in here didn't appear old or broken. The pine furniture sat close to the ground, like the Scandinavian assemble-at-home stuff popular with college kids. A duffel bag lay open on the floor, its contents over-flowing. She toed the pile of clothes. Her breath caught when she revealed a pair of jeans crusted over with a rust-brown substance. She felt Chase at her shoulder.

"Is that?"

"I think so." Her voice shook. She snapped pictures, knowing in her heart she was photographing clothes covered in blood. Was it Marjorie's? Kelsey's? Someone else's?

Chase did a sweep of the room, checked the closet.

"Anything in the bedside tables?" he asked.

Kyra searched. "No."

They returned downstairs, and Kyra tried the door, the only one in the house they'd come across that was closed. It opened to reveal a staircase down. "It's a cellar." She took a step forward, but Chase grabbed her arm and held her back.

He flicked the switch on the wall and a single bulb at the

bottom flickered on. "Me first." Kyra followed him down.

The basement was unfinished. It was musty, the field-stone walls and dirt floors doing little against the damp.

"Kyra?" Chase's voice sounded strange. He was on the other side of the stairs, in front of a giant armoire. Beside it, in an unceremonious pile, were carcasses.

"The hell?" She stepped closer. No, not carcasses. Trophies. Heads mostly. Kyra recognized deer, boar, pheasant.

"Not that," Chase said, and Kyra pulled her eyes away from the macabre pile. "That." He pointed to the large glass front cabinet. An old-fashioned key sat in the lock, a fraying tassel hanging from its bow.

Kyra stepped closer to the gun case. It had space for eight rifles and five hung in their slots. There was also a rack with spaces for handguns, but only two were being used. Kyra knew nothing about guns and didn't know what she was looking at. She snapped more pictures.

Chase's expression darkened when he pulled open the drawer. It was full of boxes of ammunition. Another drawer held knives with long, jagged blades.

"Hunting equipment?" she asked.

"And some." He pointed to one of the guns. "That's an assault rifle. And that." He pointed to the black handgun. "Looks a lot like what the Secret Service carry. You don't use that type of weaponry to hunt. Not wildlife, anyway."

A shiver ran down Kyra's spine. "You know about guns?"

"A little. I've been dragged on hunting trips with my father and other government douche bags." He checked the case was locked, and pocketed the key. "Upstairs. We need to get out of here."

Kyra went first, listening at the top, but the house was still quiet.

"I want to check the kitchen," she whispered. It was the only place they hadn't searched.

It was shabby and dated. The Formica counters were chipped and dingy and the slab door cabinets no longer hung level. The sink was one of those farm basin styles that jutted out over the lower cabinets and had a built-in drying rack. Above the sink was a big picture window covered in plastic wrap. Something dark against the gray sky caught her eye. She crept forward and peered outside.

Benny's backyard, like the front, was in desperate need of maintenance. A broken rail fence lined the perimeter of the property and beyond was a large clearing that Kyra assumed at one point had been fields. Toward the back of the yard, near a dilapidated barn, were two objects. One was a fair bit taller than the other, and both were covered in snow, but in places where the snow had fallen away, bright blue plastic tarping was visible. Thick lengths of rope tied to stakes kept the tarps in place. Kyra worried her bottom lip. She could make out the snowed over trail leading to and from the barn, but everywhere else the snow was flat, unbothered. Except near the tarped objects. The snow there was, disturbed, wavy and bumpy in the shadows of the snow-covered mounds.

"What is that?" she asked, mostly to herself.

"Kay?"

But she was already moving to the back door, pushing it open. With no concern for leaving her tracks in the snow, Kyra crossed the yard. The snow was deep, nearly up to her knees, except where it dipped down, packed in deep parallel tracks behind each mound, one set narrower than the other. *Cars.*

Kyra stooped next to the closer one. She lifted the tarp up as far as it would allow and peeked underneath. Black, scratched up bumper and a bumper sticker someone had tried to rip off. It was pink and black between the tears in the paper. Her heart beat in her throat.

"Chase!"

She fumbled, pulling the tarp farther away, causing the snow to loosen and fall around her. The license plate had been removed, leaving just the blank, black space and the rusty holes where the bolts had been. Above that was the Toyota emblem. It was Marjorie's car. Kyra'd bet her life on it.

"Oh, fuck." Chase's voice.

She wasn't listening.

She didn't even think.

Kyra ran, stumbling to the second car. She yanked on the knot holding the tarp down. She yanked again and again, until it gave, and the rope slithered through the stake, falling to the ground. The wind caught the tarp, and it flew back with a *pfft*, raining snow down on them, and revealing a battered, hunter green Jeep Cherokee.

# Chapter Forty-One

TIME STOPPED. KYRA felt her blood pulsing through her veins, heard her heart's erratic beat in her ears. Her brain struggled to process what she was seeing. Chase called her name, but it was so far away. She blinked and her eyes met his too wide ones. His mouth was set in a grim line. He was yanking ineffectively on the driver's side door, cupping his face to peer in the windows.

Tarek was here. *Is* here. There was no other explanation. He wasn't in the main house. They'd have found him. Unless he was … *No.* She wouldn't let herself think that. She squeezed her eyes shut.

She forced her eyes open, took a deep breath. Her gaze alighted on the barn. It was massive, much bigger than it appeared from the kitchen window. And it was hidden from the front of the property, from the street. Unless you knew about it, you'd never know it was there.

"The barn." It came out like a wheeze.

Chase's gaze snapped back to hers. His eyes impossibly went wider, and he bolted for the doors.

Kyra ran after him. The deep snow didn't slow Chase, but Kyra struggled. Her toe caught on something hidden below the drifts. She stumbled. She fell.

"Gah!" she hissed as her palm hit something hard and sharp. A searing pain shot up her arm. She reared back, falling in the snow, clutching her hand to her chest. Hot blood splattered red on white, leaving streaks as it melted and sank. "Shit."

"What happened?" Chase crouched beside her and gently tugged on her hand. He frowned and prodded the slice in her glove with his finger.

"Ow!" She yanked her hand, but he didn't let go.

"Are you hurt anywhere else?"

"No."

Chase helped her up. He brushed away the snow caked to her knees, her back. She felt the icy burn where it seeped inside her boot. He sucked in a deep breath and wrapped his hand around her elbow. "Come on."

Kyra let him guide her to the front of the barn, out of sight of the house.

"Call 911," Kyra said at the same time Chase said, "We should go back. Get help."

"I'm not leaving until we find him."

Sighing, he pulled out his phone and dialed.

"911. What's your emergency?"

"I'm at the Gillman farmstead near Umbagog Lake. There's been an accident."

"What kind of accident?"

"A missing person. We've located his car. We need help finding him."

Kyra shook her uninjured hand at him. "No, lie! Say there's been gunfire. Tell them it's life or death."

Emergency response prioritized their cases. If they didn't

think it was urgent, they wouldn't come right away.

"Yes sir. We will send a patrol car. Please remain on the premises." The call clicked off.

Chase gave her a helpless look and ran his hand over his head. "Shit," he said, staring at her chest where she clutched her hand. She hadn't realized how much she was bleeding. It'd pooled in the palm of her glove and was dripping between her fingers, and down the front of her new coat, across the toes of her boots, and on the snow, a ghoulish splatter painting.

She shook her head, already knowing what he was going to say. "I'm not leaving without him."

"Yeah. Alright. Let's search the barn. Keep it above your heart." He motioned to her hand.

Snow was piled high in front of the barn's heavy, wood doors, where it'd slid off the roof.

Chase reached over and gripped the metal handle. He pushed. Nothing. It didn't budge, but the latch depressed.

"Try pulling it?"

The door inched open and stopped, stuck, lodged against the deep drifts. Chase cursed and dropped to his knees. He began digging out the door with his hands. Kyra did the same. Holding her cut hand against her body, she scooped snow, shoveling it away. As she dug deeper, the snow became impacted, making it more difficult to move, and soon her breathing labored with the effort. Her knees, toes, and fingers stung from the cold. Eventually, they had enough clearance for the door to crack open, giving them just enough room to squeeze through.

They ducked inside. Chase pulled the door closed behind

him, dumping them into near darkness.

"Hold on," he muttered. A beam of weak light emitted from his phone. He shined it around the space. The barn was old, but in better shape than the house, and it was a little warmer than outside.

Metal racks of shelves were lined up against the wall and held all manner of bric-à-brac. A large industrial sink stood in the center of the room. Hoses ran along the floor.

"We should try Briscoe at Greyscale," she said at the same time Chase demanded, "Let me see your hand."

"But," Kyra protested.

Chase cut her off. "You're bleeding everywhere." He pointed to the floor, to the splotches of wet blood, bright red on the cement floors. She held her hand out for him to inspect. He pulled it closer and squinted.

"Fuck, I need more light." He swung the beam up and down the shelves. He stopped on an LED lantern sitting on a shelf with other outdoor equipment. "Nice."

He retrieved it and set it on a metal table beside the sink. He turned it on. Harsh blue-toned light illuminated the space. Kyra squinted against the brightness. He motioned for her to come closer. Chase hunched over her hand and gently peeled the glove away. Kyra tried not to react, but with each tug, pain lanced through her hand.

"Fucking hell."

"What?" she asked, afraid to look. When she did, she blinked at the jagged slice across her palm, the skin flapping over. "Oh." It came out feeble and weak. She grimaced and swallowed against a bout of dizziness.

Chase gripped her chin, forcing her to look into his eyes.

"Do not pass out on me."

"No, it's not that." She shook her head. Blood didn't bother her. Jagged chunks of skin, though ... Her stomach twisted and her mouth filled with saliva. She bit her lip. Hard.

"This needs stitches and I hope you're up to date on your tetanus vaccine."

"My what?"

"We need to wrap it. And you need to go to the hospital." Chase picked up the lantern and moved closer to the shelves.

"Call Greyscale."

"Fucking hell, Kyra!"

But she refused to back down. "Do it, Chase."

"Fine, give me your phone." He snatched it from her and dialed. She told him Tarek's security number, and he dialed in the code. A smile, or a shade of one, flittered across his lips and disappeared.

"What?"

"The code. It spells WALTER." He pressed the phone to his ear. "I need to speak with Briscoe. It's an emergency." He scowled. "They're transferring me. Dammit. Voicemail." In a few sentences Chase explained their circumstances, that Tarek was likely on the property, and they needed immediate assistance. He gave the address. "And Kyra's torn her hand open and refuses to go to the ER." He hung up and slipped the phone into her pocket. "Happy?"

"Yes. No. Why did you say that?"

"Because it's true. Now we need something to wrap your hand with before you bleed out and die on me." Chase took the lantern and started hunting through the shelves. "Stay there and keep it elevated, for fuck's sake."

She raised her hand above her heart, over the sink. Her blood hit the metal with a soft *ting*.

Chase plucked a jar off the shelf and held it up. He turned it so Kyra could see. "Oh, my god."

"No, they're fake." He set it beside her on the worktable. It was full of eyeballs, or half eyeballs, just concave lenses with dark brown irises around elliptical pupils. "Deer, I think." Chase opened a chest. "Jesus."

"What?"

"Knives, dozens of them, of all different ... it's like a torture kit." He pulled out a blade. The silvery surgical steel glinted in the lantern's light. He pocketed it and opened the next chest. "This one is needles."

"Chase, what is all this stuff?" She felt like she was in a horror movie.

"I'd guess it's Elodie's taxidermy workshop."

Chase followed the hose from the back of the sink to the wall and turned the knob. With a groan, and a flush, it plumped with water. He unzipped his coat.

"What are you doing?"

"We need to stop the bleeding." Kyra watched him in dismay as he threw his coat on the table, followed by his sweater. He yanked off the t-shirt he was wearing underneath and put his sweater back on. "We'll clean away as much blood as we can." He turned on the water and guided her hand under the stream.

It *stung*. Kyra hissed and tried to yank her hand away, but he held it steady. The water, barely above freezing, numbed away the bite. She watched in morbid fascination as the water flushed the wound, creating rivulets of diluted blood. He pried back the flap of skin and examined the gash. The sound in his throat told her everything she needed to know. It wasn't good. She hiccupped when she saw what she thought might be the white of bone.

"Don't." Chase angled his body so she couldn't see and, using the scalpel, sliced his t-shirt into strips.

"I can do it."

Chase sighed through his nose. He set the knife down and turned off the water. With a gentleness that surprised her, he dabbed the wound dry, and wrapped her hand, forcing the loose skin down. As he wrapped, the white cotton turned red. Chase stopped his administrations, and his gaze met hers. "I have to make it tight to staunch the blood flow. It's going to hurt."

Kyra braced herself. He wound the strips around her hand, and the burning sensation intensified before subsiding to a throbbing she felt in the tips of her fingers. He tied off the ends.

"How do you know how to do this?"

"Boat captain, remember?"

"Thank you," she whispered and watched as he washed his hands under the tap and pulled on his coat.

"Ready?"

Chase grabbed the lantern. Kyra walked back to the shelving units. She could see through them, to dark space beyond. The shelves weren't along the walls at all. They were standing in the middle of the barn, dividing the space into small rooms and narrow aisles.

Chase lifted the light, and Kyra yelped. Dozens of eyes reflected light back, predators staring down their prey from the floor, the shelves. She stepped back into Chase's chest and he steadied her.

"They're stuffed," he said. His voice shook. He was as freaked out as she was.

Kyra moved closer. The shelves were full of animals in various stages of being preserved. Nausea roiled through her, and she clasped her damaged palm to her mouth. "Ow!"

"This is so fucking creepy."

"*Creepy* isn't strong enough," she replied. "This is grotesque." But she couldn't tear her gaze away from the creatures.

"Kyra?" Chase croaked.

"What is it?" She turned around.

He'd lowered the light and was staring at a dark shelf. He licked his lips, swallowed. "You said Kelsey's prosthetic leg was missing, right?"

"Yeah, it wasn't at the summer camp. Why?" She inched forward.

"Pretty sure I found it." He pointed to a bundle of dirty towels on the shelf. The metal of the pylon reflected the lantern light. A ragged chunk of flesh-colored plastic was all that remained of the foot. She took a picture and let Chase tug her away.

They walked up and down the aisles, scanning the shelves, the floor.

"I don't think he's here." She was so relieved. He must have gotten away. Maybe he was in town.

They rounded a corner into another makeshift room,

and Chase raised the lantern. They saw it at the same time. In a darkened corner, on the floor, a mess of cloth, a head of dark hair.

"Tarek."

# Chapter Forty-Two

KYRA SPRINTED ACROSS the room. Her knees cracked when they hit the concrete.

"Tarek?" Her voice broke. He was prone on his back, his eyes shut, his wrists and ankles bound with zip ties.

"Kyra." Chase kneeled beside her.

Kyra pressed a hand to Tarek's cheek. It was cold to the touch. Too cold. And clammy. She jerked back.

"Tarek." Her eyes brimmed with tears.

*No. He wasn't. He couldn't be.* One drop fell, sliding down her cheek.

"Kyra."

"Tarek, wake up." She gripped his shoulder, and he moaned. It was the softest sound. "He's alive." Her grip tightened, and she froze. Fear ensnared her heart. His coat was wet and heavy. Something viscous and dark clung to her fingers when she pulled her hand away.

"He's hurt." She yanked the zipper down, exposing his shirt, and pulled at the fabric, peeling it away from his skin.

Kyra bit back a sob. She barely registered Chase's low curse as he raised the light. She couldn't take her eyes off the gaping hole amidst the bloodied mess of Tarek's chest, just below his clavicle. The skin was shredded and splayed, leaving a ragged, gory pit. It oozed blood so dark it was almost black, dribbling in thick, slow-moving streams. Her heart leaped into her throat, and she gagged. *I'm kneeling in it.* The sound she made was guttural, a half sob, half scream. The floor was a pool of blood.

"Oh, fuck!" Chase jumped back, dropping the lantern. "Shit. Shit. Shit." He pushed his hands into his hair, streaking it with blood. His jeans were stained with it. "Shit. Shit."

Kyra swallowed and pressed her bloody hands against her chest to keep them from shaking.

She stood and tore off her jacket, not caring that it fell to the floor. "We have to stop the bleeding." She pulled her sweatshirt over her head and gripped it tightly. The searing pain in her hand grounded her. Her action seemed to snap Chase out of his own panic.

"Yeah, okay." Chase's voice trembled, but he helped her shift Tarek onto his side and ease his ruined coat and shirt away from the wound.

Kyra knew nothing about ballistics, but she'd seen horror movies. She'd seen gunshot wounds on dead bodies. But this, the absolute obliteration of skin and tissue and bone as the lead tore through him … this. This she wasn't prepared for. There was a strangled sound.

"Kay."

She realized it'd come from her.

She shook her head. "I'm okay." As gently as she could, she wrapped the sweatshirt around Tarek's chest. She pulled his ruined clothes closed and pressed down to staunch the flow.

"Call 911 again." But Chase was already on the phone.

His tone was harsh, snapping at the dispatcher.

She ran her fingers down Tarek's cheek. He didn't stir. "Please don't die," she whispered. "Please." She moved her hand to wipe away the tears that stung her cheeks and hiccupped when she saw the streaks of blood she'd left on Tarek's skin.

"Fuck this." Chase yanked his hat on. "There's some highway thing. An accident or the snow ... I don't fucking know. The dispatcher said it'll take at least an hour. If we can move him, we should move him."

"What?" Kyra blinked at Chase. *Emergency services aren't coming?* Kyra thought about where they were. The middle of nowhere.

"I'm going to get the car. We'll take him to the nearest hospital."

"Wait, Chase." She wanted to tell him to be safe, but he was already gone.

# Chapter Forty-Three

KYRA TRIED TO keep even pressure on Tarek's wound. She didn't think it was working. The sweatshirt was already heavy with blood. He'd lost so much. She didn't know how long he'd been here, slowly bleeding to death. Hot rage helped to temper her terror.

"You're not dying," she snapped at him.

She pressed her fingers to his pulse point. His heartbeat was barely a flutter, soft and timid, but it was there. She'd hold on to it if it killed her.

She pulled her phone from her pocket and searched for the nearest hospital. Zooming out on the map, her heart sank lower and lower. The closest one was more than twenty miles away to the northwest. Even without a blizzard, it'd take too long. Far too long. And with the storm...

Kyra shook her head and squeezed her eyes closed. "Please, Tar. *Please.*" She fought against the despair that had her heart in its claws.

A dim light behind the shelves flickered, and Kyra froze.

"What the fuck do you want, Benny?" Chase's voice sliced through the quiet of the barn.

"Shut up," another man snarled.

Kyra inhaled, but she couldn't get air.

"Don't fucking touch me!" Chase yelled.

*Shit*, she mouthed. Kyra pocketed her phone and yanked on her jacket. She ran her hand over Tarek's blood matted hair. She didn't want to leave him, but if she was caught, they'd all be screwed.

Quieter than any mouse, cat, or ghost, she crawled away. She tucked herself into a shadowy corner, protected from the discarded lantern's fractured light. She climbed onto the low shelf and hid next to a half-finished deer. This close to it she could smell the chemicals, the fugue of decomposition. Kyra held her breath.

Boots stomped on the concrete as the men moved closer. They came around the shelves and into view. Chase walked in front; his hands raised at his sides. Benny aimed a rifle at him, the big, black one Chase said wasn't used for hunting animals.

Chase turned, and Kyra could see the fury burning in his eyes.

Benny glanced around and his eyebrows flattened out. "You came for him? The cop?" Benny sneered. "Not worth it, if you ask me. Just another piece of human trash. And you're too late. He's dead." He kicked Tarek's boot.

Kyra bit back a scream. Her fingernails bit into her palms and she felt hot blood seep from the bandage on her hand.

"What do you want?" Chase asked again, each word measured.

Benny spread his stance, straightened his spine. "I want a favor."

Surprise slackened Chase's features, but he recovered quickly. "Not the best way to ask for a favor." He nodded to the barrel still pointed at his chest.

"Your bitch mother swindled me out of my inheritance. I want it back. I want the deed back, or I want her to pay for the land she stole from me."

"What are you talking about?" Chase said, sounding bored.

"The lease!" Benny snarled. "For the summer camp! My father paid the rent every year for thirty-seven years! He scrimped and saved and every penny went to that fucking lease. It was supposed to be mine. But then my stupid mother went to her *old friend*, and she gave it up in exchange for a sealed record and a new name. I could have bought a new name with the money from that land! It's worth millions."

"Okay," Chase said, lowering his hands a fraction. "I don't know what this has to do with me."

"You don't think I've been trying to get that lease back since my mother told me she gave it away? Since she told me that Penny *saved* us from having to pay it?" His voice dripped with scorn and menace. "That bitch won't take my calls." Benny flipped the safety on the rifle. "But she'll listen to me now."

"Okay, Benny," Chase said, his tone cajoling. "You can have the summer camp back. Just lower the gun."

Kyra looked around for anything she could wield as a weapon.

Benny hitched the rifle higher. "Damn straight, I'm getting it back. Those girls' deaths will ruin that stupid theater project. That land won't be good for anything but development. Penny will have to give it back to me. It's mine," he growled.

Chase raised his hands higher. "Hey now. Mom won't listen if I'm dead. You want me to call her? I can do it right now. You let me go, I'll call her, and she'll take care of this whole thing."

"I know. That's exactly what you're going to do. But first you're going to help me get rid of that." He jerked his chin toward Tarek. "Ground's too frozen to bury him. And it's too dangerous to let the animals get to him. Pieces always end up scattered and found."

Color leeched from Chase's face. He shook his head. "I don't..."

"Dump him in the lake." Benny grinned. "We'll weigh him down, slip him under the ice. Snow will cover it up, the ice will refreeze." He raised his fist and slowly released his fingers. "Poof. Gone."

Kyra stuffed her fist in her mouth to keep from making a sound.

Chase shook his head. "No. I'm not..."

Benny lifted the rifle to his shoulder. "It's not a one-person job. You're helping me or I'll shoot you right here. If I'm going down, what do I have to lose?"

Kyra's hand curled around the rough, bony beam of a deer's antler. With each breath, her body shook. It was a miracle Benny couldn't hear her.

Oh, so carefully, Kyra brought the antler to her chest. Her body clenched as she pulled it from the pile. But nothing moved, and she blew out a slow breath.

Benny looked down at Tarek and grinned, a malignant stretching of his features and his eyes gleamed with malice.

He laughed, and shivers skittered across Kyra's skin, making her hair stand on end.

"It's good luck you came tonight. The temperature is going to drop. It'll be too hard to cut the ice tomorrow. We'll do this now."

Chase was shaking his head.

*Just agree, dammit.* She didn't know what she'd do if Benny shot him. She couldn't save them both.

"Pick him up. There's a sled in the front. We'll drag him out, cut the ice, and then you can call dear old mom to save you by giving me my land back. Penny'll do that for you, won't she? She won't do her own son like she did her best friend, will she? She acted like she was doing us some big fucking favor, and all the while, she was screwing us. Me."

Benny held the gun to his shoulder and aimed it at Chase's chest. "Pick him up."

Kyra saw the moment Chase gave up. His shoulders fell and his hands dropped to his sides.

His feet dragged as he crossed the room to Tarek's side. He glanced at the shelves, and Kyra shifted just enough so the shadows moved. When he found her hidden in the gloom, he started.

Kyra lowered her gaze to the antler gripped in her hand, clasped to her chest and back up, meeting his eyes. A message. *Get Benny close enough.*

Chase turned away and squatted next to Tarek. He moved him, trying to get behind him, prop him up. He struggled, changing his grip, twisting. Chase was thin, his body long and lean, but he was strong. Kyra had seen him working the farm and hoisting sails on the *Elpis*. It wasn't that he'd be able to easily lift Tarek, but he shouldn't be having this much trouble. He was acting.

Chase dropped Tarek, and he fell, lifeless to the floor. Kyra clenched her teeth, willing herself to stay silent.

"I can't move him with his hands and feet tied like that. He's dead weight."

"You've got to be fucking kidding me," Benny grunted. "Don't move." He slid the rifle under his arm and pulled a knife from his pocket. He unfolded it with his thumb and held it up. Kyra thought he might give it to Chase, but then Benny seemed to think better of it. "Step back."

Benny closed the distance between him and Tarek. Chase took a few steps back, giving Kyra the room she'd need. Benny squatted and began working the knife through Tarek's binds. The gun wobbled, and Chase's gaze found hers.

# Chapter Forty-Four

KYRA LEAPED OUT from her hiding place with a scream and drove the antler's tines into Benny's thigh. The gun hit the floor and Chase fell on it.

Benny screamed and swiped at Kyra with the knife. It sliced through the air. Her grip tightened, and she pushed. The sound she made when she drove the antler deeper into his flesh wasn't a sound she'd heard any human make.

"Back!" Chase yelled.

Kyra barely had time to scramble out of the way. He drove the barrel of the gun against Benny's face. Benny fell to the ground.

Chase shouldered the gun and aimed it at Benny. His mouth was set in a line. His entire body vibrated. Kyra's heart banged against her chest. *He's going to shoot him.*

"Chase. Don't."

He blinked. Again. He backed up and lowered the weapon; held it out in front of him like he didn't want to touch it.

"Help me," Kyra ordered.

She ran to Tarek, kneeled by his side. Her fingers pressed against his pulse point. It was so faint.

"He's still alive." She moved to push him up.

"You take this." Chase pushed the rifle at her. She fumbled it as Chase sliced through Tarek's bonds with Benny's pocket knife and hauled him up. Chase slung Tarek's uninjured arm across his shoulders and held him by the waist. Kyra ducked under Tarek's other side, bearing some of his weight.

Benny groaned. Bright red blood from the gash on his temple mixed in swirls with Tarek's dark pool.

"Go," she said, her voice, her body quaking with fear and adrenaline.

When they reached the barndoors Chase pushed on it. It stopped, jammed in the snow. Chase swore. "I can't carry him through. We won't fit. I need to dig it out more."

"Shit," Kyra hissed. "Take the gun. I'll do it."

Chase shook his head and eased Tarek down to the floor, leaned him against the wall.

"I'll be faster." He pointed behind him. "If that fucker comes through, shoot him."

Kyra just stared down at Chase, still squatting in front of Tarek. She'd never even held a gun before. She couldn't shoot anyone.

Chase rolled his lips, thinking. Then he reached back and swung, slapping Tarek across the face.

Kyra screamed.

Chase did it again.

"Stop!"

Tarek moaned. His eyelids fluttered.

Chase grabbed his face. "Tar, wake up. I need you to wake up."

Tarek blinked. His eyelids moved like they weighed

pounds. Confusion and pain clouded his eyes.

"Cha…" He rasped and his eyes rolled back.

Chase hit him again, hard.

"Stop doing that!" Kyra shrieked, but it seemed to work.

Tarek blinked again. His pupils expanded when he saw Kyra.

"What…"

"Gimme the gun." Kyra handed it to Chase. "Tar, listen. The asshole who tried to kill you and us is in there. If he comes out, you shoot him." Chase propped the gun against Tarek's good shoulder and wrapped his fingers around the trigger. "I'm going to get the door open. Get us out of here. Don't let him kill her."

Tarek's gaze sharpened, and he shifted his weight. Sweat bloomed on his forehead with the effort, but he held the gun steady.

"And don't fucking die." Chase disappeared outside.

Kyra strained her ears, listening for Benny. Every so often she'd hear a sound, a groan, a hissed curse, the swish of fabric on concrete. The noises became louder, more frequent.

A crash.

"Chase, hurry!" She pushed on the door, and it gave an inch.

"Just about got it. Fuck it. He's squeezing through." Chase yanked on the door, giving them an extra few inches, barely enough for them to pull Tarek through.

"Come on," Kyra put her arm under Tarek and tried to help him stand.

"Go," he whispered, his lips barely moving.

"No," Kyra said just as Chase's face appeared in the

opening.

"Shut. Up," Chase ground out through gritted teeth. He grabbed Tarek's collar and yanked him through. The rifle fell with a clatter. Kyra grabbed it and scrambled after them.

Chase pulled Tarek's arm around his shoulder and hauled him to his feet. The snow was falling faster now.

"The car?" Kyra asked.

"Yeah, we make a run for it."

Tarek's head fell forward.

"Tarek!"

"He's passed out again. We gotta move."

Despair spread through Kyra's cells like a virus, consuming and bursting each one. Even if they got to the car and got away, they'd still have to get to a hospital. In a blizzard. Tarek wouldn't make it.

She gripped Tarek's waist, and they took off toward the drive.

"Wait." Chase stopped so suddenly, Kyra stumbled and dropped the rifle. "Do you hear that?"

It came from above, a fast, rhythmic *thumping*.

Kyra stared up at the night sky. The sound got louder and louder until it was deafening. She ducked and covered her head as the helicopter appeared, descending from the heavens, causing the snow to swirl. It landed in the field beyond the fence. Snow and ice whipped Kyra's face. Her eyes streamed tears from the onslaught, and she raised her good hand to shield herself.

Three black figures jumped out and came running toward them.

A scream tore through the night, and Kyra whirled

around.

Benny came barreling toward her, a hammer raised in his hand.

She froze.

Chase screamed, "Kyra!"

*Pop! Pop! Pop!*

Benny's body flew backward.

# Chapter Forty-Five

"MR. HAWTHORN? MS. Gibson?" A man dressed in black closed in on them. He picked up the rifle and reset the safety. "Kyra Gibson? Chase Hawthorn?"

She nodded, numb, unable to take her eyes off Benny, dead in the snow.

"Dylan Briscoe. I got your message." He motioned to the other two men. They pulled a spinal board from the helicopter and came running. "Get him on board. Alert Mass General." He turned to Kyra and Chase. "Get in."

# Chapter Forty-Six

KYRA STUMBLED THROUGH the snow, rushing toward the helicopter, Chase at her heels. Inside, Briscoe pointed to the back and pulled a headset over his ears. Someone wrapped a thick blanket around her shoulders, gave another to Chase. Briscoe spoke to the pilot. She began flipping switches on the cockpit controls. The rotor blades' whir intensified.

"Load up!" a man yelled, and Tarek's body was pushed across the floor. The man jumped in behind him, followed by the other. The door slammed shut. He signaled to the pilot and Kyra felt the helicopter lurch underneath her as it left the ground.

Chase's hands tightened on her arms. The Greyscale men hooked Tarek up to machines, took his vitals. Their expressions were too serious, too grim.

"Eighty over fifty-five and dropping."

"Administering IV." The man pulled out a clear bag and hung it from the ceiling. The other poked Tarek's arm with a needle. Chase tensed at Kyra's back. Tears streamed down her cheeks. She couldn't look away.

"Shit! Briscoe! We lost a pulse!"

"Starting chest compressions!" The man tore through

what was left of Tarek's shirt.

Briscoe held gauze against the hole in his chest. "He's lost too much blood. Get a move on!" he bellowed at the pilot.

The first man clasped his hands, one on top of the other, interlocking his fingers, and heaved on Tarek's shredded chest. He counted down from thirty, while the other man placed a resuscitator pump over Tarek's mouth and nose.

"We're being routed to Maine Memorial!" the pilot yelled at them.

Kyra was shaking. Chase's grip on her tightened. His chest stuttered as it rose and fell against her back. She sobbed, great ragged breaths. She felt each compression. Felt her own ribs crack and shatter as the medics beat life back into Tarek's broken body.

*Don't die. Don't die. Please, don't die.*

She felt hot, wet tears on her neck, where Chase had buried his face. He clung to her, turned away from his friend. She clutched his hand with her cut one. He was breaking. Tarek was his, too.

"Got a pulse!" The man sat back and shared a look with the other medic.

Kyra didn't know how long they flew. The medics never stopped moving. They kept Tarek's heart beating and oxygen in his lungs.

"The hospital is ready for us," Briscoe yelled. "Three minutes. Gibson, Hawthorn, stay out of the way." He moved through the cabin, preparing them to land, yelling commands at the pilot. The medics scurried, adding more gauze to the blood-sodden pile on Tarek's chest, injecting him with something.

"Hold on!"

The helicopter dropped, and Kyra was thrown off balance. She gripped the seat to keep from falling to the floor. They tipped wildly. Kyra screamed. Supplies crashed down. The medics secured Tarek.

The helicopter righted and dropped.

They hit the helipad. They bounced, then hit it again. Briscoe hollered commands. The doors were ripped open. People in scrubs and white coats, yelling indiscernible things, yanked and pulled Tarek onto a wheeled bed. They rushed him through the hospital doors. Briscoe and the medics sprinted beside them.

And then it was only Kyra, Chase, and the pilot.

# Chapter Forty-Seven

*Thursday, February 16*

KYRA PACED. FOUR cups of cold coffee sat on the table in the private waiting room at Maine Memorial Hospital. Chase was sprawled in a chair, his hands wrapped in gauze where he'd torn his skin, digging out the barn door. He'd clawed through ice to get them out. After Briscoe and his team had disappeared behind the no admittance doors, Kyra and Chase had been directed to this godforsaken waiting room. They'd been here for hours.

One of the nurses took pity on her and told them Tarek's heart had stopped again, and he'd been rushed into emergency surgery.

Sometime later, Briscoe's men had appeared with clean clothes purchased from the hospital giftshop and then just as suddenly they'd disappeared.

She flopped onto a chair and dropped her head into her hands. The medical wrapping on her left hand pressed against her left eye. Kyra's injury mocked her. She'd initially refused treatment, but at Chase's insistence, relented. Twelve stitches and she'd need surgery to repair the damage to her tendons. Eventually. Maybe. She didn't give a single shit about her hand. She pressed it harder against her eye, needing the outlet of physical pain.

The doors opened, and Kyra shot to her feet. Chase, too. Dylan Briscoe wiped his forehead with a handkerchief and stopped in front of them. Kyra could feel the anxiety and fear vibrating off Chase. He was barely holding himself together. She had stopped trying.

"Ms. Gibson, Mr. Hawthorn."

"How is he?" she interrupted.

Briscoe smiled. Kyra's knees folded. Chase grabbed her arm and yanked her back into a chair. He collapsed beside her.

"He's stable." Briscoe let out a breath. He raised his hands. "He's not out of the woods yet, but the doctors are optimistic." His voice trailed off. "They're taking him to the ICU." Briscoe scraped his hand down his jaw. "He was lucky. The bullet hit him just below his collarbone. By some miracle, it missed every major artery. A few inches over, it would've hit his heart." Kyra stared at Briscoe. Nothing that had happened to Tarek had been lucky.

"How long was he in that barn?" Chase asked, his voice strained.

"Can't say for sure. A day, maybe two? He was hypothermic. It increases the rate of blood loss. He wouldn't have survived much longer." Briscoe assessed them, his mouth set in a line. "You should go get some rest. We'll notify you when he wakes up."

Kyra shook her head. "No, I don't want to leave him."

"He won't be alone. I'll be right here until you get back. I promise. I'll call you with any news. We can also make some calls. Let me know who we should notify."

They gave Briscoe a list. Grace and Charlie, Gully, Tarek's mother Liya, then they left and checked into a nearby hotel.

Kyra curled up under the covers. The television droned on; the sound low.

Her exhaustion was so overwhelming sleep evaded her. She'd taken a hot shower, a shower cap wrapped around her hand and redressed in her hospital sweats. Chase had needed help, with both of his hands bandaged.

"Kay?" Chase called across the space between their beds and she turned around.

His cheeks were wet, his eyelashes spikey, but his smile was all relief.

She reached across the space and met his hand. She wrapped her good fingers around his bandaged ones, careful not to grip too hard. "Me too."

# Chapter Forty-Eight

*Friday, February 17*

A PHONE BLARED, and Kyra jerked awake. Chase moved in the other bed, and he sat up, rubbing his eyes. Sunshine streamed through the window. The phone rang again, and Kyra scrambled to answer it.

"Hello? Yes, hello?"

"Ms. Gibson? It's Briscoe."

She steeled herself. She gripped the phone with both hands. "Yes?"

"Our boy's awake."

# Chapter Forty-Nine

KYRA BURST THROUGH the doors with Chase beside her. Greyscale men in suits with earpieces, looking far too much like Secret Service to be covert, stood by the door and ushered them inside.

"Room 7b, miss." The bearded one pointed.

Kyra stopped outside. She wasn't sure she could go in, terrified of what she'd see. Chase pressed his hand to her back. He opened the door and gave her a gentle push.

Tarek was in bed. He was so pale. His hair, dark and unruly, was plastered against his forehead. His arm was in a sling. The intense wrapping around his shoulder and the bandages around his chest were visible under the neckline of his hospital gown.

The monitor beeped. Its high pitched, regular *bleep* was the most musical sound she'd ever heard.

Tarek's eyes peeled open, and he blinked. It took a while for his morphine-soaked brain to focus, but then he smiled.

Kyra sobbed and stumbled to him. She wasn't thinking when she wrapped her arms around him, needing to feel him, until she heard his soft gasp and jerked back.

"Oh god. I'm so sorry."

He laughed, a dry, weak sound, and his good arm

wrapped around her, dead weight against her back. "Never be sorry."

"Thanks for not dying," Chase said, but his attempt at humor fell flat when he hiccupped. He gave Tarek's good shoulder a squeeze. "Seriously."

"I try."

Chase pulled a chair close to the bed and Kyra perched on its arm, holding Tarek's hand. She didn't want to let him go, afraid if she did, he'd slip away.

She and Chase told him what happened, going to Adele, to Errol, and the lodge. About the house. And Benny.

They would have to repeat the story. Tarek's drug-addled brain wasn't taking in any information. He quietly watched them with a soft, tired smile that never quite made it to his lips.

"The patient needs to rest." A nurse with a stern countenance entered the room and picked up his chart. "You've been here way too long."

Chase sighed and let the nurse herd him out. Kyra stood, but Tarek's grip tightened, and he tugged. She bent so she could hear him.

"You didn't leave."

Her bandaged hand pushed his hair off his forehead. He looked up at her, his expression somewhere between bafflement and wonder. She pressed her lips to his cheek, waxy and cool. "I could never. I love you."

"Miss," the nurse called, and Kyra let him go.

# Chapter Fifty

*Wednesday, March 15*

KYRA WAS IN another hospital waiting room, this time at Mass General. Tarek was being released today, and she was here to take him home.

After a week in the ICU in Maine, Tarek had been medevaced to Boston's Mass General Hospital where he'd undergone reconstructive surgery. He'd then been moved to a recovery unit, but he caught an infection and became septic. He was sent back to the ICU, where he'd remained for two long weeks.

Kyra hadn't been able to see or talk to him. Only his mother had contact, but Liya updated Kyra, Chase, and Gully regularly.

When Kyra was notified he was well enough to be released, she'd wondered if he wouldn't be more comfortable with his family.

Liya had laughed. "If you think he'd rather move home and live with his mother, you're not as smart as he says you are."

Kyra still wasn't sure they'd made the right decision. She hardly knew what kind of care Tarek would require. She was apprehensive despite Greyscale's commitment to providing whatever he needed without regard to expense, including in-home care. A young man was currently moving into her spare bedroom, where he'd live for the next few months to help with Tarek's rehab.

"Here." Briscoe handed her a cup of coffee.

In the weeks Tarek had been in the hospital, Briscoe had helped her notify Greta Koch and Peter Edwards of the truth of that night, and what had really happened to Abigail and Elodie. Greta said it was the first time she could breathe in decades. Peter's response was more subdued.

"She'd been alive a few hundred miles away all this time and we never even looked for her?"

Briscoe said that the local authorities would keep an eye on him. They'd make sure he received help if he needed it. Kyra wasn't sure they'd done Peter Edwards any favors in revealing the truth.

The last Kyra had heard—from Grace—the Pāru Group had canceled the Vineyard theater arts center project, and the property had reverted to the Hawthorns. It would be sold off for redevelopment. Phil and Margot would make a fortune.

With Benny dead, Marjorie and Kelsey's murders would not be tried, but their families and Asher urged Kyra to write an exposé. It was the first time *The Island Times* was credited with a national scoop in decades. Han, at least, was shitting himself with glee.

Kyra sipped the tepid liquid and grimaced at the bitter flavor. She forced herself to swallow. Briscoe laughed through his nose and the side of his mouth tipped up.

"What is this?" She held out the offensive beverage.

"Decaf. You're jittery enough."

"Thank you." She set the cup down. Her knee bobbed. She wrung her hands. Her left one was still bandaged and stared at the waiting room doors.

"Relax, Kyra." She shot Briscoe an annoyed scowl, and he chuckled. "You know, you and Hawthorn did well out there."

Kyra's knee stopped moving. "I'm sorry?"

"Did you know that most FBI agents and specialized investigatory consultants are actually CPAs?" She frowned, not following. "The others are mostly attorneys." He shrugged. "An enterprising, multinationally licensed lawyer would fit in well at Greyscale." Briscoe stood and slid his hands in his pockets. "Think about it."

She gaped at him, but any response she had died on her lips when the doors opened. A man in a lab coat entered, followed by a nurse pushing Tarek in a wheelchair.

Kyra jumped to her feet.

"I told you I didn't need or want a wheelchair," Tarek grumbled and stood, the action slow and labored.

Kyra ran her eyes over him, drank in the sight of him. He'd lost weight. His cheeks were gaunt and his normally bright eyes dull. His arm was set in a sling, and she could see the bandages under the collar of his shirt. He was the most beautiful man she'd ever seen.

Tears streamed down her face as she crossed the room. She stood in front of him, afraid she'd hurt him when his good arm pulled her close and she pressed her body against his. He smelled of antiseptic and stale air and nothing familiar, but she clung to him.

"Chase is seriously glad you didn't die. Again," she said

against his shirt and felt his chest rise and fall with a laugh.

"I try."

She pulled back and looked up.

He pressed his forehead to hers. "Can we please go home?"

Kyra beamed at him. Her cheeks ached with the strain. "We have the next ferry over."

## FIN.

# Acknowledgments

When I set out to write the first MVM book in 2021, I had no idea where this journey would lead me. It was a nebulous dream, and then it became real, and all of a sudden I had a website, and deadlines, and new plots and characters who have to be consistent while still growing. It's fun, challenging, sometimes frustrating, but so worth it, and I am so grateful to be here. But I can't take all the credit. So many people support me and my vision for this story and these characters, and they have encouraged me to delve into my creativity. I'm so thankful to have found such an amazing team.

Thank you to Sarah, Katie, Liz, and the amazing women at Club R.E.D. for your unwavering support and encouragement. To Mrs. Amanda for being the most beautiful person inside and out. To the Lotze and Koesler families for giving me so much access to Martha's Vineyard and the amazing people there. To the teams at AME and N.N. Lights for helping me get this series in front of readers. To my Tule family, Heidi, Jaiden, Kelly, Lee, Mia, and Monti for all your hard work on this book and its beautiful cover. And of course I could not forget my champion editor, Sinclair Sawhney, who demands the best I can give every time without apology. And finally, to the island that has inspired me.

You all have my most heartfelt thanks.

*Thank you for reading **Final Exit**, Book 4 in the Martha's Vineyard Murders series.*

*I hope you enjoyed it and if you did, please come back to see what Kyra, Tarek, and Chase get into in Books 5 and 6 coming in 2026.*

*Getting to share their stories with you means the world to me, and I'd love to hear what you thought, what you liked, loved, or even hated, what mysteries you'd like to see Kyra and Tarek solve next.*

*You can write to me at raemi.ray@gmail.com and find me on my website at www.raemiray.com.*

*Please consider leaving a review. Reviews positive and negative are how readers find writers. Here is a link to my author page on Amazon.*

*https://shorturl.at/FpnfL*

*You have my deepest gratitude.*

*Until the next ferry over ~ Raemi*

If you enjoyed *Final Exit*,
you'll love the other books in...

# Martha's Vineyard Murders series

Book 1: *A Chain of Pearls*

Book 2: *Death at Dark*

Book 3: *Widow's Walk*

Book 4: *Final Exit*

*Available now at your favorite online retailer!*

# About the Author

Photo Credit: L.A. Brown

Raemi A. Ray is the author of the Martha's Vineyard Murders series. Her travels to the island and around the world inspire her stories. She lives with her family in Boston.

Thank you for reading

# Final Exit

If you enjoyed this book, you can find more from all our great authors at TulePublishing.com, or from your favorite online retailer.

TULE
PUBLISHING

Made in the USA
Middletown, DE
23 May 2025

75960527R00222